MARTIAN RAINBOW

Also by Robert L. Forward
Published by Ballantine Books

DRAGON'S EGG

STARQUAKE

MARTIAN RAINBOW

ROBERT L. FORWARD

A DEL REY BOOK BALLANTINE BOOKS NEW YORK

SCI/ FAN

A Del Rey Book
Published by Ballantine Books

Copyright © 1991 by Robert L. Forward

All rights reserved under International and Pan-American Copyright
Conventions. Published in the United States by Ballantine Books,
a division of Random House, Inc., New York, and simultaneously
in Canada by Random House of Canada Limited, Toronto.

Library of Congress Cataloging-in-Publication Data
Forward, Robert L.
Martian rainbow / Robert L. Forward.—1st ed.
p.   cm.
"A Del Rey book."
ISBN 0-345-34712-9
I. Title.
PS3556.O754M37   1991
813'.54—dc20   90-24636
CIP

Design by Holly Johnson
Manufactured in the United States of America

First Edition: June 1991

10 9 8 7 6 5 4 3 2 1

To Martha and Eve—
for willingly joining me in the not-so-idyll wildernesses.

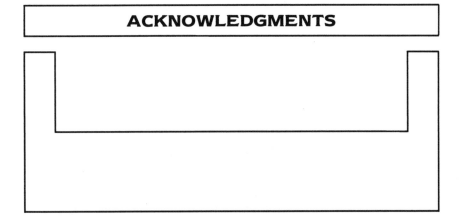

ACKNOWLEDGMENTS

Any hard science fiction novel must necessarily draw on many sources of factual information. That information has been laboriously gathered or deduced by literally armies of researchers—scientific, engineering, and literary—scattered over centuries of time. A few of the specific technical publications that I consulted the most in writing this novel are listed in the bibliography. In addition, there are many people who gave me novel ideas, valuable insight, or factual information that contributed significantly (sometimes by showing me it *couldn't* be done that way) to my fictitious regeneration of a Mars where rainbows could form.

When the story follows the reader's personal version of the "known scientific facts," the people I acknowledge below can take most of the credit. When the science unrolled in the story begins to raise doubts in the reader's mind, then it is my responsibility. Either: (1) I goofed in my interpretation of the science, (2) my interpretation of the "known scientific facts" does not agree with the reader's interpretation, (3) or I followed the Final Law of Storytelling: "Never let the facts get in the way of a good story."

With this understanding, I would like to acknowledge the help of the following people: Penelope J. Boston, Robert D. Forward, Joel C. Sercel, Paul A. Penzo, Robert M. Powers, James E. Oberg, Carol R. Stoker, Thomas R. Meyer, A. W. Gerhard Kunze, Alex and Phyllis Eisenstein, John Eades, Edward (Ned) J. Britt, H. Jay Melosh, Tom Gangale, and Lester del Rey.

Then, of course, there is Robert A. Heinlein. Without the early inspiration of his books, I probably would not have been a space scientist, much less a science fiction writer. There is nothing that I write or do that doesn't have his touch somewhere in it. Some readers, midway through this book, might have a sense of déjà vu— that they have read something like this before. They have—in "Concerning Stories Never Written," a postscript to Heinlein's *Revolt in 2100*. I was concerned when my outline for this book showed strong resemblances to the plot concepts in that postscript, and wrote to Robert. But he called me up and encouraged me to go ahead.

The same sense of déjà vu also happened to readers of my first book, *Dragon's Egg*, where my story of aliens living in a high-gravity world reminded readers of Hal Clement's classic novel, *Mission of Gravity*. (Sometimes I get the feeling that I'm the "Linda Ronstadt" of science fiction, dishing out old classics in modernized arrangements.)

My apologies to real Congressional Medal of Honor winners. I know that what Alexander Armstrong did during the battle for Mars doesn't qualify him to receive the medal. But then, he had full control of the communications links back to Earth . . . and *somehow* the real story managed to get improved upon in the telling . . .

My special thanks to the staff of the Mariner/Viking Image Library at JPL and the Mariner and Viking teams for the images that allowed my imagination to take you on a vicarious visit to the surface of a distant red spot of light in the sky.

BIBLIOGRAPHY

Boston, Penelope J., ed. *The Case for Mars*. American Astronautical Society Science and Technology Series, Vol. 57 (1984). Proceedings of the Case for Mars Conference, Boulder, Colorado (29 April–2 May 1981). Published for AAS by Univelt, Inc., P.O. Box 28130, San Diego, CA 92128.

Carr, Michael H. *The Surface of Mars*. New Haven: Yale University Press, 1981.

McKay, Christopher P. "Terraforming Mars." *Journal of the British Interplanetary Society* 35 (1982): 427–433.

McKay, Christopher P., ed. *The Case for Mars II*. American Astro-
nautical Society Science and Technology Series, Vol. 62 (1985).
Proceedings of the Second Case for Mars Conference, Boulder,
Colorado (10–14 July 1984). Published for AAS by Univelt,
Inc., P.O. Box 28130, San Diego, CA 92128.

MECA. Abstracts of papers presented at the Symposium on Mars:
Evolution of its Climate and Atmosphere, Washington, DC (17–
19 July 1986), LPI Contribution 599. Compiled by the Lunar
and Planetary Institute, 3303 NASA Road One, Houston, TX
77058.

Oberg, James Edward. *New Earths: Transforming Other Planets for
Humanity*. Harrisburg: Stackpole Books, 1982.

Pollack, James B. "Climatic Change on the Terrestrial Planets."
Icarus 37 (1979): 479–553.

Powers, Robert M. *Mars: Our Future on the Red Planet*. Boston:
Houghton Mifflin Company, 1986.

Sagan, Carl, and Mullen, George. "Earth and Mars: Evolution of
Atmospheres and Surface Temperatures." *Science* 177 (7 July
1972): 52–56.

Spitzer, Cary R., ed., and the Viking Orbiter Imaging Team. *Viking
Orbiter Views of Mars*. NASA SP-441. Science and Technical
Information Branch, NASA, Washington, DC (1980). [Obtain
from US Government Printing Office, Washington, DC 20402.]

MARTIAN RAINBOW

CHAPTER 1

ATTACK ON MARS

Two identical men floated on opposite sides of a circular railing as they looked down at a large three-dimensional image of the globe of Mars under attack by the arrowlike swarm of their invasion fleet. General Alexander Armstrong grinned with satisfaction as he looked down at the sight; and crow's-feet inherited from his famous astronaut great-grandfather formed to point arrowlike at his steel-gray eyes. He raised his left hand, brushed it meditatively over his chin, and looked up at the stocky figure on the other side of the display. His glance met an identical set of steel-gray eyes. He waited for his twin brother to say something, for Dr. Augustus "Gus" Armstrong, ranking civilian, was in nominal charge of the multinational invasion force.

Gus said nothing, but his left hand, too, raised to brush meditatively over his chin. Alexander watched the motion with detachment, noticing once again the difference . . . the defect . . . that was the only way anyone could tell them apart. The thumb and forefinger on Gus' left hand had been reduced to short stubs in an automobile accident shortly before they both were to graduate from the Space Academy. Alexander had been driving.

After waiting a while longer for Gus to say something, the smile on Alexander's face hardened into a determined look.

"It's time to go into action, Gus," he said, his jaw muscles twitching. "We passed through the L-1 point over a week ago and we're well into our free-fall drop toward the planet."

"They haven't even noticed we're here yet, Alex," Gus said

thoughtfully. "Not a sign of a spacecraft except for a few orbiters. Not even a *ping* from a radar."

"My invasion plan took them by surprise." Alexander allowed his face to return to a pleased smile. The crow's-feet appeared again at the corners of his eyes. "The new antimatter rockets gave us the power to come straight at them out of the Sun. Their spies on Earth saw us leave along the standard slow trajectory, but no one but the comets saw us leave decoys in our place—while we took a shortcut around the Sun."

"I'll call a council of war for 2300," said Gus.

Gus looked out at ten solemn faces individually inset into the high-resolution video screen covering one wall of his office on the flagship *Yorktown*. In back of the ten squadron commanders were more faces, the spacecraft commanders of each of the four interplanetary transport spacecraft that made up that squadron, the flight leaders that commanded the four attack groups that each spacecraft carried, and the attack group captains that would lead each group of landers into battle. Most of the images wore U.S. Space Force blues, with the remainder in the uniform of some friendly foreign spacefaring nation.

"Our brief trip to Mars is nearly over," Gus said. "We must now proceed with our next task, disagreeable as it may be to some of you. But as you well know, the time for negotiations passed long ago, with no success. It is now time for action.

"I would consider it a personal favor if you would all put aside your doubts and hesitations, and listen carefully to my brother, Alexander Armstrong, major general of the U.S. Space Force, and brevet general and commander of the UN Mars Expeditionary Force. The time for war is here and he is now in command. If we follow his orders, we can achieve the goals that we and the rest of Earth desire, and carry out the invasion with a minimum of damage and casualties on both sides."

Gus moved back as Alexander stepped in front of the screen. The two images were almost perfect copies of each other, except for the subtle color change as Alexander's meticulously tailored space-blue uniform replaced Gus's meticulously tailored black civilian coveralls.

"There has been no response indicating they are aware of our presence, so we will use the primary invasion plan," Alexander began. "Although the antimatter main engines are turned off, and we are well hidden in the glare of the Sun, it is important that they remain unaware we are coming. From this point on, you and your men are to obey low-observability rules. All communication is to be by direct optical link. No hot thruster is to be pointed within thirty degrees of the planet.

"Now for the plan of battle. The U.S. First Squadron augmented by Japan's *East Wind* will land on Deimos.

"U.S. Second Squadron and Ireland's *Shillelagh* will land on Phobos.

"U.S. Third through Fifth, augmented by Israel's *Shalom*, Great Britain's *King William V*, and the Royal Canadians will hit the main city at the base of Olympus Mons.

"U.S. Sixth along with *Brasilia* will neutralize the base at the North Pole, while U.S. Seventh and India's *White Tiger* will cover the South Pole base. . . ."

Each of the forty interplanetary transport spacecrafts began to unload its cargo of attack landers, medical support landers, quartermaster support landers, and robotic support spacecraft. Soon the forty interplanetary arrows aimed at the heart of Mars had been transformed into a cloud of winged bullets.

As preparations intensified, Alexander, flanked by his personal guard of crack troops, headed for an inspection tour of the fleet in his personal attack lander, *Bucephalus*. He stopped at the airlock of the *Yorktown* to put on his battle suit. This was war, and although the enemy had so far failed to notice their approach, the probability that his lander would lose air in the next few hours was not determined solely by the chance random micrometeorite.

The battle suits had self-sealing armor, with automatic tourniquets built into each extremity. In the vacuum of space or the near-vacuum of Mars, the blood in a punctured arm or leg would bubble, then freeze. But with the tourniquet operating properly, the soldier would survive—with his limb—if the rescue crews were fast enough and the doctors good enough. Even the helmet had an emergency flexible inner liner that sprang out of the neck seal area if the strong Diamondhard faceplate failed.

Alexander's personal battle suit had an extra outer plating of vapor-deposited pure gold that made him glisten in the sunlight. His gold-plated boots had risers that added a number of centimeters to his height, while his helmet sported a slotted solid-gold metal crest. Ostensibly, the crest was necessary as an antenna for the high-frequency data links needed for his unique command and control requirements. The crested helmet and the golden sheen gave him a unique profile that his troops could identify at great distances.

Alexander checked his personal weapon. It had been a long time since he had held one, but nothing could beat the simplicity, reliability, and deadliness of a .45 rocketgun. As he inserted the clip, he looked at the armor-piercing bullets, glistening slightly with their teflon solid lubricant. They were the same size as standard .45 automatic bullets, but in place of the powder cartridge was a miniature rocket engine that gave the bullet the punch of a .45 automatic without producing a recoil kick when it left the gun. He shoved the clip into the butt and pointed the rocketgun at the end of the corridor. As his gloved finger entered the enlarged trigger guard, a bright red laser beam sprang from the end of the gun and made a red dot on the far wall, showing where the flat trajectory of the rocket-propelled projectile would take it if the trigger were pulled. He cocked the weapon and returned it to its holster under his chest-pack.

"Sir!" the first sergeant in charge of his personal guard objected. "You should have your weapon on safety. If you made a mistake—"

"What's your name, Sergeant?" Alexander roared, knowing full well the name of the leader of his personal guard.

"First Sergeant Thomas L. Riley, sir!" the sergeant replied stiffly.

Alexander tongued the command microphone built into the neckband of his suit. "Sergeant Riley is relieved of his duties as of this moment." He looked up at the sergeant.

"*I* do not make mistakes, *Private* Riley! But *you* did. Report to the brig at once and stay there until I return." He nodded to a master sergeant.

"You are in charge. Hand me my helmet."

Alexander lifted the crested globe with its large battle visor and locked it into place. He pulled down the battle visor and was instantly in the center of an enormous, three-dimensional, computer-generated, imaginary control room—the Battle Control Center. The far wall of the imaginary room was covered with displays, each showing some activity that the computer was monitoring. As Alexander turned his head, more screens, containing less-important information, came into view out of the corner of his eye.

Arrayed out in radial rows in front of him were computer images of the squadron commanders, flight leaders, and attack group captains, sitting at consoles. Some of the commanders were looking at the screens on their consoles, indicating they had their battle visors up and were busy looking at things around them. Others were looking directly at him, indicating that they had their visors down and could see him in the imaginary Battle Control Center. The rows were uneven, being arranged partially by organizational grouping, partially by task grouping, and partially by physical distance from Alexander.

Each console had an identifying rectangular sign in the upper left corner. The most prominent one in the first row had the insignia of the U.S. First Squadron on a gold background. The console of the squadron commander, Colonel Bradshaw, was flanked by three consoles with signs containing red, white, and blue backgrounds to the U.S. First Squadron insignia. Beside each console sat a lieutenant colonel, each a flight leader in charge of a flight of lander spacecraft. One of the lieutenant colonels was looking at one of his console screens, his computer-generated mouth silently giving orders. Alexander identified him as Lieutenant Colonel Pinkerton. Alexander took a quick glance at the screen Pinkerton was looking at and saw a space tug chasing an errant cargo container. He blinked his left eye and the computer flagged that scene for later analysis.

"I'll make someone pay for that foul-up!" Alexander thought to himself.

Next to the three U.S. consoles was a console with a bright red ball on the sign. Admiral Takahashi sat there, his almond eyes staring blankly in Alexander's direction. Alexander looked at Colonel Bradshaw, then at Admiral Takahashi, widening his eyes each time to signal the computer. The scene zoomed down on the computer-generated images of Colonel Bradshaw and Admiral Takahashi. "Is everything in order?" he asked.

The icons came to life and replied.

"Japan's *East Wind* is ready to unleash its fury on the dark-gray dust of Deimos," Admiral Takahashi replied.

"U.S. First Squadron all ready, General Armstrong," Colonel Bradshaw said.

"I don't think so, Colonel Bradshaw," Alexander started softly. "You might have a talk with your blue flight leader, Colonel Pinkerton. I think he knows something he has neglected to tell you." He raised his voice to a roar. "And I expect you and Colonel Pinkerton to have it under control before the attack is due to start!"

Alexander gave a self-satisfied smile and switched his glance from Colonel Bradshaw to another squadron commander in front of him. It was the commander of the U.S. Third Squadron, Colonel White. Somewhere during the zoom-in on Colonel White, the computer generated image was replaced with a video image.

"Yes, General Armstrong?" Colonel White said expectantly.

"I'll be inspecting your squadron first. I should arrive in about twenty minutes."

"We'll be ready, sir," the colonel responded.

Alexander glanced around the Battle Control Center one last time. On the back wall, each screen showed a scene of activity—attack troops suiting up and filing onto the attack landers, stevedores struggling to load bulky special-purpose weapons aboard quartermaster landers, and space tugs lining up robotic support spacecraft. Off to one side, Alexander noticed with satisfaction that Colonel Bradshaw was silently jawing at Colonel Pinkerton. He raised his battle visor and was back in the corridor outside his personal lander.

The airlock to *Bucephalus* was open and most of his private guard were inside. Alexander took off his helmet and handed it to a nearby trooper. He pulled his floating body through the port and stuck his head into the flight deck. Major Thomas and Captain Harrison were there. He gave orders to the pilot, one of the best in the space force.

"Take me over to the main attack group, Betsy, and fly along each ship in turn. Start with the U.S. Third."

"Yes, General Armstrong," Major Thomas said.

"Captain Harrison," Alexander continued, "tell U.S. Fourth Squadron they're next. I won't bother with the foreigners, but will skip over to the Deimos attack group next."

"Yes, General Armstrong," Captain Harrison said.

Alexander went to the center of his specially outfitted attack lander. On a set of gimbals in the exact center of the lander was a command chair surrounded by a miniature control console. Set in the ceilings, walls, and floors were large viewports that would provide Alexander with maximum vision of what was happening outside. Alexander floated over to the command chair and the master sergeant buckled him in, while the trooper put the gold-crested helmet in the holder next to the chair, where Alexander could get it in a hurry. Alexander pulled down the battle visor built into the headrest of the command chair and was instantly back in the cavernous imaginary Battle Control Center. He searched through a cluster of support people below him and found the icon of Major Thomas, the pilot of *Bucephalus*. He widened his eyes and the computer zoomed his view in on her.

"I'm ready. Let's move it, Betsy!"

"Moving, sir," the video image of Major Thomas said, and the attack lander instantly jumped to two gravities, its gold-plating glittering in the sunlight as it moved out of the shadow of the *Yorktown*.

Alexander gave a pleased grin. He liked the way that girl flew.

Once this little chore was over, he should give her a little of his time. If she made love like she flew spacecraft, she might be worth a long weekend.

They came up on the *Lexington* from the rear. Major Thomas had reversed power and *Bucephalus* was decelerating at a half gravity. The trajectory was programmed to bring them to a halt at the nose of the two-kilometer-long interplanetary spacecraft.

With its pointed crew compartment at one end of its long open truss central shaft and the large, glowing, liquid droplet radiators at the other end, the *Lexington* looked like a flaming war arrow. It was not under acceleration, so the main antimatter engines were cold and black.

Alexander swiveled around to look through the six superconducting rings of varying sizes that outlined the shape of a spherical combustion chamber attached to a bell-shaped exhaust nozzle. Although he could look right through the structure to the stars on the other side, the blazing plasma formed by the annihilation energy of the antimatter would be trapped in the combustion chamber by the strong magnetic fields from the superconducting rings, and could only escape out through the nozzle. These revolutionary antimatter plasma engines used the new hot superconductors that stayed superconducting even when running white hot. In addition, the high operating temperature annealed away any radiation damage in the superconducting rings the instant it occurred.

Of course, no one ever had directly watched an antimatter rocket operate. Out through the same gaps in the rings came a deadly shower of gamma rays generated in the antimatter plasma. That was why the crew compartment was two kilometers away down the shaft of the ship, safe in a shadow made in the gamma ray glow by a disklike shield of heavy tungsten metal placed just in front of the engine.

Tucked up between the now-dark antimatter rocket engine and the disk-shaped shadow shield was a glowing cylinder of white-hot metal. This was the heat source that provided electrical power to operate the ship. A little under a meter long and a meter in diameter, it supplied enough energy to power a small city, which is what the *Lexington* was. A tiny stream of antimatter was injected into the center of the cylinder and annihilated. All the gamma rays and charged particles that came out of the annihilation process were stopped in the tungsten metal of the cylinder, heating it up. Through channels in the tungsten flowed hydrogen gas, which in turn became superheated and ionized and flowed out through a magnetohydrodynamic generator to produce electricity.

The waste heat from the power generator was ejected into the cold of space by the radiators that gave the *Lexington* and the other ships of its class their arrowlike shape. Squirters that stretched three hundred meters up the spine of the ship sent out a triangular spray of hot liquid droplets that were caught by three three-hundred-meter-long booms that stuck out at right angles to the spine of the ship just in front of the shadow shield. The three glowing vanes shaded from bright red near the shaft of the ship to dull gray near the catchers.

Bucephalus continued on down the shaft and came to the large tanks of liquid hydrogen propellant near the center of the ship. They were still more than half full, ready for the triumphant return to Earth. Just in front of them, huddled behind all the fuel and out of the way of the gamma rays, was the tiny container that held the small amount of antimatter that was needed to take the *Lexington* to Mars and back. Even at the one gravity acceleration that the *Lexington* and her sister ships employed, only milligrams of antimatter, no larger than a single grain of salt, were all that was needed to heat a ton of hydrogen propellant to a blazing plasma. Still, the *Lexington* was a large ship and carried a cargo of four attack landers and their accompanying medic and quartermaster landers. The antimatter storage container had once held twelve kilograms of antihydrogen ice. Now it only held four kilograms, for they would not be in as much of a hurry on their return.

Bucephalus left the hydrogen and antihydrogen tanks behind and came up on the crew compartment. It was painted in bold red and white stripes, with a star-spangled blue nose. The word LEXINGTON marched proudly across its side in gold foil letters. Major Thomas brought *Bucephalus* to a halt about half a kilometer out from the docking ports at the base of the crew section where it joined to the central truss of the ship. Alexander watched out the viewports critically.

"Take me around, Betsy," he hollered toward the flight deck. Immediately *Bucephalus* began a sideways circular maneuver around the neck of the *Lexington*, stubby wings level. Alexander swiveled in his gimballed command chair to keep the activities in view. Three of the four attack landers had undocked from the *Lexington* and were in formation, and the fourth was pulling away from its docking port to join them. One of the larger support landers was also ready and waiting. It had large red crosses on the wings and sides.

"Captain Harrison!" Alexander yelled. "Tell that med ship I'm coming aboard for an inspection. Betsy! Take me down."

While Alexander donned his helmet, Major Thomas rolled *Bucephalus* and dove the ship down to come to a controlled stop with the two airlock ports just a meter apart.

Alexander cycled through the airlocks with the sergeant, then handed his helmet to him on the other side. He was met by a man dressed in a lime-green Marsuit with large red crosses on the front and back. The man held his helmet in his left arm and extended his right hand.

"Welcome aboard the *Walter Reed*, General Armstrong. I'm Colonel Waters, chief surgeon and commander."

As Alexander shook Colonel Waters' hand, he took time to notice the special flexigloves that the medical corps wore. They were lightweight and skintight, with heater wires instead of insulation to keep the cold out. They also had active controls built into the cuff to keep the air in the glove at constant volume so the fingers didn't have to fight the pressure differential. Too delicate for fighting men, Alexander thought.

"I'm glad to see the medical corps is taking 'battle conditions' seriously and is suited up," Alexander said.

"Yes, indeed!" Colonel Waters said. "We all are in Marsuits for the duration of the battle, and our helmets are never more than an armlength away. We are firm believers in 'zero loss warfare.' "

"So am I," Alexander said approvingly. "Long butcher lists make for short careers. Show me the rest of the ship; but make it short, I have more inspections to make."

They stopped in a small room packed with eight men buckled into seats in their helmeted lime-green Marsuits with red crosses visible from all angles.

"This is our equivalent of the medivac system used in Korea, Vietnam, Kuwait, and our present Baltic-front standoff with the Russian Neocommunists, after their coup and attempted reannexation of the Baltic republics. As soon as we land near the attack group that we support, these corpsmen leave by that port there, pull out the four rocket-propelled 'hoppers' from the unpressurized bay below, and use them to take up positions behind the front lines, waiting for a call. If a trooper is injured, they fly in, stabilize the injured man, get him on a stretcher, then use the hopper to fly him back right into this transfer lock. The door closes, the room is pressurized, and the stretcher is moved into the trauma center through this next lock."

Colonel Waters moved through the lock. "If the trooper is alive when he passes through this lock, the chances of him staying alive are over 98 percent. With modern transport technology and modern medicine, a nation can now engage in limited warfare with almost zero loss of its troops."

"Politicians have changed, too," Alexander said. "They used to be able to fight wars on the cheap, by drafting warm bodies, forcing them to fight, paying them a pittance, and forgetting about them afterward. Now, when they asked me to lead this invasion, I told them what I needed, and they gave it to me—with every button and buzzer that could be attached. The last thing those pious bastards want is to be blamed for high casualties because of penny-pinching."

They entered the main body of the medical ship. There were four separate trauma centers, each with two doctors at attention. They all had Marsuits on, with their helmets in wall brackets within easy reach.

"Each doctor has a specialty relevant to the upcoming situation—burns, frostbite, compound fractures, carbon dioxide poisoning, laser eye damage, and so forth. Most have been cross-trained in other specialties as well as anesthesiology. Both pilot and copilot are cross-trained as medic-nurses, and we will use the medics that bring back the troops as surgical nurses if needed."

Alexander looked around approvingly. "Excellent, Colonel Waters. I like what I see."

"Down below are the diagnostic machines and all the medical supplies we could possibly have need for," Colonel Waters continued. "On the way out to Mars we had each of the troopers we support give six pints of blood. It is waiting here for him in case he needs it, along with plenty of artificial blood if that runs out."

"Better medicine is not the only way to achieve zero loss warfare," Alexander said—starting to brag. "The strategy and tactics I developed for this invasion will be textbook examples of that old military maxim, 'The objective of war is not to give your life for your country, but to make the enemy give *his* life for *his* country.' I have achieved complete surprise. I will overwhelm all targets with superior firepower and dare them not to surrender. And if we have to attack, it will be machines, not men, leading the charge.

"If things go the way *I've* planned . . ." He paused to poke the surgeon in the chest with a golden finger. "*You'll* never have a customer!"

Colonel Waters looked a trifle disconcerted for a fraction of a second, then recovered. "Of course . . . Of *course*! That *would* be the best result, wouldn't it?"

"Let's go!" Alexander said to the sergeant, and made his way back down the corridors.

Their last stop was a visit to an attack lander floating next to the *Bunker Hill* spacecraft. Alexander waited until his personal video specialist had passed through the air lock, then he boarded as the specialist captured the event for the battle video network.

All through the fleet, the general was seen to enter through the lock, raise his arms to remove his crested helmet from his head, then hold the helmet under his left arm like a medieval king in gilded battle armor addressing his troops.

Alexander glanced around the crowded attack lander at the troopers in their armored red-brown camouflage Marsuits. They were all veterans. No inexperienced privates or shave-tail lieutenants in Alexander's army. The troopers were in battle gear with their helmets on, their features distorted by the Diamondhard plastic bowl and partially hidden by the communication gear crammed into the interior around their heads. He knew they were watching a flat image of himself on the holographic lenses built into their faceplates as he talked to them. That same image was being viewed by all the attack troops in all the attack landers that were streaming down like an avenging swarm of bullets at their target—Mars.

Alexander frowned slightly as he saw what was obviously a woman in the second row of the attack troops. He didn't like women on the front line, but the recent court expansion of the Equal Rights Amendment into the military service domain meant he couldn't keep them out if they volunteered and qualified, *and* could overcome the hidden hurdles that were placed in their way by Alexander and the other hard-liners.

Well, Alexander thought, if the chickie got here, she must be one tough biddy. I pity the poor Martians. He put on his commander's face, activated his commander's voice, and looked imperiously around at the hold full of troopers that represented all the troops that were now watching his ghostly image superimposed on their helmet faceplates.

"Men," Alexander said, "we are about to embark on a battle that will change the tide of human history. Never before have the peoples of one planet breached the atmosphere of another planet in anger. But, as you know, we have a right to be angry. We cannot allow those on Mars to block the access of Earth to the resources of the asteroid belt and the outer solar system. We have attempted negotiations and those attempts have been rejected. It is time for Earth to take action, and you are the strong right arm of Earth." His voice grew louder.

"You must strike! And you must strike hard!

"Yet—" He paused, and his voice softened. "—you must not strike in anger. We are many. We are well trained. We have superior weapons. There is no question that we will win this battle; the only question is how many will have to die before it is over. I want you to be brave—for the enemy scatters before brave troops. But I do not want you to be foolhardy. You have superior weapons. Use them to destroy the enemy's equipment and weapons. You have superior training. Use it to frustrate the enemy's attempts to maneuver. You have superior numbers. Use them to convince the enemy that surrender is the wiser choice.

"If you use your advantages poorly, we will *still* win the battle, but in winning the battle we will have lost the war, for the casualty lists will cause sorrow to our side and produce lasting bitterness in our conquered foe. If you use your advantages properly, then we will not only win the battle and the war, but we will have gained what Earth desires, a unified solar system that is open to all."

Alexander raised his right hand in a stiff salute.

"I salute you—brave men." He paused and changed his demeanor from that of pontificating statesman to that of a commander of battle.

"We attack at 0800!" he yelled, shoving his golden-gloved fist into the air, then burst into a proud grin as the strapped-in troopers in the crowded hold returned a muffled yell and shook their weapons in the air. Alexander lifted his helmet, then lowered it over his head as if crowning himself. The last image sent to the troops was the firm grin and the famous crinkled crow's-feet on his space-weathered face pointing to his deeply penetrating steel-gray eyes.

Alexander returned to his attack lander and climbed into his gimballed command post. It was now 0450, just a little over three hours to attack time. He pulled down the battle visor and was instantly back in the imaginary Battle Control Center. He glanced quickly around the room, saw no blinking lights trying to attract his attention, and then looked down at the Signals Group immediately below him. This group was manned by people that Alexander always regarded as a little weird. Imagine, he shuddered—spending your whole life talking to and even listening to computers!

"Signals?" Alexander queried.

"There has been no significant change in the radio emissions generated by any of the sites on Mars," said the rumpled icon of a fat man with a large bald spot on top of his head and long unkempt hair that looked like the owner never had time for a barber. The image zoomed slightly and turned into real video. The fat man pushed his glasses up on his face, and Alexander noticed that he wore trifocals with an extrawide midsection designed for taking in a complete computer screen in one glance.

"Our computers tell us that it is almost certain—99.3 percent certain—that they don't know we are here. This high probability is mostly based on the fact that their radars are pointed in the direction of our decoy swarm coming along the standard trajectory from Earth to Mars."

The one that will arrive some six months from now, Alexander thought.

"Are you ready with the jammers?" he asked aloud.

The fat man looked annoyed, then resigned, as he explained it to Alexander all over again. "Please. Nothing so crude as jamming, General Armstrong. We have deployed an array of transceivers between Mars and Earth. Any transmissions from Mars will be received and used to produce amplified and inverted versions of the signals. The waves from these inverted versions of the signals will cancel out the original signals in the direction of the Earth. In their place we insert a set of computer-generated radio signals containing typical messages similar to ones they have sent before. That way their allies on Earth will not know about the attack until it is all over. The system works both ways, although we will not activate the Earth signal blocking mode unless our computers detect some sort of warning message. We also have similar arrays set to pass between Mars and its moons when we attack the moons."

"Good," Alexander said. "Continue to do whatever it is you do."

A light inset in a distant console in the imaginary Battle Control Center was now blinking. At first it had a normal white color and was blinking slowly, but as time went on, it slowly changed color from white to yellow to red, and the rate of blinking sped up. Other consoles were also starting to emit slow white blinks of light. It was approaching attack time and some of the flights had to be on their way early to arrive on target in synchronism with the main attack. Alexander picked out the reddest and fastest-blinking light. It was on the console of the commander of the U.S. First Squadron augmented by the Japanese flight. This Squadron was to attack the base on the outer moon Deimos. Alexander widened his eyes at the staring icons of Colonel Bradshaw and Admiral Takahashi, and spoke.

"I trust you are *now* ready for the attack?" he said severely, knowing full well they were, for the status board below him was all green for the First Squadron.

The icon of Colonel Bradshaw awoke and spoke briskly. "First Squadron Augmented all ready for attack, sir! The Signals Group Distant Imaging Team reports only twenty-two of the enemy at Deimos base, two outside, two in work quarters, probably awake, and eighteen in living quarters, probably asleep."

"Sixteen attack landers with 304 fighting men will give you almost fifteen-to-one odds. I expect zero losses for this objective."

"I will bring all my men back," Colonel Bradshaw promised.

Alexander paused for a second, thinking, then asked, "Were the outside men at the antispacecraft missile launch site?"

"The outside men seem to be on their way to an automated drilling site on the sunlit side of the moon. There is no one presently at the missile launch site."

"Have a few landers deployed to secure the missile site and cut the comm links," Alexander said. "We don't want anyone escaping capture and launching them off." He blinked Bradshaw's icon off before he could reply, for there were other blinking lights in the imaginary Battle Control Center that were turning redder and blinking faster as they called for his attention.

Alexander grinned and the crow's-feet crinkled at the corner of his eyes as he thought about the many surprises the power-hungry, nation-swallowing, planet-grabbing, atheistic Neocommunists down on Mars had coming this day.

CHAPTER 2

LANDING ON MARS

The attack was scheduled at 0800 Mars Zebra Time. That made it midnight at the main target, the base near Olympus Mons that the Neocommunists had unimaginatively called "Novomoskovsk." The Electromagnetic Ferret and Distant Imaging Teams in the Signals Group had identified over three hundred people stationed at Novomoskovsk. Most of them were in bed.

Except for the base-bound "rush hour" of scientific and maintenance vehicles as darkness had approached, the only significant traffic in the past eight hours had been the launch of a suborbital ballistic transport from Novomoskovsk to Novomurmansk at the North Pole of Mars. The transport must have been on an urgent mission, since it carried only three passengers, and one of those passengers was the commissar of Mars—or Novorossiysk, as he had renamed the planet. Alexander was a little annoyed that the commissar would not be captured in his home lair, but from a tactical point of view, the commissar's absence from his command center at the time of attack would make Alexander's job all the easier.

The fleet of 160 attack landers, having pulled far ahead of the still quiescent interplanetary spacecraft that had transported them there, now zoomed straight down at Syrtis Major, the midday point on Mars. They were followed closely by their 160 medic ships and 160 quartermaster ships. In the center of the pyramid array of ten Squadrons was *Bucephalus*, the golden ship of Alexander.

Soon the First Squadron broke away and headed for Deimos, around to the east of the planet. Then the Second Squadron started to decelerate to come to a halt at Phobos, doing so with fuel-inefficient maneuvers that avoided pointing the main engine exhausts of the landers directly at Mars or the moons. The remaining 384 ships hit the thin upper atmosphere of Mars at high speed, their heavy thermal insulation giving off a bright, but unseen, red glow high in the dusty pink midday Martian sky above the unpopulated Syrtis Major Plain. They showered the empty cratered highlands of Tyrrhena and Arabia with unheard sonic booms, then scattered in different directions to find their targets, some halfway around the globe. *Bucephalus* went into a low polar orbit, while robotic probes controlled by the Signals Group stationed imaging, ferret, and communications satellites in various orbits all around the globe.

Two small figures carrying a heavy metal casting between them danced slowly across the surface of Deimos. The heavy casting moved in a smooth, ponderous arc, while the bodies of the figures holding the casting bounced up and down, their toes making occasional contact with the cratered ground. The two moved out of the shadow and across the terminator into the glaring Sun. Behind them, a huge full Mars started to sink below the horizon.

"Boris calling Base. Vlad and I are over terminator. Three kilometers to drill site."

A perfunctory acknowledgment came from the base. The delay was longer than one would expect from the automatic radio relays that covered the tiny moon—the two men on duty must be playing chess again. But there was little else to do during the fifteen-hour "night" on the moon. Boris and Vladimir continued their dance with their heavyweight partner, subtly adjusting its ballistic "orbit" across the surface of the moon at each hop.

A tiny electronic chime rang at the back of Boris's helmet. It was 0800. At the same time his suit radio started to buzz with noisy static. Something must have gone wrong with his radio. Boris tongued the volume down. Then, out of the corner of his eye, Boris saw something moving rapidly across the surface of a nearby hill.

That's impossible! he thought, as he turned his shoulders to get a better look.

It was a shadow . . . no . . . four shadows . . . moving directly toward them.

He then noticed that Vladimir had stopped holding on to the casting and was trying to come to a stop while looking upward. Boris looked up, too . . . and let the casting go on its way.

Floating slowly down from the sky on soft gas jets were thirty-six armed soldiers in armored spacesuits with a charcoal-gray camouflage pattern matched to the color of the soil of Deimos. The holes in the ends of the thirty-six accuguns each looked as big as the orb of Mars, and Boris had to squint his eyes against the flickering stabs of laser light that streaked back and forth on his body as the troopers slowly fell to the surface to form a large circle around them. The static in his suit radio grew louder and Boris knew that it would be useless to try to call for help.

Boris and Vladimir waited in silence, their hands in the air, while the man in the spacesuit with the distinctive captain's bars on it made his inexperienced way across the surface toward them. A lunar lope did not work on this moon.

While they were waiting, they felt a slight rumbling in the ground. The heavy casting had finally plowed its way into the surface some tens of meters away.

As 0800 had approached, Alexander had been under the visor, his eyes scanning the Battle Control Center, looking for blinking trouble lights. Having found none, he had relaxed a little, and at 0800, when the attack started, he had nothing to do. The icons of everyone in the Battle Control Center were ignoring him and were either talking to each other or looking at their consoles.

He found the viewscreen in the back that gave an overhead view of the attack on the main base at Olympus Mons. The picture came from a satellite and was made up of a combination of passive infrared and reflected starlight images. One of the first attack landers had already landed, out of sight of the base, in a distant crater. Its quartermaster ship had pulled up beside it, while its medical ship was back a kilometer. The landers had the six-pointed Star of David, being from the Israeli spaceship *Shalom* that augmented the U.S.

Third Squadron. These were one of the three long distance "heavy artillery" attack groups that were going to take the fight out of the base.

Alexander shifted his glance back through the Battle Control Center to find the flight leader of the Israeli contingent. As he did so, he noticed that the computer had shifted the position of the U.S. First Squadron off to the side of the imaginary room. The icons of Colonel Bradshaw and Admiral Takahashi were faded in tone and still. The lights on their consoles were a soft, steady green, and their subordinates with their consoles had been erased from the volume. The attack on Deimos must be over already—and a success. He looked down at his status board. No losses yet.

Alexander found the Israeli console. The icon of the Israeli flight commander was looking over the shoulder of one of his group captains at the captain's console screen. The computer printed their names in midair below their faces, Colonel Yitzhak Begin and Captain Ben Shamir. Alexander looked at the captain's console screen and deliberately widened his eyes. Immediately he was seeing what the group captain was seeing.

If any of the commanders had used their battle visors to look around the imaginary Battle Control Center to find Alexander at that time, they would have seen Alexander's icon looking over one shoulder of the group captain, while the flight leader's icon looked over the other shoulder.

It was dark, so the group captain and all his men were seeing by using the high-sensitivity helmeyes that looked out the top of their helmets and fed the processed output into their faceplates.

"Gamma Squad!" Captain Shamir said. "Help the quartermaster set up those missile launchers. The sooner you get them up, the sooner you can shoot them."

Six men got up from the lip of the crater, where they had each been adjusting a combination console and telescope that was used to guide the precision munitions. The quartermaster left his four stevedores to finish erecting the missile launchers for the Beta Squad and led the Gamma Squad into the cavernous hold of the supply ship.

"Alpha Squad hooked up and armed, sir!" said a voice that was stereoed off to the left. The captain turned his helmeyes to the left, and Alexander saw a line of five troopers peering through their precision aimers over the crater rim toward the Neocommunist base some kilometers distant. Their sergeant was facing the captain.

"0810. Very good, Sergeant Meier. We may beat the Brits and Canucks to the target yet. The first round to the target should take out the balloon dome over the central plaza. Fire and keep firing until there isn't a structure over two meters high still standing. But keep those missiles high. We don't want to really hurt anyone." His last words were partially muffled by the roar from five fiber-optic guided rockets with pointed noses and large hooked fins.

Alexander glanced at one of the troopers controlling one of the speeding rockets and widened his eyes. Instantly he was seeing what that trooper was seeing—he was in the nose of one of the rockets, streaking low across the cratered ground. Ahead were two other rockets, and far off to the left he could see another barrage of five missiles coming in from either the Canadian or Great Britain missile unit. The lead rocket ahead of his rocket ripped through the heavy fabric of the central plaza dome, and the second rocket finished the destruction, as a fountain of dust and tons of precious oxygen and nitrogen exploded upward into the thin Martian atmosphere.

The trooper controlling Alexander's rocket directed it toward the top of a corridor. The rocket smashed through the fabric heading above an airlock and flew down the corridor, its top fin ripping up the ceiling. There was a brief image of someone, halfway into a pressure suit, scrambling down the corridor, then the missile was back outside.

Alexander blinked back to the attack captain's visor. All three of the squads were now active, firing one missile after another. Overhead roared the main wave of attack landers from the U.S. Third Squadron, each followed by its medic and quartermaster ship. The attack landers landed about a half mile from the now-tattered target building.

Now that the attack had started, the sky was turned on. High
in the sky over every battlefield, the Battlefield Illumination Team
of the Signals Group unfurled huge multikilometer reflectors in
space that sent down beams of sunlight that literally turned night
into day for kilometers around.

Alexander blinked his way back to the Battle Control Center
and looked down at his status board. Both moons, the South Pole
base, and Solis Lacus already taken. Eight troopers wounded, none
dead. No known enemy dead, but some wounded. They still had
the four biggest bases to take: the ones at Olympus Mons, Melas
Chasm, Hellas Basin, and the North Pole. He looked around the
imaginary room. The icons of many of the squadron commanders—
their objectives taken—had faded off into the corners of the room,
their subordinates erased from the volume. He glanced at the
brighter icons. They were all busy and their lights were steady and
white.

He found the U.S. Third Squadron complex and reentered the
battle around Olympus Mons. This time he found himself looking
out the visor of a group captain the computer identified as Captain
Ralph Wilson. The captain was looking at a map with his quartermaster. The captain was physically nowhere near the quartermaster,
and the map existed only in computer memory, but they both
pointed out spots on it, and each one could see where the other
one's "hand" pointed.

"I want nestguns here, here, and here," Captain Wilson said.

"You got 'em," the quartermaster said agreeably. "I got lots
more. You want one over here, too?" he asked, pointing.

"Why not?" Captain Wilson said. Then—unaware that Alexander was figuratively inside his helmet with him—continued, "Alexander the Greatest would stomp me under the high-rise heel of
one of his gold-spangled boots if I let one of my men get so much
as a stubbed toe."

Alexander's eyes narrowed. He would not forget the name of
Captain Ralph Wilson. The visor image flickered slightly as the
computer tried to interpret his eye signals. Alexander opened his
eyes to normal and the scene continued.

The heavy nestguns, hovering their heavy load of pellets and fuel on partially curtained jets of generated gas, were led out of the hold of the quartermaster ship by the four stevedores. The quartermaster fed their computers the map coordinates and the nestguns waddled their way forward into their places.

"They're all yours, Captain," the quartermaster said, turning over the controls to the nestguns. As he did so, four tiny gun icons appeared in the captain's visor. The icons were superimposed on the image of the nestguns in the visor when the nestguns were in sight, or tucked in the corner of the visor when the nestguns were out of sight.

The captain must have done something with his tongue or eyes, because the nestguns went into automatic mode, swiveling back and forth, using generated gas to shoot pellets at random times at obvious targets in the distant buildings, such as windows, doorways, or holes big enough to shoot out of. The pellets were the same ones used in the accuguns. Sharp enough, fast enough, and slippery enough to puncture nearly anything, but small enough that they were more likely to wound than kill.

"All right, troops," Captain Wilson said over the command channel, "into your foxmobiles. We're moving in."

The foxmobiles were mobile foxholes. Almost a meter high and two meters in diameter at the bottom, with tapered sides of light armor leading up to a manhole in the top, they had six tilted retractable wheels that could be used in various combinations to move it around. The foxmobile didn't have the power or traction to carry a trooper, too, so either it was moved into position and the human ran to it and jumped in, or the trooper crawled along the ground inside while the foxmobile did its best to keep up with him.

Like a chess master, Captain Wilson kept his troops in their foxmobiles, supplying covering fire from his nestguns while shifting them into position for the next attack. Alexander watched with grudging approval as Captain Wilson concentrated on the weak point in the base, a breech in an outer lock to a cargo bay that led off in three different directions.

"Ready a wire-guided rover with a pellet head," Captain Wilson said to the quartermaster.

"Already done," the quartermaster replied. "You want me to put the rover in the center of the bay as usual?"

Alexander could see the intensive training pay off. For months, these two men had taken the troops through weekly practice attacks on a mock-up of this base on the Moon, wearing weights to simulate the greater gravity of Mars.

"Right. With the pellet beamers set to shoot down the three corridors," Captain Wilson said.

"Way ahead of you," the quartermaster said. "Ready when you are." The voice of the quartermaster was artificially stereoed so that the quartermaster seemed to be right next to Captain Wilson's left shoulder.

All around the captain were the voices of his troops muttering to themselves. Over the secure spread-spectrum radio links, each voice was artificially stereoed so that it seemed to come from the physical direction of that trooper in relation to his captain. Knowing the links were secure, the troopers talked and passed on information as if they were a group of noisy, novice hunters passing through a wood.

"Still quiet on this side," a squad leader to the left said. "Saw some movement through a porthole a little while ago, but no shots have been fired."

"I wish to fuck we'd do something," a soldier muttered from front center. He gave a muffled grunt as if he was trying to change position inside his foxmobile. There was a shot and a muffled curse.

"Goddammit Captain! They got me in the hand! I was just holding the top edge to shift my weight and the bastard got me! I'm sorry, Captain."

"That's okay, Parker," Captain Wilson said with an audible sigh. "I'm glad it isn't too serious. Everybody hold up and keep down while we get Parker out of here. Turn on your medic light, Parker."

Off in the distance, Parker's half-hidden foxmobile sent up a telescoping rod with a blinking red light on the end.

"Medics on the way," said a voice stereoed to the right rear of Captain Wilson's helmet. A simulated rushing sound indicated the approach of the hopper on its jets of generated gas. As the hopper approached the enemy building it slowed and rotated around 360 degrees to show those inside the building the lack of weapons and the multitude of red crosses. It then proceeded to the blinking red light. The two medics put the hopper down next to the foxmobile as the injured trooper climbed out. They slipped a heated mitten patch over the injured hand, tightened the sealing band around the forearm of his spacesuit, and pressurized the mitten.

"I'm sorry, Captain," the trooper said again as he climbed into the stretcher pod between the two medics.

"Good-bye, Parker," the captain said sadly. The medics lowered the top of the stretcher pod over the injured man, pressurized the pod just in case, and flew the trooper back to the waiting medical lander.

Captain Wilson turned his attention to the damaged lock that waited in the distance. Murmurs came from the troops around him, muted by the communications control program.

"Alpha Squad will enter the airlock right after the rover!" Captain Wilson commanded. "Beta Squad will follow up in their fox-mobiles. Gamma Squad will redeploy outside as backup."

"All right Alphas," the squad leader said. "I want to see you tripping over that rover wire as it goes in."

"Fire rover!" Captain Wilson said, and a simulated roar sounded in back of everyone as the rover shot forward on its four down-pointed jets and flashed between the troops, who were already start-ing to move slowly forward inside their foxmobiles. The rover slowed as it neared the entrance to the airlock and brilliant strobe lights and an occasional shrapnel pellet shot forward, providing cover for the attacking troops. As the rover passed each foxmobile, the trooper inside jumped from shelter and ran after the flying ma-chine, the wheeled foxmobile doing the best it could to keep up with the legged human over the rough terrain. One of the troopers stumbled momentarily as he was tripped up by a nearly invisible

and nearly unbreakable optical fiber left from the initial missile barrage.

Alexander noticed that the leading attack trooper ran funny—
another damn woman—taking chances just to prove she was as good
as a man. She was inside the airlock with the rover when it exploded, sending pellets in all directions—except back toward the
troops that it had protected during their advance.

"All clear in here, Sarge!" a soprano voice said.

Captain Wilson and Alexander watched the Alpha Squad leader
as he deployed his troops to guard the three corridors entering the
air lock. He first made sure they were all tucked into their foxmobiles, which had ambled in after the fleet-of-foot humans, then hunkered down in his own foxmobile, his helmeyes scanning back and
forth above the lip of the foxmobile.

"All secure, sir!" the squad leader reported.

"Beta Squad!" Captain Wilson said, but the squad was already
in action. Their spare foxmobiles were already taking up positions
in front of Alpha Squad, and troopers were dashing from the safety
of their outside foxmobiles to the inside ones.

"White flag! Hold your fire!" said an override voice that was
stereoed as if it came from above. It was Captain King from the
attack group to the right.

"This is Signals," another override voice said. "We have a surrender message coming over most channels."

Objective taken, Alexander thought. But spoiled. Just because
one stupid trooper got his hand in the way of an enemy bullet.

Alexander heard a whisper from over his left shoulder. It was
the urgent message voice of his communications control computer.
Alexander had it programmed to imitate the sultry voice of a most
amazing blond bombshell he once knew. He would never ignore
that voice no matter what the circumstances.

"Urgent message from the Sixth Squadron at the North Pole,"
the computer said breathlessly. "They are having trouble subduing
the base there and are asking permission to attack unarmored enemy
individuals with missiles."

Alexander blinked back from his close contact with Captain

Wilson and looked at his status board. All objectives had been taken with the exception of the base at the North Pole. Total casualty list, two dead and fourteen wounded. As he watched, the count jumped to fifteen wounded. Another trooper had been hit at the North Pole. Alexander looked out into the imaginary Battle Control Center and found the icon of the commander of the Sixth Squadron, Colonel Melrose. Colonel Melrose was looking at him expectantly. Alexander widened his eyes and the icon image zoomed in and turned into real-time video.

"We have the base surrounded and subdued to the point where they are no longer shooting at us, but they still refuse to surrender. The real problem is that three enemy individuals had been out exploring the polar ice cap in a crawler and returned after our attack was underway. They surprised a quartermaster ship when the men were outside busy deploying hardware, knocked them down in the snow with those big, balloonlike wire wheels on the crawler, and took their accuguns, ammunition, and some hand-thrown miniseeker missiles. They're back up on a nearby glacier cliff, shooting down at us. At that angle they can shoot through the top of a foxmobile unless you keep the hatch closed."

Alexander glanced away from the video image, and it shrank as he searched out a particular screen on the back wall of the imaginary control center. He found the screen. It contained a computer-generated map of Mars covered with numerous, slowly moving, blinking dots of various colors that indicated the objects in orbit around the planet. The dot indicating his personal lander was a bright golden color. It had just passed over the equator in its polar orbit and was approaching the North Pole of Mars. He shifted his glance down to the icon of the woman sitting attentively at his feet at a pilot's console.

"Drop me down at Boreal Base, Betsy!"

"Hold tight," Captain Thomas said. The thrusters roared in reality around him as *Bucephalus* deboosted from orbit. The quartermaster and medic ships assigned to his attack lander followed *Bucephalus* down.

Alexander thought how good this would look in his biography.

After having demonstrated his superior strategic planning ability by successfully carrying out one of the most complicated military endeavors ever attempted, he then proceeded to demonstrate his tactical brilliance by personally leading the attack on the last of the opposition.

"Hang tight, Colonel Melrose," he said. "I'll be right there." He started to think of his plan of attack. It would have to be unconventional, for he was sure that Colonel Melrose had tried all the conventional approaches.

"You tried getting around behind them using three-men hoverjets, I presume," Alexander said.

"They sabotaged the ones at the quartermaster ship they attacked," Commander Melrose said. "And when the quartermaster in C Group attempted to bring in some hoverjets for the troops to use, they shot them down with the miniseekers. One dead and six injured in the crashes."

A good fraction of the total casualties in the whole damn campaign, Alexander thought. Those neocommie sons of bitches are ruining my war. I ought to let Melrose blow 'em to bloody bits with missiles. No ... would look bad if I took the easy way out. Must be *some* way to get at those pinko bastards.

"Landing in five minutes!" Captain Thomas warned.

Suddenly Alexander had an idea. "Take us in ten kilometers up Boreal Canyon from the base, Betsy," Alexander said. The *Bucephalus* tilted abruptly.

"Landing in three minutes, then," Captain Thomas said.

Alexander put on his helmet. The hold of the ship was evacuated to Martian pressure and the inner air lock door opened.

The deliberately overpowered and underloaded *Bucephalus* floated to a landing on a patch of windswept crust, the quartermaster and medic ships crunching to a halt on either side of the general's personal attack lander. His personal guards were out the airlock and deployed in defensive positions around the lander within seconds after the dust had settled. Alexander exited from the airlock and started off in a long, loping stride toward the medic ship.

———

The three Russians on top of the glacier were arguing among themselves and with their comrades trapped inside Novomurmansk base at the North Pole of Mars.

"We've just received word from Novomoskovsk that they have surrendered," a voice from the base said. "That's every base except Novovladivostok at the South Pole, and we've been out of contact with them since the attack started. It isn't any use holding out any longer. We are outnumbered and there is no one to rescue us."

"I am still commissar of Novorossiysk," the fat Russian said, firing a shot from the captured accugun at the top plate of a foxmobile below him. "And I say we will hold out as long as is necessary to achieve victory over these bloodthirsty American wolves in United Nations fleeces, and their sniveling lackeys."

"It's that sort of neocommunist rhetoric that got us into this predicament," the tall Russian shouted, also firing an occasional shot to keep the attackers below pinned down. "If you hadn't gone and claimed Mars for the New Soviet Union, we would still be in control here."

"My arm is getting numb," the small Russian said, sitting on the ice behind a rock and holding his injured arm.

"Let me take a look at it," the tall one said, bending over to release the tourniquet on the outside of the thin Marsuit and checking the patch over the entry point of the pellet. There was no way to check if the bleeding had stopped inside. "Hold your arm above your head and turn your glove heat on high. If you still feel blood trickling down your arm after a minute, I'll have to retighten the tourniquet."

"I didn't claim Mars for the Union," the commissar objected. "I said I was claiming it in the name of the New Soviet Union for the good of all mankind." He fired another shot at the base of a foxmobile that was up on its wheels and attempting to move with a trooper crawling inside. A flashing red light appeared out of the top of the foxmobile. A hopper lifted in the distance and came toward them. The commissar reached for a miniseeker.

"Don't throw!" the tall one said, holding onto his arm. "Can't you see it's a medical ship? Look at the red crosses on it."

The commissar put down the miniseeker and chuckled. "At least I dislodged another periwinkle." They watched as the medical hopper zoomed to the foxmobile with the flashing red light and stopped. Two medics jumped out, pulled the limping trooper from the foxmobile, placed him in the enclosed stretcher pod between their seats, and took off for the medical lander in the distance.

"It's still trickling," the small Russian said in a weak voice. The tall Russian went over, tightened the tourniquet, then rubbed the arm below the injury. What their side needed was one of those medical evacuation craft. The small Russian stirred and pointed off in the distance.

"There's something coming up behind us!"

The commissar whirled around to see three hoppers coming straight for them. He reached for a miniseeker, then just held it in his hand as the hoppers came to a halt some distance away. He saw that they, too, had red crosses on their sides. A voice speaking poor Russian came over the international emergency channel.

"You have injured one. Can we help?"

"I feel dizzy," the small Russian said, and slumped onto the ice. The tall one kneeled at his side. As if that were a signal, one of the hoppers moved slowly forward toward the injured man and came to a stop. The two medics aboard jumped out to help the tall Russian carry the injured man toward the enclosed stretcher pod.

As they approached the hopper, the stretcher pod popped open. A figure in a golden battle suit with a crested helmet hopped out, the business end of his .45 rocketgun making a steady bright red dot on the chest of the commissar. At the same instant the other stretcher pods on the other two hoppers opened to show armed men. Then, all the "medics" pulled handguns from beneath their red-cross-covered chestpacks and leveled them at the Russians.

The commissar froze and dropped his accugun. Then, carefully holding the miniseeker between two fingers, he lowered it slowly to the ground. While all eyes and guns were on the commissar, the tall Russian suddenly rushed the gilded trooper and started hitting him on the faceplate with both fists, screaming in English.

"How dare you violate sanctity of Red Cross!"

Alexander, surprised by the unarmed Russian, tried to fend off the unexpected blows. He was slightly shorter, but had the muscular body and training of a boxer. He went into a clinch. Peering through the visor of his captive, he saw the enraged blue eyes and short blond hair of a woman!

Suddenly, through the two tinted faceplates, she too saw his face for the first time. Her eyes opened wide in recognition, and she collapsed onto his chest and hugged him around the waist, crying and babbling in English, her voice echoing through where their helmets touched.

"It's you! Thank God, it's you! Hold me tight!"

CHAPTER 3

THE CONQUEROR

The commissar looked dourly at the sign tossed to one side of the door to his office. The sign had been broken in two by someone's knee, but he could still read the Cyrillic characters on it: *Ivan Petrovich—Commissar of Novorossiysk*. In its place on the door was a hastily written name done with the bold strokes of a black marking pen. The door now said: *Gen. A. Armstrong—Commanding*.

In permanent ink, the commissar thought. He waited patiently, hands handcuffed behind his back, while his two guards had a brief conversation with the guards on either side of the door.

"The ex-big cheese," the trooper to his left said.

"General Armstrong said to send him right in," the guard said, opening the door.

"Come right in, Commissar Petrovich," Alexander said, leaning back in the inflated easy chair in back of the commissar's desk. "You can take off the handcuffs, Sergeant, and wait outside. I'm sure I can handle him if he's so foolish as to try anything."

General Armstrong waved to a long, segmented plastic chaise lounge against one wall. Its dark blue base sections were filled with water to hold it still, while the light blue arms and backs were inflated with air. "Sit down," he said pleasantly.

Leaning back further and looking around, Alexander said, "Nice office you have here. I, of course, will be using it in the future . . . your quarters, too. I'm sure the boys can find you a bed in an apartment somewhere in the guarded wing."

Alexander suddenly turned serious, leaned forward on the desk, and stared at Ivan. The famous crow's-feet pattern formed once again on Alexander's face, but there was no smile underneath.

"I want the passwords!"

"They won't do you any good. I had the sensitive memory banks erased the minute I knew we were under attack."

"So the owlies in my Signals Group informed me. But they ferreted out the command log and found that each of the files had been copied onto holocube by your meticulous computer operators before being erased from the mainframe memory."

"The idiots!"

"And we have the holoblock," Alexander continued, finally smiling. "There aren't too many places you can hide things in a pressurized base." The smile faded abruptly. "I want the passwords!"

"No!" Ivan said, confident that there was nothing serious that these soft-hearted Americans could do to him that could make him talk. He could take solitary confinement with nothing but bread and water. Would do him good to lose a little weight.

"You, personally, killed one of my troopers and injured at least eight others," Alexander said in a low voice. "I have not yet officially declared the invasion over. We are still in the process of confirming all casualties on your side. If you do not give me the passwords *now*, you will be the last one."

Ivan remained silent.

"Guards!" Alexander hollered. The door opened and the troopers came in.

"Escort this man out the west lock—without a suit!"

"Sir?" the sergeant said.

"That is a direct order, Sergeant!" Alexander snapped. He glanced at the other troopers. "These men are your witnesses. Carry on."

"Yes sir!"

While one trooper held a gun pointed at him, two other troopers pulled Ivan roughly from the soft sofa, and the sergeant snapped on the handcuffs. Alexander came around the desk and held the door open.

"Good-bye, Commissar Ivan Petrovich. Are you sure you don't want to let me have the passwords?"

"No!" Ivan answered, sure that the general was bluffing.

"Good!" Alexander said with an evil smile, his eyes narrow slits at the ends of the furrowed crow's-feet. "For I will *never* forgive you for doubling the butcher bill in what was to be my crowning glory." He pushed his face into Ivan's and sneered.

"I don't get mad at people, Comrade Petrovich. I get *rid* of them." He stood back, holding the door open.

"Take him away, Sergeant."

As the sergeant and a trooper marched Ivan down the corridor, guns now drawn, Alexander leaned in the doorway and continued talking, almost as if to himself.

"Of course, if the passwords are ten-digit random numbers, then it will take my owlies years to find them. But if they're words, there are only some hundred thousand words in the Russian language. That should take them less than a week. Besides, we found Commissar Petrovich's publicity profile. You'd be surprised at the detail. His wife's parents' names . . . all the names and nicknames of his children . . . even the names of his two dogs . . ."

"Wait!" Ivan cried, far down the hall.

"Take him to the Signals Group," Alexander hollered down the hall to the sergeant. "And if he isn't fully cooperative, you know what to do!" He slammed the door behind him.

Tanya Pavlova's mind was churning with mixed emotions. The troopers had been kind to her, but had insisted on the handcuffs. She looked at the door ahead of her. The words *General* and *Armstrong* seemed like a contradiction in terms. But a lot had happened in the past eight years. The barriers between the two countries had slammed shut again after the Neocommunist coup and very little news about her old friends in the United States had filtered through.

The guards opened the door and she walked in.

"Tanya Pavlova," Alexander said, smiling pleasantly. "The last time I saw you, you were hitting my head with your fists. But I'm sure you won't be doing that now, will you?" He turned to the guards. "You can take off the handcuffs."

He waited until the two troopers left, then spoke to his personal guard at his door.

"We are not to be disturbed for any reason, Sergeant."

"Yes sir!" the sergeant said, a twinge of a smile at the corner of his lips as he looked at the rear of the slim, curvy woman in the two-piece coveralls.

After the door was closed, Alexander smiled and came around the desk to stand in front of Tanya. She hung her head and tried to avoid looking him directly in the face as he spoke to her.

"I also remember that you said something out there on the glacier. 'Hold me tight,' you said. It was a little hard to do it then, but I'm ready now." He stretched out his arms to her.

"I'm so mixed up," Tanya protested, putting her hands on his forearms and running them slowly up onto his massive, boxer's biceps. "My body wants me to throw myself into your arms, but my brain insists you are the enemy."

"We don't have to be enemies any longer," Alexander said, stepping closer. She took one step toward him, then whirled around and faced away.

He moved closer and slowly placed his hands on her shoulders. She tensed up. He softly rubbed her shoulders and neck until the tenseness eased. He ran his hands down her arms, moved closer, then put his hands on her waist, at the same time letting his lips brush the back of her neck. She leaned back into his arms.

He kissed one side of her neck, then the other, as his hands moved up her body. Slowly he cupped his hands around her breasts. She did not protest.

Suddenly she grabbed his left hand with both of hers and looked down at it.

"You're not Gus!" She whirled around in his arms to look him closely in the face for the first time.

"I'm better than Gus. I've got all my fingers—the better to feel you with, my dear." His fingers squeezed her from behind as if to illustrate.

"Stop!" she said, reaching down to take his hands off her.

"Why should we stop?" Alexander argued, grabbing one wrist and putting it behind her, pulling her close once again. "You were certainly enjoying yourself. Why not continue? We even have a soft sofa to finish things off with." He started to unbutton her shirt.

"No! Stop! I'll scream," she said, backing away.

"The guards won't come in," he said, grabbing her short blond hair roughly with his other hand. He pulled her head up and his tongue raped her mouth.

She wrestled away, but he finally got both her hands behind her back. He started walking her toward the couch.

"You can't deny you came here ready for this. You know you're enjoying every moment. But if you're going to play at being a tease, first turning me on, and then saying 'No,' I may have to get rough with you."

He threw her on the sofa.

There was a loud, insistent knock on the door.

"I said I was not to be disturbed!" Alexander shouted at the door.

The loud, insistent knock was repeated and the door opened.

"Gus!" Tanya said, trying to button up her shirt.

"I see you've met Alex," Gus said. He turned to Alexander.

"We still have an invasion to finish off, Alex. Don't you think Tanya should return to her quarters and you two could continue this discussion at some other time?"

"Gus! I—he—" Tanya stammered.

"Sure . . . we'll continue our *conversation* at some other time," Alexander said with a smirk, regaining his composure and taking command of the situation. "Guards! Take her away!"

Tanya gave one more embarrassed glance at Gus and went quickly out the door.

Alexander returned to his seat behind the desk, while Gus paced firmly back and forth in front of the desk.

"I hadn't heard from you in some time, Alex," Gus said. "Since there was a shuttle coming down bringing the technicians to repair the base, I got a ride on it. According to our situation analysts up with the fleet, you have things completely under control. Isn't it time we reverted to civilian command?"

"I still have to collect all the neocommies on Mars here at Olympia base, then ship them up for the return flight back to Earth," Alexander countered. "But first I have to find out who the KGB agents are, so I can keep them under tight security. I should have that information shortly, once we get the passwords to the personnel files."

"Alex, I agree that the politicians and the KGB agents should go. But the knowledge that the technicians and scientists have about running the base and exploring Mars will be valuable."

"Every technician is a potential saboteur and every scientist a probable spy," Alexander said. "I say we should send them all back!"

"I still think the technicians and scientists can be useful," Gus insisted. "I know most of them from before the Neocommunist coup. They're the top people in their field, and they've got more years of field experience than our best planetary scientists. I've even coauthored papers on near-Earth asteroid composition with Viktor Braginsky and lunar vulcanism with Tanya Pavlova."

"That Tanya is some volcano, herself." Alexander laughed. "You two must have done more than coauthor papers together."

"We did spend a couple of months together on the Moon in a solar-powered crawler," Gus admitted. "We were exploring the Aristarchus Crater volcanic field."

"Now I understand why you want her to stay here on Mars," Alexander said, a smirk growing on his face and his eyes disappearing in the crow's-feet folds. "No, dear brother, she goes back with me as a prisoner, and I get a chance at taming the blond vixen."

"To you, she's nothing but a woman to screw!" Gus yelled, his fury at what his brother had tried to do breaking through. He took a deep, steadying breath. "We need her planetary expertise here on Mars," he said firmly.

"Not if I have anything to say about it!" Alexander shouted.

There was a pause as the two glared at each other.

"You *don't* have anything to say about it," Gus said grimly. "As of right now, I am reassuming command of the expedition."

Alexander stopped. His brother had won this one. It wouldn't look good on his record if he tried to violate the almost sacred principle of the United States that the military was controlled by civilian authority, even though this was nominally a UN mission. He wanted his four-star brevet rank for the expedition made permanent. Then, within a few years, he would be the top candidate for chief of staff of the whole U.S. defense force.

"With your permission, *sir*," he said to his brother, "I intend to include in my summary report back to the president and Congress, the recommendation that *all* the Russians be removed and replaced with a pure U.S. contingent."

"You may do that, Alex. But don't forget our allies—Japan, India, Canada, Brazil, Australia, Israel, and the Europeans. Some of them have excellent planetologists."

"You know as well as I do that they were only along to make it look good in the history books—a UN force instead of a U.S. force. They only suffered one casualty. We did the fighting, we should get the spoils."

"The war is over, Alex," Gus said soothingly. "Mars isn't booty that belongs to the United States, it belongs to the whole world. Maybe with this incident out of the way, the peoples of the world can stop bickering among themselves and work together to utilize the immense resources of the solar system."

"I'll never trust those atheistic neocommies," Alexander said. He paused and looked around the room. "Well, I guess you'll want to take over this office, it being the biggest on Mars. All you'll have to do is scratch out the word *General* on the door and put in *Doctor*."

"No. You keep it," Gus said. "I'm going to take an office over in the science wing. As soon as I can get my administrative assistant down here and set up, I'm going to take some time to do some science."

Four days later, Gus found enough free time to visit Tanya in her apartment. Her roommate had already been shipped out up to the *Lexington* for eventual transfer back to Earth. After a tense and perfunctory greeting, Gus slumped into a magnesium-frame hammock chair. Tanya stood behind him and ran her fingers through his short, dark hair, graying at the temples.

"Alex won, Tanya," Gus said in a discouraged tone of voice. "I had hoped that we could limit the number of Russian people removed from Mars, so that we could all work together, explore the planet together, face common dangers together, and show both our nations that it is possible for us to cooperate. But when the Signals Group finally broke into the security files, it seemed like practically every person on Mars was a KGB agent. Even your roommate."

"But Maria was a nuclear engineer," Tanya said, resting one hand on his shoulder. "She ran the second shift at the main power plant for the base."

"Her grandmother was Jewish," Gus said. "And in return for letting her grandmother go to Israel to die, Maria became a KGB agent at sixteen. They didn't ask her to do very much. But one of the things she did was to file daily reports on your behavior."

"Maria!" Tanya exclaimed. "I can't believe it. Why were they interested in me?"

"You had been under suspicion ever since you and I explored Aristarchus together," Gus said. "In fact, the way we finally decided on the list of those that could stay was to pick those that the KGB didn't trust. That only left some twelve scientists and thirty techs out of eight hundred people on Mars and the moons."

"I guess I can understand their suspicions about me. We did get pretty friendly during that trip."

"Yes," Gus agreed, looking uncomfortable and turning red.

"You're blushing!" Tanya said, turning his chin with her hands so she could see his cheeks.

"If you remember," Gus said, "that was a Russian-built crawler."

"Why is that important?"

"There were electronic bugs all through it. In your computer dossier is a complete transcript of everything we said during those weeks. Alex had a great laugh reading it. Especially your 'Gussie, dearest . . . let's do it again' phrase."

Now it was Tanya's turn to blush. He looked up at her, then they both laughed together. Tanya dropped her hands and walked to the small porthole in her room that looked out at the Martian surface through thick glass.

"Do you remember how at the end of a long day out on the lunar surface, we would come inside, help each other out of our suits, and then after a wash-up with a damp rag and a hot-tray dinner, I would stare out of the porthole at the distant crater rims . . ."

"Then you would say that phrase, and I would come over." Gus got up, walked up behind her, and slowly placed his hands on her shoulders. She was tense, wondering if he would be like his brother or the tender Gus that she had loved so long ago. Technically, he was still her enemy.

He softly rubbed her shoulders and the back of her neck until he felt her tenseness ease. He moved his hands down her arms, then put them on her waist, his lips kissing tenderly at the back of her neck. She melted back into his arms with a sigh.

"This is a Russian base," Tanya warned. "My room is probably full of electronic pickups, since I am so untrustworthy."

"I had them turned off."

"Well, in that case . . ." She paused, then her voice switched tone.

"Gussie, dearest . . ." she said, and turned to smile coyly at him. "Let's do it again!" She took his hand and led him across her room to her plastic water bed framed in thick slabs of diamond-sawed Martian volcanic rock.

Two weeks later, it was time for the invasion fleet to return home in triumph. Gus walked into Alexander's office to say good-bye to his twin brother. Alexander would be returning with the troopers and the captured Russian prisoners of war, while Gus would stay with the replacement group made up of technical people from the United States and their allies. In one hand Gus carried a sheet of fax-erase paper. It contained the condensed and reduced contents of the news portions of the *New York Times*. Even at reduced size, the headline was visible across the room.

ARMSTRONG TAKES MARS! it proclaimed. Just below Gus' mangled thumb stub was a large picture of Alexander. The news article went on to describe the almost zero-casualty-loss capture of Mars, the recently released details of the battle, and the plans to return most of the Russians back to Earth.

"Look at the caption under your picture," Gus said. "Alexander the Great!"

"Fits me, don't you think?" Alexander preened.

"You know, with your present popularity you'd be a shoo-in for president of the United States in forty."

"You're probably right," said Alexander, with a thoughtful expression on his face. "But I think I'll stick with the military for a while. If you're a president and give an order, the civil servants say 'yes sir' and do what they've always done. In the military, when I say 'shit,' people squat."

He held up his collar tip and looked at the four gold stars with pride. "Once these four stars are permanent, I'll have more *real* power than any president." Alexander looked up from his collar at his brother.

"Are you sure you don't want me to take the rest of the Russkies back, Gus? I know why you want to keep Tanya around, but Viktor Braginsky and the other neocommie scientists will give you nothing but trouble."

Gus shifted uneasily in the inflated sofa in Alexander's office. "They may be Russians, Alex, but they are not *neocommies*. They're scientists. Good scientists. To them, discovering the truth is more important than petty politics."

"Well, don't say I didn't warn you." He got up from behind the desk and came over to shake hands with his brother.

"We part once again, Gus. I really didn't know whether I would be able to stand being subordinate to you after we'd been off doing our own things for so many years, but you weren't a bad boss—at least you didn't get in my way." Alexander pumped Gus' hand and slapped him once on the shoulder.

"Good-bye, O old and wise one," he said.

Gus watched his twin walk out the door.

"You have been rebelling against that one-minute time difference your whole life," he mused.

"I wonder . . . Would you have been a different person if you had been the first born?"

He paused and thought some more.

"I wonder?

"Would I have?"

CHAPTER 4

INDEPENDENCE DAY

After the departure of General Alexander Armstrong and the main body of troopers, the crowding eased at the various bases on Mars. Not all the troops went home. Some of the original contingent had taken up the offer extended by Gus to stay on Mars and help rebuild the bases they had made so thoroughly unlivable when they had first arrived.

Practically the whole Israeli contingent decided to stay, one of them remarking, "This place will be easier to reclaim than the Sinai desert—at least it has some water in it!" The *Shalom* stayed in orbit around Mars with two others of the original invasion fleet of transport spacecraft, while the remaining thirty-seven ships returned, carrying the victorious troops and their prisoners back to Earth.

The attack trooper barracks that had been added to the original complexes were partitioned into individual quarters. The ripped dome at the main base at Olympia had been repaired and there was now a large domed commons plaza that could be used for group meetings and sports activities that needed lots of volume, especially altitude.

Gus had punfully renamed the covered plaza the "Boston Commons," after an elderly planetologist back on Earth. She was still strong in spirit, but her body was now too frail for her to make the trip to Mars. The pressure inside the dome was kept at three-quarters of an Earth atmosphere, a compromise between engineering and comfort, although those from Denver, Los Alamos, and Mexico City found it perfectly normal. Around the base of the dome were exercise rooms with improvised weights, and handball courts made of thick slabs of diamond-sawed Tharsis Ridge lava.

Gus had adopted the Russian calendar system for Mars, which divided the long Martian year into ninety-five weeks of seven sols each, then added holidays—holisols—outside the weekly calendar at the solstices and equinoxes to make up the 669 sols of the year. Today was the apsolstice, the solstice closest to the aphelion of Mars. It was the summer solstice and the longest sol of the year in the northern hemisphere. With Sunday, the first sol of summer, coming tomorrow, this was the start of a two-sol holiday weekend for the hardworking scientists and engineers who normally got only one sol off a week. They had endured the twenty-seven weeks of spring, the longest season of the year, since their last two-sol weekend at the spring or apequinox, and now the commons and the courts were full. Gus was playing handball with Jay Plantagenet, specialist in impact crater dynamics.

"Your serve, Gus," Jay said, tossing him the ball. "Make it a good one, or I'm coming back!" They were both breathing hard in the rarified atmosphere and their breathing echoed loudly around the court. Gus stood at the serving line, bouncing the ball nervously on the floor and wiping the sweat from his forehead. He glanced back at his younger opponent. Jay was Gus's height, but thin and wiry, chocolate-brown, with a large head—to hold all those brains, Gus thought—and glasses held on with an elastic band. Jay let a boyish smile spread across his strong-jawed face as he pushed back a strand of straight black hair.

"Getting tired, old man?" he chided.

Gus bunched his massive, muscular frame and slapped the ball down the court. Jay dove to make the return, but was in no position to follow up as Gus sliced one into the corner to win.

"Great game!" Jay said as Gus helped him up.

"Better let the next pair have the court," Gus said. As they walked out he asked, "I understand you're off on an extended field trip?"

"Yep. Now that summertime is coming to the northern polar

regions, I and a few techs are going to make a traverse of Lomonosov and Kunowsky craters in a crawler."

"That's a long one!" Gus said as they went into the shower. The showers had been one of the benefits of the invasion. The originally spartan Russian base now had an adequate closed-cycle sewage system incorporated with the gardens, pens, and ponds that provided their food.

"Eight hundred kilometers from Boreal Base and a thousand-kilometer traverse," Jay said, peering nearsightedly for the cleansing lotion. "And there's lots of interesting impact structures, so we'll be taking cores along most of the traverse. I expect it to take all summer."

"I'll see you around the perisolstice holisol, then," Gus said, heading for the dressing room.

As Gus left the dressing-room door leading into the commons, he was nearly knocked over by three men in shirts trying to run down a tall, shirtless man with a mass of curly, sandy hair carrying a volleyball negligently in one hand. It was Chris Stoker, playing goalie for the "Skins" in the game of air polo that he had invented. Chris had just run around behind his goal after making a save. Using his almost two-meter height to advantage, he leaped into the air and threw the ball down the field to another Skin, keeping it high.

As the ball approached, the receiver jumped high, caught the ball, landed on one foot, hopped up easily in the low Martian gravity, and fired the ball to another Skin, who was in full running stride. This one made a high leap after the catch, but, surrounded by Shirts, he couldn't get a good pass off during his trajectory and finally had to touch down with a shoulder. He grounded the ball and took off back toward the Skins goal, along with the rest of the forward Skins.

After a pause to regroup, three backfield Shirts started running toward the motionless ball sitting on the ground. Gus expected the lead shirt to make a flying kick, since the main rule of air polo was that you must make initial contact with the ball while in midair, and except for the goalie, you could only touch the ground once between a catch and a throw, and then with only one foot—or hand, or shoulder, or elbow, or head. Other than that, there seemed to be *no* rules.

Instead of kicking, however, the lead Shirt made a leaping somersault over the ball, picking it up as he went over and flipping it sideways to one of the Shirts beside him. That Shirt took his allowed step, leaped, and fired it downfield to a Shirt running across in front of Chris, anxiously guarding the goal. The Shirt slipped a toss under Chris' lanky reach and scored. Chris called a timeout and went to the sidelines for a drink, where he was immediately surrounded by his teammates and admirers. Gus crossed the field to the center of the dome where the Icarbatics net had been set up.

Icarbatics was only for the lean and wiry. It also helped if you had some experience with Icarbatics on the Moon. The one-sixth gravity on the Moon made it easy for practically anyone to glide down from the ceiling of the tall hangars there with large bat wings strapped to his—or her—arms. The smaller and leaner could even fly up and around for a short while before their muscles got too tired. Icarbatics on Mars was a combination of gliding, diving, gymnastics, and aerobatics, with an emphasis on perfection of technique and beauty of form.

Practitioners of the sport dove from a platform up near the top of the dome. Then, using their custom-made, highly maneuverable arm and leg "wings," they did midair rolls, somersaults, twists, and all the maneuvers of divers on Earth and more as they fell, but in slow motion. In addition, by adding powerful beats from their arm wings, then locking the wings in a back brace at the right instant, they could pull out of a dive like a glider, then carry out different maneuvers on the way up, for all the world like an aerobatic airplane.

Tanya was accomplished at Icarbatics, having practiced extensively when she was on the Moon, although she was a little too large and getting too old to carry out some of the newer routines. Gus watched as Tanya developed a new finale.

"I call it the 'Wounded Phoenix,'" she said, strapping on her wings. She wore a sky-blue skintight leotard that matched her eyes and contrasted nicely with her light-blond hair. It also showed off her small but still firm breasts, narrow waist, and full hips. Strutting stiff-legged in the braces, she walked over to Gus, gave him a pat on the cheek, and headed for the hoist.

Gus watched her approvingly as she grasped the bar on a rope hoist and a motor pulled her up to a narrow platform at the top of the dome. She poised for a moment, spread her sky-blue wings, and dove headfirst toward the ground. After a fairly standard dive routine with a "Falling Leaf" thrown into the middle, she locked her wing struts for a high-speed pullout and went into a spiraling climb that went straight up. Near the peak of her trajectory, she stopped her spiral by stretching her wings and legs out to her side. Her momentum continued to carry her motionless, spread-eagled body straight up.

Suddenly, she collapsed, as if pierced by a bullet, her arm wings and leg flaps flailing randomly, her body seemingly tumbling out of control. Gus felt his heart skip a beat. But just before she hit the safety net, her body was in the correct position to bring her fall to a halt with two strong down beats of her wings. She came to a proud, spread-eagled halt, standing motionless in the exact center of the landing pad at the center of the safety net.

Gus and the others watching clapped appreciatively as Tanya bounded to the edge of the net, her flapping wings extending her bounds more than normally in the low Martian gravity. Gus reached up his arms to help her down, but she shook her head and, grinning, flapped over his outstretched arms and landed in back of him. As he came up, she turned her back to him, and he obediently held the titanium-lithium alloy tubing brace-frame while she pulled her arms free from the wings and unbuckled her chest and leg straps.

"I'll take it now," she said, collapsing the wings and folding them up into a long cluster of tubing, wires, and blue fabric. She reached out to squeeze him on the arm.

"You had better get the commons ready for the meeting."

Gus then noticed that some of the bystanders were already loosening the ropes on the safety net. He looked down at his watch, then shook his head in disgust. He had forgotten to reset the watch the previous night to add in the forty minutes that was the difference between a Martian day and an Earth day. He had thought there was still an hour before his speech. Now it was only twenty minutes away, and people were already gathering.

Someday, he thought, we will *have* to come up with a proper clock system for Mars.

He hurried off to help the rest of the group roll up the safety net and put it along one wall of the commons.

Gus looked out at the small crowd that nearly filled the Boston Commons—most of the five hundred people in the main base at Olympia were there, spreading out blankets or blowing up inflatable hassocks. Toward the back, Gus could see the curly head of Chris Stoker sticking up out of the crowd of friends he always seemed to have around him.

There were some fifteen hundred more people elsewhere on Mars and its moons. They would watch the meeting on video. The population was roughly one hundred fifty each at Boreal Base and Austral Canyon at the north and south poles, another one hundred each on Phobos and Deimos, with the remaining thousand spread around the planet at various bases.

It took at least twenty-four jack-of-all-trades technicians just to keep a base operating around the clock, with more needed if the base was large or being expanded. The bases where there were significant potential resources, such as the moons, poles, and Solis Lake, had teams of exploration engineers taking detailed core samples and carrying out topographical, gravity, acoustic, microwave, electric current, and chemical surveys. These bases also had process engineers running selected batches of soil through pilot processing plants and scaling up the designs into full-scale plants.

Finally, sprinkled nearly everywhere, were the small group of scientists, less than twenty percent of the population, that went out to explore the regions of the planet that weren't obvious sources of useful resources. The scientists might find some new resources, but that wasn't their main objective. Their job was to understand how

Mars formed some five billion years ago, what it was like originally, how it developed over the intervening billions of years, and why it had become the way they now found it in 2038. What that knowledge would ultimately be good for was unknown.

Gus looked at the video technicians at one side of his platform. He could see the side of his face in the monitor screen coming from a camera at the back of the commons.

"A few more seconds, sir, and Phobos will be over the horizon," one of the technicians said. Gus waited.

"We have a lock. You may proceed, sir."

Gus looked into the video camera in front of him. He gave a smile and his face crinkled up to form the two well-recognized crow's-feet that pointed arrowlike at his half-hidden steel-gray eyes. He dropped into his deep, resonant, speech-giving voice.

"Guds'l," Gus said, using the greeting that the small Australian contingent had made popular. A ripple of laughter ran through the crowd.

"As you know," Gus continued, "this meeting is to formally announce the end of martial law on Mars, and the start of a new independent territory of the United Nations, operating under the protection and the laws of the United States.

"As of the close of this meeting, I will resign as the administrator of Mars for the Reformed United Nations and will assume a position more to my talents and interests, director of the newly formed Sagan Mars Institute and chairman of its planetary physics department. With Fred Whimple as my administrative assistant, I hope to spend most of my time poking my nose into some of the interesting volcanoes around here.

"Since nearly everyone here, scientists, engineers, technicians, and service personnel included, is an employee of the Sagan Mars Institute, and therefore technically a civil servant of the United States, and nearly all our supplies come, at great expense, from the United States, and we operate under the laws of the United States, then you might well ask, 'What's all this nonsense about an independent territory?'

"Well, there are many here on Mars who are *not* employees of the Sagan Institute, and it is the intention of the UN and the U.S. that there be many more in the future. There are the foreign scientists, engineers, and technicians who are guests of the institute, but whose expenses are paid by their governments. There are those who are sponsored by major corporations seeking to generate major profits from space resources, such as the twelve scientists and engineers presently here from Rockwell International, Exxon Energy, Space General, Europlanet, and Rising Star. They can come and go as they like and stay as long as they like, provided their company covers their costs. We hope many more will come and that they will not only make a profit supplying the services that the Sagan Institute presently has to supply for itself, but that they will also find resources of value here on Mars and its moons that are needed on Earth or elsewhere in space. Then there are the group of Russian scientists, engineers, and technicians that remain. Technically, they are still prisoners of war, but at the conclusion of this ceremony, they will become guests of the institute. All of these people should have a voice in running their own affairs.

"Therefore, although U.S. federal law will apply, the people on Mars will have the rights normally reserved to the states and the local governments under the U.S. Constitution and laws. Each permanent base can set up its own city government, with a mayor and council if you want one, but I recommend a town meeting format as long as we're this small. There will be an elected governor of Mars, who will supply guidance to the director of the Sagan Institute on the disposition of the resources allocated for personnel maintenance and services. The election will be held in thirty days, so start campaigning if you are interested."

Gus paused and put a determined look on his face before proceeding in a dead-serious voice. "And . . . for your information . . . I am not running . . . and I will not serve if elected."

A tall figure unfolded himself up off the ground in the back of the crowd.

"If you aren't going to run, then I will!" Chris said.

Immediately a chant started up around him. "Chris for governor! Chris for governor! Chris for governor!"

"Anyone else?" Gus asked, with a pleased smile. "Don't forget the people out at other bases. Some of them would make excellent candidates. Ernest Licon, director of Boreal Base, for example. They don't even have to be U.S. citizens . . ." He leaned forward to look at Boris Batusov, the internationally known antimatter engineer who won the Nobel Prize for the theory behind the Batusov reactor that provided prime electric power for their larger vehicles. "How about it, Boris? Would you like to be governor of Mars?"

Boris grinned and shrugged. "We talk about it later," he said with some embarrassment.

Gus returned to his normal booming formal-speech voice.

"There is one other thing. I was able to convince the Reformed United Nations and the U.S. government that employment in the Sagan Mars Institute should have no strings attached. If you are not happy with your job and cannot find one that suits you, then you can quit at any time. After all, the last thing the institute needs is a disgruntled employee. If you want to go back to Earth, we will send you back on the next available ship. If you want to stay on Mars, you can stay as long as you support yourself by providing services that people will pay for. I will leave it up to the town governments how long they will tolerate nonworking spongers. Actually, we hope that you stay. It saves the institute the cost of shipping you back, and we will always need more people on Mars."

Gus reached into his pocket and pulled out some coins. He walked over to the technicians at one side of the podium and handed them down. Soon the video screen above the podium and similar video screens around the globe and on the moons showed the faces of five coins of graduated sizes and different colors.

"Speaking of paying for services, we now have money you can use to pay for those services. There will be a Mars currency, issued and controlled by the governor of Mars. We have chosen coins of hardened anodized aluminum, so they won't wear out. The one-dollar coin is yellow and has the Viking lander. The ten-dollar coin is green and has Mount Olympus on it, while the one-hundred-dollar coin is blue and has the distinctive pattern of the northern polar ice cap on it. We also have the red cent, a small red aluminum coin with the number one on one side and Deimos on the other, and the orange dime, with the number ten on one side and Phobos on the other. Since we are starting out fresh, the money will make some sense. The thickness and diameter of a coin is proportional to its value, and the colors of the coins follow the colors of the rainbow."

"Those who work for the Sagan Institute have a contract that provides for free room and board while on Mars, in addition to a salary. They can decide how much of their salary they want to draw for use here on Mars, and how much they want to have banked on Earth for use when they get back. We have set an artificially low exchange rate for the Mars dollar at one hundred U.S. dollars for one Mars dollar." There was a gasp from the audience.

"That's to keep people from importing unnecessary items," said Gus. "Don't forget, a kilogram of books, soap, junk food, or practically anything ordinary on Earth costs only around ten U.S. dollars. But to ship that kilogram of junk food to Mars costs over five thousand dollars, a five-hundred-to-one ratio. Thus, the true exchange rate should be something like five hundred U.S. dollars for one Mars dollar. However, if you create that kilogram of junk food, or whatever, on Mars, using Martian resources, then you have created something worth five thousand dollars and you can easily find buyers for it on Mars at one thousand U.S. dollars or ten Mars dollars. It will be one of the unenviable tasks of the governor of Mars to adjust exchange rates and the amount of money in circulation to keep the monetary system working smoothly."

Gus reached under the podium and brought out a large sheet of paper. He waited until the audience quieted and started reading.

"By the authority vested in me by the Reformed United Nations on the planet Earth and the United States of America, I hereby declare the end of martial law on the planet of Mars, and the formation of an independent territory, to be known as the Territory of Mars, with the status of a nonvoting observer at the deliberations of the Reformed United Nations. The Territory of Mars shall be a protectorate of the United Nations, with the protecting nation being the United States of America."

He put the paper on top of the podium and signed it with a flourish.

"I hereby declare sol three hundred and forty-five of Mars year twenty, previously known as the sol of the summer or apsolstice, to henceforth be known as Mars Independence Day!"

A cheer went up from the crowd in the Boston Commons, and he had to lean forward into the microphone to make his last sentence heard.

"Now let's all get to work and get this planet moving!"

He leaped off the platform and Tanya ran up to give him a hug. Then, her arm still around him, they walked together through the crowd to his office.

CHAPTER 5

RETURN OF THE HERO

The returning portion of the invasion fleet was under acceleration, bringing the troopers back home to Earth and a hero's welcome. Alexander's flagship, the *Yorktown*, led the way, its antimatter plasma engine glowing an electric blue from inside its nest of white-hot superconducting magnet rings, its three-fletched tail a bright glowing yellow as the flowing stream of hot metal drops traversed their trajectory through empty space from spine to spar.

Inside, Alexander was just finishing his second holovideo interview of the day. This interview was a joint one with Lieutenant General Antonio Cabral, the head of the Brazilian contingent, for release over the Brazilian video network. General Cabral's three stars was one of the reasons it had been felt necessary to give Alexander a temporary promotion to that of a four-star general in the U.S. Space Force.

Because of the long time delay between Earth and the *Yorktown*, the interview was being conducted by the publicity officer of the general's staff, with Alexander and the general recording their replies. Later, Alexander's words would be translated into Portuguese and the program assembled.

"And what part did our brave Brazilian troopers play in this first-ever invasion of a planet?" the interviewer asked, reading the first question from the prepared list. Alexander let the general answer that one.

"I led our men in the attack on the Russian base at the North

Pole, which they had provocatively called Novomurmansk," the general said in Portuguese. Alexander, listening to the simultaneous translation provided for his benefit, knew the general had really been up in space in his command post on the *Brasilia*, where he belonged.

"In fact, my brave men from Brazil were the first to strike a blow against the enemy!" the general continued. Alexander had to admit that what the general said was true, since the Brazilians, like all the other foreign troops, had been assigned to backup and support roles, such as the "heavy artillery" units that tore up the living quarters on the base to keep the Russians busy while the attack landers were getting in close with the U.S. shock troops.

"Yes," Alexander interjected, his politician's smile and crinkled crow's-feet drawing the attention of the camera and the potential viewers. "The troopers from Brazil were the first to land at the North Pole base and their rockets were the first to strike to free Mars from the domination of the atheistic Neocommunists. Their efforts made the work of the American troops all the easier."

"Wasn't there some trouble subduing this base?" asked the interviewer, switching to English as he directed his attention to Alexander. Alexander grew a little annoyed with the way the interview was going, but he carefully hid his annoyance and carried on.

"There were three individuals out on the glaciers that proved to be a minor problem," Alexander admitted.

"They caused many casualties!" the general blurted. "Those casualties could have been prevented if they had allowed my artillery unit to strike a blow against them." Now Alexander allowed himself to look annoyed.

"We would have called on the brave Brazilian troops to shoot their missiles at those three if it had been necessary, but one of them was the commissar of Mars, and we wanted him taken alive," Alexander said. His face returned to its pleasant politician smile as he continued. "Fortunately, I was able to catch them unaware and capture all three of them alive, thus personally ending the battle for Mars."

The interviewer departed from his list of questions to blurt out a question that had suddenly occurred to him. "I wonder what the Russian commissar was doing out on a glacier?"

Alexander almost let his surprise show. What *had* Ivan Petrovich been doing out on that glacier? Going out on the surface of Mars, especially the North Pole during early spring, was what scientists did, and Petrovich was no scientist. An inspection visit to the base itself could be understood, but going out on the glacier? Also, Alexander now remembered that the Signals owlies had told him, just before the battle had started, that the ballistic transport that had carried Petrovich to the North Pole had carried only three passengers . . .

The interviewer, getting no immediate reply, turned to the next of the prepared questions and the interview continued.

Alexander sat in the flag chair on the small deck above and in back of the command chair of the spacecraft commander of the *Yorktown* and surveyed the busy scene below him as the *Yorktown* accelerated at a tenth-gravity, enough to allow walking and to keep people in their seats. The Sun shone through the side of the forward view window above his head, making it difficult to see the double-planet that was their target, as their nearly straight-line trajectory took them inside the orbit of Venus to the Earth on the other side of the Sun. There would be a free-fall period of flight around the turn-around point to save on antimatter, but they would be home in a little over a month.

There was a momentary turning of heads as the door to the spacecraft deck opened and shut with a pneumatic double-*whoosh*, admitting a fat man in a rumpled short-sleeve shirt, sweatpants, and Velcro deck shoes. He had a large bald spot sticking out of the top of a long mop of unkempt hair that made him look like a hippie monk. The door was normally silent, but the fat man had supplied the *whoosh*ing sound effects as he passed through.

He peered nearsightedly around the deck through trifocal glasses, tilting his head up and down, trying to choose the right lens, then noticed Alexander on the flag deck above him. His flabby arms and belly jiggling in the low gravity, he made his way up the steps like a dancing elephant. On the rear of his sweatpants, right where it would be sat on, was a cloth patch with an embroidered silver oak leaf, the insignia of a lieutenant colonel in the space force. Alexander looked at him with a combination of anticipation and annoyance. Although the man was technically a lieutenant colonel under his command, the military had long ago learned that the only way to keep their bright scientist "owlies" in the service was to give them all the toys they wanted to play with and tough problems to solve, but otherwise treat them as civilians and leave them alone.

"Jerry Meyer, head of Signals Group, General Armstrong. I thought you might want to have this information kept confidentially, so I brought it up on hardcopy rather than blatting it out on your screen." He handed over a piece of fax-erase paper and Alexander read it.

"So . . . the passengers on that urgent trip to the North Pole were the same ones that went out on the glacier—and incidently loused up my invasion. Ivan Petrovich, Tanya Pavlova, and Viktor Braginsky. Did you find out why they were on the glacier?"

"Nothing obvious came up in the records," Jerry answered, pushing his glasses back up on his nose. "And I have holocube copies of all the computer records from all the bases. Viktor Braginsky is a permafrost and glacier expert. He had been engaged in research at the North Pole base for some months, and he and his technicians went out on the ice cap about twice a week to take deep core samples of the ice. Then, according to the vehicle and personnel logs from the North Pole Base, he cancelled his standard requisition for a crawler and caught the next ballistic transport to the main base. He must have gone straight to the commissar and told him something important, because within a few hours after he arrived, he and the commissar were on their way back to the North Pole, with Miss Tanya tagging along. They wasted no time at the base, but immediately commandeered a crawler and took off over the ice. We attacked shortly after."

"Where did they go?" Alexander asked. "One of your imaging satellites must have had them under surveillance."

"They had started east around the base of the main glaciers, but hadn't gone far when our attack landers roared overhead. They turned back, caught our guys unaware, and began to raise hell."

"Don't remind me," Alexander snarled, crumpling up the paper and tossing it to the deck. Jerry wheezed as he leaned over to pick up the piece of fax-erase paper. He smoothed it out on his ample thigh so the fax machine could erase, iron, and ready the paper for use again.

"What did they want Tanya for?"

"Beats me. According to the records, she's an expert on volcanoes, but there are no volcanoes at the poles. But she is also a backup medical doctor, one of the two at the main base that day. Having both a Ph.D. and an M.D. is probably why the KGB let her go to Mars, even though they didn't trust her."

"Well, both Tanya and Viktor are back on Mars. But I've got someone here on the *Yorktown* who can clear up the mystery for me." Alexander's fingers flew over the icons on his screen. "Bring me Ivan Petrovich from the prison section!" he said to the face that appeared on the screen.

"That brings me to the other reason that I showed up in hardcopy," Jerry Meyer said, handing over another sheet of fax-erase paper. "Here are a couple pictures of your Ivan Petrovich—taking his time in the toilet!"

"What is he doing standing on the seat?"

"Getting access to the conduits in the ceiling. It turns out the main comm links from the bridge to the central computer are routed through that region. We noticed some funny things happening to the computer system, failed password attempts, loused up files, stuff like that. We set up imps at all the known terminals and the input ports to the computer, and found that one line was inputting requests that were never sent by its transmitting terminal. That line passes right over the toilets in the prison section. It didn't take us long to locate the position of the tap, and security installed some hidden cameras. They were triggered just an hour ago, and I brought you the pictures as soon as security could get them enlarged. He still doesn't know we caught him in the act."

"Spying!" Alexander's face broadened into an almost evil grin, the steel-gray eyes slitting up as the crow's-feet appeared. "What did he use to get past the computer's defenses?"

"I'm afraid there *aren't* many defenses built into the *Yorktown* computer," Jerry said with a shrug. "The *Yorktown* is what we would call a 'secure facility.' It was built to hold loyal fighting troops, not strangers or prisoners. The fiber optic cables have armor to protect them from enemy attack, but none of the normal security precautions to protect them from enemy spying. The I/O software is also fairly lenient, since it is only designed to keep underlings from reading the mail of their superiors. Otherwise it assumes everyone talking to it is on our side."

"As for what he used," Jerry continued, "according to the security people, it is a normal-looking video reader with expanded I/O capability and a hidden compartment containing a device for tapping into fiber optic lines. Also, according to them, he must be high up in the Dirty Tricks Department of the KGB as well as the Communist party to be allowed to have one of those."

"A *KGB* spy!" Alexander said with pleasure. He dismissed Jerry with a wave of the hand and started touching the icons on the control screen in front of him. The deck vibrated slightly as Jerry went down the steps, followed by two pneumatic-sounding *whooshes* as he passed through the door.

"You have heard what these two gentlemen have reported to me," Alexander said to the prisoner standing on the other side of the table. On the table were pictures of Ivan standing on the toilet and the video book with the fiber optic tap pulled out of its secret compartment.

"The Signals Officer has reported clandestine attempts to obtain information from the classified weapons operations files of the *Yorktown* battle computer. Those clandestine attempts were traced to a certain compartment in the prisoner section of the ship. The photograph shows you in that compartment operating a video book in an unorthodox fashion.

"The security officer has testified that the video book in the picture is the one on the table that was found in a search of your room. The security officer has also testified that the video book is capable of tapping into a fiber optic line and attempting clandestine contact with a computer. Thus, you had put yourself into a position and made yourself capable of clandestinely gathering information that would be of assistance to the enemy.

"The security officer has additionally testified that the video book also contains a provision for using the video laser to produce a burst code message on a tightly focused laser beam. The laser beam can be sent out any Earth-facing porthole to the well-known 'photon bucket' telescope the enemy has established on the back side of the Moon. Thus, you had made yourself capable of transmitting that clandestinely gathered information to the enemy."

Alexander paused, and his crow's-feet crinkled slightly as if he was enjoying himself. "In view of the sworn testimony and the physical evidence, I pronounce you guilty of spying and sentence you to the fate of a spy in wartime—*death*!"

Ivan stiffened a little at the verdict, then relaxed and smiled. "Surely you are joking with your little mock trial. You are merely a general and have no authority to judge me. We are not at war. The hostilities on Mars ended many weeks ago."

Alexander's face turned serious, and he leaned forward to stare directly at Ivan's eyes. "The battle for Mars was but a skirmish in the long war of the free world against the atheistic forces of communism," Alexander said. "The U.S. and the New Soviets still have armed troops facing each other all along the Baltic front. Technically our nations are still at war and technically, as commander-in-chief of this theater of operations, I can try, convict, and execute you . . . and I did . . . and I *will*!"

He got up and laughed. "Of course, it won't be possible to hang you in one-tenth gee. But given unusual circumstances, one must make do with what one has."

Ivan stood impassively, his hands handcuffed behind his back, while two large troopers, feet firmly implanted in footholds on the deck, held him by the elbows.

"Guards! Take him to personnel lock 180. I'll be right behind you." The guards unplanted their feet, lifted Ivan in the one-tenth gravity like he were a doll, and carried him out the door, with Alexander following.

They came to the lock. "Put him in," Alexander said.

"Sir?" one of the troopers said.

"That is a direct order."

"Never mind," Ivan said, stepping into the lock. Alexander walked over to the door and stuck his face close to Ivan's.

"I don't *like* you, Mr. Petrovich," Alexander said slowly, his face mean, and his eyes nearly hidden in his space-wrinkled face. "You killed my men and doubled my butcher bill. I told you before, I don't get mad at people, Mr. Petrovich, I get *rid* of them." He reached back and started to close the door to the inner lock, then paused.

"I might consider letting you appeal your sentence back on Earth if you tell me a story," Alexander said.

"A story?" Ivan asked, puzzled.

"Yes. What were you, Viktor Braginsky, and Tanya doing at the North Pole?"

Aha! Ivan said to himself. All this trial nonsense was to make me talk. Well, *I* won't—and Tanya doesn't know why we went there. Once I get back, I'll have to make sure Viktor *never* talks. He raised his eyes in simulated bewilderment.

"The North Pole?" Ivan repeated to gain time. "I was just on one of my usual inspection trips."

"I know better!" Alexander yelled. "The commissar of Mars has better things to do with his time than take long trips out onto the glaciers of the North Pole when winter is barely over."

"Why don't you look in the computer files, like you did the last time?" Ivan chided. "Your 'owlies,' as you call them, have told you everything else, surely they could do this little thing for you."

Alexander closed and bolted the airlock door. He went to the controls and activated the intercom. "One last chance. What was important at the North Pole and where is it?"

"There was nothing and it is nowhere," came the echoing reply from inside the lock.

Alexander turned a control and the outer door started to open. The air pressure in the lock started to drop. For a fraction of a second there was a flicker of concern in Ivan's eyes, then he laughed and spoke over the hiss of escaping air.

"Go ahead, lower the pressure. Threaten me all you want until I pass out from lack of air. But you'll learn nothing from me. I'm a Neocommunist. I'm brave. Not like you cowardly Americans who go into battle hiding in tin cans and with many pretty doctors and nurses just the throw of a stone away."

Alexander turned the control more. "What is it and where!"

Ivan was in pain from the growing bubbles of gas in his bowels and obviously having trouble breathing. His eyes were rapidly blinking slits to protect them against the near vacuum. The pain in his gut made him want to strike back. He leaned close to the window, motioning Alexander toward him. As Alexander drew near, he *spat* at him, the spittle freezing as it bubbled down the window.

"You asked for it, you neocommie bastard!" Alexander yelled, suddenly losing his temper. "Nobody spits at *me*!" He slammed his palm onto a red button and blew the outer lock.

There was a loud bang and a wide-eyed Ivan Petrovich went tumbling off into space.

CHAPTER 6

OVER OLYMPUS

The sun was rising in the east as Joseph Stanislavsky nudged the large crawler forward through the narrow confines of the north-side vehicular airlock of Olympia.

"You have fifty centimeters this side," Tanya said, looking out the copilot window at the tip of the springed "feelers" that marked the outer edges of the huge hollow spring-wire wheels that the crawler used for traction. Joseph pushed forward evenly on the two forward motor controls and increased the speed of the crawler as it came out into the pink morning sunlight. Mount Olympus loomed off to the left. Its nearby steep rampart cliffs reached high above them, nearly blocking their view of the top of the gigantic volcano.

"It's been a long time since I've been outside," Gus said, his voice echoing from the observation dome in the top of the middle section of the three-segment crawler. "I hadn't realized the base had this much equipment."

"Every spare moment we have, we go out and salvage what we can find from what the troops left lying around," Mike McGuire said from the engineering console in the middle segment. "Never can tell when it might be useful ... Say! Joe! I forget. What does 'phi oh tee' mean on a circuit breaker?"

"Photon, Mr. Mike," Joseph called back from the pilot's seat. "That is protector switch for photoflash circuits of panoramic camera."

The six huge wheels of the crawler slowed slightly as they came to the end of the graded roadbed that led away from the base and continued north across the rusty-colored rolling ground.

"We have less than one hundred kilometers of travel," Joseph said as he swayed back and forth from the motion of the articulated crawler over the rough terrain. "But this route is not served by autobahn, so it will take some hours."

Gus looked back along the way they had come. The base, which had loomed so large in his life on Mars up until now, was rapidly shrinking into the distance. He nodded to Ozaki Akutagawa, who was looking out a similar dome above the living quarters in the back segment, then turned toward the front to watch the sparse scenery of Mars flowing toward him as the crawler made its way toward the southeast lift station at the base of the Mount Olympus ramparts. He could see the curly mass of Chris Stoker's sandy hair matted up against the top of the dome in the front segment. He, too, was obviously enjoying the view.

"Hold up!" Mike said suddenly, looking at the indicators on the engineering panel. "The left rear wheel motor is heating up."

"I, too, now see the problem," Joseph said, looking at a corner of his pilot's console. "The wheel must have picked up another optical fiber from the American missiles."

"I'll go out and clear the tangle," Mike said, getting up. "We made the mess, we should clean it up."

"Watch yourself," Gus warned. "Those fibers are nearly unbreakable."

"Not if you know the technique," Mike said as he put on his helmet.

Soon they were on their way again.

"Wow!" was all Gus had to say as he stepped out of the crawler at the foot of the rampart cliff and looked upward. Chris had loped off a distance away from the rest of the party in the upwind direction to run a sample of air through his atmospheric analyzer.

"Yeah, wow!" Mike said quietly. The cliffs looked as if they were about to fall on him.

"It is indeed impressive," Ozaki agreed, shading his eyes with his glove. He turned to Joseph. "How many meters, please?"

"It is little over five kilometers, three English miles," Joseph said. "But there are higher ramparts on north side." He, too, shaded his eyes with a glove and pointed with the other one.

"The Sun angle is now high, so is hard to see, but careful looking will observe distinctive layering of ash and lava flows. Howsoever, the lava layers are too thick for the viscosity I calculate from samples I obtain."

"You've been up that cliff to get samples?" Mike said.

"Many times, Mr. Mike," Joseph replied. "But is easy when you rappel down from the top."

He turned to look at Ozaki and Gus, and continued. "In my professional opinion, this is an example—an extreme example—of a table mountain, such as is found in Iceland. This volcano grew up out of a large ice field. The hot lava and ashes melted a hole out to this point, then got too cold."

"Five kilometer sheets of ice!" Tanya injected. "Ridiculous! You should stop pushing your crazy theories on these polite foreigners, Joseph. Are you asking us to believe that Mars was once covered by many kilometers of ice? If so, where is it all?"

"I do not say all Mars covered with ice," Joseph replied angrily. "Just northern hemisphere. Both Olympus Mons and Tharsis Ridge volcanoes grew through the ice. As to where ice went, what didn't evaporate into space is trapped under dirt at poles, I bet."

"Anybody with any sense knows that ramparts are caused by gravity thrust and hydraulic-aided shear wasting," Tanya replied. "The growing volcano puts great weight on the surface—after all, it is twenty-seven kilometers high and six hundred kilometers in diameter. The surface around the periphery fractures and thrusts up under the pressure. Trapped underground water heated by the volcano aids in creating fractures." She tossed her head and continued. "I, at least, have some evidence to back *my* theory."

"You and your pissoir waterfall," Joseph said, angrily turning away. "Come Mr. Mike," he said to the engineer. "Let me show you how to drive this monster back to base."

"You found a waterfall?" Chris asked in surprise.

"Yes!" Tanya said. "A very pretty one, maybe tallest in the

whole solar system. I noticed a clue on the survey photo and found it for certain during our first expedition around the base of the mountain, so they named it Pavlova Falls. Because the most famous Pavlova was a dancer, the name makes a joke in English. Anyway, I will show it to you when we get to the north side. But first we must go up and over."

She led the way to the southeast lift station at the base of the cliff. It was a simple motor-driven pulley system with two cables that went up into the air at a sharp angle and disappeared in the distance. Gus pulled down his visor and, by zooming the magnification of his helmeyes, he could follow the dual cable up until he could see a similar pulley system in a metal frame some five kilometers up at the top of the cliff.

"The size of those cables isn't very comforting, even if there are two of them," he observed.

"Come now, Gus," Tanya said in a chiding tone, putting a gloved hand on his arm. "These are made of the latest in polymer tether materials. Each one has been tested at one million Newtons—they can lift one hundred metric tons in Earth gravity. Surely two of them can lift you in Martian gravity. Besides, I go up first." She reached for a harness hanging from a carrier frame attached firmly to the two cables.

"I'll go first," Gus suggested, starting to take the harness from her. She snatched it away, and standing on tiptoe, used her height advantage to look sternly down at him while holding the harness in back of her.

"Do you know what the landing site looks like?" Tanya asked. "Do you know how to stop the cable at the right time?"

"No, but—" Gus protested.

"I do," Tanya said, coming down off her toes and closing out any further discussion by patting him dismissively on the chest. "So I go first, then help you to a safe landing." She turned her back to him and got into the harness. By the time she was ready, Joseph Stanislavsky and Mike McGuire had returned. Between them they carried a heavy bag of supplies and oxygen bottles.

"What is the channel of the motor, Joseph?" she asked. He

looked down at an instruction card in Cyrillic next to the control panel on the southeast lift station.

"Channel ninety-six," he said. "Three ones for checkout, three twos to start motor . . ."

"Three threes to stop, and single twos and threes to speed up and down," Tanya continued. She paused for a second, as if listening to something. "Motor says it is okay and the battery has lots of power. I'll go now." She tongued the number two button three times and the electric motor hummed to life.

Following the slowly moving carrier frame overhead, Tanya ran up a slight slope and then flew up into the air toward the distant point on the cliff top above. Gus watched her go, then switched to his helmeyes as the speed of the motor increased and the tiny figure became even tinier. She was obviously enjoying the ride, swinging her legs back and forth to make herself move in large, birdlike swoops as she rapidly rose up along the kilometers of cliffs. The silence was eerie as the five men waited, looking always upward.

After about twenty minutes, Gus noticed something coming toward them down the cable. It was another carrier frame with harnesses hanging below it. The motor changed speed a number of times, slowing each time, then came to a complete halt. The incoming carrier frame had just passed the drive wheel.

"Everything's okay," Tanya's voice said over the radio. "Hut's holding pressure and has plenty of reserves of water, air, and batteries. You can come up."

"We are on way," Joseph said. He reached up to the two-meter-long carrier frame and unloosened three more harnesses.

"Let me ride up front," Chris said, reaching for the first harness. "I want to analyze some air samples as we go up."

Joseph helped them with their harnesses and, as soon as he was sure they were all properly buckled in, he started the motor on slow. Gus walked a few steps, then found himself treading air, while Chris's long legs took him to the peak of the slope before he started flying. On the way up, Joseph gave them a guided tour of the lava layers they passed on the cliff face.

As they approached the top, Gus could see no sign of Tanya. He was slightly worried, thinking that she might have fallen while they were traveling up, but then they got a call over the radio.

"You traveled faster than I expected," Tanya's voice said. "I thought from what I heard over the radio that Joseph was going to show you every little ice crystal he could find in the cliff face to support his silly notion of Mars covered with glaciers ten kilometers thick. I'll be right out."

The outer airlock door opened in a small yellow plastic prefabricated hut snuggled up to a boulder. Tanya exited and came bounding over to the cliff edge where they would land.

"Not glaciers, Tanya," Joseph said in annoyance. "Frozen oceans. And not ten kilometers deep, just five or so."

"*Just* five. Five's still ridiculous. Quiet, now. I'll bring you to a halt." The motion of the cable slowed and halted. Gus also noticed with relief a long red lever connected to a transmitter box that he could have slapped, and a red pull-cord at the turn wheel that would have shunted the carrier frame and its cargo off the cable and onto a siding track with a decelerator section.

As Tanya helped them out of their harnesses, she babbled on happily. "I warmed up the hut for you while you were coming up the cable. It felt good to get out of the suit for a while and clean up. Now you can, too—without a woman in the way. Go ahead—while I monitor lifting the supply load."

"We lost one and a half millibars on the trip up," Chris said, peering at the readouts on his portable analyzer. "I'll have to get well upwind from the hut before I do any composition measurements, though. I'm sure the water vapor and the hydrocarbons I'm seeing are coming from leaks during the airlock cycle."

Leaving Tanya talking by radio to Mike McGuire below, the four men cycled their way into the hut. Gus was the first one through the air lock into the cramped six-person hut. Two paces took him from the exit door of the air lock to the entry door to the toilet. As he took off his helmet, he smelled a combination of mustiness from the plastic walls and scorched dust from the hot coils of an electric heater. The smells were faint in the half-atmosphere air pressure of the Russian-built hut. There were six bunks, three each along two walls. He put his helmet on the bottom bunk and started getting out of his Marsuit. By the time Joseph had finally cycled through the lock, he had to wait to open the door in order to give the other three men enough room to struggle out of their suits.

Gus went into the tiny bathroom. Because it didn't have zero gee facilities, it reminded him of one on an airplane back on Earth. The sink was damp—recently wiped clean—and there was a small wet hand cloth folded neatly over one of the drying racks on the wall overhead. He picked it up and brought it closer to his nose. The faint scent of womanly sweat mixed with cleansing lotion brought back memories of hardworking but idyllic days on the Moon in a crawler.

That afternoon, they walked along the edge of the cliff a number of kilometers, Tanya pointing out different lava flows that she had dated. They came to a long, rounded ridge that went straight down the mountain. Gus started to look for a way to climb it.

"Come this way," Tanya said, pulling on his elbow. She led them to a crevice and they walked through into a large, underground cavern that arched high overhead. The crevice had formed at the site of a large fault plane that had sliced right through the cavern, opening it to the sky and letting a two-meter-wide sheet of sunlight in.

"A lava tube!" Ozaki exclaimed. "But such an immense one! There is nothing like this on Earth."

"A big volcano deserves big lava tubes," Gus mused, looking around. He walked out of the patch of sunlight into the darkness on the uphill side of the cavelike tube, pulled down the viewer on his helmet, and activated his helmeyes. Using the zoom feature he looked up-slope. The larger the zoom, the more sensitivity the helmeyes had to use, and still there was no end to the cave. He centered the viewer reticle at the darkest point in the image, triggered the laser range finder, and waited. The range indicator came up all nines.

There had been no return. Chris walked by him, holding his analyzer out in front of him, the light from his chestpack making a
pool of rippled brightness and shadow on the rugged gray floor.

"We have walked up the tube for fifteen kilometers," Tanya
said. "There was no end in sight. We can trace it on survey photographs for over two hundred kilometers."

"The down end empties over the cliff edge," Joseph said.

While he had his range finder activated, Gus took quick range
measurements in the other directions.

"Fifty meters high by three hundred meters wide," he said as
he raised his visor and rejoined them in the sunlit section of floor.

"Truly immense," Ozaki said upon hearing the numbers.

"No traces of hydrogen sulfide. Must be a pretty dead vent,"
Chris reported from the gloom.

"We have dated this flow at two hundred ten thousand years,"
Tanya said. "The youngest one we have found in this region of the
volcano is over one hundred thousand years old."

"We haven't been all the way around yet," Joseph said. "There
is still a lot to do." He led the way back out of the lava tube.

"Mars is a big place," Gus admitted.

"With exceptionally big structures," Ozaki said, coming out the
crack in the gigantic lava tube. He once again stood looking in awe
up toward the peak of the planetoid-sized volcano they were climbing. It was seventeen kilometers above and three hundred kilometers
distant from where they were. "I am so used to volcanoes like
Mount Fuji, or the Hawaiian Islands, where you can get close
enough to the structure that the sides are steep and the peak towers
over you. Here on Olympus Mons, once we are on top of the steep
ramparts, the average slope is only a few degrees, and the top of the
peak is barely visible over the curvature of the horizon."

When evening came, they gathered in the hut, stored their suits
and helmets in storage lockers, and raised one rack of bunks to give
themselves a little more room. They cooked one of their more substantial meals in the compact microwave oven, then pulled down
the table from the ceiling to eat and plan their next day's journey.
There were no chairs, the middle bunks doubling for that duty.

There was also the inevitable housekeeping. Tanya did the dishes, Chris resorted their supplies, Ozaki filled and checked the air and water tanks in their suits, Joseph cycled and checked the hut utilities, and Gus did everyone's dirty laundry in the miniature ultrasonic-washing, microwave-drying launderette.

They got to bed early, since the next day would be a long one. Chris went to sleep nearly instantly in one of the top bunks, despite the fact that he had to sleep curled up since the bunk was substantially shorter than his nearly two meters. His snores reverberated in the chamber formed around his head by the top corner of the hut and the flimsy wall of the toilet.

Gus had a hard time getting to sleep and lay in the bottom bunk, his eyes wandering over the dimly illuminated curved shapes formed in the bed above him by Tanya's body. The curved shapes moved as Tanya rolled over, and a thin hand reached down over the edge of the bed. He reached up and squeezed it. It squeezed back and withdrew up under the cover.

The next day was more riding on cable lifts. There was a crawler at the top of southeast lift that they could have used, but since this was just a fast, get-acquainted visit to Mount Olympus for the "foreigners" taking over the planet, it was faster to use the cableway the Russians had installed during their first few crawler transits of the superlarge volcano. The cableway was in thirty-kilometer segments, so there was never more than a fifteen-kilometer walk if the cable broke or a motor failed.

"We all go together, this time," Joseph said as they approached the end station of the southeast cable-way.

"I see we get seats this time," Gus said.

"Three hundred kilometers in a harness wouldn't be fun," Tanya said. "I had to do some thirty-kilometer segments that way in the early days. Sling seats are much better. Here, let me show you how to adjust it."

With Chris and his analyzer in the lead and Tanya at the rear, followed by the bag of supplies, they started slowly up the slope. As they gained experience balancing and handling the jolts as they passed over idler pulleys along the way, Tanya increased the speed by sending radio commands to the motor at the base station.

"We are moving with exceptional rapidity," Ozaki said, looking down at the volcanic blocks streaking by underneath his feet.

"Forty kilometers an hour," Tanya replied. "I can go faster if you want."

"Great!" Chris said, obviously enjoying the ride. "Jack it up higher!"

"No!" Ozaki said. "This is sufficient speed."

"I agree," Gus said.

They came to a flat plateau region about ten kilometers in diameter. Five kilometers to the north was a triangular rock jutting a few hundred meters up out of the plateau. Five kilometers to the south was a larger rock, even more triangular, with sharp edges, that jutted up more than half a kilometer. As the cable-run took them between the two jagged spikes, Tanya slowed the cableway to a stop.

"Now," she said, "I would like our three distinguished foreign scientists to observe the formations to the north and south of us. Although Comrade Kilometers-high-glaciers up front has ridden over this plateau many times, he has failed to comprehend what is right before his eyes. You will observe that these formations have sharp edges and nearly vertical faces on *all three sides*. Do they look like a flow of volcanic lava that has run into a glacier? No! They look like up-faulted rocks, exactly what one would expect around the edges of a massive volcano. I rest my case."

"Tanya!" Joseph said in annoyance. "I have already admitted these massifs along the cliff edge are suggestive of up-faulting, but only on this southeast side. You don't see them anywhere else around the periphery. Let us go on."

"Well, Ozaki," Gus said, "it looks as if the Russians have left us plenty of research questions to work on here."

"Indeed," Ozaki said, allowing a soft chuckle in his reply.

After they left the small plateau, they came to the end of the first cable-run.

"Southeast Eleven!" Tanya announced as they arrived.

"Eleven?" asked Gus. "Shouldn't it be two?"

"We numbered them according to altitude," Joseph said, pointing to a sign. The sign had "11,030 m" painted on it. "We are now over eleven kilometers above Martian 'sea level.' We have sixteen more kilometers to go."

After a few minutes of stretching their legs and looking around, they switched to the next cableway and continued their long climb to the top.

It was four hours later and the sun was nearly overhead, when a station came into sight that was more than just a motor and a frame. This one boasted another hut.

"Southeast-Eighteen," Tanya reported. "Halfway point and some welcome relief."

"Thank goodness," Gus said as he felt the cable slowing. "I was about to have to use my suit system."

Joseph slipped from his seat while the cable was still moving and ran quickly toward the door of the hut. Gus was right behind him. Chris went off away from them to make some measurements of the atmospheric composition.

"Raise the seat!" Tanya yelled after them as she helped Ozaki out of the harness. The two of them followed the rapidly moving form of Gus up the well-trod path to the hut.

Chris was the last one through the airlock. "Only a little over one millibar pressure," he reported. "We are five-sixths of the way to space. I'm also seeing a different mix. Five percent nitrogen instead of the two and a half percent at Martian 'sea level.' Also higher concentrations of carbon monoxide, ozone, NOX compounds, and ions."

After an energy-bar lunch and a small sip of water, they were back in the sling-seats again. Chris came down from a small rise where he had been scanning the horizon.

"The mountain just seems to disappear, the closer we get," Chris said plaintively as he got into his seat.

"The caldera is eighty kilometers in diameter and we are one hundred fifty kilometers away," Ozaki said. "It should not be a surprise."

"The only way to really 'see' this mountain is from space," Gus said.

"Yes," Ozaki replied, nodding in agreement. "It is extraordinary from there."

Tanya tongued them into motion and they started once more up the gradual slope.

It was sunset when they reached the last station at the edge of the Mount Olympus caldera. While Tanya and Joseph went off to use the facilities of the large twelve-person cabin at this research station, Chris, Ozaki, and Gus, awed by the majestic wonder of the scene, forgot their bodily discomforts and moved closer to the edge. They were right on the edge of the steep slope of the deep southwest collapse crater.

"Holy moly!" Chris said quietly to himself as he looked over the edge of the three-kilometer-high cliff.

"It must have been some sight when it was active," Gus said, looking down at the nearly flat surface far below. "A twenty-kilometer-diameter pool of glowing, molten rock."

"Or the larger caldera during an earlier day," Ozaki said, waving his arm at the horizon. "Molten lava as far as you could see."

The next day they spent exploring the caldera. Tanya showed them the samples she and others had collected and the take-apart model that they had constructed that allowed one to visualize the sequential history of the various eruptions that had been identified by caldera overlapping and sample dating.

"Our youngest sample is a core from the floor of the northeast collapse crater," Tanya said. "It dated out at only thirty thousand years."

"Young, by geologic standards," Gus said, impressed. "The mountain is no doubt still alive."

"Any signs that the fire dragon inside is stirring?" Ozaki asked.

"Our seismic net has not picked up anything significant yet," Tanya replied.

"I pick up an occasional whiff of volcanic-type gas molecules," Chris added, "but nothing significant."

Gus and Ozaki took the model outside and compared it with what they saw. They then took another cable ride, this time down into the caldera of the volcano.

"I see you have started drilling a coring hole," Gus said as he looked around after reaching the bottom of the southwest collapse crater. Chris stuck the port of his analyzer down the borehole.

"I had a team of technicians carrying out a detailed core-sample survey program, but their work was interrupted by some unannounced visitors," Tanya said dryly.

"Let me know what you need for a crew to get it operating again, and I'll get them for you," Gus said. "As a guest of the Sagan Mars Institute, you have equal rights to support equipment and manpower."

"Thank you." Tanya patted him on the arm. "When we return, I shall form a crew and set them to work."

Once back up top, they boarded a crawler and made their way around the caldera to the other side. Chris insisted that they take the long way around, since according to the topographic map, the highest point on the volcano—and probably on Mars—was in that direction. When they came to the middle of the 26,500-meter contour on the crawler's map they found a sign reading "26,551 m." Below it was a long list of names written in Cyrillic, and a date.

"Tan ... ya Pav ... lo ... va ... A.D. 2035," Gus said, spelling out the last name on the list and the date. For the first time in a long time Gus felt second-rate. The Russians had been here first—years ago. Now the U.S. was reduced to stealing the planet away from the Russians. But the Russians had been greedy; now Mars belonged to itself—and all the people who cared enough to come there to settle.

"Joseph is on list, too," Tanya said.

"I want to make a composition measurement," Chris said. He got quickly into his Marsuit and cycled out the crawler air lock.

"Now go back a ways and wait until I call you," Chris said from outside through his suit radio. "You're polluting the air—what there is of it!"

Shortly after Joseph had driven the crawler away, Chris called them back again and he climbed back in.

"Things stabilized fairly fast once you were a few hundred meters off," he reported as he took off his Marsuit. "Total pressure only 439 microbars, less than a half a thousandth of an Earth atmosphere. In the old days you could have packaged that and sold it as a vacuum. Carbon dioxide down to ninety-one percent instead of ninety-five percent, and lots of interesting excited molecules to stick into my stratospheric model."

They had dinner at the edge of the northeast collapse crater, the near twin to the southwest crater. Joseph had maneuvered the crawler so that the view window of the crew quarters in the rear segment of the crawler was looking out over the cliff. There was another Russian cabin there, but they decided to stick with the facilities in the crawler.

They continued on around the caldera, stopping occasionally to visit a site that the Russian scientists had found interesting. It was night again when they finished the 180-kilometer journey.

"Here we are at Northwest Twenty-six," Joseph said as he brought the six wheels of the crawler to a halt beside the twelve-person cabin. "Time for dinner and early bed. It will take all day to ride down the north side of the mountain tomorrow."

"I have an idea," Tanya said brightly from the couch-bed in the living quarters. "So that we all have more room, why don't you, Chris, and Ozaki sleep in the cabin, and Gus and I can sleep out here in the crawler?"

"Fine by me," Chris said, reaching for his Marsuit.

"But . . . the cabin," Ozaki objected, very perplexed. "The cabin . . . it holds twelve people. Plenty room—"

"Very good idea, Tanya," Joseph said loudly over Ozaki's protestations. "Come, Ozaki, let us suit up."

"But . . ."

"Come!" Joseph said, handing him his Marsuit and helmet.

Gus continued to sit looking out the window from the copilot seat and said nothing.

The ride back down the northwest side of the mountain was long and tedious. Although Gus tried to keep a vigilant scientist's eye looking at every rock and vent and lava tube, he often found his head jerking upright as he was lulled to sleep by the hum of the cableway and the rocking of his harness by the periodic bumps as they passed over the idler wheels that kept the cable off the ground.

"Too big," Ozaki observed during one long boring stretch. Gus could only agree.

Finally they came to the end of the line.

"Northwest Ten," Tanya sang brightly. "Time for dinner—and then we go to see Pavlova Falls!"

Gus, who had found it necessary to use his suit system an hour previously during the long last leg of the journey, cooperated by staying outside and dumping his suit tank into the holding tank through an outside service tube, while the others crowded into the cramped six-person hut and took turns using the tiny bathroom. They cooked one of their larger meals and, at Tanya's urging, left the housekeeping chores for later.

"The falls are thirty kilometers away and we want to get there before the Sun is setting," she said, getting into her Marsuit.

Tanya drove them up the volcano a little to get around the end of a ridge that towered above their campsite, then around the flank of the volcano toward the west. Far ahead of them they could see a long sheer scarp formed in the northwest flank from a large slumping of the side of the mountain. The scarp extended a third of the way up the side of the volcano from the rim. After about an hour and a half of travel, Tanya turned the crawler to the right and headed for the rim. There was a deep gash in the slope, indicating a canyon below, and she drove to the sunward side of the gash, stopping about halfway along. They climbed out of the crawler and walked carefully to the edge of the rim.

"There is Pavlova Falls," Tanya said, pointing proudly.

Gus looked across the canyon to the cliff face on the other side.

The setting Sun was almost behind them so the cliff face was in full sunlight. About three hundred meters down from the rim of the cliff was a thick dark red-brown layer over a lighter gray-black layer. The softer red-brown layer had eroded away at one point just above the harder gray-black layer to form a cave, and from that cave came a small stream of water and steam.

The steam rose into the air and dissipated, while the water flowed to the lip of the gray-black layer and fell off down to the surface of Mars, some six kilometers below. The waterfall broke up into a veil of droplets almost immediately and slowly trailed away to the south and west, carried away by the thin cyclonic Martian trade winds that made their way around the base of the Olympus Mons cliffs. On one side of the falls was a semicircular band of reflected sunlight, brightly colored near the top and fading into white.

"A rainbow!" Gus said. "A Martian rainbow."

"Technically a spraybow," Chris injected.

"I notice that colors only last for a few hundred meters, then rainbow turns white, although back reflection is quite strong," Ozaki said. "Water must be freezing as it falls and turning into ice crystals."

"What is the temperature of the emerging stream?" Gus asked.

"I climbed down and obtained samples," Tanya said. "The water is superheated by the volcano to one hundred three Celsius and has dissolved many minerals."

"That's why I detect plenty of volcanic gasses," Chris said, looking at the readouts on his atmospheric analyzer.

Tanya continued. "This waterfall shows that there was plenty of water in the ground to lubricate faults and cause the kind of uplift faulting needed to make these ramparts around Olympus Mons."

"They are just the proof *I* need to show that thick ice existed at these altitudes above the Martian surface," Joseph countered loudly. "Ice intruding on an old, cold, dormant layer was later covered by ashes from a subsequent eruption. You are now seeing this trapped ice finally find its way out."

"Ashes? Ashes?" Tanya said, looking around. "If this volcano has ash eruptions, where are the cinder cones you see on every other ash-emitting volcano. No ash cones, no ashes."

"Every other *Earth* volcano, Tanya," Joseph said. "This is Mars, and things are different here."

"The sun has set," Ozaki interrupted. "It will be getting dark soon."

"All right," Tanya said, swallowing her reply to Joseph. "We should go now." She grabbed Ozaki and Chris by the elbows and led the way back to the crawler.

The next day they got up early, cleaned up the hut and crawler, and went out on the level plain around the Northwest Ten cableway station.

"How do we get down off this cliff?" Gus asked, looking around for another cable station.

"We have to go up first," Tanya said, putting one hand on his shoulder and pointing to the top of a nearby ridge with her other. Gus looked up and saw a tiny cable station perched high above them.

"Ohh . . ." he groaned.

"It's only two kilometers away," Tanya said with a grin in her voice.

"Yeah—but one of those kilometers is up!" Gus objected.

"You are getting too heavy anyway." Tanya dropped her arm to hug him around the waist. "Exercise will help you lose weight."

"Too *heavy?*" Joseph chided. "Tanya, how would you know?"

Tanya was glad her helmet tint was set on dark. She didn't answer, but dropped her arm from Gus' waist and started off on the path to the steps cut up the side of the nearby ridge.

"This ridge we are on is really something," Gus said as they reached the northwest lift station sitting on a ledge halfway down from the crown of the ridge. "It goes all the way down to the plains below. Looks like you should be able to climb down along the spine of the ridge all the way to the bottom without too much trouble."

"That's how we got first cable down," Tanya said. "We drove

a crawler up the east side lava slope to get on top of the mountain, then came to this point on the northwest cliff face. We couldn't throw a rope over, since the cliff face was not steep enough; so two techs with mountain experience and I went down the spine of the ridge, leaving a length of light tether behind us as we went."

"How far was it?" Gus asked.

"The ridge is sixty kilometers long and drops eight kilometers in that distance, so the average slope was not bad," Tanya said. "Once we got to the bottom, they tied the tether to the crawler and pulled it northward, keeping it taut, until the tether came free. Then they moved it over to the middle of the valley to the east of the ridge and used it to haul up the first cable from the bottom lift station." While she had been talking, Gus had been using the magnification capabilities of his helmeyes to scan the distant ground below them.

"I can see the bottom lift station now," Gus said. "It's much further away than the southeast lift."

"That's because there is more slumping at the base of the cliffs on the northwest side, and the station has to be placed further away."

"I can see the hopiter waiting for us," Gus said. "They must have landed yesterday. Their refueler modules are all spread out.

"Give them a call," Tanya said.

"Gus Armstrong at Northeast Ten Lift Station calling Hopiter Eight," Gus sent.

"Thank goodness you have arrived," a strained, high-pitched voice replied.

"Fred Whimple!" Gus exclaimed. "What are you doing here? I thought you were running things at the institute!"

"I'm sorry, Dr. Armstrong," the reply came. "But it was very important. I received a message for you. From your . . . from General Alexander Armstrong. It starts out with top secret, NOFORN, eyes only, and other classification statements. Then there's a short message in code. Only I didn't decode the message, since I didn't know if you would want me to. I came with the message and your codebook. Since the codebook is top secret and the hopiter has no classified storage facility, I've been staying awake to keep it safe."

"How long have you been without sleep, Fred?" Gus gently asked.

"Only thirty-six hours, sir . . . but I am doing fine, sir," Fred replied, but there was a stifled yawn at the end of the transmission.

"I'll be right down. Tell the hopiter engineer to monitor the cable-lift station down there in case I don't handle the radio controls right." He turned to Tanya, but she had been listening and had the harness ready for him.

"I'll go with you," she said, pulling down another harness. "The others can ride down with our supply bag."

The two of them stepped off the edge of the ledge and the cable whirred softly up to speed as they glided down alongside the ridge into the valley below. Gus tried to take a professional interest in the ridge formation as he moved along it, but his mind was busy trying to puzzle out what could be in the message from Alex.

Tanya pushed the cable-lift to its maximum speed, but it was still over ninety minutes before they came to a landing.

"Mr. Whimple is waiting for you in the hopiter," the engineer said as they landed. "He gave me instructions that no one else should come in until *you* say so, sir."

He looked at Tanya. "He was especially specific about you not being allowed in, Dr. Pavlov, because of the NOFORN restriction. You'll have to wait in the hut over there with the hopiter pilot, I guess."

"Humph," Tanya said. "I'll stay here and monitor the cable-lift station while the other two come down. You had better go read your secret message, Mr. Director."

Gus headed for the hopiter. The airlock door didn't open as he approached. He had to cycle it by himself. When he reached the main cabin, he found Fred Whimple, toppled over in a chair, sound asleep.

Fred Whimple's small body was as thin as that of a starving street waif. Everyone else in space wore coveralls and boots. But

Fred's expensive, tailored, brown-vested business suits with the padded shoulders and the custom-made brown Italian shoes for his tiny
feet gave his body a substance that it lacked when unclothed. Even
now, sound asleep, the large head with the bulging brow under
neatly combed, thinning brown hair still looked as superintelligent
as ever. Fred had a Ph.D. in chemistry—magna cum laude—but as
he had never had the self-confidence needed to write a convincing
research grant proposal, he had drifted into administration. The envelope containing the coded message was still gripped in the slim,
manicured fingers of his right hand, but the top secret codebook
had slipped to the floor.

"You did well, Fred," Gus said as he quietly removed his helmet
and Marsuit. "And no, I won't accept your resignation for failing
to stay awake. You're too talented to lose. If only you had some
tiny little bit of self-confidence . . ." He reached down and picked
up the codebook, then gently extracted the envelope from Fred
Whimple's fingers.

With the message decoded and read, Gus woke Fred up by starting
a conversation with him and then speaking louder and louder.

". . . and so in view of the content of the message, Fred, instead
of returning to Olympia, I'm going on to visit Boreal Base at the
North Pole. If you are not too tired, Fred, please arrange for another hopiter and pilot. You are *not* too tired, are you, Fred?"

Fred struggled awake, "Oh! No, sir! Not too tired . . ."

"Good. Please arrange for another hopiter and pilot to take me
to Boreal Base."

"Yes sir. Right away." Fred Whimple staggered to his feet,
blinked himself awake, and headed for the radio on the control
deck.

It turned out to be impossible to get Tanya alone to talk to her for
almost a full sol. If it wasn't Joseph or Chris or Ozaki in the hut,
it was the pilot or engineer either in the hut or in the hopiter. He
couldn't talk to her outside, because then anything they said could
be heard over the suit radios, which were automatically monitored

by the hut and the hopiter. Once the second hopiter had lifted off from Olympia and was on its way, Gus gathered them all in the hut to try to explain what was going on.

Tanya was sitting opposite Gus, her arms draped in a friendly fashion around the shoulders of the hopiter pilot and engineer. Chris was curled up in a top bunk overhead, for his knees kept banging the hanging table when he sat on the middle bunk.

"I can't tell you why, right now, but it's important that I go on to the North Pole from here as soon as possible. The rest of you need to get back to your activities at Olympia, so I've called a second hopiter to hop you back. It's now on its way, so I'll be leaving shortly in the hopiter that is here."

"Good thing we stayed an extra day," the hopiter engineer said. "I was able to process a lot more CO_2 with the extra time, and now we got plenty of LOX and carbon monoxide for the big hop to the pole."

"Tanya will be going with me," Gus went on bluntly, not knowing any other way to do it.

"Me?" Tanya exclaimed, bewildered and a little annoyed at not being consulted. She pulled down her arms from the two men on either side of her and leaned forward on the hanging table.

"I've got to get my team together to restart the caldera core survey program," she said intently.

"It's important, Tanya," he replied. "I'll have to let you know why later . . ." He reached across the table to put his hand imploringly on hers. "Trust me."

Tanya hesitated. But one thing was sure—she trusted Gus. "Okay," she said.

"I am completely at a loss, Dr. Armstrong," Fred Whimple said, turning to look at Gus. "You *do* recall the NOFORN designation on the message."

"I do, Fred," Gus said patiently.

"Then I can conceive of no logical reason for Dr. Pavlova to accompany you on this classified mission."

Joseph leaned back in the bunk with a smirk on his face and reached around Gus to tap Fred on the shoulder. "Some day I'll have to tell you a little story, Fred," he said in a fake whisper. "About unusual uses for crawlers."

"Tanya will be going with me," Gus repeated. He paused to see if there were any additional protests. Then he rose and pushed the table between them up to the ceiling.

"Now, if those waiting for a hop back to Olympia will climb into the right-side bunks with Chris, the rest of us will raise the left-side bunks and have a little room to get into our Marsuits."

The stubby, pointed body of the hopiter stood some distance away from the hut on its five landing legs, looking rather like a wounded scarab beetle with its nose pointed straight up into the air and its eviscerated trachea spread out on the ground around it. The hopiter was a suborbital rocket that was the vehicle of choice for exploration of the vast land area of Mars—nearly equal to the dry land area of Earth.

Starting from any point on Mars, a hopiter could fire its carbon monoxide–liquid oxygen rockets and "hop" off in a suborbital trajectory that could go to any other point on Mars in less than an hour. Once there, it did not need a prepared landing field, but could hover on its rockets, find a reasonably level place to land, and set down on its superstable platform of five actively controlled feet, any noncontiguous three of which would suffice to hold the ship upright.

Once landed, converters would be deployed to suck up the carbon dioxide atmosphere of Mars, decompose it into oxygen and carbon monoxide, and store the resultant propellants in tanks ready for the next takeoff. The only limitation of the hopiter was the time and energy it took to make the fuel. If the energy supply was weak, such as that provided by solar cells, then the time between hops could be weeks or months. With a Batusov reactor aboard to efficiently convert a few hundred micrograms of antimatter into electrical energy, the fuel needed could be generated in a day or two.

Tanya and Gus helped the pilot and engineer of the hopiter fold and store the air ducts, fans, and radiators that were the outside portions of the fuel manufacturing facility of the hopiter. There was still a lengthy checklist to go through, however, so they had a few minutes alone in the large passenger compartment in the base of the hopiter while the pilot was busy on the control deck up above and the engineer worked outside.

"What were you, Ivan Petrovich, and Viktor Braginsky doing on the North Pole ice when we attacked?" Gus asked in a whisper.

"So that's why you want me to go with you to the North Pole," Tanya said, quickly catching on, but not really answering the question.

"What was out there that was so important that the commissar of Mars had to go there to see it in person?" Gus insisted.

"Why . . ." Tanya hesitated, suddenly looking truly bewildered. "I don't know!"

"You don't know?" Gus asked in an unbelieving tone. He looked away from her.

"*I don't know,*" she repeated firmly, stroking him across the shoulders with one hand and pulling his chin back around with the other so she was looking straight into his eyes. "I know it sounds strange, but so many things happened that day and the following days, that I never had time to wonder about the reason we three went to the North Pole Base."

She paused to think, her brow furrowing. "I do remember . . . when I was called into the commissar's office that morning . . . I was warned not to say anything to anyone. I was to pack an overnight bag, bring my surgeon's kit, and report to the launch facility within the hour. But such false urgency and unnecessary secrecy is not uncommon in Neocommunist bureaucracies."

"You were specifically told to bring your surgeon's kit?" Gus asked. "Then the reason you were brought along was because you were a surgeon. Why did they chose you and not someone else?"

"Simple," Tanya said. "The primary surgeon in Novomoskovsk was operating on an appendix in Novobaku. The other backup surgeon was the one on call, and I was the only one free. The smaller bases like Novobaku have paramedics, but no surgeons."

"Where were you going that day? To tend to someone hurt out on the glacier?"

"Very unlikely. The base paramedic is supposed to stabilize any patient needing surgery, get him under pressure, bring him back to base, and keep him alive until I arrive. There was no indication of trouble when we landed at the base. Whatever I was supposed to do, it wasn't to treat someone."

"What place were you going to?"

"I really don't know," Tanya said, looking puzzled. "When you are a woman, a woman the KGB doesn't trust, and the commissar says to come along, you come along without asking questions." She leaned close to him and put her hand on his chest. "I'm sorry I'm not much help. Is it important?"

"Important enough to die for," Gus said, frowning.

"Die?" Tanya asked in a quiet voice, suddenly scared. She removed her hand from his chest and straightened up.

"Ivan Petrovich is dead," Gus said. "I don't know the details, but he died rather than reveal anything about where you three were going or why. Now, since he can't talk and you don't know, the only one left who can enlighten us is Viktor Braginsky. Viktor is at the North Pole, so that's where we're going."

CHAPTER 7

THE MAKING OF A GOD

It had been the first time in memory that the mayor of New York City had *asked* for airborne noise pollution. Alexander Armstrong Day in New York City started out with a bang. Two bangs, in fact—sonic bangs from the golden nose and wingtips of *Bucephalus*, bringing General Alexander Armstrong back to Earth. Having been designed to fly through the almost vacuum of the Martian atmosphere and land unaided at any point on the rocky surface of that planet, *Bucephalus* had more than enough lift and power to allow Major Thomas to land it at LaGuardia Airport. After a tour of the world, *Bucephalus* would find a permanent home in the Smithsonian Air and Space Museum.

Alexander was met by Mayor Diane "Di" Perkins, the "Bronx Bombshell." A tall, striking, blond-haired, fashionably dressed woman with steel-gray eyes like Alexander's, she was single and used her dating opportunities to political advantage. Always on the go, she strode out to *Bucephalus* with her three-man police escort and met Alexander at the exit lock instead of waiting for him back in the terminal buildings. A chartered helicopter took them into the city to the start of the parade. Di had brought along three newspapers.

"This is the *Times*," said Di, holding up the front page. HAIL THE CONQUERING HERO, said the headline.

"The *Daily Mirror* is a little more dramatic," she went on, holding up, PLANET BUSTER BACK.

"While the *Fax/Facts* electronic newsheet . . ."

ALEXANDER THE GREATEST, it said.

She leaned forward to hand them to him.

"I agree. You are the greatest," she said breathlessly.

Alexander, interested only in what the papers had to say about him, glanced briefly through the columns, noticing the photographs. There was an especially good one in the *New York Times* that showed him in his battle suit, the helmet under his arm. The gold color came out well.

Di was sitting in the small helicopter passenger seat facing him. She undid her seat belt and slipped forward until her knees were between his. She took his free hand.

"After the parade," she said, "there will be a reception and dinner at my mansion. I'd be very willing to put you up for the night." She squeezed his hand slowly and with feeling.

"Well . . . Di," Alexander said, dragging his attention from the newspaper clippings and squeezing her hand in return to play for time. "I would really like to do that, especially if we could get some time alone together. But . . . Major Betsy Thomas and I are already booked into the top floor suite at the Hilton Kilometer." He paused, then added brightly, "Perhaps I can spend a night in the mayor's mansion the *next* time I'm in New York."

"Or the White House, if you happen to be in D.C. next year," Di said with a wink. "I don't intend to be mayor of this little burg forever."

"May I quote you on that?" a rough-sounding voice said from up front. The copilot turned in his seat and shoved a microphone between them. He took off his huge pair of sunglasses and pushed his too-large borrowed hat to the back of his head, revealing a coarse, friendly face topped by curly sandy-red hair with prominent white streaks along the sides. The most noticeable feature of the face, however, was a bulbous, red-veined, five-martini nose. The smell of vodka saturated every word he breathed.

"Maury Pickford!" Di shouted furiously. "You drunken, brown-nosing, prying asshole! What the fuck are you doing flying my helicopter!"

Maury feigned shock at the reply, then looked down at his recorder. "My goodness, Di, I do believe you have burned a hole in my nanodisk."

He looked up from the recorder and answered her seriously. "The copilot owed me one for saving his life in the Baltic fiasco."

He turned to Alexander and his face broadened with an ingratiating grin that made him look like an aging, dissipated leprechaun. Alexander was forced to like him.

"In case you missed Di's introduction, I'm Maury Pickford— my father's idol was shortstop Maury Wills. I work for the *Daily Mirror*—the one with tits on the third page ... Tell me, General, what's it like to be a worldwide hero, with all the girls, even mayor-type girls, throwing themselves into your lap?"

Maury stuck close by them as they landed at the starting point for the parade. Alexander lost sight of him as the video cameras crowded in, but somehow Maury ended up sitting between the driver and the security guard in the front seat of the limousine that took Alexander and Di through the streets of New York City. From there Maury got the famous shot of Alexander and Di that for once made the front page of the *Daily Mirror* more titillating than the third page.

The picture showed the pair twisted around and looking back over the trunk of the limousine at some commotion that had taken place as the limousine had passed by. The wind had blown Di's skirt up and Alexander's left hand was on her stockinged thigh.

Alexander had a difficult time explaining that one to Betsy when he showed up back at the hotel suite that evening after the reception. Shortly afterward, he traded in his kilometer-high view of the city for a midnight taxi ride to the mayor's mansion.

Late the next day, after a short plane hop down the coast, Alexander found himself back in Washington, D.C., at the center of U.S. military power—the Pentagon.

America may be getting too old for its own good, Alexander thought as he made his way around a construction area inside the Pentagon. The five-sided building was approaching one hundred years old. It should have been torn down and replaced, but it was now an "historical monument." Instead of getting a new building, the armed forces were reduced to demolishing the inside portions of the Pentagon one-fifth at a time and rebuilding the inside to modern standards while keeping the outside looking the same.

This was the one building in the country where the brass on his visor and the two stars on his shoulder brought few glances from passersby, although one kid in the shopping concourse had recognized him, while he was getting a shoeshine, and tried to bother him for an autograph until he shooed the little pest away.

Alexander made his way through the rings and corridors to the office of the chairman of the Joint Chiefs of Staff, General William Macpherson. He took special note of the layout of the office as he entered and saw some things that he would do differently once it was *his*.

It wouldn't be long now. "Billy" Macpherson had specifically asked him to stop off before he gave his invited speech to the joint session of Congress the next day. The only reason for the invitation would be to make permanent the four stars that Alexander had worn as commander of the UN Invasion Fleet and to tell him of his nomination to the General Staff of the U.S. Space Force.

The secretary sent him right in. General Macpherson was in the white uniform worn by the members of the Joint Chiefs of Staff. The four gold stars on his shoulders glistened nicely on their white-worsted epaulets. General Macpherson did not come out from behind the desk to shake Alexander's hand, but sat back in his chair and looked at him from a distance.

"Good afternoon, Alex," he said. "New York City certainly gave you an outstanding welcome yesterday."

"That's only the beginning," Alexander bragged. "After the speech to Congress tomorrow, I will be off on a tour of the major cities of the United States. Then I'll have to visit the capitals of our allies that supplied troops to give a UN flavor to the invasion." He shook his head and shrugged. "I'm afraid it will be some weeks before I am free enough to take up my General Staff duties here at the Pentagon."

A frown crossed General Macpherson's face. "I'm afraid your next duties for the Space Force are not going to be at the Pentagon."

"What do you mean?" Alexander asked, puzzled.

"A two-star general is usually assigned to a base," General Macpherson said.

"You mean," Alexander said, getting angry, "that after leading one of the most successful campaigns in history and winning back a whole planet—a whole solar system—you're not going to promote me?" He lunged forward over the desk and grabbed a white lapel. General Macpherson stared impassively as Alexander yelled in his face, "You can't do this to me!" Suddenly realizing what he was doing, Alexander let go of the lapel and stood back in shocked silence.

"I didn't do anything to you, Alex," the general said. "You did it to yourself when you spaced Petrovich. Although everything you did was technically correct and the Board of Inquiry whitewashed the incident and cleared you, as far as the rest of the Joint Chiefs of Staff and I are concerned, it was murder. Besides being murder, it was stupid. Both military intelligence and the CIA wanted to get their hands on Petrovich."

The general slowly and deliberately reached up to straighten his lapel, then continued. "Until you learn to control yourself better, you don't belong on the Space Force General Staff."

Alexander could feel his anger returning. His face stiffened. He stood at attention. "Very good, sir," he said, turned on his heel, and walked out.

Macpherson will pay for this, he promised himself as he left.

The warm welcome he received at the joint session of Congress partially made up for the previous day. The news that he had not been promoted had rapidly leaked around Washington. Most who heard about it thought he had been unfairly treated, and one senator had already started a call for an investigation.

The announcement of his name as he entered the House chambers was buried under an avalanche of applause that went on and on for twenty minutes. The video cameras followed his every move as he shook hands with the president and his cabinet in the front row, pointedly walked by the Joint Chiefs of Staff, also in the front row, then shook some more hands. Taking his time, he strode to the podium, waved to the video cameras, and waited, nodding his acknowledgment to the crowd, his face periodically crinkling up into the now famous smile with the space-weathered crow's-feet arrows pointing at his deep-set eyes, then relaxing as he leaned over to listen to someone trying to talk to him from below.

After the tumult had died down, there were the ceremonies. The Speaker of the House and the vice-president gave welcoming speeches. The president, knowing this was not his day, gave a brief speech as commander-in-chief of the armed forces, thanking Alexander for a successful campaign with minimum casualties.

Then came the awards. The first was a special gold medal authorized and presented by the grateful members of the Reformed United Nations. The medal had a picture of Mars on one side and the arrowlike shape of the *Yorktown* class of spacecraft in full acceleration on the other. Next was a certificate containing a joint declaration of the two houses commending him as commander of the UN Invasion Fleet and leader of the U.S. forces.

Finally, he was awarded the Congressional Medal of Honor, the only one awarded in the Mars campaign, for—as the Speaker of the House intoned in his stentorian voice—". . . his personal bravery and risk of his life above and beyond the call of duty, while personally engaged in hand-to-hand combat with only a pistol against enemy forces armed with missiles and rifles . . ."

The applause started again as the medal was put around his neck and went on another fifteen minutes, Alexander nodding his thanks and waving occasionally to the video audience as he waited for the chambers to quiet down. They finally did, and he began to speak.

"I want to thank you, Mr. Speaker, all the members of this Congress, and all the people of the great city of Washington, D.C., and the rest of the United States and the world, for the warm welcome and the great honors you have bestowed on me. I also want to thank all of you assembled and the president for your help prior to the Mars campaign by giving me a blank checkbook for the soldiers and equipment that I needed to oust the planet-grabbing Neocommunist occupiers from their illegal bases on Mars." He paused, then his face took on a serious tone.

"Although the Russians no longer control Mars, they still threaten us all along the Baltic front. They also still threaten us from above with their military bases in orbit and on the Moon. What I won on Mars was not a war. It was only one battle of our still-continuing war against worldwide domination by the atheistic rulers of Neocommunist Russia, aided by their socialist sympathizers and their cowardly Neocommunist propaganda dupes."

Alexander stopped smiling and turned grimly serious. "And those people that are duped by Neocommunist propaganda not only exist in foreign nations, they have come to exist here in this country. I know they even exist at the highest levels of our unified military command—*right now!*"

There was a gasp from the audience, and General Macpherson and the rest of the Joint Chiefs of Staff started to frown.

"I call on you to listen to me!" Alexander said over the crowd noise. "In my great victory on Mars, I have shown that it is possible to attack the Neocommunists *directly*, drive them away from the stolen lands they illegally occupy, and send them crying back home to 'Mother' Russia, *without* the cowardly Neocommunist government doing a thing in return. If *I* could get the Neocommunists off Mars—" He paused and his forefinger swept accusingly over the Joint Chiefs of Staff. "—why can't these so-called leaders of the armed forces get them out of the Baltic . . . and orbital space . . . and off the Moon?" His finger came to rest on General Macpherson.

"Because that man and the rest of the Joint Chiefs of Staff are Neocommunist dupes that have bought the Neocommunist propaganda line that the Russian armed forces are invincible. They are cowards who are afraid to fight!" A murmur started in the audience and the commander of the U.S. Space Forces started to rise, but General Macpherson placed a hand on his shoulder and restrained him.

"I was proud to serve my country and the world against the atheistic evil of neocommunism!" Alexander continued, shouting against the rising voices. He raised one hand after the other to his shoulders and pulled the loosened double-star bars off his uniform epaulets. "But I can no longer serve under leaders who are *cowards*! I resign!" He flipped his stars to the floor, where they slid to the feet of General Macpherson. He then turned to grasp the podium and stared fiercely at the audience while the video cameras closed in on the steel-gray eyes.

The chamber quieted to a deadly silence as he continued in a low voice. "But unlike another brave but battered general who once stood at this podium, I will *not* fade away . . ."

He rose up on his toes and stood straighter, arms stiff on the podium. "Instead," he said, "I shall return . . . to drive away the evil forces of atheistic neocommunism that threaten the peace. I will bring everlasting freedom to the United States, to the world, and to the solar system!"

He strode off the podium and made his way unescorted out the doors of the chambers to loud but scattered applause that switched to a puzzled buzz as soon as he cleared the door.

The space force limousine was waiting for him at the bottom of the Capitol steps. The driver raised his eyes questioningly as he noticed the missing stars on the general's shoulders, but said nothing as he opened the door, then went around to the driver's seat.

"Take me back to the Crystal City Pyramids," Alexander said to the driver. As the driver started toward the Fourteenth Street bridge, Alexander started to think about what he would do next. This would be the last time he would be able to call on the space force for a limousine.

He wasn't too worried about money; the Scott Meredith Literary Agency in New York City had sold world rights to his life story for one hundred million dollars to Ballantine, Interplanetary, half the money up front, and had found somebody to write it for him. The immediate problem was staff to take care of all the piddling details in order to free his brain for the important decisions.

Perhaps he should take his brother's advice and run for president. But no one in their right mind would want that bean-counting, hand-shaking, baby-kissing job. The president had a lot of power, but what the office of the president needed was a good adjutant—a prime minister or something—to take over all the drag work. Unfortunately, the U.S. Constitution didn't allow for that and made it so the president had to do everything. Then again, if he did get himself elected president, the first thing he would be able to do would be to kick Macpherson off the Joint Chiefs of Staff and send him into obscurity . . .

As they crossed the bridge, the Pyramids loomed ahead. The largest hotel complex in the Washington area, it took up four blocks in the Crystal City area and consisted of five pyramids—a tall central one, and four slightly smaller pyramids around it. Inside each was a pyramidal atrium.

Alexander had asked for the top floor suite of the central pyramid. His original request had been rudely rejected—the top floor suite was permanently unavailable. But shortly thereafter an apologetic manager had called back to say there had been a terrible mistake and he could have the room after all.

The suite was magnificent, with solid-gold doorknobs and plumbing, a separate office with twenty-four-hour rotating secretary service, complete computer and communications capability, and a full personal staff, including a butler, a chef, and a buxom maid in a skimpy French outfit who giggled instead of slapped when he copped a feel. Best of all, the hotel told him some admirer of his was picking up the tab. They declined to tell him who.

The space force limousine dropped him at the special outside elevator. The doorman held the door and sent him on his way up the forty-five-degree incline to the top of the pyramid. As he rose to the higher levels, he could see into the five-sided central court of the Pentagon a few kilometers off. He wished that he had a nuclear tipped miniseeker in his hand instead of the Congressional Medal of Honor.

At the top he was met by the butler, who took his hat, medals, and jacket—while looking disapprovingly at the epaulets with their ragged holes.

"There is a gentleman to see you in the View Room, sir," he said.

"Who is it?"

"He said to say, 'An admirer of yours,' " the butler answered. "Hotel security assures me that he has a legitimate reason for seeing you. *I* can also vouch for him, sir."

Alexander went up the winding steps to the View Room. The room was the apex to the central building of the Crystal City Pyramids and had an unobstructed view in all directions. Standing there looking out one of the triangular floor-to-apex windows was a large man in a white silk suit and white suede shoes. They went well with the thick mane of white hair on his head. He was over six feet tall and looked like he weighed 250 pounds or more. He was holding a glass in a huge paw of a hand whose fingers seemed to be cluttered with masses of gold rings sparkling with huge diamonds. The glass was full nearly to the brim with brown liquid. There were no ice cubes.

"Straight malt scotch," Alexander muttered to himself, noticing the bottle of Old Pulteney sitting on top of the liquor cabinet. The hand raised, there was a long pause, and the hand came down. The tumbler was one-third empty.

"Enjoying the view?" Alexander asked.

"Ha-hah!" the man replied in a loud voice that echoed strangely in the pyramid-shaped room. "The conquering hero returns!" He slowly turned around and Alexander could now see that in addition to his white silk suit and gold rings, the man was wearing a gold-thread brocade vest that stretched across his ample chest and belly. Under his ruddy, cherubic, smiling face was a white silk tie in a Windsor knot with a gigantic gold and diamond stickpin. As he stretched out his other gold-ringed paw to shake hands, Alexander noticed that he didn't try to come in close in order to overawe him with his height, as so many large people did.

"I know *you*. You are the great General Alexander Armstrong, conqueror of Mars," the man said heartily. "Excuse me . . . *ex-*General Alexander Armstrong—for I have just finished watching your recent performance on television." He paused, took a sip of scotch, then continued.

"I am a great admirer of yours. In the past I have admired you from afar, since you were doing very well on your own. But now I have brought my admiration closer, for I believe that I can be of some benefit to you in your present situation. And perhaps . . . you can be of some benefit to me." He took another long, slow drink of scotch, swishing it around in his mouth as he did so, obviously enjoying the taste as well as the alcohol.

"Enjoying the scotch?" Alexander asked, one eyebrow raised.

"Should," the man said, filling his tumbler again from the bottle of Old Pulteney. "I had my butler order this case after sampling it during my last golfing trip to the Sandside Dome Golf and Beach Resort on the north coast of Scotland."

"*Your* butler?" Alexander said, finally beginning to understand.

"Yes. I own this place. In fact I own the whole damn Pyramids Hotel. When I heard you were coming to town and wanted the top floor, I just hopped over to one of my guest suites on top of one of the other pyramids and let you have it. Use it as long as you like— the maid, too; she's not there just for dusting . . ." He paused for another sip of scotch. "Like the place?"

"Yes, it's very nice. Thank you, Mister . . ."

"You don't know me," the man said. "I am burdened with the terrible moniker of . . . Robert L. Krapp. Why my father never changed his last name, I'll never know—although I never did, either. Once you have fought for your name all through grade school, keeping it is a badge of courage. Just call me Rob."

"But if you are rich enough to own the Pyramids Hotel, why haven't I heard of you?"

"When you have a name like mine," Rob said, "you use someone else's. For the expenditure side of the ledger I use Pyramid Trust. For the income side of the ledger I use the Prophet Muhammad Sheik and the Church of the Unifier."

"The religious nut who has half the population of California and the East Coast believing he is the pipeline to God?"

"That's my boy," Rob said proudly, taking another gulp of scotch. "But it isn't half the population, we only get tithes from twenty-eight percent of the East Coast and thirty-five percent of California—as of last week's figures."

Rob suddenly got serious. "But the real problem from a market-growth point of view is that Muhammad doesn't seem to be transportable. He does real well on the coasts, where people have more cosmopolitan tastes and are willing to listen to a foreigner, but when I try to market him in the central states, or across the border, the customers stay away in droves.

"What I need is someone with a broader appeal, someone who is known around the world, someone with strong and proven leadership qualities, someone who shows up well on video—although I can make anyone look good on video—someone who has an important mission to carry out . . . like a mission to save the world from evil . . ."

"Like the evil tyranny of atheistic neocommunism that threatens us now!" Alexander said, phrases from his recent speech still echoing in his brain.

"Exactly. Wouldn't it be wonderful if we could use modern mass-media technology to aid you in ridding the world of the atheistic rulers of Neocommunist Russia, their socialist sympathizers, *and* their cowardly Neocommunist propaganda dupes?"

Rob put down his tumbler and started to pace around the room, his voice rising and falling in a hypnotic pattern. He pounded one huge fist into another. "You must strike. You must strike now! You must strike during your upcoming tour, while the world hangs upon your every word." He stopped pacing and, stooping slightly, put both hands on Alexander's shoulders to stare straight into his eyes.

"Together," he said, "we must drive away the evil forces of neocommunism that threaten us and bring everlasting freedom to the United States and to the world!"

"Yes," Alexander agreed, under his spell. "We must! But how?"

"Come!" Rob said. "I will show you."

He led the way down the winding stairs from the View Room to the built-in office of the central pyramid suite.

"Alert Eric and the media magicians, Jane," Rob said as he led Alex past the secretary. Rob moved knowingly across the room, touched some hidden controls, and soon a triple-video-screen console rolled into view out of an inner wall. Rob sat down before the central screen.

"Let's have a 'naked' of Muddy, Eric," Rob said to the console.

"Are you sure you can stand it?" a voice said from a speaker.

"Warts and all," Rob assured him. On the central screen appeared a picture of a skinny, rheumy-eyed, muddy-skinned Arab with a poorly wrapped turban, a ragged wispy beard, and a strongly hooked nose with a horrendous hairy wart on it. He was giving a speech. The voice was reedy, monotonous, and heavily accented.

"Is that the real Muhammad Sheik?" Alexander asked in amazement. "I've seen him on video occasionally while scanning across the channels, and he doesn't look like that!"

"Cut the fooling around," Rob said to the console. "This is serious business. I have Alexander Armstrong with me." The hairy wart vanished from the nose of Muhammad Sheik. "Sorry, Rob—just kidding."

"*That* is the way he really looks," Rob said, pointing to the reedy Arab guru. "Before Eric and his media-magicians 'smooth' up his image a little.

"Now give me the Southern California standard on the left screen, Eric," Rob said. Almost instantly the same view of Muhammad Sheik appeared on the left-hand screen, but now the turban was spiraled perfectly, clear eyes sparkled intensely from a lean, aesthetic face with a flowing beard. The color of his face was a clear light brown, while the hook in his nose had been softened considerably. The voice was strong, clear, and hypnotic.

"That's the Muhammad Sheik I remember," Alex said.

"The New England version on the right," Rob said, and a third image appeared on the right screen. The color of the skin of the image was whiter in tone and the nose straighter. The voice was broadening its a's and swallowing its r's.

"Our across-the-border attempt now." The New England image was replaced with another version of Muhammad Sheik. This one had a skin tone that was close to the original, but the beard had completely disappeared. The voice now spoke in fluent Spanish.

"I don't know Mexican, but it looks like even his lip motions are correctly synchronized!" Alex said in amazement.

"Nothing to it, once you have built up a library," Eric's voice answered from the speaker.

"With these software tools," Rob bragged, turning around to look at Alexander, "I can make a silk purse out of a sow's ear. But in your case, I don't have to. It does really help to use Eric's program, however, when you want to switch languages." He returned to face the console.

"Dump Muddy, Eric," Rob said. "And let me have some of that demo tape of General Armstrong you've been working on for the past half-hour."

"It's still a little rough in spots," Eric warned.

The three screens blanked, then the central screen lit up with a picture of Alexander at a podium. The podium and microphone height, the background, and the camera angle had all been adjusted to make Alexander look over six feet tall. Instead of a military crew cut, he had a wavy hair style that even Alexander had to admit made him look handsomer than ever. His face smiled, and the famous crow's-feet wrinkles appeared, but now they didn't add to his age, just his character. His eyes seemed to burn and sparkle with inner fire.

His uniform had been replaced with a golden buttonless tunic, with a cadet collar and padded shoulders. His voice had not been changed much, although it was somehow richer, more articulate, more fascinating, and more hypnotic in its ability to hold the attention of the listener.

"My people," his image said. "My people! Come to me. Come to me and listen. I call on you, my people! Come and drive away the evil forces that threaten the peace. The peace of the United States. The peace of the world!

"They now threaten to grab all the planet. You know them . . . the atheistic rulers of Neocommunist Russia, their socialist sympathizers, and their cowardly Neocommunist propaganda dupes! But they are not invincible. I can drive them away. But I need your help!"

The image pointed its finger down over the podium and the camera point of view switched to one that looked up from below at a towering, awe-inspiring image of a golden-tuniced Alexander, his finger pointing straight down at the camera.

"*You* can help! Get your checkbook . . . and send a check . . . *right now*! To the Church of the Unifier, Washington, D.C."

The motion of the image stopped. "The only words I had to piece together were *church* and *unifier*," Eric's voice bragged from the console.

Alexander stood in amazement.

"That was me?"

"That was only a first approximation of what could be you," Eric replied.

"Now that you no longer have the staff and resources of the Space Command to draw on, perhaps you could use a little assistance in managing your media appearances in the U.S. and around the world in the next few months? Pyramid Trust would be glad to take on the responsibilities, in return for a small commission."

"How much?" Alexander demanded, suddenly suspicious.

"Muhammad Sheik retains eighty-five percent," Rob said. "But since you are so much easier to market, Pyramid Trust would be more than willing to only charge a ten percent fee."

"Fine," Alexander said, having recently negotiated a ten percent fee plus expenses contract with Scott Meredith Literary Agency for his book.

"Plus expenses," Rob added, almost as an afterthought.

"Okay," Alexander replied, unconcerned about details.

"Excellent," Rob said, pulling out a small piece of paper. "Sign here."

Alexander signed with a flourish—two ornate capital A's, each followed by a squiggle. He then went back and carefully stroked in the single straight back cross through the invisible *x* in the first squiggle that distinguished his signature from that of his brother Augustus.

The next day Rob took Alexander off to Eric Oldenburg's studio, which was full of high-tech cameras and image processing computers. Physically, Eric was almost the exact opposite of the other computer wizard that Alexander knew.

Eric was compact, well-built, and handsome, like Alexander, but with nowhere near the shoulders or biceps. Although buried alone in a complex console room, surrounded only by computers, and communicating with the outside world only through computer links, he wore an expensive, impeccably tailored business suit, a fashionably thin narrow-striped tie, and a carefully color coordinated two-tone tailored shirt with ruby cuff links that occasionally clattered on the keyboard when he reached to touch a screen icon. Eric was obviously doing well working for Rob.

A cross between a rich movie star and an IBM salesman, was Alexander's final analysis.

They had Alexander give a speech. There were a lot of strange sounding phrases, many from the Bible, and some from other books. Eric then had him repeat the alphabet and read a list of words and phonemes. It was late that night, in the Pyramid penthouse, before the tailor finally finished his last measurements and Rob left for the guest penthouse. Then the maid started to make a pest of herself.

The following afternoon, Alexander, Rob, and Eric met in the penthouse. The tailor had delivered Alexander's suit that noon. It consisted of a modernistic tunic and tights made of scintillating gold cloth, with high, raised golden boots that made him look taller. The buttonless tunic had a high cadet collar that lengthened Alexander's neckline, and space-age winged shoulder pads that made him look like a hero from the future.

Alexander looked himself over in the three-sided mirror in the cavernous clothes closet. "Looks nice!"

"Yes, it does," Rob and Eric agreed.

Rob came over and adjusted a shoulder. Eric activated the video cameras behind the mirrors to get sample images of Alexander from all sides.

"I canceled your tour of Philadelphia tomorrow, Alex," Rob said.

"Why?" Alexander demanded. "That's the home of liberty! Surely we will need Philadelphia to fight neocommunism."

"Because the organizers couldn't get a hall big enough, and I didn't want to start off your tour with a riot," Rob said. "Besides, tonight is your debut as the new leader of the Church of the Unifier."

"But isn't that Muhammad Sheik's church?"

"Not anymore," Rob said. "Muhammad has decided to take his millions and return to Lebanon."

"Not to mention the fact that someone reported to the Immigration Service that his visa had expired," Eric said under his breath. "Twenty seconds to nine," he called to Rob.

"I'm sure there will be a request for press interviews after the broadcast," Rob said. "I assume you will be up to it?"

"Of course," Alexander said. "I've handled hundreds of press conferences before. What room will we be using for the reporters?"

"We don't do face-to-face interviews anymore," Rob replied. "All interviews are now done by remote, with everything passing through Eric's computers before it goes out to the public."

"But the public will certainly see the real me when I give my speeches during the tours," Alexander objected, slightly bewildered.

"Not the way I have your tour rearranged," Rob said. "I only booked you into large domes and football stadiums, and then insisted on a fifty-meter clear space between the podium and the first seats—for security reasons, of course."

"Nobody can see any sort of detail in a face at fifty meters or more," Eric said. "So then I come in by supplying a large-screen video replay of the speaker to the stadium audience. Suitably massaged—of course."

"The main reason I'm doing this," Rob said, "is that after a few weeks, you won't even have to bother going to the stadium to give speeches. I have a search out for some six-foot look-alikes. As soon as we get them signed up and trained, they can take care of that minor detail for you."

"Not very minor sometimes . . ." Eric said under his breath.

"Later, Eric," Rob hushed, but Eric wasn't in the mood that day to hush.

"We lost a Muddy look-alike last year." he said. "Being a profit-making prophet is not the safest job in the world. That's why Rob takes refuge behind his name and lets other people front for him."

The Sunday evening broadcast of the Church of the Unifier came on at nine P.M. eastern standard time—six, pacific standard time. Prophet Muhammad Sheik started with his usual introductory message and the call for pledges and tithes. Then he startled the audience by saying that he had a revolutionary message for them. They were to call their friends and make sure they were listening.

Then came the break for the demonstrations of the Muhammad Sheik 'Healing Chair,' the advertisements for the potions to stop drug addiction, alcohol hangovers, cigarette cough, overeating, poor circulation, herpes, AIDS, backache, and the common cold. After long minutes, the prophet returned to the screen, looking as good as he had ever looked, his face radiant with joy.

"For long I have been a prophet telling you of the future coming of God the Infinite Lord! God the Unifier of all," he said. "I am now a prophet that has great joy!" His face lit up even more. "Because today I am the prophet that will introduce God himself to you, the living Unifier, the Infinite Lord incarnate!"

The camera drew back, making Muhammad Sheik a small figure in the left foreground. In the distance there shone a golden light, a golden light that grew larger and brighter, until it almost filled the camera lens. An angel chorus raised a trillion hosannas in the background and a thousand organs seemed to expand the very space-time with their sound.

Muhammad's voice came in over the music. "I am privileged to present to you today, the Infinite Lord, your God. God the Unifier. The Unifier of your life. The Unifier of your country. The Unifier of your world. The Unifier of the solar system. The Unifier of the universe!" He paused.

"This is Alexander. The Infinite Lord—and this is his sign."

Muhammad Sheik made the sign of the infinity symbol, but vertically, like a propeller. The animation artists behind the television camera captured the symbol as he drew it and raised it high overhead. "Heed his sign," Muhammad Sheik said, fading. "Heed the Infinite Lord . . . and obey him."

The camera point of view moved forward until Muhammad Sheik slipped off the screen into obscurity, leaving only the vertical infinity symbol in the distance. The camera point of view then zoomed down from the symbol to a glowing point below it. There, growing larger as the camera point of view zoomed in, was the golden figure of Alexander. He stood there, like a golden god from the future, arms outstretched.

"Come, my people," the golden figure of the Infinite Lord said. "Come unto me."

CHAPTER 8

BOREAL BASE

The hopiter punched upward at high gees through the thin Martian atmosphere on a slightly smoky orange exhaust of carbon dioxide, unburnt carbon monoxide, and the occasional carbon particle. Just after leaving the upper atmosphere, it switched off its engines to coast on its ballistic trajectory the rest of the way to its destination at the North Pole of Mars—one quarter of the way around the planet. Once the engines were turned off, the pilot rotated the vehicle so they could look back at the gigantic volcano they had left behind.

"We will be flying right over the aureole of Mount Olympus on our way north," Tanya said, loosening her seat harness and floating free to the window. Gus followed.

"The Sun angle is good," she said. "See how the aureole is made up of lobes on the downhill side of the Tharsis bulge?" Holding onto Gus with one hand, she pointed with the other. "See that each lobe has its outer edge tilted up, and the part back toward the volcano is depressed? That is not an ash flow from the volcano. It is an obvious indication of gravity-driven thrust faulting. Same thing occurred in the Bearpaw Mountains in U.S.A."

"But look at that old meteor crater down there," Gus said, pointing. "See how the striations in the lobe pattern seem to be laid down over top of the crater pattern? Joseph would say the old meteor crater was covered with ice, and the lobe pattern was caused by an ash flow that took place over the surface of the ice. Then later the ice melted or evaporated, lowering the ash field pattern gently down over the meteor crater pattern."

Tanya chewed thoughtfully on her lower lip. "Well, maybe there was *some* ice," she finally admitted. "But not ten kilometers' worth."

Their journey peaked just past the still-unexplored Milankovic Crater that stood large and lonely in the middle of the nearly craterless Arcadia Plain. They started their descent toward the Martian polar ice cap that was coming up over the horizon in front of them.

Gus pulled out a blue "polar" from his pocket and rotated the large, thick, one-hundred-Martian-dollar coin until he could match the swirling pattern on its face with the swirling terraces and canyons in the ice cap showing through the porthole. The spiral-pattern canyons so visible from space and so distinctive on the blue "polar" were not permanent, but were slowly shifting over the aeons, uncovering ancient deposits at the bottoms of the canyons, then covering them again with fresh deposits.

"We start deceleration in five minutes," the pilot warned from above. "Get buckled in."

The descent to Boreal Base was just as crude and basic as the lift-off—a high-gee, preprogrammed deceleration maneuver that used maximum advantage of aerobraking to minimize fuel consumption. Since they were landing at a prepared site, there was no period of hovering to find a flat spot; they just dropped down the last five meters onto the landing struts.

They were met by the base director, Ernest Licon. His primary job was head of Boreal Base engineering. He had the difficult task of designing, constructing, and maintaining buildings that would keep everyone alive and warm during the long, cold, sunless winter season when the very atmosphere condensed and fell from the sky as carbon dioxide snow. The next winter was many sols away, however, and there was sunlight for a good part of the day.

Even with the Sun up, it was cold, and Gus felt the heaters in his Marsuit switch on high as he stepped out of the hopiter. They hurried across the field, cycled through the air lock, and got out of their Marsuits. Ernest hung his up next to the air lock, but Gus and Tanya folded theirs up, bagged them with their helmets, and carried them.

"Your office is right down here," Ernest said, leading the way. "We might as well talk there."

"*My* office?" Gus asked, as they entered a good-sized room with a large rough-cast aluminum table surrounded by tech stools, a desk with a full comm-comp terminal, and an inflatable plastic lounge seat that could unfold into a single bed.

"Your administrative assistant, Mr. Fred Whimple, contacted me before you arrived," Ernest said. "I was instructed to clear out an office for your use and to give you every assistance. He even gave me a special unlimited charge number for any expenses. He wouldn't tell me much else."

"That's because I am here to explore a little mystery," Gus said. "I can't tell you much about it yet, partially because I don't know much myself. Where can I find Viktor Braginsky? I'd like to talk to him."

"While I was waiting for your hopiter to land I saw Viktor and his two techs returning from a field trip with a rack of cores. You should find him at the core storage building."

"It might be better if we went and visited him," Gus said, reaching for the bag containing his helmet and Marsuit. "Where is the core storage building?"

"As you exit the lock, it's the long building off to the left by itself. Make sure you have plenty of charge in your heater batteries. The building is refrigerated."

"Refrigerated!" Tanya exclaimed. "At the North Pole?"

"We keep it well below the freezing point of carbon dioxide," Ernest replied. "We don't want the contents of the cores to melt or evaporate until they've been analyzed."

Tanya and Gus found the core storage building with no trouble. Outside one end of the hut was a crawler hitched to a six-wheeled trailer carrying a coring rig and a set of storage racks that carried about three or four dozen plastic coring-tube liners, each ten meters long. Two men were pulling the tubes off the racks, one by one.

Another man was noting the numbers engraved on each tube, entering notes into a vidofax, and giving instructions as to where to store the tube in the building.

"*Kak pozevaetye*, Viktor," Tanya said as they walked up to him.

Viktor looked up with surprise at the two. "Tanya! And Dr. Armstrong! I thought you two were exploring Olympus Mons."

"We just finished," Gus said. "I wanted to make an inspection trip of Boreal Base and the North Polar region now that its summer, so I came up on hopiter. Tanya, having been here briefly only once before, took the opportunity to come with me."

"Before?" Viktor said, then remembered. "Oh! Yes! The day I was shot." He turned to Tanya. "I still have aches in that arm," he said plaintively.

"What were you doing out on the ice that day?" Gus asked.

Viktor paused in his answer, then finally stammered, "Why . . . trying to defend our base, of course." He grew slightly defiant. "Did you expect me to do anything different at the time?"

"I mean *before* the UN forces arrived," Gus persisted. "Where were you and Ivan Petrovich and Tanya going? What did you expect to see there?"

Viktor hesitated, stammered, then finally said, "Nothing. Nothing! It was just an inspection trip—just like you, the new commissar of Mars, are doing."

Gus fought down the temptation to explain the difference between his job and that of the old commissar. "We'll wait here while you and your men finish unloading," he said. "Then perhaps we should have a little talk."

"A—a talk?" Viktor stammered. "About what?"

"About your status as a guest scientist at the Sagan Mars Institute," Gus said with finality. He turned, walked a few paces away to stand near Tanya, and waited.

The technicians continued in their task of pulling cores from the rack, taking them by Viktor for recording in his vidofax, then placing them in the designated racks in the refrigerated core storage building. The men cycled through into the hut by a simple insulated double door system that kept the predominantly nitrogen-argon atmosphere inside from diffusing out. The core sample tubes were slid through a sleeved hole in the side of the wall.

Gus noticed that the tubes were covered with frost. The core samples had been pulled up from the frigid depths of the glaciers that formed the northern polar caps, and the carbon dioxide in the air had frozen to the surface of the tubes, hiding the contents. Where the technician's gloves had wiped the snow away, Gus could see thicker layers of white ice alternating with thinner layers of rusty brown dust. Just like tree rings, except that the white ice layers became more compressed with depth.

Viktor finally finished and they went inside. Gus took Viktor into his office alone. Tanya went off to find their personal quarters.

"Are you a scientist?" Gus asked Viktor bluntly.

"Yes!" Viktor said, somewhat surprised.

"The Sagan Mars Institute is open to any competent scientist, no matter what his race, national origin, religion, or political beliefs are," Gus started. "As long as that scientist acts like a scientist and does not allow his scientific behavior to be distorted by his national patriotism or beliefs. A scientist, first and foremost, is a searcher for truths. Truths about nature. But that is not all. The scientist must transmit to others the results of his searches. He cannot hide his findings for personal gain or political advantage.

"Now ... there are some reasons to *delay* publication," Gus continued. "For example, when you have not yet finished analyzing your data, or when you work for a corporation that needs time to file a patent application. You don't work for a profit-making corporation, so that's no reason for not telling me. Is the reason you're keeping silent because you still have further work to do? If so, then let me know so I can make sure you have the resources you need."

"Tell you about what? There was nothing out there!" Viktor replied angrily.

Gus looked pained. He took a small card from his pocket and, using the scribbled notes for guidance, began talking in a dry monotone, like the canonical mystery detective summing up a case after having assembled everyone in the drawing room.

"0800 Zebra Time Monday Week twenty-five: You and two techs took out a crawler, as usual, to continue your ice core drilling survey program. 1410 Tuesday Week twenty-five: You and two techs returned in the crawler, as usual, with a trailer load of core samples. From 1705 to 2200 Tuesday: the core storage building refrigerator system indicated a six-hundred-watt heat load, typical of one person working in heated Marsuit. 2220 Tuesday: You checked out a crawler with a trailer containing a manhole-sized auger drilling rig. You went out alone at night despite warning by vehicle depot supervisor. 2025 Wednesday Week twenty-five: Twenty hours later, you returned crawler and trailer and canceled your crawler for the next day, after having used a crawler regularly every Monday and Thursday for weeks. 0000 Thursday Week twenty-five: You caught next hopiter to Novomoskovsk, arriving 0025 Zebra Time or 0825 local time. 0140 Thursday or 0940 local time: You have appointment with commissar. 0220: Tanya Pavlova summoned to commissar's office. Told to get surgeon's kit and report to launch site. 0420: You, commissar, and Tanya leave on nonscheduled flight on hopiter back to Novomurmansk. No other passengers on a twelve-passenger vehicle. 0445 Thursday Week twenty-five: Hopiter arrived at Novomurmansk. 0600: You checked out crawler with trailer containing backhoe and blade machine. Passengers were Petrovich and Pavlova. You went east along base of ice cap. 0800 Thursday Week twenty-five: The UN forces attacked and you turned back."

Gus looked up. "What did you find in those core samples that made you go back out on the ice alone, at night? What did you find there that made you go immediately to the commissar of Mars? What did you say to him that made him drop everything else and order a nonscheduled hop back to the North Pole? And why did you need a surgeon and a digging machine?"

"It was nothing! I tell you," Viktor insisted. Inside he was petrified with fear. Ivan Petrovich, upon hearing what Viktor had found, had immediately classified it as a state military secret and forbade him to discuss it with *anyone*. "This is our chance to pull far ahead of the capitalist imperialists!" Ivan had gloated.

"If you have nothing to hide," Gus said, putting out his hand, "then let me make a copy of the contents of your vidofax where you keep your daily notes."

Victor hesitated for a second, then passed his vidofax over.

The next afternoon, Gus and Tanya were waiting in Gus' office for the arrival of another glacier specialist, Dr. Phyllis Eisen. She was an American scientist who had come with the UN fleet and who had been working since that time with Viktor Braginsky, trying to catch up on what the Russians had found in their exploration of the North Pole ice cap.

The woman who showed up looked like a trim, middle-aged high school teacher, with intelligent, vigilant eyes, a thin nose, slightly graying curly brown hair, and a pleasant but controlled face that was allowed to smile, but not to grin.

"I'm Phyllis Eisen," she said brightly, then turned to the man a half step behind her and smiled at him. "And this is my 'right-hand man,' Al Eisen." Al was sandy-haired and wiry, about her size, and wore the standard-issue coverall of a technician.

Al stepped briefly to the front and shook hands, saying, "You've heard of secretaries marrying the boss? Well, I'm the tech that married the scientist." He laughed, and Phyllis frowned slightly, but Al always felt better getting their relationship right out on the table the first time they met someone new. Al stepped back to his shadowing position behind her.

"Have you had a chance to go over Viktor's vidofax?" Gus asked.

"You were right, Dr. Armstrong," she replied. "The records for Week 25 were missing."

"Not only were they missing," Al interjected, "they were carefully 'wiped' to make sure someone didn't resurrect them with an UNERASE program. I tried."

"But having worked with Dr. Braginsky for some weeks now, I know he is a very thorough and very methodical scientist. I pulled up a map of the North Polar region and plotted all the boreholes he had taken up to that time, and after that time. I can show you on your console."

Al went to the console, inserted a nanodisk, brought up the image of a map, and stood back. Phyllis went forward and started to point to a series of red dots on the map. They had dates marked next to them.

"East, or clockwise, from Chasma Boreal is a series of wide spiral terraces of thick glacier ice, spaced by narrow canyons where the wind and sun have eroded the glacier ice away. As you can see from where I marked the bore sites, Viktor has placed his past bore sites right along the eighty-first north latitude line. He spaces them such that he cores on one edge of an ice terrace, in the middle of the terrace, just back from the other edge of the terrace, at the base of the terrace cliff, then in the middle of the canyon, the base of the next cliff, and so on. He also takes detailed pictures of the layers visible on the sides of the cliffs. By piecing together the spacing patterns of the alternating dust and ice layers, combined with radio-isotope dating of samples from the deeper cores, he has been able to put together a detailed date map of layer pattern versus age.

"You will notice," she said, pointing to one dot after another, "that the string of boreholes stops right here, with the bore-hole dug on Thursday and Friday of Week twenty-four being right at the base of this cliff face. If he followed his normal pattern, the next borehole he would have dug would be right in the middle of this canyon. When he resumed research after the invasion, however, he did not continue at that point, but started a new string going west, or clockwise from the base."

"How far is that point from here?" Gus asked.

Phyllis measured off some distances with her fingers and compared the spacing with the scale at the bottom of the map. "Three hundred kilometers east along the base of the cap to the entrance to the canyon, and two hundred kilometers up the canyon," she said.

"We can be there tomorrow during daylight if we start to-night," Gus said. "I'll order a crawler prepared."

"I can even tell you how far down you are going to have to dig," Phyllis said with a slight smile.

Gus turned around with a surprised look.

"Al and I did an inventory of the core sample tubes in the core storage building."

"Cold work, that is," Al interjected, slapping his arms around himself.

"There is one core tube missing, serial number 202," Phyllis continued. "If Viktor had followed his usual pattern of using core tubes sequentially, it would have been tube two in a ten-tube core. Whatever Viktor is trying to hide, it is between ten and twenty meters down at eighty-one degrees north and twenty-five and a half degrees west."

"I'd better have a crew of technicians follow us in another crawler with a manhole auger, and a backhoe and blade," Gus said, turning to the comm-comp unit.

Gus insisted that Viktor come with them in the crawler, but Viktor spent his time sulking in the living quarters segment in the back, headphones on, listening to hard metal rock. Al was in the driver's seat, but he let the autonomous vehicle program drive the crawler. Behind them, following their trail, was a second crawler pulling a trailer carry an auger and a digging machine. Shortly after they left camp, they came to a large dune field. Instead of ice or permafrost, they were now driving over a few dozen kilometers of rolling dunes. The crawlers made their way up the fifty-meter-high slopes, then down the other side, while Al just watched the sandy ripples passing under the glare of the headlights.

"I did a quick check of the layer patterns in core tubes 201 and 203," Phyllis said from the jump seat in back of Al. Gus turned around in the copilot seat to look at her.

"The dates in 201 weren't hard to establish using Viktor's dating chronology. They are amazingly old. Two billion years—some two and a half billion years after the formation of the planet."

"Back when Mars had an atmosphere," Gus mused.

"The bottom part has a disturbed region, as if there had been an avalanche," Phyllis said.

They drove on through the darkness.

It was early morning when they reached the mouth of the canyon and the two vehicles started into it. There was a thick layer of ground fog, and the going was slow since the autonomous vehicle program could not use its video or laser ranging sensors, and was limited to radar. Al was up in the dome where he could look over the fog, while Gus monitored the radar screen from the pilot's seat. As the Sun rose higher, the wind started blowing down the canyon, the ground became visible again, and their speed picked up.

As they penetrated deeper and deeper into the canyon, the wind-etched ice-canyon walls became higher and higher.

"Stop for a second," Phyllis said from the middle dome in the engineering segment. "I want to get a photo survey set of that cliff side on the right. The top part is overhanging and the orbiting imager wouldn't be able to get pictures of the layer pattern."

Al rolled the crawler to a stop while she activated the external long-focus camera. Once they were stopped, she used the laser range finder to designate a series of points from the base of the cliff to the top and the camera took overlapping high-resolution pictures of the cliff side.

Gus looked out the copilot's window at the cliff side, squinting his eyes until they were almost hidden in the crow's-feet wrinkles.

"If you squint your eyes to lower the resolution so you can't see the yearly bands," he said, "you can see large light and dark banding."

"Those are the long-term variations in dust level caused by axial tilt variations," Phyllis said. "There are even longer cycles of two million years caused by variations in eccentricity of the Martian orbit."

She sang forward to her husband. "You can take off again, Al," she said. "I have the sequence in the can." She climbed down from the dome and came forward to the jump seat behind Al.

She leaned across to look through Gus' window up at the cliff top high above. "From the laser ranging data I calculate it's over two kilometers high," she remarked.

"Pretty impressive for ice," Gus replied.

"Ice with a lot of dirt in it," Phyllis reminded.

They continued their way up the curving canyon. Viktor had put away the headphones and was looking gloomily out the back window while mechanically cutting up a minipig pork chop he had warmed up for himself in the microwave.

"According to the navigation system, we are approaching eighty-one north, twenty-five thirty west," Al announced.

"Do you see anything, Tanya?" Gus asked as he peered through the front windows at the horizon.

"Nothing yet," Tanya said from the dome above him.

"Here we are," Al announced, bringing the crawler to a halt.

"Nothing," Tanya reported.

"Nothing here, either," Phyllis said from the middle dome.

"I guess I'll have to ask Viktor," Gus said resignedly. "I hope he—"

Just then, Viktor burst from the rear of the crawler, shouting *Nyet!*" and brandishing his table knife.

He lunged toward Gus, but Tanya dropped from the dome above and grabbed his arm from behind.

"Traitor!" Viktor snarled in Russian. He whirled around and stabbed Tanya in the chest just as Gus felled him with a rabbit punch. Tanya screamed and fell to the floor under Viktor's unconscious body.

Gus bodily picked up the small Russian scientist and tossed him down the corridor, then bent over Tanya. She was holding her chest and groaning. She got control of herself and slowly took a deep breath, listening carefully.

"No lung puncture," she said finally. "But . . . Oh! It hurts!"

Gus felt Al's hand on his shoulder.

"Let me take over, sir," Al said. "I've had paramedic training."

Gus tied Viktor firmly in the engineer's chair in the midsection. As he finished, Phyllis came out of the crew quarters in the back.

"The table knife just slid off the breast bone and down the rib cage," she reported. "She has a long skin gash and a badly bruised breast, but otherwise she's okay. She insists that as soon as Al gets her bandaged up we are to continue on our way. She doesn't want us to turn back now."

After forty-five minutes, they were ready to go again.

"I guess the only thing we can do is start a search spiral," Gus mused.

"Wait," Phyllis said. "Viktor always chose the point exactly midway between the canyon walls. Maybe I can refine our guess with a few range measurements." She climbed into the dome above the still-unconscious Viktor and brought up the laser range finder. She fired once at the cliff face on the right-hand side of the crawler, then again at the cliff face on the left-hand side. Then she hopped down from the dome and came up behind Al.

"Three hundred forty meters to the west," she told him. "Make sure you stay on eighty-one north."

The crawler crept forward and mounted a small rise. On the other side was a disturbed section in the snow. Although an attempt had been made to remove the traces, there was a mound of removed snow beside a man-sized depression in the ice. The crawler stopped beside it. The other crawler pulling the trailer with the auger and digger came to a halt on the other side. Everyone went outside except Viktor, who was groggily awake but still tied in the engineer's chair.

"Here's where the original coring hole was," Phyllis said, kicking at a small depression a little over a meter away from the larger depression.

"Rebore the larger hole," Gus instructed the technicians. "But after the first ten meters, go very slowly. When you hit new ice, stop."

The techs maneuvered the trailer containing the augur into position and started drilling. Almost immediately there was a loud clank.

"Stop!" Gus yelled, but the technician was ahead of him. The auger was lifted and everyone looked in. About a meter down was a threaded metal cap on the end of a plastic tube. Al jumped into the pit and brushed away the snow.

"Number 202! The missing core tube!"

"Pull it out, then continue digging," Gus directed the techs.

The technicians jury-rigged a hoist with rope and the auger's lifting mechanism and slowly worked the ten-meter-long segment of tubing out of the ground and laid it flat in the gritty snow. They went back to digging, while Phyllis crawled slowly along the tube, brushing frost away and peering carefully at the layered contents before the frost reformed. Suddenly, about a third of the way down, she stopped short. Her voice over the Marsuit intercom was almost a whisper.

"This isn't ice or dirt," she said. Tanya and Gus bent down and looked, too.

"There is about forty centimeters of dark-red material with centimeter-thick gray end-caps," Tanya said. "How do we open the tube to get a sample?"

"The tube is really two tubes, each with a centimeter-wide slot," Phyllis said. "You just twist the ends to make the slots line up and you can pick out a small sample."

Al and Gus rotated the opposite ends while Tanya got out a small knife and some self-sealing bags from her medi-pack.

"The dark-red material is icelike, but fibrous rather than brittle," she reported. "The gray material is like rubber." She rose and started toward the crawler. "I'll take it inside and look at it under the microscope as it warms up."

"We've reached the bottom," a tech's voice reported over the Marsuit intercom.

"I'll be right there," Gus said. He walked over to the edge of the pit.

"Fourteen meters deep," the chief technician said. "The side wall toward the borehole is soft. Obviously someone dug through there from the bottom of the hole. Shall I have the men clean it out?"

"My helmet has a helmeyes built into it," Gus replied. "That can let me see in almost total darkness; plus, it can store in memory everything it sees. I'll go down, unless you have an objection."

"No sir!" the chief technician said. "Just don't panic if the hole collapses on you. You have plenty of air in your suit and your head is only twelve meters down. We can dig you out in no time."

Gus had plenty of time to contemplate the idea of being trapped at the bottom of an ice-hole as they rigged up a safety harness. He climbed down using a rope ladder they had found near the bottom of the hole. He was gaining a measure of respect for Viktor Braginsky's courage in going down into the hole alone, with no one to rescue him if anything had happened.

The chestpack light, combined with the helmeyes, gave him excellent vision. The built-in thumb and finger extenders in the custom-made left-hand glove of his Marsuit worked well in the compacted snow, and he pawed away at the snow in the wall of the hole until his knees were covered. He climbed up the ladder, the techs cleaned out the hole, then he went back down again. He started in digging again and his hand struck something large and stiff!

Just then Tanya called over a special Marsuit frequency they used for private conversations.

"Gus?"

"Yes?" he replied, continuing to brush away at the snow.

"Both of the samples are organic! They have cellular structure with differentiation. Although there are major differences from their Earth counterparts, if I had to say in one word what they are, the dark-red material is 'meat' and the gray, rubbery material is 'skin.' The skin is more like that of a dolphin than a human, though."

"The skin may be like a dolphin's," Gus said, looking down at a frozen, gray-skinned, hairless foot with six large clawed toes, "but the feet are more like a bear's!"

He then noticed that what he thought was a badly crushed foot was really the way it was designed. There were three clawed toes to the left and three clawed toes to the right, with a gap between them. They could be brought together to make a powerful digging shovel, or spread apart to pick up a ball—or grasp a victim between the two opposing sets of talons.

"Toes arranged like a koala bear . . . a big, gray, hairless koala bear," he added as he uncovered a massive gray leg as big as his arm attached to the middle of a body that extended under the packed snow in both directions. This was not a hindquarter or a forequarter, but a "midquarter."

"What are you talking about?" Tanya said.

Gus switched over to the common intercom channel.

"I think we've found the remains of a Martian!" he said.

There were gasps from above.

"Frozen there for two billion years," Phyllis whispered in awe.

"Was it intelligent?" someone asked.

"No sign of clothing or other artifacts," Gus said. "Probably just an animal. But it has legs and grasping claws, so it's fairly complex. It's also large. Too large to dig out from down here." He stepped back.

"I think we better get out the backhoe and blade and make a ramp down to here," Gus said. He made sure his helmeyes had recorded a good overall picture of the portion that he had uncovered, then turned and climbed up the ladder.

The excavation went rapidly at first, then more slowly as the three-meter-wide, fifteen-meter-high artificial cliff face began to approach the point where Gus had uncovered the foot. They found one end of the creature next. About half a meter from the end was a set of two feet attached to opposite sides of the body, much the way a bear's would be. This was probably the rear end since the claws on each foot pointed in the other direction. The rear end had a fan of long, hexagonally shaped crystal rods growing out of a muscular skirt, somewhat like the display feathers on a male peacock.

"Don't uncover too much," Tanya protested, too excited over their find to be concerned about her injuries. "We have to keep it well frozen until some real experts get here. I am only a surgeon, not an xenobiologist." She did, however, work the stiff joints to get some idea of the bone structure and manipulated the crystal fan to see how it attached to the muscles under the skin.

"Mars has always been pretty cold," Phyllis said, "especially up here at the North Pole where this poor fellow got caught in an avalanche. Why doesn't he have any hair?"

"Whales and dolphins do fine in the polar oceans without hair or feathers," Tanya replied. "This fellow has thick, blubbery skin to keep him warm. No pores in the skin, either."

"It would make a good space suit, then," Al said.

"Very interesting point, Mr. Eisen," Tanya said. "Very interesting point."

They found the next pair of feet, then, a little further on, another collapsed fan of hexagonal crystals—more of them this time—then another set of feet, another chunk of body, then another set of feet, then another fan of crystals. Each segment seemed to be about one and a half meters long.

In the middle of each segment, between the two pairs of feet, the normally gray skin changed to a pattern of black and white stripes. They were symmetric about the middle, but the group of stripes on the second segment had a different pattern than the group of stripes on the end segment.

"Curiouser and curiouser," Gus said. "A bear-clawed, koala-toed, hula-skirted, zebra-striped icepede."

They continued on, taking pictures and measurements of each segment before covering them again with a layer of snow. On the backbone of segment three was a crumpled mass of what looked like black velvet cloth. Tanya carefully pulled at it and half straightened out a jet black wing with fragile sticklike stiffeners.

"It would be over two meters from wingtip to wingtip if other side is like this one," Tanya said in amazement. She tenderly folded the wing back up.

"Add bat-winged," Gus said.

"It surely couldn't fly!" Phyllis exclaimed.

"Bones too heavy," Tanya replied. "Wings are probably for heat control. Like lizards."

It was segment four that Viktor had bored through with his core-sampling equipment. A half meter one way or the other, and the Martian would have slept on undisturbed underneath the snow for billions of more years. Both segments four and five had wings.

"Segment six," Gus said as Tanya uncovered another fan of crystals and the body continued on. "Nine meters long and still the creature stretches onward in a seemingly never-ending lineup of segments, one after the other."

"This pattern looks familiar," Tanya said as she uncovered the black and white section. There was no wing this time.

"Let me check," said Al, who had been taking the documentation pictures with a vidofax. He flashed back through the images and halted at one. He held it down so Tanya could see and compare.

"Almost the same," Tanya said. "But the last outside stripe is black instead of white."

"I wonder why the segments on these lineup creatures don't have the same pattern?" Al asked.

"Perhaps we shall never know," Tanya said. "I am sure they are extinct. The lineups, as you call them, are so large they would have been easily seen from orbit if they were still around."

"I've been wondering what to label this file of critter pictures!" Al said. "The name 'Lineup' fits him perfectly. He even has his prison stripes on already."

Even Gus had to groan.

"I think we have come to the other end," Tanya said as she brushed away the snow to find the expected fan of crystals. "There are only half as many crystals here, and the skin texture changes on the other side."

She worked more slowly as she uncovered the head end. There was no neck. The head was conical in shape, like that of a tapir, and narrowed rapidly to a flexible snout. There was nothing that looked like eyes or nose, but the snout was a complex, multifingered structure. It had been badly crushed, so it was hard to figure out its exact structure.

"I don't want to damage it further by prying at it," Tanya said.

"Get me something to shield it and I'll cover it back up with snow to keep it frozen."

"Hold it up, so I can get one last close-up picture," Al said. He looked through the viewfinder and zoomed the vidofax camera in on the nose section. "Through the zoom lens I can see some featherlike structures under the fingers," he reported as the vidofax clicked a number of single-frame shots.

"Probably the smell organs," Tanya said. "Like antennae on moths. They can smell single molecules."

"I can just see my report now," Gus said. "We have found a Martian frozen in the ice at the North Pole. He is called a 'Lineup.' What does Lineup look like? Well, imagine, if you can: a moth-nosed, finger-snouted, tapir-faced, pig-bodied, bear-clawed, koala-toed, bat-winged, hula-skirted, zebra-striped, six-segmented, twenty-four-footed, ten-meter-long, two-billion-year-old icepede."

Gus watched as Viktor flipped the vidofax through the images Al had taken of the Lineup. When he came to the end, Gus said, "If you had behaved like a scientist and had let us know of your discovery instead of trying to hide it, then I would have put you in charge of the expedition. Then it would have been *you* uncovering the Lineup and *you* taking the pictures and *you* announcing of the discovery of the century. As it stands now, you'll have to share the credit."

"So," Viktor said, slamming the vidofax back in Gus' hands. "You are going to let me *share* the credit for *my* discovery."

"A scientific discovery is not a discovery until it is reported to the rest of the scientific community," Gus reminded him. "You forfeited your priority when you tried to hide your findings. You didn't even tell your fellow Russian scientists at the base. Instead you tried to advance your political status and curry favor with your bosses by running to them with it first."

"It was *my* discovery! Then you and your nosy friends came and stole it from me!" Viktor retorted. "You rapacious, capitalistic Americans are just like the Nazis, stealing whatever you can get your hands on. I spit on you!"

He spat into Gus' face. Gus pulled back, shocked. He reached for a handkerchief, found he had none, then wiped the spit off the side of his nose with his sleeve. Viktor stood petrified as Gus' face curled in anger, the crow's-feet furrows pointing arrowlike at the slitted steel-gray eyes.

"I hate your guts, Mr. Braginsky," Gus growled. "You have done nothing but cause me trouble since I came. You lie to me, you threaten me, and you tried to kill Tanya. Now—after I have tried to be nice to you—you spit on me."

Gus' voice lowered even further. "Because of your recent behavior, I would be fully justified in canceling your guest visitor status at Sagan Institute and sending you back to Russia immediately."

"Don't do that!" Viktor said, panicking. "They will never believe I didn't lead you to the site. Petrovich didn't understand. He thought I had discovered an ancient Martian civilization. He dreamed of finding new weapons. I couldn't convince him otherwise. He made it a state military secret—and the penalty for revealing state military secrets is death. They'll kill me!"

"Good riddance!" Gus said, his face still clouded with anger.

"Please don't send me back," Viktor said, his hands waving helplessly, wanting to hold on to Gus to plead with him, but fearing to touch the angry-faced man. "I'm sorry I spit on you. I'm sorry I hurt Tanya. I was just so angry with myself, so frustrated . . ." Tears started to stream down his thin, rawboned cheeks and off his small, pointed chin.

Gus let his face and shoulders relax, then finally said in a resigned tone of voice, "All right, Viktor. If Tanya will forgive you, I won't send you back." Then his face hardened again, and the deepset steel-gray eyes were almost hidden in the crinkled crow's-feet arrows that formed. "But I must insist you finish this piece of research like a true scientist."

"I will! I will!" Viktor promised, sniffling heavily.

"You are responsible for the full scientific investigation and detailed reporting of all aspects of the finding of the alien. You will start by staying here with the technician team in their crawler, making sure nothing happens to the find. I will arrange for portable buildings and a long refrigerated hut to be sent out to hold the specimen. I will also arrange for xenobiologists to be sent by express transport from Earth. You are to stay out here on the ice at all times to work with and coordinate their efforts. Finally, you are responsible for the collection and editing of a full and comprehensive report. It will be a lot of work."

"I'll do it," Viktor said, a little appalled by the job ahead of him, but relieved at the same time.

"See that you do—or else!" Gus, still angry, marched to the front of the crawler.

CHAPTER 9

THE CHURCH OF THE UNIFIER

Under the expert guidance of Rob and his highly efficient organization, fueled with all the funds and manpower needed to take care of every little detail, Alexander's tour of the major cities of the United States grew from a smashing success into an unbelievable phenomenon. The publicity surrounding Alexander was so great that when the news of the discovery of the alien "icepede" on Mars arrived on Earth, it only lasted two days on the news. Even then, it was relegated to the "science" sections.

Cities for miles around each of the planned stops would empty on the day that Alexander was to arrive. The people would go to stand hundreds deep around the boundaries of the nearby airport, just to watch Alexander borne overhead in his gigantic gold-leaf-gilded private Boeing 7ZX macroliner *Bucephalus* as it rumbled in to land. More thousands would line the streets from the airport to the dome or stadium where he would speak.

Thousands of well-dressed "Unies," all third level or higher in the Church of the Unifier, served as ushers at the domes, impressing people with their neatness, calmness, dedication, and helpfulness. In addition to directing and controlling the crowds that came primarily to see General Armstrong, they made converts to the Church of the Unifier. They passed out literature and politely answered questions—sometimes even rude questions—about the Church of the Unifier and the brightly colored Caps of Contact that they wore. The ushers would let little children in the crowds try on their caps, so the little ones could see the video image of Alexander on the built-in viewers that flipped around in front of the left eye of the wearer.

It was the amplified and glorified vision of Alexander presented by Eric and his media magicians, however, that made the most converts to the Church of the Unifier. People who had come to see Alexander the Greatest, conqueror of Mars, left with a sense of worshipful awe at having seen and heard Alexander the Unifier, Infinite Lord.

Those who came to see the general could also not help but be impressed with the sight of the infield. For all around Alexander, in all directions, were seated rank upon rank of devoted leaders and followers of the Church of the Unifier. The first rows were always filled with the white caps and robes of the level nine Leaders, those who owned and controlled the franchises in the local units of the Church of the Unifier.

The next rows were packed with the violet, then blue, caps of the eighth level Senior Watchers and the seventh level ordinary Watchers. Then came more colors of the rainbow, each descending level moving further down the rainbow and filling more rows, all wearing Caps of Contact.

After a successful sweep of the United States, Rob took the show on a world tour. With Eric's computers working overtime, Alexander spread the word in every country in every tongue outside the New Soviet Union. In those countries around the Mediterranean and in the Near East, whose history and culture had been strongly influenced by the original Alexander the Great, Rob had Alexander ride through the streets on a mechanized version of Alexander's famous horse, Bucephalus, wearing a modernized golden helmet with a built-in communications system and occasionally raising a gilded short sword in salute to the adoring crowds, many of whom were converted on sight.

All of these scenes of adoring crowds, of course, found their way back to the United States, where they were broadcast over Rob's captive television stations, and especially through the left eye viewer of the Caps of Contact of the faithful. Rob had bought at least one television channel in every city and boosted its power so that its continuous transmission of inspiring messages by Alexander and the various advertisements for religious products could be received at all times not only by any television, but by a Cap of Contact anywhere in the surrounding area. In addition, there were three direct-broadcast satellites, with the combined ability to reach a Cap of Contact anywhere on the globe, with different channels for each of the different major languages.

In larger cities, in addition to the inspirational channel, there were other channels that scheduled programs of instruction in the mysteries that needed to be memorized in order to attain the next level in the Church of the Unifier. Like the secret societies, Rob had realized the importance of making a follower feel superior to those of lower levels, while still feeling unsatisfied by not knowing what was going on at higher levels.

To receive each level of instruction required a different video decoder chip, and it was supposedly the cost of these "custom" chips that justified the enormous initiation fees that were imposed at each change in level. By the time followers had attained the fifth or sixth level, they had usually turned over all their property to the Church and were either full-time "slaves" to the higher level instructors in the Church, or were working outside at good jobs and turning over all their salaries to pay off the ever-growing interest on their debts. In return they received free room and board, sometimes in their own former homes, now turned into dormitories full of other Unies.

The Caps of Contact were not just continuous receivers of inspirational messages, they were two-way. If some follower of the Church of the Unifier had a question or a problem, all he had to do was press a button on the side of his Cap of Contact, and soon he was in direct contact with someone higher in level who could help him or switch him to someone that could. Like the old-time big-city political ward organizations or the Japanese criminal protection gangs, Rob knew that if you took care of the little problems of the little people, they would be so grateful they would let you get away with murder.

Only Rob and the Watchers knew that each Cap of Contact

also continuously broadcast a coded spread-spectrum signal containing a modest resolution picture of what the wearer of the cap was looking at. The view seen from any cap could be separated out from the transmissions of millions of other caps by merely punching in the identity code of the wearer.

By the time Alexander returned from the world tour, the Church of the Unifier was solidly established everywhere in the United States and growing exponentially around the world. "Palaces" had been established near every major city for the use of Alex, Rob, and their entourage. Once each Sunday, they moved to a different city, where Alexander gave the weekly inspirational message, always to a packed house in the largest dome or stadium available. Alexander's large and loyal following was not lost on the political leaders of the United States. Diane Perkins was a frequent visitor to the "Staten Estate" off New York City and the "Potomac Palace" outside Washington, D.C., when Alexander was on the East Coast.

Rob was careful to maintain quality by personally running spot checks on the performance of the Watchers and instructors. Punching in a number at random on his monitor console one day, he found the video monitor looking down into a small cubicle. There was a single table with a single lamp, shining directly at an insecure-looking young man with a worried frown.

The young man shifted nervously in the small, hard, armless chair. His black first level cap of contact was new and had not been worn long enough to shape itself to his head. The view-plate had been flipped back so the novice could concentrate on the shadowed figure in the dark orange robe and cap of a fourth level instructor sitting on the other side of the table. The computer read the bar code pattern on the caps and inserted their identifications on the screen under their images. The novice's name was Fred 1-13,404, and the instructor was Janet 4-121. Although Unies were allowed to keep their first names, a follower of the Church of the Unifier was expected to forgo family names and family ties for the broader ties of church fellowship.

"I dunno . . . If the boss had found out I'd been tapping the till he would eat me alive—then fire me."

"You want to be an honest employee, don't you, Fred?" the shadowed figure said in an unctuous voice. Janet reached into a rack of literature, took out a pamphlet, and handed it across the table, the fingers on her thin white hand extended out from the long orange satin robe far enough that the novice could see the massive silver ring of an instructor embossed with the vertical infinity symbol of the Infinite Lord.

The young man glanced down at the title of the pamphlet. It said, "The Honest Employee—A Servant of the Infinite Lord Can Be Trusted." He started to open it.

"Don't read it now," the instructor said. "I will tell you what's in it, then you can study it in detail later. Now, our overall objective is to have everyone love and obey the Infinite Lord, is it not?"

"Yes," the young man agreed.

"And if the Church of the Unifier can assure an employer that those of his employees who are members of the Church will be scrupulously honest, unlike his average employee, then he will like the Church, and someday come to love and obey the Infinite Lord as we do. Correct?"

"Yes," the young man said, his forehead beginning to sweat, "but I don't see how teaching me to steal from him can do that."

"We are not going to teach you to steal, we are going to teach you *not* to steal. I think for your situation we will want to go to page seventeen, Erroneous Shipment Addresses. Open to that page and read it."

The pale young man leafed nervously through the pamphlet and started to read, haltingly. "A mail clerk in a large merchandising store . . ." He stopped and looked over at the shadowed figure. "Say, that's me, isn't it?" He bent over the pamphlet again and continued. ". . . should *never* succumb to the temptation to place fake telephone orders for expensive merchandise that is charged to a wealthy customer and mailed as a gift to a nonexistent address, then change the address on the package to his own when it passes through the mail room." He looked up at the dark figure, surprise on his face. "Say, I never thought of that. Sounds easy."

"It *is* easy, as all sins are," the dark voice said, assuming a commanding tone. "And to make sure that you do not fall prey to that particular sin, I command you, in the name of the Infinite Lord, to commit that sin. Once you have sinned, and know the suffering and shame that arises from committing a sin, the Infinite Lord will absolve you of that sin, and you will never commit that sin again."

"I don't know . . . the boss . . ."

"The Infinite Lord is your only 'boss'!" the shadowed figure interrupted. "The Infinite Lord wants to save you from sin. But to be saved—"

"I must sin," the young man agreed resignedly.

"You are showing great promise, Fred," the instructor said in an approving tone. "If you do well, you should be ready soon for second level training sessions."

"But I can't do it," Fred complained. "If I asked any of my so-called friends in the credit department for some charge numbers to use, they would probably turn me in, and the boss would skin me alive!"

"I have already taken care of that," the instructor said. "Here is a list of credit card numbers of people who charge a lot at your store, and here is the list of items. As you receive each one at your house, destroy the wrappings and any tags that indicate the store name, and bring them to me. I will see that they get back to the proper person."

Fred looked down at the list and his face whitened visibly with shock. "There are over thirty items on this list!" he whispered in a strained voice. "Jewelry . . . watches . . . vidofaxes . . . Each one costs over a hundred dollars!"

The jerk has overreached herself with that one, Rob thought. The mark will lose his nerve and quit.

"The Infinite Lord wants you to be so appalled at the enormity of your sin that you will never do it again. The sin is appalling, isn't it, Fred?"

"Yes, but—"

"Won't you feel relieved when the Infinite Lord absolves you of that sin?"

"Yes . . ." Fred agreed reluctantly.

"When you are free of sin, I can guarantee entry into the second level mysteries," the instructor promised.

"I'll get started today!" the excited youngster said as he bolted out of the cubicle.

Rob could now see great Watcher potential in Janet and made a note in her personnel files.

A message appeared at the top of Rob's screen.

Andy 8-10 on Channel 32. "Would you or Alexander like this one?"

Rob switched his viewscreen to Channel 32. There were two people sitting at opposite ends of a comfortable sofa in a large, well-appointed office. Both wore Caps of Contact. His was the eighth level violet of a Senior Watcher, while hers was a second level brown. He was in his violet robe, while she wore a short skirt that showed shapely legs and a blouse whose buttons were under considerable strain. The computer identified the young woman as Susan 2-132,030. After seeing Susan's face and figure, Rob understood why a level eight was stooping to individual instruction of a level two.

"I understand you are married, Susan?" Andy asked, putting a violet-robed arm up on the back of the sofa.

"Yes," Susan said. "He's John 2-321,556. We met eight months ago at a first level retreat."

Rob zoomed the monitor image in on Susan and looked her over with an experienced eye. She was too skinny for his tastes, and Alexander preferred blonds.

"Tell Andy, 'No thanks.' " he instructed the communications computer. The computer instantly flashed the message to Andy through the viewer on his Cap of Contact.

"Then you know how very important it is in a marriage for the partners to be sexually faithful to each other. In the Church of the Unifier, it is a sin to have sex with someone other than your husband. In order to move up to the third level you must be saved from this sin of extramarital carnal pleasure."

"Oh," Susan said, her face suddenly blushing. "Then that means I must . . ."

"Yes . . ." Andy said, flipping back his viewer and moving closer until he was staring straight into her eyes. "You *must*! The Infinite Lord commands it! If you don't sin, how can he save you?"

"I do so want to become a third level . . ." Susan said, pondering. Then she looked puzzled.

"Who?" she asked innocently.

CHAPTER 10

THE CALM

The xenobiologists came and spent a dozen weeks out on the ice cap examining the Lineup. The general physiology turned out to be similar to that of an animal on Earth, with the exception that there was no breathing system. The lack of eyes was puzzling at first, but the multitude of rods between each segment seemed to play that part, somewhat like the compound eyes of an insect. Amazingly enough, the eyerods were pure diamond—dense glassy diamond at the center, graded to less dense diamond crystal around the outside— so the eyerod acted like a light pipe. The Martian creature was the first example of a carbon-based life form that could produce a pure carbon structure.

The most unexpected discovery occurred during the preliminary exploration of the body cavities with fiber-optic probes. The long, segmented creature seemed to be made up of six individual units lined up end-to-end. The xenobiologists had not yet attempted to separate out one of the units, since they were extremely tightly bonded, sharing digestive tracts, bloodstreams, and possibly even nervous systems. A puzzling feature, and a disappointment to that type of specialist, was the lack of parasites. No fleas, no mites, no cysts, not even gut bacteria.

The region of the ice canyon for hundreds of meters around the find and tens of meters down was carefully mapped, excavated, and screened for artifacts. The only object found was an unrelated three-centimeter-diameter iron meteorite.

As fall turned into winter in the northern hemisphere and the population at Boreal Base shrank in proportion to the amount of daylight, the xenobiologists carefully packed up the creature in a surplus quartermaster lander modified with a refrigerated hold and took it off to Earth. There, they would use whole-body scanners to image its insides before they started cutting.

The weeks passed, and soon the short northern winter was over. The Sun began to rise above the horizon once again, and Boreal Base slowly became alive. The arrival of spring brought the independent prospectors, lured by the dream of finding armloads of diamond eyerods in some hypothetical Lineup graveyard.

The first to arrive was Red Storm, and she caused a minor sensation when she landed her asteroid belt tug, *The Billionaire*, at Boreal Base. She was tall and angular, pretty in a skinny sort of way, with a long, thin, space-weathered face innocent of makeup, and a narrow nose covered with freckles. She had shoulder-length, curly orange-red hair falling in a mop of hundreds of straggly ringlets, and large innocent-looking blue-green eyes that had stared at vacuum more than once.

Her first stop was at the "Bore Hole" beer garden on the bottom floor of the central hub of Boreal Base. It was early morning and there was no one at the bar. The combination bartender, postmaster, and banker was busy sorting mail into mailboxes, for some things just don't transmit well over computer links.

"Hi!" Red said loudly to attract his attention, and when he came to the counter she leaned forward to shake his hand firmly. "Red Storm," she said. "They say you can set up a bank account for me."

"Mike," the bartender said. "You don't need a separate account here. All the bases on Mars are linked. You can use your account at your home base."

"Don't have a home base," Red said. "Just dropped in from the belt to do some high-gravity prospecting. Will have to buy some supplies. Got a few bucks on Earth. What's the procedure to get them out here?"

"Got an eye-card?" Mike asked.

"Sure." She reached into her grimy, well-worn, pale green coveralls and pulled out a small wallet. Peering down into it, she pulled out a silver-colored card. As she looked up, she caught Mike's eyes roving over her face and hair. He had that intense, bemused look of a man that hadn't seen an unattached good-looking woman in a long while. Suddenly flustered, she blushed, then brushing ineffectually at her unruly mop and, unable to look him in the eyes, she pushed the card slowly across the bar. Mike looked down at it and his eyes popped to attention.

"Wheeoo . . ." he whistled softly. "I've heard about these before, but never saw one." He lifted the heavy, metal card and his eyes widened further. "Real platinum . . ."

He put the eye-card in the scanner and raised the wand. She obediently leaned forward and opened her right eye wide as he waved the infrared beam over the beautiful blue-green iris.

"Well, the card says its you, Octavia," Mike said, looking at the scanner display.

"Red!" she snapped, suddenly glaring.

Mike raised both hands in surrender. "Okay! Red it is," he said agreeably. He glanced again at the scanner. "The card number isn't on the wanted list, so you're good for a thousand instantly. Heck, the card by itself is worth a thousand. An account transfer will take about half an hour because of the time delay in the Earth comm link. How much do you want shifted?"

"I'll probably have to lease a crawler and I'll want to top off my H-bar tanks before I leave, so make it a hundred million U.S. to start," she said thoughtfully. "What does that amount to here?"

"A hundred million! That's a million spiders!" Mike spluttered.

"Can't make money without spending money," Red said, unconcerned. "Is that what they call the local money here—spiders?"

"Spider is the local slang here at Boring. The usual name for the Mars one dollar coin is the viking, since it was a picture of the Viking lander on it. How much pocket cash do you want?"

"I'll take a full thousand. Make most of it large bills."

"Sorry." Mike opened his cash drawer with a key. "Bills wear out. Hope you've got big pockets." He took out five stacks of coins from the racks in the drawer and piled up the colorful graduated stacks one by one in front of her.

"Nine blue polars for nine hundred dollars, nine green olys for ninety dollars, nine yellow vikings for nine dollars, nine orange potatoes for ninety cents, and ten reds for ten cents—one thousand Mars dollars even."

"Pretty," Red said, picking up an oly and admiring the intricate bas-relief carving of the Mount Olympus volcano. She shoveled the money into a pocket and, clinking slightly, stood up.

"I'm going to want a room tonight," she said. "The bunk on my ship isn't designed for high-gee sleep. Does this place have a hotel?"

"The base director's office will assign a dorm room to you. Three stories straight up," Mike said, pointing. He leaned forward to put his elbows on the counter and raised his eyebrow at her. "But you don't have to bother with that. Why don't you just sleep at my place tonight?"

"Look!" Red said, clouding up like a thunderstorm. She pointed a finger at him. "Let me get one thing clear at the start. I don't fool around, and I always pay my own way . . . with *cash*!"

Mike raised both his hands once again in surrender. "Sure, Red. I understand."

Red turned and clanked her way over to the stairwell to the offices above.

Night came to Boreal Base, and when Red returned to the Bore Hole, there were already a few customers there, sipping Mike's homemade brew while waiting for the dinner serving at the lab cafeteria to start. One of them, too hungry to wait, was gnawing away at a plate of pickled minipig feet and hard-boiled bantam eggs he had selected from the little deli Mike ran at one end of the bar. Red now wore clean, well-worn coveralls, dark green this time. Her hair hung in a shoulder-length mop of limp, rusty ringlets—clean, but still damp from the welcome hot shower. She smiled and waved at Mike—their past little run-in forgotten—and clinked her way to the nearest table.

"Hi!" she said, shoving out a hand. "Red Storm. Join you?"

"Sure!" one of the men said, starting to get up.

"Siddown," Red said, pushing on his shoulder and grabbing a chair. "Mike!" she called to the bartender. "A round of drinks here . . . and see what the boys at the next table will have."

More people came in, most of them men, and Red kept introducing herself and buying drinks until she finally cornered her target. Dinnertime came and the men at her table started to get up to leave.

"Why don't you come to the cafeteria with us," one of them said. "Only costs visitors two spiders for a good meal. We're having catfish and fries tonight—better than Mike's pig feet."

"I just may," Red said, putting a restraining hand on the man next to her. "But why don't you five go ahead? I want to talk to Viktor some more about the critter he found."

Viktor, with three beers on an empty stomach and a pretty woman paying attention to him, was feeling on top of the world. As soon as the others had left, Red got serious.

"I've made arrangements with the base director to lease a crawler with three techs to run it around the clock," Red said. "I've got a microwave sounder to scan under the ice for objects and a coring rig to get samples. I've got a fossil hunting license from the governor of Mars and an agreement with the director of the Sagan Institute that I can sell what I find to the highest bidder, once the scientists have had a chance to study it.

"But I need someone that knows their way around the ice cap, someone who can tell me where the ancient ice beds have been uncovered, so I spend my time prospecting in the best places." She poked him in the chest with a finger. "Everyone tells me you're the expert. How about taking an unpaid vacation from the institute and working for me? Name your own fee."

"I don't know," Viktor said, uncertain. "I'm still editing the last volume on the Lineup findings."

"You can work on it in the crawler," Red suggested. "We'll be spending most of our time either traveling from one spot to another or doing slow search spirals. How about it?"

"I guess that will work . . ." Viktor replied, still uncertain.

"How much do you want?"

"I don't know . . ."

"Let's make it a thousand a day," Red said. "A sol," she corrected herself.

"A *thousand*!" Viktor said in a whisper.

Oops . . . Red said to herself. Guessed a little too high. Well, if you want the top, pay the top.

"Sure!" she said out loud. "A thousand Mars dollars per sol. Okay?" She held out her hand.

"Okay!" Viktor grabbed the thin hand and shook it vigorously. He got up, wavering a little. "Shall we go eat now?" he asked, pointing the way to the cafeteria.

"You'd better pack, instead," she replied. "The techs say if we leave this evening, we can get to the site of the finding at dawn tomorrow." She grabbed him by the arm and headed for the dormitory wing.

"Lead me to your room, and I'll tell you about my plans while you pack. We'll have dinner on the crawler while the techs drive. I supplemented the usual crawler food selection with some items from the larder on my spaceship. We have five jars of sterlet caviar, six bottles of Stolichnaya Vodka, four tins of . . ."

The long spring dragged on as Mars climbed slowly out of the Sun's gravitational well on its way to aphelion. It took a long time coming, but finally the twenty-seven weeks of spring were over and it was Independence Sol again. The governor of Mars and de facto Mayor of Olympia was leaning over Gus' desk, his badge of office, a violet thousand-Mars-dollar "globe" coin in a silver holder, dangling from around his neck on a rainbow-colored ribbon some woman had donated from her personal baggage allowance stores.

Gus knew the picture on the rare coin well—a beautifully detailed bas-relief map of the northwest hemisphere of Mars—the north polar spiral pattern at the top, Olympus Mons lifting its peak above the west horizon, the three volcanoes of Tharsis Ridge prominent near it, and the Mariner Valley stretching across the lower middle from horizon to horizon. Gus had the only other thousand-Mars dollar-coin ever minted in his desk. He often took it out when he was thinking through some tough administrative problem and used it to go through the exercises designed to maintain the dexterity of the stubs on his left hand.

"The guys have it all figured out, Gus," Chris said. "We'll bring the beam off Max MacFadden's materials diagnostics bench, send it out through the lab door, down the corridor to the southwest hub, up the light well, then along the ceiling of the ground floor corridor, through the window of the airlock into the commons, right into Seichi Kiyowara's lasermonium, and—bang! Multicolor laser fireworks for Independence Sol all over the inside of the Boston Commons dome!"

"I don't know," Gus said, shaking his head and looking concerned. "That diagnostic laser is powerful enough to blast holes in rocks. I don't like the idea of having that powerful a beam bouncing all over the institute."

"Come on, Gus. It'll be Independence Sol. Everybody will be on holisol anyway and we'll just lock off those corridors. Max has fixed his laser modulator so that the output beam has a large diameter that won't cause any damage and can be transmitted over those distances without loss. Seichi's tied in the laser frequency control on Max's bench to his jury-rigged harmonium-vibrator keyboard so he has control of the color and rep rate as well as the position on the dome."

"It should be spectacular!" Gus agreed, leaning back. "Sure. You can use Max's laser for the fireworks show."

"Great! Can I count on you for a speech sometime during the ceremonies?"

"Isn't that your job?" Gus replied. "One of the reasons I didn't want to be considered for governor was that I wanted to spend less time attending meetings and giving speeches, and more time doing research." He waved at a screen full of messages awaiting his decision or reply. "Although, being institute director, it doesn't always turn out that way."

Chris' face lost its boyish glee and turned pensive, almost sad.

"I'd really like to have you give us a pep talk, Gus. It's our first Independence Sol and we're all a little concerned."

"About what? Things are going fine here."

"Funny things are happening on Earth," Chris said. "People here are wondering how that will affect our support from Earth in the future."

"Oh," Gus groaned, forced to think about things that he tried not to think about. "My brother . . ."

When the first news stories about Alexander becoming the Infinite Lord of the Church of the Unifier had come in from Earth, the staff at the Sagan Institute had made jokes about it.

"Where's your golden tunic, Gus?"

But after Alexander had finished his world tour and the Church of the Unifier started to grow, Alexander's success scared people and the jokes stopped. It got really serious when Alexander announced his candidacy for president of the United States in the upcoming elections, with the widely popular Diane "Di" Perkins as his running mate. They had formed a new "Unification" party dedicated to unifying all the disparate parties, people, and cultures of the U.S. under Alexander's banner of the vertical infinity symbol.

Alexander's speeches over Ron's captive television channels were sent to Mars on the laser comm link along with all the rest of the television channels. Fortunately, they seemed to have lost their ability to persuade by the time they got to Mars, and the Church of the Unifier made no converts there. Either it was the generally higher intelligence level of the average inhabitant of Mars, or more likely the harsh reality of a life of hard physical and intellectual activity on a hostile planet.

The latest crew rotation ship from Earth, however, had brought a number of Unies—two scientists and five techs. It was weird to see them carrying out their normal duties—Gus had no complaints about their competence or work habits—while all the time, through nanodisks in their Caps of Contact, their left eyes were feeding their right brains a continuous replay of Alexander and his messages. Even more appalling was that lately, in any crowd scene shown on normal network television, more than a third of the people in the crowd were wearing the multicolored Caps of Contact. Even a significant number of those running for congressional seats in the upcoming elections wore their caps while on the stump, trying to ride into office on Alexander's coattails.

"I just had my third 'Dear John' case," Chris said. "Only this time it was a 'Dear Gladys.' Gladys Polatkin's husband has divorced her because she wouldn't come back and join the Church of the Unifier with him. Not only that, he sold their house, emptied their joint savings accounts, and gave it all to the Church."

"She's a tech on the Sagan Institute staff," Gus said, bewildered. "Why didn't she come to me?"

"Can't you guess?" Chris replied quietly.

"She's probably furious with Alex," Gus admitted. "It must be all she can do to keep from throttling his carbon copy."

Chris came forward once again to lean his tall, lanky frame on Gus' desk, his face still serious. "You're our hero, Gus. We need you. Come out on Independence Sol and let us hear the real you. Give us some hope. Give us some inspiration. Give us a future to look forward to."

The Independence Sol ceremonies and laserworks were over, and it was now just past midnight on Sunday of Week 50, the first week of summer. Seichi Kiyowara was still going strong on the lasermonium, but the music was now soft and dreamy, and the multicolored laser beams waltzed smoothly in spirals around the inside of the darkened dome of the Boston Commons. Gus and Tanya were sharing a large tarp with Chris and his mob of friends. Gus had his head in Tanya's lap, and she was running her fingers through his hair while he looked at the colorful display on the domed ceiling. Chris had taken off his governor's medallion and was sipping a glass of home-brew hopless beer he had bought from an enterprising vendor who had convinced a few handfuls of northern Scotland barley to grow in a makeshift greenhouse.

"That was just the right speech, Gus," Chris said. "It helped for you to remind people that the Earth had gone through periods of religious fanaticism before, and even if religious fanatics did take over some countries, like Iran in the 1980s, the checks and balances of the U.S. Constitution would keep any religious group from doing the same in the U.S."

"Yeah, and remember: Mars is an *independent* territory and not part of the U.S.," Gus said. "I'd like to see the Russians come back here in force, and other nations, too, so we're less dependent on support from the U.S. Congress."

"Well," Chris said, ostentatiously getting out his governor's medallion and slipping the rainbow-colored ribbon back over his neck, "as governor of the sovereign and independent Territory of Mars— *I* shall invite them."

"Great idea!" Gus said, rolling his head out of Tanya's lap and resting on one elbow to look at him. "Since ninety-five percent of the Lab budget comes from the U.S., I've been hesitant to make any overtures to the Russians since the U.S. is technically still at war with them along the Baltic front because of their invasion of the Baltic republics after the Neocommunist takeover of Soviet Russia."

"The Territory of Mars is not at war with Russia," Chris said. "They're more than welcome—just bring money."

"And I can guarantee adequate funds to support your personal research if anyone is so politically stupid as to try to cut them off," Gus assured.

"I'll do it day after tomorrow, on Monday," Chris said, looking at his watch. "Oops—past midnight. I'll do it tomorrow."

"Past midnight? Time to reset." Gus lay on his side and fiddled with buttons on his wristwatch. "Damn!" he cursed, sitting up and taking off his watch so that he could manipulate the buttons better. "Got it wrong. Now let's see, subtract forty minutes and add twenty-five seconds . . ." He finally got the watch reset and put it back on his arm. "We've got to do something about this thirty-nine minute, thirty-five second set-back-every-night nonsense!" He turned to Chris. "Has anything come of your contest for a new clock system to subdivide the Martian sol?"

"Got lots of suggestions. But nothing as clean as the calendar system we adapted from the Russians."

"What were the best clock suggestions?" Gus asked.

"The simplest one was to adjust our watches so that they run 2.7 percent slow. But that brought a storm of protest from the scientists. You would think the second was their god from the defense they put up. 'A second is a second is a second—throughout all space and time,' one said." Chris paused to grin and take a sip of beer. "I reminded him of the slowdown of time near black holes and he shut up. The trouble is, most modern watches are so accurate when made, they don't have a 2.7 percent adjustment in range. We would have to have a new chip designed, and if we are going to do that, we should consider other options that save the second for the scientists.

"I also got one from somebody who must have labored for days over it. It has twenty-four Martian hours, called maurs, but the maurs have eighty-six Martian minutes, or marmins, and the marmins have forty-three seconds—with the Martian second exactly equal to the Earth second. This results in a clock sol of 88,752 seconds, twenty-three and a quarter seconds less than the physical sol of 88,775 and a quarter seconds. There doesn't seem to be any other combination of prime factors around 88,775 that does any better. Close, but not close enough, since it would add up to over four maurs over the Martian year.

"The one that seems to be the best is a compromise between commerce and science, but it looks like it was designed by a congressional committee trying to meet a holiday recess deadline."

"Most successful compromises do," Gus said, rolling back to put his head in Tanya's lap again. "Let's hear the gory details."

"The second stays the second to keep the scientists happy," Chris started. "The day—excuse me, sol—has twenty-four hours, or maurs if you want to get technical, and the hours have sixty minutes, or marmins, each averaging 2.7 percent longer than Earth hours and minutes. Since time cards, appointments, and schedules are in hours and minutes, but seldom in seconds, this makes businessmen and administrators happy."

"Sounds great so far."

"Now comes the complication," Chris said. "Let's see if I can remember the details . . . The minutes have either sixty-one or sixty-two seconds. The shorter sixty-one-second minutes in each hour are the 00 and 01 minutes, every minute divisible by three, and in three sols out of four the 02 minute of the 00 hour. That produces three sols of 88,775 seconds and one sol of 88,776 seconds for an average of 88,775 and a quarter seconds. That's close enough to the physical sol that the scientists can include the clock drift in their normal leap second adjustments to the calendar to accommodate the slowing down of the planet's spin rate."

"That's not bad," Gus said. "The only people who would really care whether a minute or an hour or a sol had an extra second or two in it would be the scientists, and they can learn the system. Everybody else wouldn't have to be bothered."

"Since all watches are controlled by chips anyway, nobody has to remember," Chris said. "Just program all the details into the chip, along with the calendar and its leap mears."

"Sounds great! Why don't you go ahead and get some watches made?" Gus said. "We'll want one for everybody and extras for vehicles and consoles. Get bids for a batch of twenty thousand and I'll arrange payment out of the institute administration budget."

"Don't need to," Chris said nonchalantly. "I awarded the first Martian patent to the inventors last week—Al and Phyllis Eisen. They formed a partnership with Charles Kim, who has a brother in the solar-powered watch business in Korea.

"The first shipment should be on the next crew rotation ship. They didn't want to wait for the slow freight supply ships, so they'll pay someone to include it in their personal baggage allowance. Since I gave them a patent monopoly for ten mears, they should make a killing."

"How much are these going to cost?" Gus asked, the administrator in him concerned about buying one for nearly every office, lab, and vehicle owned by the Sagan Institute.

"That's up to them. If you don't like the price, Gus . . ." Chris

said, pausing to take another sip of beer. "You can always just reset
your watch every night."

Gus groaned.

Twenty-six weeks later, they were back under the dome in the Boston Commons for the periequinox holisol. Chris had been unani-
mously reelected governor of Mars thirteen weeks before, but had
requested that someone else be elected mayor of Olympia. Being
governor of Mars was no longer a part-time job. First there were
the negotiations with the Russians and Japanese on sites for future
expansion bases and the ratio of supplies to personnel. Then there
was the hassle of trying to reason with newly elected President Alexander Armstrong's transition team, led by the very firm and even
more demanding future Vice-President Diane Perkins.

With fall coming and the days getting shorter and colder, the
diamond prospectors at the North Pole had given up and departed,
their searches unsuccessful. The woman prospector had told Chris
she would be back next spring, however, and paid for her fossil
hunting license in advance.

The new mayor of Olympia was playing his lasermonium. He
was wearing the badge of his office, a somewhat battered collapsible
top hat someone had unaccountably brought in as part of his personal baggage allowance and even more unaccountably had donated
on the night of the election.

"It's nearly midnight," Seichi Kiyowara said through his microphone to the crowd under the dome, the top hat sitting jauntily on
the back of his head. "Time for 'Auld Lang Syne'!"

As he started in on the introductory chords, Gus looked down
at the thin plastic decal pasted over the face of his old wristwatch.
The two rows of numbers on the liquid crystal display said, "M021
75SAT" and "23:58:35."

Gus had deliberately sought out and sat with Chris and his
friends for the periequinox celebration, for it was lonely with Tanya
off on a field trip around Elysium Saddle. Fortunately, he would be
taking some time away from administrative duties at the institute
for the next few weeks and would soon be working with Tanya's

survey team on Hecates Tholus. He joined in the singing, but soon developed a catch in his throat and had to quit for a while, eyes damp.

"... take a cup of kindness yet, for auld lang syne ..."

The singing stopped and the countdown began, with Seichi swinging the laser beam back and forth like a metronome.

"fifty-eight ... fifty-nine ... sixty ... sixty-one ..."

As Gus stared at his watch, the display switched from "M021 75SAT 23:59:61" to "M021 PEQUI 00:00:00."

Seichi repeated his fireworks finale from Independence Sol, and the two-sol holiday started.

"They really *do* have everything all programmed in," Gus said, impressed. "All that in a stick-on decal no thicker than a fingernail. Almost makes it worth four olys."

"I'm sure glad the Eisens suggested a five percent 'government royalty' or tax on the gross receipts of patent-protected monopolies," Chris said. "Now the Territory of Mars has enough money to run for years at its present rate, without bothering with other taxes."

"Maybe the institute should start charging you for your telephone calls," Gus said. "You certainly have spent enough time talking to the State Department and the secretary general, as well as the Russians and Japanese."

"Well, I finally have the Russians convinced that they are going to have to name everyone they send ahead of time, so the CIA can make sure they're really technical people and not just KGB agents. Now all I have to do is convince the transition team and the State Department that every scientist is not necessarily a technology spy. It just takes jawboning. They'll come through."

Early the following week, Gus finally wiped the last of the urgent chores from his administrative disk files and made a reservation on the evening west-bound hopiter flight. The hopiter caught up with the Sun during the rapid suborbital flight and it was afternoon when he landed at Elysium Saddle. Tanya was not there to greet him, but there was a note for him on the message board outside the Down

There cafe and beer garden on the lower level of the central hub of Elysium Saddle base.

"Techs bringing in trailer load of cores on 77THU. Ride back out with relief crew. Miss you. Tanya." Gus looked at his watch. "M021 77TUE 21:15:33," it said. He set it back five hours. He had two days to spend. He went to the local office of the Sagan Institute and found that Andrew Phillips was taking a crawler out to Elysium Mons early the next morning and he could go with them.

It was only sixty kilometers from the base to the Stygis Fossae, part of the circular fracture zone that almost completely surrounded Elysium Mons. The crawler had been over this territory before, so the autonomous vehicle navigation program took them there swiftly and smoothly.

"This is where I stop," Andrew said. "I want to collect some samples at a few more places to make sure I have the whole fault structure properly mapped. But right now it looks like a simple thrust fault. The volcano built up, got too heavy for the crust, the crust cracked, the mountain sank down like a stone on rubber ice, and the edges of the crack came up."

"Like Olympus Mons," Gus suggested.

"Well . . ." Andrew said doubtfully. "I don't really buy Tanya's theory that the two are the same. Those ramparts around Mount Olympus are mighty high. I have to agree with Joe Stanislavsky that there might be other explanations. For example, just to the west of us, in Granicus Valley, are some ridge-shaped, serrated mountains, very similar to the moberg ridges on Earth that form from volcanic fissure eruptions underneath glaciers—only much—"

"Larger," Gus interjected.

"Right! Anyway, the size of a moberg ridge is limited by the thickness of the ice above the erupting fissure lava. The height of the moberg ridge in Granicus Valley is two and a half kilometers high, indicating that the preexisting ice sheet was at *least* that thick."

"So maybe Joe is right, after all," Gus said.

He looked out the front window of the crawler. "How do you get from here onto Elysium Mountain? That ditch in front of us has some pretty steep walls on the far side."

"The Russians installed a cable-lift north from here," Andrew said. "It connects to the cable system going up to the top of the mountain. If you'd like to go up to the top for a look around, I can spare a tech to go 'buddy' with you."

"I'd appreciate that," Gus said. "It wouldn't do for the director to flaunt institute safety regulations and travel alone."

The crawler took them to the start of the cable-lift system and they rode their way up the two-hundred-kilometer-long slope of the medium-sized volcano. Gus noticed as they traveled that the volcano was significantly different from other volcanoes on Mars. The lava that formed it must have been less fluid, since it produced hummocks of lava rather than featherlike flows. It was more like an Earth volcano. Except for the lack of large cinder cones, it had a great deal of similarity to the Emi Koussi volcano in northern Chad, just south of the Sahara Desert in Libya.

"Only bigger, naturally," he said to himself. "Being it's on Mars, it's twelve kilometers high instead of three and a half."

They spent the night in a twelve-man hut on the top with a small group of technicians that Tanya had left behind to continue a core-sampling survey across the diameter of the fourteen-kilometer-wide caldera. Gus cycled through the airlock into the hut and was taking off the helmet of his Marsuit when one of the techs lounging around inside the hut reacted with surprise.

"My Infinite Lord!" he cried, flipping back the viewer on his yellow Cap of Contact and falling to the floor on his knees, his hands clasped together in ecstasy.

"Get up!" Gus said somewhat angrily. "I'm his brother."

That evening after dinner, the scientific curiosity in him having overcome his natural reluctance to pry, Gus asked to try on the technician's Cap of Contact. The cap was willingly turned over by the still-awed tech, and Gus watched a full fifteen minutes of his brother blathering on about ridding the world of atheistic neocommunism and other forms of venial sin, and unifying all mankind into one great Church family.

He thought it hadn't affected him, but he had a difficult time getting to sleep and, when he did, he had a terrible dream. He was

standing on top of a tall volcano on Earth, dressed in a golden robe.
Next to him, standing on a bubbling pool of molten, bloodred lava,
was the Devil. The Devil was pointing to the world spread out
below them, promising Gus it would all be his, if he would but sign
a pact with him. Gus, to his horror, saw himself scrawling his signature at the bottom of the proffered piece of scorched parchment,
two ornate letter A's, each followed by an illegible squiggle. The
instant he signed, the Devil gave a long echoing laugh, the volcano
exploded, and the whole world was turned into a roiling ball of
molten lava.

Gus awoke to find that he had left the hut heater on high and
it was stifling inside. He turned the heater down and slept fitfully
until dawn came.

He would have liked to have spent more time on the volcano,
but he had to get back. Besides, the Unie made him nervous, the
way he followed him around with his eyes. The trip back to the
Elysium Saddle base was uneventful, and Gus made arrangements
to go back out to Hecates Tholus with Tanya's relief group of techs
early Friday morning.

The domed shape of Hecates Tholus seemed to grow abruptly up
out of the plains surrounding it like a gigantic rotten mushroom
cap dropped on the floor. The Russians had not installed a cable
system here, since the volcano was only ninety kilometers from base
to caldera and only six kilometers higher than the saddle point on
the ridge where Elysium Saddle base sat perched five kilometers
above "sea level." The crawler only took three hours to cover the
one hundred kilometers to the base of the volcano, including a half-
hour stop to untangle some fiber-optic strands that had wound
around one of the wheel hubs. The crawler then started up the steep
slopes of frozen lava, all on autonomous guidance, since it had been
this way many times before. About halfway up, the slope decreased
and they came onto the relatively flat region on top of the volcano.
There they found Tanya keeping two crews of techs busy drilling
cores and taking samples, working their way from the bottom of
the mountain to the caldera.

The next ten weeks of Gus' life were the most blissful he had ever spent, even though he never got a moment alone with Tanya. The two volcano specialists divided the sol into two twelve-hour shifts and, adding another group of techs, kept two coring rigs working day and night. One or the other would be out on the surface, looking at the cores as the crews pulled them from the ground, deciding what segments to leave there, what segments to take inside for a quick look, and what segments to take back to base.

"That last segment shows evidence of a different flow layer at twelve point three meters," Gus said through the crawler comm link. "Very thin, though. You must have caught the edge."

"I'll start the next core thirty meters over," Tanya said from outside. Through the crawler cockpit windows, Gus could see her different-shaped, curvy figure silhouetted in the glare of the flood-lights among the bulkier man-shaped Marsuits of the techs.

"I'm going to hit the sack," Gus said, stretching.

"Spokoinoi noche," Tanya said sweetly over the general comm channel. The morning-shift techs were already snoring in the back of the crawler, so Gus switched the crawler comm to the channel he and Tanya had selected for private conversations. The sound of a kiss came over the speaker. He sent one back.

In the middle of Week eighty-seven, they reached the bottom of the slope on the north side of Hecates Tholus. The days were getting shorter, and it was time to come in out of the cold and turn the data they had collected into a first guess at the flow history of the volcano. They returned to Elysium Saddle, spent another two weeks selecting segments from the cores that they had sent back to the base, and arranged to have them shipped back to the diagnostic and dating labs at Olympia.

The flight back on the east-bound hopiter from Elysium Saddle to Olympia was crowded. By the time Tanya and Gus got to the launch pad, the passenger compartment was full. Rather than wait, they crammed into the jump seats behind the pilot and engineer. The hop was a relatively shallow one, since they didn't have far to go. As they rose up over the Tartarus Mountains the pilot tilted the nose of the hopiter toward the south so his guests could see Orcus Patera, a still largely unexplored giant dike-rimmed oval lake of frozen lava four hundred kilometers long and one hundred fifty kilometers wide.

"A caldera as big as the San Joaquin Valley," Gus said, impressed.

"Mars is a strange place," Tanya said. "The planet is smaller than Earth, but the structures are bigger."

"Gravity," Gus suggested.

"Maybe," Tanya allowed.

Tanya and Gus were first through the airlock and soon were back inside the familiar corridors of Olympia. Their walk from the hopiter pad corridor to their underground dormitory rooms took them through the Boston Commons and past the tables set up outside the Olye Olye Outs Inne.

"Tanya!" a voice called from a small crowd gathered to watch the Icarbatics practice at the center of the commons. They stopped and a young woman came running over. "Thanks for letting me use your wings while you were away. They're so much better than the clunky things you can check out from the equipment desk. I just put them away in my room, let me get them for you."

"I'm glad you put them to good use, Penny," Tanya said. "I'll come with you."

Gus watched them go, then heard someone calling him.

"Hello, Gus, you handsome devil. Where have you been all these weeks?"

Gus turned to see a young woman get up from a table and strut over to him. She was dressed in a short red skirt that showed off a pair of black net stockings with elaborate designs cascading down her long legs and into her red high-heeled shoes. His view of these delights was soon blocked by the nearby presence of an obviously unencumbered swaying bosom barely contained in a deeply scooped peasant blouse. The light color of the woman's hair had been aided by peroxide, probably obtained from some rocket engineer, and the ruby-red lips, rouged cheeks, and long artificial eyelashes must have been brought in as part of her personal baggage allowance. He tried to place the face. Finally he remembered.

"Rose! Rose Wood. One of Jay Plantagenet's techs," he said, finally remembering. "Hi, Rose. What can I do for you?"

"What can I do for *you*, is the question," Rose replied with an inviting smile. "You've been away for a long time. Would you be interested in having a little company for a while? Hummmm?"

She came closer and her fingers started walking up his chest. His eyes flickered nervously, very aware of the two mounds exposed to view below. She tickled his chin. "Very *friendly* company," she promised, lips pouting slightly.

Suddenly there was a loud explosion of Russian words that Gus had never heard before. He turned his head to see an enraged Tanya spluttering in indignation. There was another long burst of Russian, ending in ". . . swine!" and Tanya stomped off. Rose had backed off during the outburst, but now she started to come back.

"Thanks, Rose," Gus said, shaking his head and waving her off with his mangled left hand. "Not interested."

He turned to go. It was no use talking to Tanya now. He might as well dump his bags in his room and go to the office.

Fred jumped up from his tiny desk in the outer office when Gus entered the institute door.

"I'm so glad you're back, sir," Fred said, greeting him with concern. "Something terrible has happened since you left."

"Really, Fred?" Gus replied. "You could have contacted me, you know."

"Oh! No!" Fred said with horror. "I couldn't have told you over the comm links! Someone might have overheard!"

"Sounds serious. What's the matter?"

"Well . . ." Fred said, nervously, his voice lowering almost to a whisper. "One of our techs decided that she didn't like spending over half her time outside in a Marsuit and quit."

"She has a perfect right to do that," Gus replied. "I tried to make that clear in my speech on Independence Sol. The last thing I want is a disgruntled employee. Is she going home or staying?"

"She said she wants to stay," Fred said. "But you'll *have* to send her back," he continued, his voice becoming more agitated and rising in volume. "We can't allow her kind to stay on Mars!"

"What on Earth are you talking about, Fred?" Gus said, puzzled. "Who is this person?"

"Her name is Rose Wood. And she's become a . . . a . . ." His voice failed him.

"Ah-hah!" Gus said with a loud, relieved laugh that took Fred aback.

"I've met your Rose," Gus said, slapping him on the back. "Just recently, on the commons." He walked into his office.

"Then you're going to send her back?" Fred asked, following along behind, relieved that he didn't have to explain.

"Why?" Gus replied, stopping beside his desk. "Just because she's a prostitute?"

"A-a-a—" Fred stammered, both shocked and bewildered.

"Is she not supplying a service? A badly needed service on a planet with six men for every woman?"

"Well, yes." Fred admitted.

"And is not everyone who comes to Mars checked to make sure they're free from venereal diseases?" Gus continued. "So no one can accuse her of spreading disease."

"Yes." Fred admitted.

"And is she not making enough money to support herself, so that she is not a burden on society?" Gus continued.

"At a polar a trick, she ought to!" Fred exploded. "She makes more a day than *I* do!"

"Well, the price will come down once she gets some competition," Gus said, sitting down at his desk console and opening his message file.

"You mean you aren't going to do *anything*?" Fred exclaimed in exasperation.

"If the governor of Mars or the mayor of Olympia is foolish enough to want to pass, then attempt to enforce, blue laws to prohibit victimless behavior like prostitution and gambling, then they are welcome to try," Gus said, looking up. "But I'm counting on the general good sense and intelligence of those who have been selected to come to Mars to keep such activities in perspective in their lives."

He got up from the desk, came over to Fred, put his muscular boxer's arm tenderly around Fred's thin, sloping shoulder bones, and slowly escorted him to the door.

"Y'know, Fred," Gus suggested as they walked, "you've been under an awful lot of pressure lately and been getting very tense and uptight. Perhaps . . . maybe . . . you should consider a visit to Rose yourself?"

He gave Fred a friendly slap on the back as he pushed him gently through the doorway, then closed the door on the wide-eyed, open-mouthed, speechless face.

CHAPTER 11

DEFIANCE

Chris came into Gus' office to tell him the latest news. Gus, eyes red from lack of sleep, just glared at him.

"I don't want to know," Gus said irritably. He had been deliberately avoiding the news about his brother, somehow feeling that he was partly at fault.

"It only took fifteen days, but its all nice and legal," Chris said. "Your brother is now 'president-in-perpetuity,' and the new regent took over this morning."

"Regent?" Gus asked.

"You don't expect the 'Infinite Lord' to be bothered with the petty duties of being president, do you? He'll let Di Perkins take care of those details. Some say it was part of a deal he made with her before the elections. They call her regent because she isn't elected, but appointed by your brother to run the country in his place."

"Appointed! What happened to the Constitution?" Gus blurted.

"The Constitution is still there." Chris said. "But parts of it got drastically amended by the overwhelmingly pro-Alexander Congress. Almost all of the new House of Representatives are Unies, and they've got a large majority in the Senate, enough so they can elect the Senate majority leader and control committee appointments. Using that power, and with Vice-President Di Perkins controlling the floor, they rammed the amendments past the few raw-throated filibustering senators who dared to oppose them. Their constitutional amendments were ratified in record time by more than enough equally intimidated state legislatures. Even the Supreme Court admitted that they couldn't stop it, since every step along the way was allowed by the old Constitution.''

Gus grimaced and gave a sigh.

Chris continued. "So they've changed the executive branch and even renamed the old U.S. of A. the 'Unified States.' The government will run very much like it did before, except that the regent has veto power over everything, and her veto can't be overturned. Her appointments can't be blocked, either. To keep individual civil servants and congressmen under control, the regent has line-item veto power in budgets. She can not only eliminate support for a congressman's district, she has the power to line out an individual's salary."

"That explains this, then," Gus said, his fingers moving over his portable flatscreen. "But I don't want you to worry about it." He searched through his message file, then handed Chris the flatscreen with the short message on it.

> Pending review, further support is canceled for Sagan Mars Institute Research Grant NSF 33-1087, "Seasonal and Altitude Air Composition Models for the Martian Atmosphere," Principal Investigator, Christopher Stoker.

Chris' stomach sank. Being governor of Mars was no longer a lark. The new U.S. secretary of state had warned him that Alexander was pretty annoyed when he learned that the governor of Mars was inviting the Russians back to the planet that he had just kicked them off of. Then, to top it all off, just this morning Chris had received a message from the Russians saying they were backing out of their agreement to send a large contingent of scientists. Something about the shortage of antimatter for their spacecraft and surface transporters because of the Russian military building up its stockpiles.

"Sir?" came a voice from the doorway to the office.

"Yes, Fred?" Gus said, looking up.

"I hate to bother you and Dr. Stoker, sir," Fred said hesitantly. "But an important message just came for you. You might want to read it while Governor Stoker is here."

Gus took back his flatscreen and pulled up the most recent message.

The government of the U.S. Protectorate of Mars is hereby put under the control of Dr. Augustus Armstrong, director, Sagan Mars Institute. All local elections are hereby voided and all local officials are dismissed. Dr. Armstrong is directed to detain all non–U.S. citizens in quarters and prepare a schedule for their removal from the planet. The Sagan Mars Institute budgets are suspended pending review of alien citizen removal schedule.

By Order of The Infinite Lord and President-in-Perpetuity:

Di Perkins,
Regent of the Unified States

"She can't do that!" Chris said. "The Territory of Mars is a protectorate of the United Nations."

"Yes, but it's supposed to operate under United States laws, and in the new Unified States, Alex's every whim is law. My brother never did like sharing the spoils with the other nations, much less letting any Russians stay behind. I figure he is counting on my concern for the Sagan Institute to force me to help him renege on the independence agreement the old United States government made with the Reformed U.N. and the Territory of Mars."

"What are you going to do, Gus?" Chris asked, concerned. "You might be able to protect me from budget cuts, but you can't protect the whole institute. You'll have to go along."

Gus leaned back pensively in his chair. "It isn't what *I'm* going to do, Governor Stoker, it's what the people of the Territory of Mars are going to do. My brother is too used to being a military commander. I can't carry out his orders without cooperation from the people here. Are the people of Mars going to cooperate with this new dictator? Or are they going to fight back?"

"I'll have Seichi call an Olympia town meeting," Chris said. "But I'll have him schedule it late so most of the other bases can join in via video link and we can turn it into a Territory of Mars meeting."

The Boston Commons was packed with a huge but strangely silent crowd. The beer vendors moved among the tarps, folding chairs, and inflated pillows, but many sitting there just waved them away. This was no time for relaxing. Seichi Kiyowara, the mayor of Olympia, opened the meeting as soon as both moons were over the horizon.

"We'll be making some decisions today," he said. "So I shall officially open this town meeting of Olympia. Anything decided here by a substantial majority of the people will become a law of the city of Olympia, subject to the usual appeal and approval process. I'd now like to turn the floor over to the governor of Mars, Chris Stoker. Chris?"

Chris took Seichi's place in front of the video camera. "I'll wait a few minutes while the mayors and conveners of other bases formally open their town meetings," he said. "Turn on your attention switch when you're done."

Chris looked over at the bank of flatscreen sets showing the pickups from the other bases in and around Mars. Each had superimposed across the top of the screen the name of the place, Phobos, Deimos, Boreal Base, Australe Canyon, Hellas Plains, Mutchville, Isidis Basin, Melas Canyon, Sinai Springs, Tharsis Saddle, Elysium Saddle, and Solis Lacus—twelve isolated communities trying to comprehend and gain control over an unknown, untamed planet. One by one the red attention lights blinked on at the upper right of the screen. Chris returned to the video pickup. When all the attention lights were on he started to speak again.

"I have asked the cities and bases to call town meetings simultaneously so we can all hear and discuss what has happened recently

and come to some joint decision as to further action. If you want
to speak on an issue, go to your mayor or convener and have him
blink the attention light.

"I want to reiterate that *anyone*, U.S. citizen or not, has a right
to speak *and vote*. You all know that, but why I'm emphasizing it
now will become obvious later.

"You are all aware of the news that has come in concerning the
restructuring of the United States of America into the Unified States
under the control of President-in-Perpetuity Alexander Armstrong
and his appointed regent. This has affected some of us personally
already. Now it threatens to affect all of us here. I would like Dr.
Augustus Armstrong to read us a message that was sent to him a
short time ago."

Gus got up and slowly read the message from the regent from
his pocket vidofax. The mutterings from the crowd grew as he went
along, and when he got to the phrase, ". . . directed to detain all
non–U.S. citizens in quarters . . ." he had to stop because of the
noisy protests.

"Who does she think she is!" came a voice from the crowd.

"It's not her, its that egotistical bastard, Alexander the Greatest."

Gus waited until they had quieted down, then continued to
read. When he got to the phrase ". . . Institute budgets are suspended pending review . . ." the crowd became deathly still. By the
time he had finished the ending he could hear the echo of his voice
bouncing back from the Deimos pickup.

Almost immediately people were on their feet at the Boston
Commons, waving their hands for attention, and attention lights
started blinking on the bank of remote video pickups. Chris came
up beside Gus and spoke.

"Before I open the meeting for debate, let me clarify the issue
before us. We were established as an independent territory under
the protection of the United Nations—"

"Some protection they are!" someone yelled from the audience.

"But we are supposed to operate under the laws of the United

States," Chris continued. "Now, things have changed and it's the Unified States. The question is, shall we knuckle under to the new regent and send our friends packing, or do we resist?"

"We can't win a war!" someone said. "They'd smother us with nuclear warheads."

"Doesn't have to be a war," Gus said, stepping forward again. "Could be just a little civil disobedience. You know, the civil kind of civil disobedience you learn in the civil service."

A laugh rippled through the crowd.

Chris started recognizing speakers, trying to alternate between those on the floor of the Boston Commons and those behind the blinking red attention lights on the flatscreens from other bases.

"I can live without a salary," a researcher said from Boreal Base.

"I can't!" a tech shouted from the commons. "I have a wife and kids back in the States."

Boris Batusov waited politely with his hand raised, and Chris finally noticed him and gave him a chance to speak. The crowd hushed as they waited for the famous Russian Nobel Prize winner to speak. "I don't think we non–U.S. citizens should ask our American friends to sacrifice their careers just to keep us here," he said.

"I think there is a more fundamental question," Max Mac-Fadden said. "Are we going to accept the domination of Alexander and become part of his Unified States, or are we going to assert our independence? Even if it means losing the support that allows us to carry on pure research."

"Forget about research," Ernest Licon said from the Boreal Base pickup. "I don't think we can even survive for long without massive support from the U.S."

"I cannot speak for my country," Ozaki Akutagawa said from the Elysium Saddle pickup, "but it would seem likely to me that under the circumstances, Japan's support could be increased in those areas where you need supplies that cannot be locally fabricated, such as electronic components and antimatter."

"All we have to do is hold out until someone shoots him or he dies," a belligerent tech in the front row said. "Even if he is president-in-perpetuity, the bastard can't live forever—maybe he's one of those kind with a weak heart that pops off at forty-five or fifty."

Gus walked to the microphone. "I believe I might have something pertinent to say along those lines."

The crowd quieted, and the tech who had made the comment blurted out an apology. "Sorry, Gus. Didn't think . . ."

"It's all right," Gus said, waving his left hand as he took the microphone from Chris with his right. For some reason, the mangled fingers on the left hand seemed especially noticeable in the floodlights bathing the platform.

"Our father died at fifty-eight. Heart attack—didn't believe in doctors. But our mother is still healthy at sixty-eight. We are both forty-three and in general good health, but I have high blood pressure which I keep controlled with some medicine." He turned to look at Tanya. "What is it, Tanya?"

"Atenolol—a beta blocker," she answered.

"Something else we can't produce here on Mars," Gus reminded. "If Alex takes his pills and avoids bullets, he could easily last another twenty-five years—or more."

The discussion went on until way past midnight at Olympia—with everyone allowed to say his piece. Finally, there was a call for a vote. There was no question of the result.

"Okay, it's decided then," Chris said. "We will attempt to make it on our own, with help from our friends in other countries on Earth. Those that don't agree and want to return to Earth have five days to close down their affairs here. The next crew rotation ship arrives Thursday of Week twenty-one." Gus came forward at the last to take the microphone.

"In the meantime," he said, "I can recommend a couple of good stories to download from the library into your vidofax. Read *The Moon is a Harsh Mistress* and *Revolt in 2100*, both by Heinlein."

The following Thursday the Unies, those with families trapped under the new dictatorship, and a few others, crowded onto the crew rotation ship that had been in transit out to Mars during Alexander's takeover, and went back to Earth.

The Regent Perkins next demanded the return of the three remaining Yorktown class space transports that had been left in orbit about Mars. But their engineering crews kept finding serious problems with the propulsion systems that seemed to require many months to fix. Meanwhile, some of the kilograms of antihydrogen ice remaining in their storage tanks were extracted and used to fill up the storage canisters in the hopiters, crawlers, and orbital shuttles needed to keep the transportation system on Mars going.

Chris and Gus were very busy the following weeks pleading for support from Japan, Australia, the EEC, Brazil, and other countries. The responses they got were sympathetic, and soon they had received "foreign aid" gifts and loans that allowed them to bring in the medicines, precision equipment, electronic components, and antimatter needed to keep the planet going. The Russians, however, deathly afraid of Alexander and his paranoid anticommunism streak, retreated behind their borders and raised their defenses.

Independence Sol finally came again. The laser fireworks show was just as spectacular as before and the speeches had a flavor of defiance in them, but the crowd had to go to bed early, for many now had to carry on their scientific work on the side, after they had worked on their "Independence Task."

The already-existing factories that produced raw stocks of metal and plastic from the Martian soil and atmosphere were now expanded in size and diversity of output. A Marsuit factory had been started to make replacements for the major components of the suit that received the most wear, but there were critical components, such as valves, that had to be salvaged from the old suits and hand-reworked to restore them to safe operation. One of Chris' best foreign "handouts" was a computer-controlled minimill that could cut any 3-D shape in metal directly from a computer-generated drawing.

Chris and Gus, whose Independence Tasks were administrative and full time, stopped by Gus' office after the celebration to check for messages. Fortunately, there were none, so they both could relax for a while.

"Do me a favor, Gus?" Chris asked.

"Sure," Gus said.

"We're off to a good start. But I noticed today that people are getting tired of the grind. They need pepping up. You're their hero and can do that, but video won't really do the job. I need you to go around to all the bases, meet the people, show you care, slap them on the back, and send them back to work. Will you do it?"

"If you'll come with me," Gus said, getting up and heading out the office door. "You're their governor."

"Great idea!" Chris said, draping one lanky arm around Gus' broad, muscular shoulders. "The two of us together—like Damon and Pythias . . ."

Gus looked up at the young mop-head towering over him and laughed. "More like Mutt and Jeff, you mean!"

Their first hop took them westward to Elysium Saddle. There Chris and Gus kept their political fences mended by having dinner with Ozaki Akutagawa.

"This is excellent sushi," Gus said, picking up another delicious morsel carefully with his chopsticks. "Where did you get the rice?"

"It is a special dwarf strain that we developed for space," Ozaki responded. "Grows well, even when crowded, and all it needs is a modest amount of soil and water. I must show you our gardens after dinner. We have the fish ponds and rice paddies laid out with bridges and benches so that a stroll through them allows one's spirit to think it is back on Earth. It is very important for those who work here with me."

"How many are there now at the Nippon Mars Volcanic Studies Institute?" Chris asked. "I understand your fourth ship arrived last week."

"We now number fifty-two," Ozaki said. "Our plans are to expand on the preliminary survey that Dr. Pavlova and Dr. Armstrong carried out. It will take that many people to completely map all the volcanoes and fossae on the Elysium bulge within a reasonable period of time."

Gus had a wonderful time the rest of the evening drinking warm rice wine and talking volcanoes with Ozaki. Chris was bored, but polite.

The next few sols they spent walking around the base, visiting with the workers at the superconducting wire plant that was one of the Independence Tasks assigned to the Elysium Saddle base.

"Because of our lack of equipment, we have to make the stuff by a batch process," the foreman said. "So we only make about thirty kilometers a day."

"Doesn't sound like enough," Chris said. "What do you need to increase your production rate?"

"Don't really need to. As long as you keep plugging away, thirty kilometers a day is a cable around the circumference of Mars in one mear. We'll be ready to tie the electrical grid together by the time the bases have their solar cell farms deployed." He took them to a crawler trailer, which had been modified to hold a big spool of wire. At the rear end was a plowlike attachment.

"The superconducting material we can make with our crude metallurgical control is the old-fashioned type that only stays superconducting if kept below freezing. This plow will bury it in the permafrost to keep it cold."

"Where do you plan the first line?" Gus asked.

"We've already started on the run from Elysium Saddle to Isidis Basin," the foreman replied. "It was only three thousand kilometers and a straight shot across the Elysium plains once we got around the fossae."

"Isidis," Chris said. "That's where we go next."

Isidis base was relatively small. Like all the bases, it had a nuclear reactor as the prime power supply. However, the initial charge of uranium fuel would not run forever. Like all the bases, Isidis had as a primary Independence Task the job of surrounding the base with a growing field of solar cells that would carry the electrical load during the day. Once all the bases were connected together with a grid of superconducting wires, those bases still in the sunlight could help power those bases where night had fallen. They were shown the multiple drill-hole aluminum bus bar installation near the power station where the direct current coming in over the superconducting link from Elysium would be sent into the ground to complete the circuit.

After the obligatory pep talk after the evening meal at the base cafeteria, Chris and Gus had a few minutes to relax at the Insidious Delight, the local cafe and beer garden.

"I've got a remote station monitoring the atmospheric composition at the low point in the basin," Chris said. "While I'm here, I think I'll take a crawler out this evening and check the calibration. It's only twenty kilometers away. Want to come?"

"No." Gus feigned a sigh. "You go off and play scientist while I slave away at being an administrator."

After Chris had left in the crawler, Gus found a chance to play scientist and attend an evening lecture by Joseph Stanislavsky, who had been out exploring along the southern perimeter of the Isidis Basin. Joseph used a large high-resolution flatscreen on the wall for his presentation and first put up a standard map of Mars with the topographic contours at one-kilometer intervals.

"Now, notice," he said as he tapped the icons on his control flatscreen. "If you draw a line around Mars at the *one* kilometer contour interval, not the zero contour—after all, that was chosen arbitrarily—you will see what I call the true 'sea level' of Mars."

The one-kilometer contour shifted in color from black to a bright blue that contrasted well with the rusty color of the map. The blue contour snaked above and below the equator all across the map of Mars.

"Note how, except for the Olympus and Tharsis volcano complex, all the highly cratered highlands of Mars lie south of the one-kilometer contour and all the uncratered lowlands lie north of the contour." He touched an icon and a dashed blue line appeared that dipped below the Solis plain south of the Tharsis Ridge, again separating heavily cratered territory from smooth plains.

"It is my thesis," he said, touching another icon on his screen so that the uncratered plains north of the blue contour line turned light blue, "that all this area was once filled with water—the Boreal

Sea. But water covered with ice. Thick ice, in many places frozen all the way to the bottom—a glacier. When the Olympus and Tharsis volcanoes grew, they grew up out of those thick layers of ice to form the shapes they now hold.

"If my thesis is correct, then Isidis plain was once a bay in the Boreal Sea. And since it is on the equator, it may have become warm enough at various times that the ice would melt, forming a bay of liquid water. If my thesis is correct, then when I look around the southern perimeter of Isidis plain I should find—at the one-kilometer contour level—evidence of terraces formed by water action at the shores of the Isidis bay."

He switched the picture to one taken of some terraces. "Ladies and gentlemen," he said, proudly pointing at the terrace features, "a picture of the terrain at one-kilometer elevation, directly south from here."

Gus was impressed, although some of the others weren't. The argument was still going on when Gus went to bed, knowing he had a busy day tomorrow.

Their next hop took them south across the equator to Hellas, the lowest point on Mars. After touring the various facilities, giving little pep talks to small groups and answering questions and trying to solve problems, both Gus and Chris were tired and went to relax in the Hell Hole beer garden in the basement of the hub building. There was someone familiar there.

"Jay Plantagenet!" Gus said, coming up and slapping the young man on the back. "What are you doing here?"

"Giving my crew of techs a little break in civilization before we start off on our crawler trek again," Jay said. "I'm combining my research with my Independence Task, which is prospecting for heavy metal ores. We spent the last six weeks in the Hellespontus Mountains. Now we're on a survey traverse of Hellas Basin on our way over to Hadriaca Patera, to see if that volcano spewed up anything worthwhile."

"You've got a crawler free?" Chris asked. "I'd like to borrow it to go check out my automated station."

"Sure," Jay said. "I've got lots of free time, I'll 'buddy' you."

"I'd like to come along, too," Gus said, then dredged up a hoary Mars joke. "Feels good to go outside and get a breath of fresh air."

"At least you'll have a little more to breathe than usual," Chris said. "The air pressure here at four kilometers below sea level is nearly twice that over most of Mars."

"How deep would it have to be to get up to one atmosphere?" Jay asked, curious.

Chris did a quick mental calculation. "The present air pressure on Mars is less than one percent of Earth's, so we have to go up by a factor of more than a hundred. Three scale heights is a factor of twenty. Four is a little over fifty. Four and a half scale heights would do it. The scale height on Mars is around eleven kilometers, so you'd need a hole about fifty kilometers deep."

"Only forty-five if you started digging here at the bottom of Hellas Basin," Gus suggested.

"If you'd been around at the right time, Hellas would have been dug that deep," Jay said with a smile. "But I don't think you would have wanted to be around. A little dangerous."

"What do you mean?" Chris asked.

"From what I've found so far, I'm now almost positive that Hellas Basin is really an impact crater. A *huge* one. It could have easily been over forty-five kilometers deep."

"But it instantaneously filled in due to isostatic rebound," Gus said. "Look at it now, only four kilometers deep."

"Instantaneous to geophysics people like you and me that think a thousand years is a short interval of time," Jay said. "I'm still working on my crater impact and rebound models for Mars, taking into account the thicker crust and the lower gravity. It may have taken hundreds of years for the hole to fill in. My model also predicts something that may be of interest to you volcano types."

"Really?" Gus said, interested. "What?"

"According to my model simulations, the shock waves from the meteorite that caused the Hellas Basin were so strong, they upset the inner core and fractured the crust on the opposite side. That led to the growth of the Tharsis Ridge and its volcanoes."

"Your volcano theories are like your handball," Gus objected.

"Full of tricky off-the-wall shots. I'd believe it more if the ridge were directly opposite the basin. As it is now, that meteorite would have had to come in at a steep angle."

"Stranger things have happened," Jay said, shrugging and starting off toward the stairwell.

From Hellas Basin, Chris and Gus took off in a hypersonic single-stage-to-orbit vehicle to visit the bases on the two moons about Mars, Phobos and Deimos. The orbiter had an engine that scooped in the relatively thick air at the bottom of the basin, heated it to high temperature in an antimatter-powered heat exchanger, and exhausted it at high speed to accelerate the vehicle up to almost orbital speed before switching to rocket mode for the last portion of the climb. It was nerve-racking to zoom at hypersonic speeds low across the cratered terrain, but the air there was like the air at thirty kilometers altitude on Earth.

Chris and Gus spent a great deal of time talking with everyone on the two moons of Mars. These people, isolated from the social contacts enjoyed in the larger bases on Mars, lived and worked under difficult and dangerous conditions. Yet they were essential to the long-term survival of the Territory of Mars. Their last get-together was with the entire contingent of the base on Deimos. They met in Asaph Hall, the small communal dining area and meeting room of the base.

"I want to let you all know how much we appreciate your work here," Gus said to the small group of forty men and eight women crowded into the small room. "To survive, the Territory of Mars must import its medicines, its antimatter, its electronics, its precision machinery, and the other things that we need to keep alive. A nation cannot import forever, it must export something to balance those imports. The only thing exportable from the surface of Mars that is light enough to justify the cost of shipping it back to the Earth's surface is knowledge. Scientific knowledge." He paused to shake his head, then continued.

"Until recently, we had a customer for that knowledge, the United States. Now that customer has become aberrated and no longer desires knowledge. We have found other customers for scientific knowledge, but they in total do not provide sufficient imports to keep us going. We must have something other than knowledge to export. That's where *you* and your Independence Task come in." Gus patted the shoulder of a man sitting next to him.

"Your director, Tom—oops!" Gus had patted Tom too hard and now found himself floating upward in the low gravity. Tom, legs twisted around the rungs of his floor-fixed chair, pulled him back down to titters from the amused crowd.

Gus, embarrassed, fixed himself firmly to a table and continued. "As I was saying before my oratory took me to such great heights," he joked, "your director, Tom Manley, took me out on a visit to your materials separation facility today. It is marvelous what you have done, using electrostatic and diamagnetic forces to separate out the different elements and compounds. He tells me you should have your first shipment ready to go in a few weeks. A cluster of graphite fiber storage tanks containing hundreds of tons of water, hydrocarbons, and nitrogen fertilizers destined for the gardens of the EEC Eurospace Hotel at L-5. What really impressed me was that except for the engine, the whole ship is cargo, all built right here on Deimos. You even supply the water for the reaction mass to push the cargo there. I applaud you." He clapped his hands and Chris did, too. Smiles spread around the room.

"Of course," Gus continued, "the reason the EEC is buying your products is that they can't get them from the Moon, and they find it is cheaper to ship those vital compounds in from Mars than haul them up out of the gravity well of Earth. Also, because of the facility you have built here, you deliver processed products, ready to use, while the asteroid prospectors can only deliver unprocessed carbonaceous chondrite asteroids. The EEC benefits from lower costs and Mars benefits from an improved balance of trade."

Chris then added, "We flatfooters really appreciate what you tippy-toers are doing. Let me know if there is anything you need."

"Just keep the Hellsbridge scotch whisky coming," one said. Although every base found room to grow barley and brew beer, only one place made decent whisky. Everybody concluded it must be something in the permafrost field in Hellas Basin where they drew their meltwater from.

"A few more good-looking dames would be nice," a man's voice said from the back, knowing that with an overall Mars ratio of six to one, Deimos, with its five to one ratio, had more than its share.

"A few more decent gentlemen would be even nicer," a woman's voice retorted.

Chris and Gus took the orbiter down to the Chryse spaceport, a little to the northeast of Mutchville in the middle of the Chryse Plains. At 3.5 kilometers below sea level, it was the second lowest spot on Mars. After visiting the hopiter refurbishment depot there, Chris and Gus took the almost-obligatory crawler visit to the Mutch Memorial, one hundred kilometers away to the southwest. Although Gus had been there before, Chris, like many who came to Mars, had not had a chance to see it yet.

The Viking 1 lander was sitting out in the open, just as it had been doing for sixty years, its top surfaces covered with a slight film of red dust. There was a low wall of rocks in a circle around it that hinted to the visitors to keep their distance. Inside the ring, however, there were some footprints leading up to the lander and back again. The older, faded ones had been made by the first human visitors to Mars, Russian cosmonauts. At the request of NASA, they had removed one of the cameras, obtained samples of paint and plastic-covered cables, and brought them back for analysis to look for any signs of degradation caused by the Martian weather.

"There is one set of footprints inside the ring that looks fresh," Chris said, sitting on "Big Joe" like many another tourist before him. "I wonder what thoughtless jerk made those."

"I did," Gus said quietly. "One of my first assignments after taking over Mars was to restore the camera to the lander and install the plaque dedicating the Viking 1 lander as the Thomas A. Mutch Memorial."

"Oh . . ." Chris said.

The next hopiter jump took them to Melas Chasm in the middle of the Mariner Valley. The rest of Mars seemed to disappear as the hopiter dropped into the five-kilometer-deep canyon and came to rest on the landing pad beside Melas base.

Because of the copious quantities of sandy soil and subsurface water available, and its near-equatorial latitude, the Independence Task of Melas was to be the farm belt of Mars, supplying the smaller bases with food varieties they could not afford to grow themselves. Gus and Chris visited one typical farm.

"Watch out!" Chris yelled, as something struck Gus from behind.

Gus turned around to find out it was a brown and white miniature goat, and it lunged again, this time at his kneecaps. Gus fended it off.

"I'm sorry about that," the keeper said. "We've bred milk production into them so that they produce as much as a cow, but we haven't been able to breed out the butting instinct."

"That's all right," Gus said, nursing the bruised stubs on his left hand. "It didn't hurt much. Just surprised me, that's all."

The next base was a small one just up the valley from Melas. It was called Sinai Springs, and was close enough that it was reachable by crawler. Gus and Chris got a ride to the base on the weekly crawler that brought in food supplies. The frozen food rode uncovered in the trailer, where it stayed deep frozen in the Martian sunshine. Their driver was Ben Meier. He let the crawler move through the deep Ius Canyon on autonomous guidance while he told old war stories to Chris about how his Israeli squad had made the first strike against the Russian base at Novomoskovsk.

They slept through the night while the crawler traveled onward on automatic; they awoke to find the Geryon Mountains had closed off their horizon to the north, while the view toward the south had also shifted closer and now looked more like a normal Earth mountain range, with branched valleys coming down to the floor, rather than the precipitous cliffs usually found in the Mariner Valley. Chris and Gus were up in the observation domes, taking in the scenery.

"Looks like the Owens Valley region in California," Chris observed from the middle dome.

"Except there are no tourists with ski racks on their cartops," Gus called back from the front dome. "Say! What's that up ahead? I could swear I saw something large and white—and it seems to be moving!"

"That's our slush-glacier," Ben said proudly. "Must have built up enough pressure to break through."

"Glacier?" Gus said. "On Mars!?"

"Man-made," Ben said. "We'll start selling ski racks for crawlers any time now."

They drove north of the spreading glacier field. Off in the distance Gus could see a large stream of water shooting over a rise and down the valley toward them, where it joined a lake of slushy water ponded in by frozen ice flows. The water obviously came from a large pipe that plummeted down the side of a steep cliff to the south of them. At intervals along the pipe were small blockhouses.

"That's our Independence Task," Ben said proudly. "A rural electrification project. I'll let Colonel Begin and Captain Shamir tell you all about it."

A little while later they came to the end of the Geryon Mountains.

"We're going to turn here up Lightning Canyon," Ben said. "But if you look off to your right through that cut in the mountains, you can see Hoofprint Slump, one of the biggest single landslides on Mars. Its almost fifty kilometers wide, twenty kilometers in, and five kilometers deep. The modeling studies insist that there had to be water inside to make the flow as big as it was. That's one of the reasons we knew we would hit water when we drilled wells."

He turned the crawler south and entered the wide canyon.

"Our scientists are positive that this canyon was formed by water during a warmer period on Mars. The water would come out during the warm days, but freeze at night, forming the strange valleys that look like Earth erosion features, but fatter. Lightning Canyon reaches well into the Sinai Plains from the Mariner Valley, and the tip of the furthest tributary is not far from a 'splosh' crater. The big pile of wet-looking debris around the crater indicates that there's plenty of liquid water not too far under the surface."

Shortly after entering the canyon, Ben turned the crawler sharply left. "The grade up Lightning Canyon is easier," he said. "Only five percent. But this crawler has good motors, so we take the steep way—the Valley of Aqaba—five kilometers up in fifty kilometers."

The whine from the motors lowered in pitch, and the crawler climbed straight up the steep, Swiss-like valley, as if it were on a cog-wheel track, with only the occasional swerve to avoid a soft sandstone boulder that had rolled down to the bottom without fracturing. After three hours they reached the top.

"Welcome to the Sinai Peninsula," Ben said. "It's even shaped a little like the Sinai Peninsula of Earth, except it's a lot smaller." He headed the crawler north. "Off to the left is the Mediterranean Valley. No water in it, but then, once upon a time, the real Mediterranean Valley was dry like this one. In less than an hour, you'll be at Sinai Springs, the watering hole of Mars . . ."

Gus and Chris were met by Yitzhak Begin, director of the Sinai Springs base and former commander of the Israeli contingent during the invasion of Mars.

"We originally started our work at Solis Lacus, where the Russians had set up the base they called Novobaku," Yitzhak said. "Admittedly there are frozen salty-sand marshes there that melt into shallow ponds during the day at midsummer. That is why radar returns from the flat surfaces had been seen on Earth. But as we started building up our water table models, we were led to explore regions that were closer to the source of underground heat needed to melt the permafrost into water—in this case, the Tharsis Ridge. We kept drilling test wells along the edge of Marineris Valles until we got here. I'll let Ben Shamir, one of my ex-captains in the Israeli UN contingent, tell you the rest. He's now head of our construction team for our hydroelectric power station."

Ben Shamir took them to the edge of the Suez Cliffs along the Sinai Peninsula's northern edge, which fell precipitously into the Ius Canyon that they had traversed not long before. He pointed out the pipeline down the cliff, the many stations along the way, and the growing flood of glacier ice moving its way slowly down the valley to the right.

"When we drilled our test wells, we found liquid water at half a kilometer below the surface. The ground turned out to be porous enough that we can get a high rate of flow. So, we pump the water up to the top, pipe it over here to the edge of the Suez Cliffs, and send it back down that pipe into the valley. We have turbines at about every kilometer of drop to extract electrical energy from the falling water.

"The water goes from seventy-eight hundred meters elevation at the top of the cliff to eighteen hundred meters elevation at the outflow nozzle, a six-kilometer drop in only eighteen kilometers of pipe. Although we have to invest the energy to pump the water up half a kilometer, and we have some friction losses, we get back more than ten times as much energy as we had to put in. Later on, we hope to extend the drop pipe another twenty-five kilometers to a hole in Ius Canyon that is actually thirty meters below 'sea level,' and extract even more energy."

"What's your power output?" Gus asked.

"If we ran our wells at full output, we could easily generate a hundred megawatts with the present system."

"The energy problems of Mars are solved," Chris said.

"We've still got to get the superconducting DC power grid installed," Gus said. "And we're still going to need antimatter for the hopiters and crawlers."

"Some of our engineers have been discussing antimatter factory designs with Nobel Laureate Batusov, since it would be an ideal way to utilize electrical power that is not needed elsewhere on the planet. He has some novel ideas that would increase the antimatter production rate. The question is, should I have my engineers continue to work on increasing the output of our electrical power system, or should I have them start work on an antimatter factory?"

Gus looked at Chris with a pleased expression.

"Decisions . . . decisions . . ." Chris said with a bemused frown.

CHAPTER 12

THE SHADOW OF HIS WINGS

It took a lot to awe Jerry 5-9753, but he had to admit to himself that he felt a little scared as the military limousine dropped him off at the entrance to the Potomac Palace of the Infinite Lord. He now wished that he had something else to wear than his usual sweat suit outfit. He adjusted his yellow Cap of Contact, which was bringing him a replay of last week's inspiring sermon by Alexander, and jogged solidly up the steps, the patch that signified his two-star military rank jiggling slightly on his plump bottom.

At the top of the steps, two large women of Alexander's new Amazon Bodyguard Corps started to block his way, but some unseen Watcher, monitoring the scene through an array of video cameras, recognized him and let him pass. After walking down a long hall, Jerry came to a large room overlooking the Potomac River flowing by down at the foot of the grassy bluff that the palace stood on.

The Infinite Lord was there in all his glory, looking so wonderful that Jerry wondered how he had ever taken Alexander for granted back when he was on Alexander's Mars campaign. As Jerry had expected, the Regent Di and the head of the armed forces, General "Sam" Samuelson were there, their purple and white Caps of Contact on, but their visors flipped back. There was also another man that Jerry didn't recognize. He didn't wear a Cap of Contact at all.

"Welcome Jerry," Alexander boomed as Jerry walked into the room. "You are looking remarkably well."

"Becoming one of your devoted followers has been the best thing that ever happened to me, your Infinite Lord," Jerry replied, beaming with pride at the praise. "I found friends who loved me and respected me, and soon I finally began to like myself. I've dropped fifty pounds, exercise every day, and now feel better than I ever felt before in my life. I owe it all to you, my Lord."

"I'm glad things are going so well for you personally," Alexander said with a pleased smile. "How are things going with my Strategic Offense Initiative?"

"Very well, sir," Jerry replied. "With all the resources you and General Sam have supplied the SOI office over the past eighteen months, my owlies and metalbenders have made great progress." He held up a nanodisk. "I'm prepared to give you the briefing you requested . . ." He hesitated, looking at the strange man in the white suit without the Cap of Contact. "It's highly classified . . ."

"Don't worry about Rob," Alexander said. "He's okay. He's my right-hand man, you might say."

"All right," Jerry said, looking around for a flatscreen. General Sam went to a wall switch and curtains pulled back from one wall to reveal a floor-to-ceiling flatscreen. Jerry put the nanodisk in the slot, picked up the controller, and stepped back.

"The three major components of the SOI program are: the Winged Eyes of the Lord, to search out evil wherever it can be found; the Nuclear Rapier of the Lord, to make those that live by the nuclear sword die by their own chosen weapon; and the Silver Scythes of the Lord, to cut down those who would still resist the will of the Infinite One." He switched to the next picture; it had obviously been taken from some point on the Moon. It showed the Earth half-lit by the Sun from one side. Hanging over the dark side of the Earth were two bright arcs of points stretching nearly from pole to pole, like two giant silver scythes, one over the evening side and one over the dawn side.

"The Silver Scythes were the easiest, so they are already up and in place. Everyone has seen them drifting across the sky above them at night, but few know yet why we put them up. Each of the points in the arc of a Silver Scythe is a solar sail a few kilometers across.

They are not in orbit around the Earth, but instead hover motionless over the dark side, the downward gravity pull of the Earth being counteracted by the light pressure from the Sun."

Jerry switched to a close-up scene showing a cluster of long rods, each the size of a crowbar, hanging from the central truss structure of a solar sail that stretched on out of sight.

"Hanging from each sail are hundreds of heavy rods made from slag left over from processing the asteroid used for the sail material. Twice a day, at dawn and dusk, nearly every person on Earth passes underneath the Silver Scythes, and if that person is so rash as to incur the wrath of the Infinite Lord, *nothing* can protect him!" One of the rods gave a shiver as its connection was cut, then it started to fall to the earth below.

The image switched to computer animation showing the rod falling through the air, perturbed by random buffeting. Tiny fins in the nose and tail of the rod flicked back and forth under the control of a tiny inertial guidance unit, keeping it on course.

The next scene showed a crude building out in the middle of a test range, cameras and instrumentation all around. The camera dwelt on the thick reinforced concrete ceiling of the building, then zoomed through the open doorway to the figure of a dummy sitting in a chair inside. The dummy wore a rubber Halloween face mask of the present Russian premier, Alexin Gorki. There was an explosion downward from the ceiling. When the concrete dust had cleared, pieces of the dummy were scattered around a deep hole in the floor.

"Our CEP is down to less than one meter," Jerry said proudly.

"And believe it or not," General Sam joked, "our CIA boys say they have the toilets in the Kremlin pinpointed to the centimeter."

Alexander laughed loudly at that one and took a long time to recover.

Jerry was waiting with the next scene when Alexander had finished laughing. This showed another structure in space, a fat rectangle made up of millions of tiny components in a regular array. "The Winged Eyes of the Lord was also relatively easy, since we only need three to observe any point on Earth, and it was just a matter of adding a floater to existing facilities at geosynch. The only trick was making all the software play—I got to write some of this code myself." He switched from the picture to a diagram.

"It's basically simple optics. If you are a long way away from something, like thirty-six thousand kilometers away from the surface of the Earth out at GEO, and you want to see something small, like the half-millimeter dot at the end of a sentence on a piece of paper, then you need an eye that is one hundred kilometers across."

"You must have used some of your owlie magic to build that one," Alexander interrupted. "You certainly didn't cast a hundred kilometer diameter telescope lens."

"You're right, sir," Jerry said. "Instead of combining the light in phase using a lens, then detecting it, the Winged Eye of the Lord has millions of photodetectors that detect the light first, keeping the phase information, then combine it using the computer equivalent of a lens. The result is the same, except the computer version of a lens can also compensate for atmospheric distortion and any vibrations and motion of the Eye itself. With your permission, sir, I'd like to give a live demonstration."

"Sure!" Alexander said, pleased. Jerry tapped the control buttons on the side of his Cap of Contact.

"Break Potomac region block and commence with zoom," he ordered. He took out his leather-bound, real paper, gold-leaf-edged pocket Bible of the Church of the Unifier that he had bought from an advertisement on the church video channel—guaranteed to have been blessed by the Infinite Lord himself. He opened it to the Prime Principle and walked over near the window. On the flatscreen a picture of the full Earth in sunlight appeared, growing larger as the computer in the Winged Eye of the Lord stationed over the Americas zoomed in on the East Coast of the Unified States.

"There's Washington, D.C.," Jerry said as the zoom continued. "I've removed the block that prevents anyone from imaging in the area around the Potomac Palace. There's the palace now . . . and now the window . . . Hi, there!" He waved out the window with one hand, still holding the Bible with the other; and in the image on the flatscreen a figure inside the window waved a quarter of a second later. The zoom continued in until it focused on the opened page of the Bible.

"For the Infinite Lord to absolve you of sin, you first must have sinned," it read.

"Do you mean that thing can peek in my window any time day or night!" Alexander exploded, his face red with rage.

Jerry, having been pleased with himself, now realized that the live demonstration was about to turn into a disaster. He quickly flicked the flatscreen blank.

"Oh! *No!* Sir!" he assured him. "I have set the Eye up with strict blocks on viewing *any* of your residences."

"You'd better," Alexander grumbled, still angry.

"I assure you, sir!" Jerry said, quickly manipulating the screen controls. "Now, let me show you some other scenes that the Watchers have collected in the past few weeks.

"This is the Fifth Red Army tank battalion on maneuvers in the occupied portion of Latvia.

"This is the right shoulder of General Kalensky, head of the Russian Air Force, holding a classified document. Those large red letters at the top mean 'top secret' in Russian."

The general turned the page, then picked his nose. Alexander laughed.

The next picture showed a man in bedouin garb furtively pouring himself a drink of scotch whisky, then hiding the bottle in a hidden compartment of a cabinet. "This is the most influential and most righteous Muslim in all of the Arab world. He must have picked up some bad habits at Cambridge. If this picture got out, he would be lucky to escape with only a loss of all his influence."

"The man has good taste," Rob said. "That was Old Pulteney."

"This last one is in multispectral infrared," Jerry said. "Even the darkness of night is as daylight to the Winged Eyes of the Infinite Lord."

"Oh!" Di exclaimed when she finally realized what she was seeing. "Look at the fucker hump!"

"Who is it?" Alexander asked, eyes fixed on the titillating infra-red scene.

"The prime minister of Australia," Jerry replied. "And the young lady is not his wife."

Alexander continued to watch with interest until the scene faded. "There is a lot we could do with that," Alexander finally said. "All it takes is for the people to lose faith in their leadership, and they will turn to someone stronger."

"Now for the third element in the Unified States Strategic Offense Initiative—the Nuclear Rapier," Jerry said.

"Yes!" Alexander said, sitting back. "How do we keep the Russkies from blowing us all to hell with their damn atomic bombs? Until we can solve that problem, we can't do anything to stop the evil tide of neocommunism."

"We just had our first tests of a full-up operational system last week, and it exceeded our expectations," Jerry said. "We have always known that a neutrino telescope could spot the position of a nuclear warhead or nuclear reactor with great accuracy. That is one of the reasons that the nuclear stalemate with the new Soviet Union has been so stable: We both know where each other's bombs and nuclear submarines are at all times. But until now, it has not been possible to reach those weapons and destroy them. They are too protected by distance and hardening. The Nuclear Rapier will solve that problem."

"Great!" Alexander said, beaming. "We'll blow the bastards off the face of the Earth."

"Actually," General Sam injected, "they'll blow themselves off the face of the Earth. The beauty of the Nuclear Rapier is that it only works on those nations that have nuclear weapons. It turns the weapons on those that brandish them."

"The explanation of how the Nuclear Rapier works is a little complicated," Jerry said, "so I had my CAD scribblers make some animated diagrams." He showed the first picture. It was an ordinary nuclear power reactor. Little white animated balls bounced randomly around inside the reactor.

"Nuclear reactors work by using neutrons. A uranium atom in

the reactor emits a neutron, it bounces around for a while until it slows down, then it gets absorbed by another uranium atom, which fissions and makes three neutrons. They bounce around for a while until they slow down, then they fission three uranium atoms. Each fission releases three new neutrons, for a total of nine, and the chain reaction builds up. If there are no controls, it builds up fast and you have a bomb. If there are proper controls, it only builds up until the reactor is hot, and you can get power from it.

"The main thing to remember is that slow neutrons cause uranium to fission. If you had a gun that shot neutrons, you could shoot a flood of neutrons at a subcritical assembly of uranium or plutonium and make it explode. Unfortunately . . ." He switched to another diagram showing a white ball representing a neutron sitting next to a ticking clock. The clock rapidly ticked off the minutes, and when it reached eleven, the white neutron split into a fat red particle, a small blue particle, and a fast-moving wavy line.

"The neutron has a half-life of only eleven minutes. It then decays into a proton, an electron, and a neutrino—which is why we can spot bombs with a neutrino telescope. They are always giving off a few neutrinos, even when subcritical. Now, it's possible to build bottles that will hold ultraslow neutrons without loss—the Russians have been making such bottles for years—"

"They aren't working on a Nuclear Rapier, are they?" Alexander asked, concerned.

"No," General Sam assured. "I have a special group constantly monitoring their activities in that area. They haven't hit upon what our owlies have.

"So, although you can bottle neutrons, they decay away before you can use them." He switched to the next animated diagram. It showed four white balls orbiting around one another. Each ball was also spinning about its axis and had an arrow coming out of the top. The four arrows pointed in the same direction. Vertically through the image flowed rippling blue lines.

"Then, one of our particle pushers at Los Alamos National Lab was playing with a new ultrahigh-magnetic-field solenoid made from the new hot superconductors . . ."

"Like we used in the antimatter rockets on the *Yorktown?*" Alexander asked.

"Exactly," Jerry said. "In fact, this discovery was made back in '38, before we were Unified. It was brought to my attention when I set up the SOI office and asked for new ideas. Los Alamos had done a lot of the background engineering. All my SOI office had to do was grab it and run with it.

"Anyway, he had put a bottle of ultraslow neutrons in a high magnetic field to see if he could produce a bottle of polarized neutrons, with their magnetic spins all oriented in the same direction. It would be useful as a target in some types of particle experiments. To his amazement, when the end of the day came and he turned off the superconducting magnet, there was a crackle of radiation from the bottle, which he had last filled with neutrons four hours ago. He had made the first spin-polarized tetraneutrons. Unlike single neutrons, they are stable."

"Spin-polarized tetraneutrons?" Di asked, trying to get it straight. "What the shit does all that gobbledygook stand for?"

"The scientific name isn't important," Jerry said. "It's just four neutrons bound together in an excited state. It takes a very strong magnetic field just to form them, that's why they were never observed before. Once they are formed, however, they are quite stable. Since they have all their spins pointed in the same direction, they are also magnetized. So you can use magnetic fields to pipe them from one point to another, shoot them out of guns, and store them in bottles. We have almost a hundred kilograms of liquid tetraneutrons in orbit now in the three orbital forts equipped with neutrino telescopes and the Nuclear Rapier." He switched the flatscreen to an image of a standard orbital fort, with its long particle-beam weapon, laser mirrors, and racks of defensive and offensive hit-to-kill kinetic energy weapons. The image zoomed to a short barrel made of loops of wire on a swivel mount.

"Is that it?" Alexander asked, not very impressed.

"With the new high-magnetic-field hot superconductors, you don't need much length to get the tetraneutrons up to speed," Jerry said. "Makes the gun easier to repoint for the next target, too. Let me show you some of the test results."

The next image was back at a test site out in the desert. A missile tipped with a nuclear warhead was lowered into a deep hardened silo and the thick concrete lid lowered into place. An array of boxes with lights were placed on posts all around the site.

"Those are battery-powered neutron detectors with lights, so you can see the neutrons when they hit," Jerry said. "Otherwise, you wouldn't see anything happening."

Suddenly a large patch of the lights lit up, the center of the patch slightly to one side of the heavy silo door. The next instant the heavy slab of concrete was flying into the air, and the glowing hell of nuclear fire was rising from the depths of the silo.

"The tetraneutrons stop in the first few meters of soil, but then continue to bounce around and penetrate further until they are absorbed by the uranium in the weapon or an occasional rare isotope in the dirt. That test took only ten milligrams of tetraneutrons. If we were trying to get a submarine a few hundred feet down, we would keep the beam on longer and flood the area with a few grams."

"Milligrams? Grams?" Alexander said. "Didn't you say you had hundreds of kilograms of those tetraneutrons in orbit?"

"Why, yes . . ." Jerry admitted. "We thought it would take a lot more particles to make a kill, so we collected plenty for our test plan."

"Forget the test plan," Alexander said. He turned to General Sam. "How many nuclear missiles do the Russians have?"

Sam raised his eyebrows, reached under the front of his Cap of Contact to scratch his bald head, and replied carefully, "Two thousand four hundred and sixty-eight missiles that can reach the Unified States directly. Another one thousand sixteen aimed at other countries, and twenty-four submarines, each with twelve to eighteen missiles. The submarines are being phased out, now that everyone has neutrino telescopes and knows where they are."

"Less than four thousand targets," Alexander said. "You could throw a gram at every one and still have tetraneutrons left over."

"Yes," General Sam admitted.

"Do it," Alexander said firmly.

"Sir?" General Sam replied, taken aback.

"Now!" Alexander shouted, jumping to his feet. "The minute the next orbital fort with a Nuclear Rapier passes over Russia, I want it to start firing, and keep on firing until every single one of their missiles has blown up in their neocommie pinko faces!"

"Oh, my God!" Rob muttered into his hands.

"Yes, my Infinite Lord," General Sam said, flipping his viewer in front of his left eye. He paused with his fingers on the control pad of his Cap of Contact, then turned to Alexander. "May I wait until we have *two* orbital forts within firing range?"

"If it would make you feel more comfortable," Alexander said calmly and agreeably, his recent passion over. He walked over to a cabinet and, getting out a bottle, poured himself a drink. Rob got quickly to his feet and poured himself one, too.

"But I haven't finished the testing program yet," Jerry objected. "What if we don't get them all, and they start launching missiles at us? Whole cities would be destroyed."

"I'll just launch our missiles back at them," Alexander said, unconcerned. "We'll come out ahead in the end, because they don't have the Nuclear Rapier, and I do." He smiled and came over to pat Jerry on the shoulder. "Thanks to you and your fine bunch of owlies. You have served your Infinite Lord well, Jerry."

Hearing these words of praise from his master sent Jerry's spirit soaring. He was loved, he was wanted, he was appreciated. He would do anything for this man.

"Stations Alpha and Charlie will be in good position in about ten minutes," General Sam reported.

"We're in luck!" Alexander said, pleased.

"If you don't mind, I'd like to go down the hall to the office and switch over to a data console with a high-res screen and a faster data rate," General Sam said. "I need to put our boys on alert. In the meantime, perhaps Jerry can arrange a real-time link from the Winged Eyes and you can watch the show."

"Great idea!" Jerry said. He activated his Cap of Contact, and in a few minutes the large flatscreen had a number of views on it. One was of a stretch of open ocean off the icy coast of Greenland. The peaceful floes suddenly bulged upward in a roil of radioactive water.

"Got the bastards!" Di yelled, clapping her hands and bouncing in her seat.

Rob stared at the smug, self-satisfied look on Alexander's face as the Infinite Lord watched a field full of Russian missile silos blowing open one after another in rapid succession. He shook his head and buried his face again in his pudgy gold-ringed fingers.

"Oh, my God . . ." was all he could say.

It was all over in twenty minutes, the time it takes for a space fort to orbit from Minsk to Petropavlovsk. The Russians had managed to get three missiles away, but they were stopped in midflight by the standard laser and particle beam defenses of the decades-old orbital forts.

Alexander was enjoying another drink. Rob wasn't enjoying his.

"Tell them they have one hour to surrender," Alexander said to Sam when Sam returned from the office after the engagement was over. "The terms are unconditional surrender, complete disarmament, disbanding of their armed forces, and incorporation into the Unified States."

"I don't think Gorki is going to accept all that without argument," Sam said. "He knows as long as he tells his troops not to shoot at us, we won't use our nuclear warheads."

"What do you mean?" Alexander blustered. "If he doesn't agree, I'll blast his whole damn country off the Earth!" He paced back and forth a little. "No." He shook his head. "Can't do that . . . would look bad in the newspapers." He turned suddenly to Di.

"Get him on direct video contact, with Eric's translator program operating, and start negotiating with him," Alexander said. "But have the CIA boys figure out where he is and pass the coordinates along to Jerry. If he gets hard-nosed, he can expect a visit from the Silver Scythes. Keep working your way down the chain of command until you find someone who will agree to unification.

You can promise him he can be my regent and run things pretty much as he did before, but that damn neocommunism has got to go, and they have to become unified with the rest of my people."

"I'll have the State Department set up the link right away," Di said, flipping the viewer of her Cap of Contact in front of her left eye and starting to finger the control pad on the ear flap.

"But Alex," Rob objected. "The Church of the Unifier is just a gimmick. You're taking it too seriously."

Alexander stopped abruptly. He turned around slowly. "The Infinite Lord, Unifier of All, is always serious," he said. He stared at Rob, steel-gray eyes slitting, the deadly arrows forming.

"Do you understand?" he asked menacingly.

"I understand!" Rob agreed, acquiescing.

"Good," Alexander said, brightening the mood with a broad smile. "You have been very helpful to me, Rob. I would hate to lose you."

Somehow, Rob didn't feel comforted by those last words.

With Di and Sam busy talking over their cap comm links, Alexander paced up and down the room, musing to himself. "Once I have the Russkies saved from neocommunism, then I should start working on the rest of the world. That's going to be a little tougher. Can't just go marching in with armies. Doesn't look good in the history books." He then remembered the infrared pictures of the prime minister of Australia; that was some broad he was humping. Maybe the prime minister would prefer the job of being the regent of Australia instead of having no job at all . . . It was blackmail; but then, political blackmail was just another form of diplomacy . . . He stopped pacing.

"Jerry," he said, putting his arm around the shoulders of the eager young man.

"Yes, Infinite Lord?" Jerry replied, basking in the warm friendship.

"I'd like you to assemble a large stable of Watchers. Have them keep a careful eye on all the influential people around the world. Whenever you catch them doing something they shouldn't, make a careful record of it."

"Like the Arab and the Australian prime minister? No problem. In fact, most of the Watchers I've been using seem to be very good at catching that kind of stuff . . . Second nature, I guess."

"Give the information to Rob," Alexander said. "He'll make sure it gets to the senior people in the Church of the Unifier in that country. Then they can see that these improper leaders are replaced with good ones who are properly respectful of the Infinite Lord and his desire to unify all the world into one great family."

"That will be a wonderful day," Jerry said, beaming. "I will do all in my power to hasten it."

CHAPTER 13

FOUND UNINTERESTING

The crawler humped itself over the peak of the frost-covered reddish-brown dune, its articulated frame twisting as the engineering and living sections started to follow the cockpit section down the other side. A red warning light flashed on the control console.

"Damn!" the driver said.

"What's the matter?" the copilot asked.

"The right center wheel motor is running hot," the driver said, bringing the crawler to a halt.

"I'll suit up and check it," the other said, getting up.

A mop of stringy, orange-red hair turned around in the engineering section above.

"What are we stopping for, Pete?" Red Storm asked.

"Must be another damn missile fiber wrapped around the hub," the tech said, putting on his helmet. "I'm going out to untangle it."

"Oh . . ." Red turned back to continue planning the next day's survey with Viktor.

The tech was cycling the inner airlock when Red's head swiveled back around. The wide blue-green eyes had a questioning—almost eager—look, as if they were on to something important.

"According to Viktor's map," Red said, "we're almost a hundred eighty degrees around the polar ice cap from Boreal Base. It's over fifteen hundred kilometers as the crow flies—or the missile flies, in this case. I don't know much about missiles, but I doubt they would have that much fiber in them." She reached for her helmet on the rack. "I'm coming with you to take a look."

Red stuck her helmet on her head with a practiced twist and crowded into the airlock with the tech. The outer airlock door was almost opposite to the right center wheel, and sure enough, there was a glittering nest of fine fiber wrapped around the hub. Red reached for a loose strand.

"Careful, Miss Storm," the tech said. "That stuff is tough. You could slice a gash in your glove. Here, let me show you how to break it."

He laid a strand across his forefinger, held it down with his thumb, made a large loop in the fiber, and slipped the free end between his thumb and forefinger so that it overlay the beginning of the loop. Then he pulled on the fiber, making the loop tighter and tighter, being careful not to let the loop slip over his pinched thumb and finger. The loop finally became so small it disappeared under his thumb. Suddenly the fiber snapped and he was left holding the two ends.

"Fibers can't take a small radius of curvature," said the tech, handing one end to her.

Red let the tech work away at untangling the mess while she broke off a short piece to look at. It was clear and uncoated. Acting on a hunch, she raised an end up to her Diamondhard faceplate, just above the neck fixture, and rubbed it hard. She peered down and her eyes widened.

"Coming in!" Red called, cycling the lock and leaving the tech outside. She was soon seated at the science console in the engineering section, looking through a microscope and busy with some liquids. By the time she was finished, Viktor had gotten up from the flatscreen plotting table and was standing beside her on the tilted floor. She turned around and, using the technique the tech had taught her, snapped off a ten-centimeter length of the fiber and handed it to Viktor.

"Have a diamond," she said with a pleased smile, blue-green eyes sparkling.

"A diamond!" Viktor exclaimed, looking with surprise at the glassy thread.

"Crystal diamond on the outside and glassy diamond on the

inside—just like the eyerods on those Lineup critters," Red said. "I
read all about it in volume three of a nanodisk series edited by one
Viktor K. Braginsky. It was in a paper called 'The Optical Properties of Lineup Fanrods.' I forgot the author's name, but I didn't
forget his techniques for measuring the density and index of refrac-
tion. It's diamond all right. It even scratched my Diamondhard faceplate."

"A very strange diamond," Viktor said, looking at the fine
thread. "Not very large . . ." he said dubiously.

"What you have is small," Red agreed. "But while I was measuring I was calculating. That fiber is about ten microns in diameter,
not much per meter, but that comes to two carats per kilometer!
And there may be thousands of kilometers of the stuff lying around.
And as for it being strange, why that just jacks up the price. You'd
be surprised at what people will pay for oddities."

"That sounds wonderful!" Viktor said in a pleased tone.

"Wonderful for me. Not so wonderful for you."

"Not so . . ." Viktor said, a little bewildered.

"You're out of a job," Red said in a matter-of-fact tone, but
biting her lower lip as she did so. "You'll have to go back to being
a scientist at practically nothing a day."

"I guess you are right," Viktor said with a shrug. "But it was
fun while it lasted. I will miss being around you, Red."

"Don't give me that malarkey," Red replied with a wave of her
hand. "What you'll miss is the caviar and vodka."

"That, too," Viktor agreed with a nod.

Red slid open the partition to the crew quarters.

"Hey, Charlie!" she yelled. A muffled "What?" came from one
of the insulated sleeping bunks.

"Rise and shine," Red hollered. "We've got to make some mods
to a wheel and we'll need everybody. Get a move on. The sooner
we get it done, the sooner you get back to the sack."

A few hours later the crawler was moving off over the sand
dunes again, only now, instead of following a previously determined
course, they followed the lead of a thread of diamond fiber that

glistened in the glare of a floodlight beam as it was lifted from the sand by a hook stuck out ahead of the crawler on a long, jury-rigged pole.

The fiber was directed by wire loop guides around the body of the crawler, there to be wound around the right center wheel, which had been converted into a take-up reel. The wheel suspension system had been adjusted to keep the wheel clear of the ground, its load-bearing task now shared by the other two wheels on that side, and the speed of its independent electric motor was varied to keep the fiber taut.

The fiber took them north—toward the North Pole.

"We're coming up to an ice canyon," the driver said after a number of hours.

Red was up in the hemispherical dome in the top of the engineering section, watching the huge spool of fiber grow thicker. They had collected over a hundred kilometers worth already—and only one break where the fiber had been buried under a large dune. Fortunately, it had been easy to pick it up again on the other side.

"What's our coordinates?" she asked, jumping down.

"Eighty-five north and one hundred eighty-five west," the driver said.

"Keep on going," Red said.

"I'm having to take it slow, since the fiber is buried under a lot of snow," the driver said. "Fortunately it's strong and cuts its way out if I don't hurry it."

Red brought up the map on the large high-res flatscreen in the plotting table and located their position. They were entering a complex of canyons that started from the edge of the polar cap and spiraled in around the North Pole. One canyon was over six hundred kilometers long.

"Good thing it's just past summer solstice," Red said. "We can work twenty-four hours a day."

"I bet the Simon Legree in you really chortles over the extra forty minutes a day you get out of your slaves," the driver said.

"Well-paid slaves," Red retorted. "I didn't have to give you a supplement when I rented your services from Base Ops. If you're not happy with the arrangement—"

"Oh, we's happy slaves, Miss Red Legree," the driver joked, turning and tugging at his imaginary fetlock. "Please don't sell us down the river to Base Ops. They don't have truffles in their pâté de foie gras."

"Pole bending," the copilot warned, reaching for the speed control and slowing the crawler down. The pilot jerked his attention back, the pole lifted as the fiber worked its way up through the snowdrift, and they continued slowly on.

"Only two degrees from the pole," Viktor said, watching the red line that showed their course on the plotting table as it moved slowly along the spiral canyon. Red was still up in the central observation dome watching the spooling of the precious fiber.

"The fiber seems to be taking us toward the inner wall," the driver said from up front. "There's an overhang. Shall I follow it under?"

"Hold up," Red said, jumping down. The copilot moved back to a jump seat and she took his place to peer out the window. The Sun was low and around at the wrong angle, so the cliff face was in dark shadow despite the reflection from the snow. She turned on a floodlight and scanned the beam over the underside of the overhanging cliff face. It was ancient polar cap material, dark with the dust layers left behind as the ice had slowly sublimed away over the aeons. As Red swept the floodlight beam across the base of the cliff there was a momentary reflection. She went back and stopped the beam. There was a bright reflection, as if from a mirror.

"A door!" she exclaimed. "A crystal-clear circular door set in a crystal-clear frame . . ." Her blue-green eyes widened and stared intensely out the cockpit window. "Ten to one it's solid *diamond*!" she whispered.

"Whe-e-e-w," the driver whistled, staring at the unbelievable sight in front of him.

"Move on in," Red instructed him. "Slowly . . ."

The crawler moved slowly forward, the thread of fiber leading them directly to the door in the base of the cliff. By the time the driver had brought the crawler to a halt, Red and Viktor had suited up and were out the airlock, walking along under the body of the crawler.

The door was a circle about sixty centimeters in diameter set low to the ground. They went carefully up to the door, hunkered down on their heels, and peered in. The door was set in a clear frame not quite a meter wide and a meter high, with a flat bottom and an arched top. Around the center of the circular door were six indentations. On the other side were six more indentations, offset by thirty degrees. Red had come prepared with a diamond ring she had dug out from her personal baggage and she scratched the large diamond hard across the face of the frame.

"Not a scratch," Red said, examining where she had scribed the point of the hard gem. "*Got* to be diamond."

They looked inside with the flashlight. A meter and a half away was another frame with another circular door. Between the two doors was a small room with a flat floor and arched roof that followed the contour of the outside frame.

"Obviously an airlock," Red said. "What's beyond that?"

"It's hard to see," Viktor said, waving the light beam from his flashlight around. "But it looks like a long tunnel, the same cross section as the airlock."

"Let's go in," Red said eagerly, putting her fingers into the six holes around the center of the circular hatch door. The holes were slightly smaller than her gloved fingers, but fingertips were all that were needed. The door started to rotate.

"Stop!" Viktor said, grabbing her arm.

"Whatdaya mean, stop!" Red shouted, angrily slapping his arm away. "This is my find and I can do what I damn please with it."

Viktor forced his way between Red and the hatch door, his back covering the finger holes.

"This belongs to the human race first," he said firmly. She glared at him. "Then you second," he reassured her. "Just give me time to get some equipment and cameras here to make measurements and document everything while we open it up. Once we have the information, you can have the artifacts."

"Okay! Okay!" Red said in frustration. "That's what my fossil hunting license says anyway." She patted the nearly meter square frame of centimeter thick diamond. "With building stones like this, I won't even need artifacts." She got up from her crouch and shook her cramped legs. "I'll call the director of the Sagan Institute and let him know of our find."

"Go ahead," Viktor said. "I'll use my suit laser range finder to see how far back the tunnel goes." He fired the laser down the tunnel a number of times in slightly different directions, trying to make sense of the multiple returns.

"I'll have to make a computer model," he finally decided. He got up from his seat in the snow, brushed off the seat of his Marsuit, and trudged back to the crawler.

"Signaling/strange/from outside. Replying."

No one saw the short answering flash of blue laser light that shot out the transparent doorway and momentarily illuminated the snow outside.

"Signaling/strange/from outside/stop."

The base had been called, the experts were on their way, and there was now nothing to do but wait. Red was exhilarated by her find and was tingling all over. She began to look at Viktor as a man rather than as an employee. He was kind of small and thin, but it had been a long time since she had let herself relax in the arms of a man. The champagne they had shared with the techs had loosened both of them up, and now they were alone in the back, sipping vodka and nibbling on Bremner Wafers piled high with caviar.

"This is very good, Red," Viktor said, beaming.

"I'm glad you like it, Viktor," Red replied, sitting next to him.

"Y'know, I'm going to miss you." She patted him on the shoulder and then left her arm there.

"I'm going to miss you, too," he said, putting an arm around her waist and giving her a hug. She relaxed against him and turned her head. Their lips came close together. Suddenly she pulled back a little.

"Say . . . you aren't married are you?" asked Red.

"Well, yes," Viktor admitted. "She's a physicist at Novosibirsk." He tried to pull her close again, then added, "But she doesn't understand me!"

Red put on a grim smile. That was the line her ex-husband had always used to use on the other women he seduced. The resultant divorce had hurt her so badly she had dropped out of her chief pilot's job at Lunar Spaceways in midcareer and had become another bum netting rocks in the belt. Fortunately, she had been lucky and ended up rich instead of dead, but she had sworn she would never hurt another woman like her husband's girlfriends had hurt her. She put both arms around Viktor, gave him a solid kiss, then disentangled herself.

"That's your reward for being honest," she said. "But that's all you get." She got up and headed for a bunk.

"It's going to be busy once those scientist-types get here, so let's get some shut-eye—in separate bunks."

By the time Red and Viktor had finished their short vigil of self-enforced fitful catnaps, there were three hopiters landed at varying safe distances away down the canyon and three dozen excited specialists trudging through the snow carrying their instruments. Chris was there with his atmospheric composition analyzer, Max with a portable version of his materials composition analyzer, and Tanya with her medical bag in case they found another Lineup. Gus had just pulled rank. Another volcanic specialist was not needed, but he was not about to be left out of the find of the century. All the explorers wore surplus battle helmets fitted with helmeyes that would not only allow them to see in the darkness of a tunnel, but were modified to record everything they saw on nanodisk.

"Your guess was right, Red," Max MacFadden said as he lifted his portable pulsed laser materials analyzer from the face of the frame surrounding the circular hatch door. "Nothing but carbon—must be pure diamond." He looked closer at the readout. "With maybe a tiny bit of nitrogen added for strength." He used the analyzer to check the hatch door. "That's diamond, too."

"Look down here," Gus said, bending down and brushing away the snow. In one corner of the frame were four fibers of glasslike material. One of the fibers turned out to be the one Red had been reeling up. The others went off under the snow, one down the canyon and two up the canyon.

"You can have those," Red said, patting the door frame. "I'll take this."

"I can't really tell, but it looks like there's an optical coupler built into the frame," a tech said after examining Gus' find. "There's four other fibers on the other side. But there are no connectors. They look as if they had been butt-welded to the frame."

"Anybody want to do anything else before we open the first door?" Chris asked. Nobody answered, so he taped a plastic bag around the circular hatch door and the nozzle of his analyzer, used the analyzer to suck the residual Martian atmosphere out of the bag, and started to turn the door through the collapsed plastic material. Suddenly the bag started to inflate.

"High pressure!" Chris said, quickly twirling the hatch door shut again. He read his display.

"Nitrogen sixty percent, argon six percent, oxygen fifteen percent, carbon dioxide fourteen percent, methane three percent, other junk two percent. You could breath it, but not for long. The carbon dioxide level is toxic. Wonder what the pressure is?"

He turned the door open again while he monitored the pressure indicator on his analyzer. The bag ballooned up and the tape gave way.

"It got to 620 millibars," he said. After six turns, the door unscrewed and fell outward. He climbed in. "Only room for one at a time," he said, picking up the door and screwing it back in place with the six offset holes in that side of the circular plate. He made a tare measurement of the Martian atmosphere trapped in the air-lock with him, then opened the inner circular hatch. It rotated as easily as the first one.

"Basically the same composition as the first one, but some water vapor this time. Total pressure is 690 millibars," Chris reported. "Shall I go on, or let someone else go first? We can change places by crawling over each other, but it's basically single file on hands and knees, unless you are good at the frog walk."

"The next obstruction is 122 meters in and slightly upward," Viktor said.

"How's your air supply?" Gus asked.

"Fresh tanks," Chris assured.

"Let's cycle Max and his laser analyzer through," Gus said. "He can take a few hundred meters of rope in with him and feed it out to you. Hook your helmeyes video output to the optical fiber in the rope so we can monitor your progress. If you find another crystal airlock like this one at the other end, you can analyze what's on the other side. If you find anything else, come back and let Max measure its composition before we proceed further."

Chris screwed the hatch door closed and Max cycled through. Then Chris crawled off into the dark tunnel, his flashlight getting fainter and fainter in the distance. Gus found the channel where Chris' helmeyes output was being broadcast from Max's suit, and pulled down the visor in his helmet to watch along with Chris.

"It's getting lighter," Chris said. Gus could see an illuminated door ahead through Chris' helmeyes.

"Looks like another airlock," Gus said.

Chris crawled to the door, his head-down position leaving the vicarious viewers only a view of dusty diamond floor moving downward across their visors. He reached the door and sat down in front of it, looking out.

"Well, I'll be a monkey's uncle," Chris said, holding his head still for the benefit of his coviewers. "Lookit that . . ."

"A live Lineup!" Tanya said as a six-segmented creature undulated past in the distance, its twenty-four legs working much like that of a caterpillar. The gray portions of the Lineup were much darker in color than the one found in the snow, and the zebralike black-and-white striped middle section on each segment seemed more complex. The eyerods were the most fascinating part of the creature, however. Instead of sticking stiffly out in a fan, as many of the computer reconstructions had shown them, the rods at the rear and front opened and shut like a sea anemone, while those between segments waved back and forth in a coordinated pattern that spiraled around the body.

A five-segment Lineup passed by off in the distance and disappeared behind some plants.

"The middle segments don't seem to have those black wings," Tanya remarked.

"Let me get closer," Chris said. "I can't see the whole room from way back here behind this airlock."

"Wait!" Gus said, but it was too late. The hatch door was soon unscrewed and Chris crawled into the airlock. He leaned forward until his helmeyes were pressed up against the last transparent door and scanned his viewer around the room.

"It's a huge room," Chris said. "All full of beds of different kinds of plants, most of them dark gray or black, but some have a reddish or purplish tinge. The Lineups seem to be tending them." As they watched, the six-segment Lineup raised its first four segments four meters up in the air—twice as tall as a man—while balancing on its eight hind feet. Its front fan of eyerods clustered into six bunches pointed at the end of its elephantlike snout, while the prehensile fingerlike structures on the end of the snout carefully trimmed some ragged-looking dead white fronds from a tall fernlike plant that nearly reached the arched ceiling some five meters overhead. To get at the tallest of the dead fronds, the Lineup had to pull the top of the plant downward using the tender touch of six interleaved claws around the stem, three on each side. It ate everything it cleaned off the plant, then dropped down to loosen the soil at the base of the plant with its clawed paws.

Chris tilted his head to scan along the ceiling. An upside-down spray of bent hexagonal rods with bright light emanating from the ends came into view.

"Those must be light ducts coming down from the surface above," someone said.

"Probably made of solid diamond," Red said. "Why did we have to find the place inhabited! The whole place—walls and ceiling, too—must be made of solid diamond slabs. How big is that room anyway?"

"Let me take some measurements," Chris said. He activated the laser ranger built into his helmet and shot it at the far wall.

"Signaling/strange/from outside."

The six-segment Lineup bunched a number of its midsection eye-rods together and sent a bright flash of blue light in Chris' direction.

"Replying."

A sudden cacophony sounded in Chris' helmet as if he were listening to a hundred shortwave channels at the same time.

"What was that?" Gus asked.

"I think its the Lineup equivalent of 'Hello,' " Chris said. "It must have splashed over into the emergency channel on the optical link option to my helmeyes system. Let's see . . . How do I reconfigure my laser range finder into a laser communicator?"

"Hello," Chris said, flooding the not-too-distant Lineup with a modulated beam of low-level laser light from his helmet-mounted laser. He hoped the Lineup would take the hint and lower the intensity level of its reply. As a precaution, however, he darkened his visor and lowered the volume on his helmet audio system. To make sure he heard any reply, however, he opened all the optical channels of the helmeyes comm system.

"Signaling/strange/from outside. Replying."

There was another bright blue flash and again the helmet was filled with a multitude of teletype sounds, but at the end came a distinct "Hello."

"Investigating."

"One word down, a few hundred thousand to go," Chris said over his fiber link back outside. "Now what?"

"Look at that!" exclaimed someone watching the view through Chris' helmeyes. "The blooming bug is coming apart!"

"One of the segments is detaching itself," Tanya said.

The foremost section of the six-segment Lineup pulled free from the remaining five, revealing a snout identical to the one on the first segment. The remaining five-part creature continued on the task of tending the plants while the single segment came over to the airlock where Chris sat.

"I was wondering how such long creatures were able to use these airlocks," Gus said. "Now I see. They just go through one segment at a time."

"I think I'd better get out of here," Chris said, climbing through the airlock back into the tunnel and screwing the door closed. "I don't like the looks of those claws."

The single Lineup stopped at the door and made no attempt to open the hatch. Chris felt better and stayed where he was. The Lineup pointed his forward fan of eyerods at Chris and started scanning them over his body. After a few scans they started to give off a bright ultraviolet that changed to blue, then green, then yellow . . .

"You're a specimen being laser analyzed for composition content," Max said, watching the performance of the Lineup through Chris' helmeyes. Show him your joints and hold up your equipment. Make his job easier."

Chris waved his fingers "hello" at the Lineup, crawled a little way down the tunnel, then back again, held up his analyzer, pulled his visor up and down, turned on his flashlight and waved it around.

"Consisting/of hydrocarbons/with artifacts/manufactured/this creature. Concluding/organism/living/intelligent."

"Commanding/communicate/maximum."

The Lineup then proceeded to do something down at the left corner of the airlock frame at the same time it flooded Chris' helmeyes with a hundred multicolored beams of laser light.

"Turn it off!" Chris yelled, lowering his helmet volume to a relieving silence.

"Hey!" came a voice over the common suit channel. "The coil of diamond fiber on the crawler is all lit up!"

Gus looked around. The Sun was behind the cliff, and in the shadow, the coil of fiber was glowing with multicolor flashing laser light leaking out due to the curvature in the optical guide.

"They're trying to communicate with us," Gus yelled. He ran to the crawler. "Where's the end?" he asked.

"I'll make you one," said a tech standing there. He quickly grabbed a loose strand of bright fiber and looped it expertly between his thumb and forefinger. Suddenly a large segment of the coil went dark. He handed the still-glowing end to Gus, who put it up to the laser unit on his forehead.

"Hello?" he said.

"Hello . . ." the voice from the fiber repeated. It was an almost perfect rendition of his voice.

"Communicating."

"Here," Gus said, holding the fiber up to the laser unit on the tech's helmet. "Say something to it until I get inside and raise the computer gang at the institute. We need to get that Lineup talking with our neural net computer with a language learning interconnection program set up in it."

"What'll I say?" the tech asked, bewildered.

"Sing to it," Gus suggested. "But while you do, climb to the top of the crawler until you can stick the end of the fiber into our optical comm link. Hold it there until someone relieves you with a piece of tape."

"What shall I sing?" the tech asked, starting to climb the ladder up the side of the crawler, while holding the glowing fiber to his forehead laser unit with one hand.

"Anything!" Gus said out the closing airlock door.

"Oh-h-h," the tech started, "Mamie minded Mama till one day in Singapore . . ."

Within less than an hour, the instructional link had been set up. Gus thought things were going well—but obviously the Lineup didn't think so.

"Needing/cogitation/increase."

"Something is happening," Chris said from where he had been watching the nearly motionless single Lineup crouched beside the airlock door, one of its lower eyerods hooked over a fiber that passed through the frame. "The five other segments are coming over here. I'll be! They just plugged back into the single Lineup like pop beads."

"What happened out there?" came a voice over the common suit link. "Our neural net computer is now reporting a huge jump in learning speed for the Lineup."

"Get ready for more jumps," Chris said. "Here comes a seven-segmenter and two more fives."

The language lessons stretched on for hours. Finally Chris had enough. He crawled back down the tunnel and cycled out. Viktor, who was planning to go back to take Chris' place and install a permanent monitoring camera, was just starting to crawl up the slope when he heard through the thick air in the tunnel the sound of claws tick-tacking on a diamond floor. He backed out rapidly and was through the airlock before the Lineup got down to the bottom.

Everyone gathered around at a respectful distance as the single Lineup segment expertly manipulated the hatch doors in the airlock with the six prehensile fingers in its snout and climbed out the circular door, which just fit its long cylindrical body. Gus and the others tried to talk with it using their laser communicators, but it just ignored them.

The Lineup felt around with its snout where the four fibers came through the door, and when it was finished, there was a fifth fiber attached to the door, glowing slightly from scattered laser light. Spinning out more diamond fiber from under its snout as it went along, the single Lineup started off down the canyon, following the tracks of the crawler.

"It's replacing the fiber you wound up," Gus said to Red. He paused and gave an apologetic cough. "You might say it's mending the telephone lines after the Storm has passed."

After the Lineup had left, Viktor tried to open the outer hatch door. It would not rotate.

"Locked," he said with a shrug.

A group of scientists followed the Lineup on foot, while others made arrangements to leapfrog ahead in hopiters to take their place. At the first rendezvous the Lineup arrived way ahead of the predicted time, with only one human, a former marathon runner, able to keep up the pace.

"It's getting faster as it goes," the marathoner said, panting. "It grabs mouthfuls of snow and dirt as it moves along and eats them. It has already grown a full set of wings, and the larger the wings got, the faster it moved. I don't think the wings are just for heat rejection. I think they are its energy source—that animal is solar powered!"

The Lineup moved swiftly over the kilometers, never stopping or resting, and continuously spinning out diamond fiber. Now that its wings were grown, it stopped eating so much, and only snacked occasionally on carbon dioxide snow.

Chris and Tanya were together at one hopiter landing site and managed to keep up with the fast-moving Lineup for a mile before tiring out. They were lucky enough to catch the Lineup in the process of eliminating.

"I definitely caught the emission of oxygen," Chris said, looking at the indicators on his air composition analyzer. "The creature must be breaking down the carbon dioxide in the snow and turning it into carbon and oxygen. The carbon is used to make the diamond fiber." He looked at Tanya. "Find anything in the stuff it eliminated?"

Tanya looked at the loose pile of dry granular material in the sealed bag she held in her glove. "I'll take a good look under the microscope when I get back to the crawler," she said. "But this is not the waste of a biological creature."

Her later analyses backed up her first evaluation.

"There is no organic material in it whatsoever," she reported to the investigating team. "The creature eliminates nothing but aluminum oxide, silicon oxide, and iron oxide—sand—very clean sand with every bit of usable minerals and nourishment taken out of it."

After three sols the Lineup came to where Red's crawler had started to pick up the fiber in its wheels. The Lineup went a few kilometers beyond that point, then started to dig with its powerful, clawed feet. The rusty sand flew in all directions as the trench grew deeper. Suddenly the Lineup stopped and picked up a buried strand of fiber. It did something with its snout, then climbed out of the trench and headed back the way it had come. A tech slid down into the trench, uncovered the reconnected fiber, and looked it over carefully. He was unable to determine where the joint had been made.

The fiber continued south.

How far south, no one yet knew.

By the time the fiber-laying Lineup returned to the entrance to the underground cavern, it had reabsorbed its wings.

"They just got smaller and smaller, and then they were gone," Tanya said in amazement.

"How are the language lessons going?" she asked Gus.

"Fairly well. They use a strange form of grammar, but had no trouble learning English. And they must've kept adding more segments, since toward the end they were reading videobooks from the library as fast as we could transmit them.

"Now I guess it's time to get to know them better. I hope this one's been keeping in touch with its fellows." He walked over to where the single Lineup was standing outside the hatch door, its fiber-coupler eyerod hooked over the fiber that the Lineups used to talk to the language computer.

Gus activated his helmet laser communicator. "Now that we

can converse, we should get to know each other. My name is Gus Armstrong. What is your name?"

"Belonging to this segment is name Badepi."

"We would like to come inside your remarkable home, Badepi."

"Surviving of Gus Armstrong outside is possible."

"Yes," Gus admitted. "But—"

"Going of Gus Armstrong inside is not necessary."

The Lineup turned and ran its snout around the periphery of the hatch, somehow unlocking it, then, using its six-fingered nose, easily unscrewed the door and started inside the air lock.

"But we need to talk, get to know each other better," Gus protested as the Lineup screwed the door into place. Fortunately the laser link went easily through the transparent material.

"Continuing of tasks on inside of importance higher," Badepi responded firmly.

The Lineup spent some time going around the periphery of the circular hatch door with its snout. It looked almost as if it were erasing the fine line between the circular door and its frame where they screwed together with a six-turn thread. Tanya leaned down to look closely.

"It's welding that diamond door shut with those fine feathers under its snout-fingers!" she exclaimed.

The Lineup went through the next hatch door and welded it shut, too. As Badepi started up the long sloping tunnel its rear eyerods gave one last burst of light.

"Communicating terminated," Badepi said with finality.

Gus stood there in a daze, shaking his head. Red Storm went over to the now-solid diamond wall in the cliff face. She stuck her fingers in the six outer finger holes and gave a fruitless twist, then kicked viciously at the base.

The crowd of scientists and techs finally realized that everything was over. Picking up their instruments and tools, they started back to their vehicles. A note sounded at the back of Gus' helmet and he switched the comm channel to the secure one Fred Whimple used to contact him with confidential messages.

"I thought you ought to know right away, sir," Fred said. "There was a series of coordinated coups around the world this morning. The leaders of most of the major countries on Earth that weren't already in the Unified States have been replaced with regents who pledge their loyalty to Alexander, the Infinite Lord." There was a long pause.

"That's not all," Fred continued. "He is now demanding the closing down of all lunar and planetary bases and the immediate return of everyone back to Earth."

CHAPTER 14

RESCUE FROM THE MOON

By the time Gus and Chris got back to Olympia, their message files were full and people were lined up outside their offices. They decided to handle them together, since the future of Mars and the future of the Sagan Institute were now inseparably entwined. The highest priority item on Fred Whimple's appointment list was a video call from Dr. Ozaki Akutagawa, the head of the large Japanese contingent at Elysium Saddle. Japan was one of the major financial supporters for both the institute and the Territory of Mars.

"My government has called upon me to return and it is my duty to do so," Ozaki's emotionless face said.

"But it is no longer the same government," Gus protested. "You should feel no sense of duty to some regent put in place by foreign forces."

"The new regent is not a foreigner, but a young Japanese politician who was well known to be next in line for prime minister—after the old one had died or lost his influence," Ozaki said. "And if recent rumors about the old prime minister's behavior with young men are true, he would not have had his influence much longer, anyway.

"Also," Ozaki continued, "you did not see the television broadcasts from Japan, showing the mobs overrunning the diet and the offices of the prime minister, as I did. The faces under the Caps of Contact were all Japanese. If this is what the people of Japan want, then I must go along."

"If you insist," Gus said.

"I have already initiated procedures to close down the Nippon Mars Volcanic Studies Institute and transport our contingent back home. The last of our contingent will be going up to our transport ships in two sols."

"No, they won't!" a voice interrupted, and the face of a young Japanese scientist leaned over Ozaki's desk to look into the viewer for the comm link. "These old ones with their traditional ways may feel obligated to go along with everyone else, but I and a lot of others aren't about to return to that insanity. We want to stay here. I know you have more volcanists than you need, but I worked my way through college at a sushi bar and won't be a burden. Can we apply for Martian citizenship?"

"You've got it," Chris said. "But I'm sure we can find a better use for your talents than running a restaurant."

"You may go now, Yoshida," Ozaki said, only mildly perturbed by the interruption. After the young man had left, Ozaki confided to the viewer. "The young ones are probably correct in their decision," he admitted. "But I must return to add my voice of age and reason to the discussion, for though it may take years, or even centuries, we must return the misled people of Japan to the old ways." A slight smile formed on his round face and his eyes twinkled. "Besides, the Territory of Mars will certainly need people they can trust inside the Unified States. I, of course, having once been on Mars, will always be under suspicion. But I can identify people who would be sympathetic to your cause and put you in touch with them."

"A fifth column!" Gus said. "Just what we'll need! Why didn't I think of that?"

"Because we're trained as scientists, not politicians," Chris said. "We'll just have to sharpen up our devious streaks."

"It won't do to recruit people if we can't talk to them," Gus said. "I'm sure the Unified States will soon shut down all communication links between Earth and Mars."

"I believe I may have a partial solution to that problem, also," Ozaki said. "Because I will have showed my loyalty by returning, and because of the strong respect for age and authority in Japan, I expect to retain my position as director of geophysical studies at Tokyo University. We have at the university a roof-mounted laser radar system capable of ranging off the Moon. It should be relatively simple to convert it into a low data rate communication system to Mars. You will want to establish other links, of course."

"To be sure," Gus said. "But you, of course, must remain unaware of them, just as Chris and I will tell no one else of your plans."

"You are rapidly learning to become properly devious," Ozaki said with a slight smile. "Look for my transmissions after midnight Tokyo time at the time of the new moon. The students will be asleep and the laser will not be in use for measuring the orbit of the Moon."

"We will miss you," Gus said. "I enjoyed our trip up over Olympus and the delightful walk through your garden."

"We have decided to leave our garden intact as a gift to the people of the Territory of Mars in thanks for the hospitality they have shown us," Ozaki said. "Unfortunately, that will be the last gift you can expect from the state of Japan of the Unified States of Earth."

"Your continued friendship is gift enough," Chris said, surprising himself with his diplomatic tongue.

Their next visitor was a nervous young computer programmer, Bill Boswick, who had hopped in from Austral Canyon. Gus wasn't sure but that Fred hadn't sent him in just to get rid of the incessant clinking from the stack of yellow vikings the man was continually riffling between his fingers. As Bill came into the office, he dropped the stack of coins into a pocket of his rumpled overalls. Ignoring the chair in front of the desk, he started pacing back and forth. Soon one hand was back in his pocket and he was fooling with the coins again as he talked.

"I hate to do this," Bill said. "But I gotta to go home . . . I got a spacegram from my wife saying she's been a Unie for nine months, how wonderful it is now that the world is unified, and asking me to come back." His pacing became more agitated and his voice started to crack as he continued.

"She's also pregnant . . . and I've been here for twenty months . . . slaving away . . . trying to earn enough money so we could start a family . . . and now she's pregnant . . ." Tears started to pour down his face. "She calls it 'her blessing from the Infinite Lord incarnate' and isn't even *ashamed*!" He suddenly pulled the stack of coins from his pocket and threw them viciously at the far wall, yelling, "How I'd love to *smash* that bastard's face!"

He collapsed into the chair in front of Gus' desk, face in his hands, sobbing.

"If only there were some way to bring him down . . ." he muttered through his tears.

"There is a way," Gus said. "But it will take calm and patience, not anger."

"What?" Bill said, looking up with hope. "I'd do anything!"

"Even becoming a Unie yourself?"

Bill hesitated for a second. "Sure—if I had to. But how will that help?"

"We need people we can trust in the Church of the Unified. I *know* we can trust you. Would you be willing to swallow your pride, accept your wife and the baby that isn't yours, and not only join the Church of the Unified with a glad smile, but become one of its most devoted followers?"

"You're asking an awful lot," Bill said, hesitating. Gus kept silent. "What do you want me to do once I get in and accepted?"

"I don't know yet," Gus said. "We've only begun our long-range planning. But if you can be our white knight, overlooked in a notch among the black pawns, ready to assist at the right time . . ."

"I'll do it," Bill said, brightening. "How do I keep in touch?"

"Don't call us. We'll call you," Gus said. "Do you have a relative other than your wife and parents?"

"Sure, Uncle Dave—David Boswick, my father's brother."

"Good. Once every few weeks or so, you'll get a telephone call from 'Uncle Dave.' That's your signal to blab on about everything you have been doing in the Church since the last call, so we can monitor your progress. We'll also set up a drop where you can send information that can't go over the telephone. Other than that, keep moving up in the Church and volunteer for everything that sounds interesting. When we finally have something for you to do, we'll simply write you a letter.

"So, if you ever receive a letter from Uncle Dave, never open it up while you are wearing your Cap of Contact. Smuggle it into the shower to read . . . and then read the small print on the inside of the envelope."

"I'll be waiting eagerly for Uncle Dave's every call and letter," Bill said, a grim, determined smile on his still tear-marked face as he shook hands good-bye. Fred, annoyed, carefully picked up every viking coin before he ushered the next visitor in.

Red Storm was one of the last they talked with.

"I've sorta been asked to be an ambassador of sorts," Red started apologetically. "When I heard the news about Alexander taking over the Earth, I borrowed your deep-space dish to make contact with some of my friends out in the belt. They'd already been talking together and asked me to talk to you." She looked down at her feet and then looked up again, lips firm.

"We're a pretty independent lot . . . *have* to be out there . . . We hate to ask favors . . . don't like to be obligated . . . But we need help," she finally blurted out. "We all had grubstake contracts with the big space processing firms. Except me—I got lucky a few years ago and could grubstake myself. But all the contracts have been voided. Even my Swiss bank accounts have been frozen. We can last a year, maybe two, without resupply, but after that, we either have to give in and become ground-pounders under a religious dictatorship—or literally starve to death. We have no farms like you do."

"We've got plenty of food," Chris said. "You're welcome to take a cargo load back with you."

"We want to pay our way," Red said proudly. "What do you want? Heavy metals, organics, or ice?"

"We have plenty of ice at the poles and our own carbonaceous chondrite asteroids in orbit," Chris said. "But if we are to become truly independent of Earth, a few nickel-iron mountains to mine would be helpful."

"They'll be on their way," Red said, perking up. "Normal delivery is five to ten years, but we'll just divert some that were scheduled for delivery on the canceled contracts. Make sure you return the nets with the sails, they'll be getting scarce."

"Nets?" Gus asked.

"The job of a belt prospector is to find a suitable asteroid, assay it with a few test borings, then wrap the asteroid in a net that ends in a long pull-tether with a radio beacon on the end," Red said. "That's why one person can do the job, if they're motivated enough.

"The big space processing firms then send huge automated perforated lightsails speeding out to the belt, where they home in on a beacon, hook onto the pull-tether, and start the long slow haul back toward Earth. The outgoing sails usually carry food, antimatter, and other supplies for our grubstake. We collect our own propellant from the icy asteroids."

"You'll be needing some antimatter then?" Chris asked.

"Nope," Red said. "We decided we can't ask you for that. You need it more. We'll just use our auxiliary solar-powered ion drives and coast between asteroids instead of rushing to get there first. We're going to be cooperating now instead of competing. All we need is food."

"It's a deal, Ambassador Storm," Chris said, rising to shake her hand. Red shook hands and smiled, pleased with the way things had gone, then turned and strode out the door, the muffled clink of polars coming from the deep thigh pocket above her right knee.

The most difficult messages to handle were the ones from the scientific bases on the Moon and the outer planets. The time delays ran from minutes to hours and relatively simple interchanges took hours to complete. Chris had discussions with the scientists from various nations who were in observation platforms in orbit around Jupiter; exploring the icy worlds of Europa, Callisto, and Ganymede; or buried under the murky skies of Titan. All of them were concerned about what had happened on Earth, but felt protected by the large distance and the infrequent visits by resupply and crew rotation ships.

"We have a few who want to go home," Giovanni Ricci said from the EEC base on Titan. "But the rest have voted to defy the Dictator Armstrong. We will stay here, doing our scientific duty, for as long as possible. Then we will use our transport spacecraft, not to return to Earth, but to come to Mars to accept your kind offer of asylum."

"That takes care of all the outer planet bases," Chris reported to Gus. "With the exception of the misguided loyalties of the Japanese contingent exploring Callisto, all the rest have taken us up on our offer. But we don't have to worry about them for a long time. Most of them have supplies for a year, if not a mear, and will continue their work as long as they can before we have to support them. How's the Moon coming?"

"I'm afraid we're going to lose everyone on the Moon," Gus said. "They're too close to Earth and its spacecraft and missiles. I've talked with Charlie Forbes, head of the big U.S. base at the north pole ice mines, and Carlo Vulpetti, head of the CERN circumlunar accelerator project, while Tanya and others have contacted some of the other national groups with bases on the Moon. The general feeling is the same. Only a few want to return. They were delaying, hoping something would happen, but Alexander is getting angry. He wants to see ships coming home *now*, and anyone left on the Moon after seven days is going to be visited by a nuclear warhead!"

"Why don't they just fly off here to Mars? Surely we could accommodate them. How many are there, anyway?"

"Over two thousand. But all their transport spacecraft are designed for going from the lunar surface to lunar orbit, or lunar orbit to Earth orbit. They don't have ships that can get here. They don't even have ships to hold two thousand people."

"We have ships that can get *there*," Chris said. "The three *York-town* class ships the UN forces came in."

"Yes . . ." Gus said, thinking. "And being warships, they were designed to go fast. Given enough antimatter, they can hit two gees. But even one gee would be enough . . . We could be at the Moon in a few days."

"Well before Alex's deadline."

"But those long, flimsy interplanetary spacecraft can't land on the Moon," Gus said. "How do we get the people off the Moon and onto the ship? We can't run a shuttle service using just the few ships they have. We'd have rescued only a few hundred before the Unies would figure out what was going on and launch their nuclear warheads, with everyone getting killed, including the rescue crew."

"There must be some way," Chris said. "But I can't think of it."

"Neither can I," Gus said. "But we're not the only brains on Mars. Let's call a planet-wide council of war."

Within an hour, the emergency meeting had been called, and even though people were still trickling into the Boston Commons, Gus started the meeting going by explaining the problem and asking for suggestions.

The first speaker was Yitzhak Begin, former commander of the Israeli contingent during the invasion of Mars, speaking over the Sinai Springs hookup. "We Israelis would like to volunteer our ship, the *Shalom*, as the rescue ship, since many of its original crew are here on Mars. All it needs is some antimatter and propellant transferred from the two other ships."

As Yitzhak stepped back from the camera, his place was taken by Ben Shamir. "I say we don't worry about the amount of antimatter we use up in the rescue. If we can bring back Carlo Vulpetti and his top-notch particle accelerator team, they can quickly build us an antimatter factory that will make us independent of Earth supply."

There was a general murmur of agreement.

"Okay," Chris said. "We won't worry about running the rescue ship at high gees to get there in a hurry. But how do we get the people off the Moon?"

"Take lots of landers," someone suggested. "We have plenty of those trooper attack landers left over from the UN invasion."

"That's a start," Gus said. "But the *Shalom* can carry only sixteen landing craft, and even if we crowded in thirty people instead of the twenty they were designed for, that's less than five hundred people, and we have two thousand to rescue—in a hurry."

"If they won't fit inside, let 'em ride on the outside," someone yelled from the center of the commons. There was a short burst of laughter, which quickly died away because of the seriousness of the situation.

"That's it!" Red Storm yelled, getting up from her seat at the Olye Olye Outs Inne bar and striding through the crowd, clanking slightly at every other step, until she reached a microphone.

"We're going fishing," she said as she started to explain her plan. "With nets . . ."

The *Shalom* was ready to go in twenty-six hours. Lander pilots who had been converted into hopiter pilots were now retreaded back again into their old landers, which they flew up and docked into the berths at the base of the pointed head of the arrowlike interplanetary transport spacecraft. But instead of the troop-carrying attack landers, they flew the quartermaster ships. In each hold was one of Red Storm's asteroid-gathering nets, a large spool of high-strength cable stripped off the chair lifts on Mount Olympus, and four medivac jet-powered hoppers rescued from the junkyards of the base motor pools.

One gee for two days was enough to cover one AU, so it was less than two days before they reached the halfway point between Mars and Earth in their separate orbits around the Sun. The anti-matter engines on the *Shalom* flickered into darkness and the two-kilometer-long interplanetary spacecraft started its long, slow, majestic turn, end over end. Then Colonel Yitzhak Begin began deceleration. The dull-red liquid-droplet radiator "feathers" on the tail end of the long, narrow, arrowlike *Shalom* changed to bright yellow as the gamma-violet plasma in the antimatter engines turned back on again.

"I've got the Moon between us and Earth, but they're bound to see us coming sooner or later. Then it's a race to the Moon, and the winner has two thousand souls."

"Or dead bodies," Gus said gloomily.

"We will win," Tanya said reassuringly. "We *must* win!"

Four hours before arrival, the Moon was starting to loom large around the *Shalom*'s gamma ray shield in the rearward-pointing monitor. Gus gathered the lander pilots and their helpers in the briefing room and went over the details once again. There had been precious little time to practice, and none of it on real hardware, only crude computer simulations.

"You all have your assignments," Gus said finally. "Good fishing!"

Laughing, they went down to their ships. Gus and Tanya went with them.

The sixteen landers pulled away from the large interplanetary transport, its antimatter engines temporarily silent during the maneuver. The landers spread out in all directions and soon pulled ahead as the *Shalom* started decelerating again, for they had to be down and back with their catch before it came to a stop. Some headed for the north pole of the Moon, others for the south pole, both sites of ice mines. Others aimed at points on the lunar limb, their real targets somewhere over on the dangerous, Earth-facing side.

Gus was in the leading lander. He raised his contacts on the Moon and told them to spread the word.

"We're coming to rescue you! Tell everybody by all means at your disposal. We'll be there and gone in less than two hours, so it doesn't matter who hears. If anyone wants to go to Mars, they are to get suited up immediately, go to a clear place outside, and form a group for pickup."

"What are you going to do, Gus?" Charlie Forbes said from his north pole site. "Beam us up?"

"Almost," Gus said with a rare laugh. Then he added, "By the way ... only one piece of carry-on luggage will be allowed per passenger."

The Chinese helium-three strip-mining facility in the Bay of Tranquility was coping with a number of problems that day. One was an air leak in the underground west dormitory that seemed to defy detection, the second was a major policy debate between the administrators, the engineers, and the scientists over the proper response to the recent return ultimatum they had received from the new regent of the state of China, and the third was how to cope with their very strange visitor.

They had treated him most politely, had assigned him one of their best translators, Lap-Wai Wong, and had fed him well—pressed duck last night. But he still kept coming up with the most unusual requests instead of following the tour that the administrators had planned for him.

"Tell them to do that triple somersault onto the ten-man pyramid again, Lap-Wai," Maury Pickford called, running around to the other side of the group of amateur Chinese acrobats. "I want to get a video of it from this angle."

"These people really must get back to their helium harvesting work," Lap-Wai protested.

"But think of all the publicity I can get!" Maury stopped and everyone stiffened as an emergency siren went off through loudspeakers in the dome of the exercise room and an excited voice speaking Chinese immediately followed.

"What's going on?" Maury asked, grabbing Lap-Wai's arm. Lap-Wai flinched from the alcoholic breath.

"The Americans have said that there is someone coming to rescue us from the Moon and take us to Mars," Lap-Wai replied. "Those that want to go must get into spacesuits and gather outside." Lap-Wai pulled away and started toward the dormitories.

"Mars! Can I go, too?" Maury called after the retreating form.

"I don't see why not. After all, you are an American," Lap-Wai said. "But you can take only one small bag," he warned.

Maury looked down at the pile of video and photographic equipment he had been hauling around. There would be little need for that on Mars. People there would want information from their newspapers, not entertainment. How was he going to pay his way once he reached Mars?

He reached into a bag and pulled out a plastic squeezer of Chinese beer and sucked thoughtfully at it. Suddenly he bent down, opened up a battered aluminum briefcase with a vacuseal rim, dumped the expensive zoom and wideangle lenses from the padded interior onto the dusty floor, and ran down the corridor toward the farms he had been shown earlier.

Ten minutes later he was standing in line at the exit air lock, waiting his turn in a line of patient Chinese. He carried his helmet in one hand and a battered aluminum briefcase in the other. A good-looking young Chinese woman was in front of him. She turned and, when she saw the American stranger, she greeted him politely.

"I see you are joining us in our flight from the devil Alexander. I know a little English, so let me know if I may be of any assistance. My name is Sui-May."

"Hi, Sui-May. I'm Maury Pickford, reporter for the New York *Daily Mirror*—the one with tits on page three. Thanks for letting me come along."

"Anyone that wants to get away from what is happening on Earth is welcome. Why were you visiting the Moon, Mr. Pickford?"

"I got myself sent here to do a series of articles on sports in space. I figured it was a good way to get as far away as possible from all those Unies, so I kept finding new sports and writing them up, like your acrobatics team. My best was on swimming—even got on the third page with that one." He pulled out his filofax from his chestpack—it was the old kind with paper pages—and extracted a folded newspaper clipping from a pocket in the back. He unfolded it tenderly and proudly handed it over to Sui-May.

"I call it 'Boobs in Space.'" The clipping showed a well-endowed young woman shooting out from the surface of a spherical swimming bubble at the zero-gee pool on some large space station. She was wearing only her bikini bottoms.

Sui-May's eyebrows raised.

"It's lovely what zero gee does to a woman's figure," Maury said as he took the clipping back and tenderly returned it to his filofax. He looked down at Sui-May.

"Say!" he said, shifting back a little. "We haven't had a Chinese chick on page three in ages . . . Pay's good . . ."

"Not interested," Sui-May said dryly and looked away.

"I forgot . . ." Maury said to himself, taking another sip of beer from his suit supply. "I'm not in that business any longer . . ."

The most difficult rescue involved the people at the large Russian radio and optical astronomy observatory at the "quiet" spot on the Moon, right in the middle of the side of the Moon that always faced directly away from the Earth. It was at this same point that Colonel Begin was aiming his ship *Shalom*, although it would come to a halt many tens of thousands of kilometers up, then take off again toward Mars.

For this pickup site, the rescue lander had to zoom out away from the Moon, then turn back to pass over the back side. Tanya was riding shotgun on one of the hoppers in the cargo bay of that lander.

The large door on the quartermaster lander slid open with a rumble Tanya could feel through her thighs as she sat astride the jet-powered medivac hopper, now stripped of the dead weight of the clamshell stretchers.

"Twenty-five minutes to target," the pilot, Michael Wolfe, said through the suit radio.

"Time to go," said Tanya's driver, Roscoe Razinski, an ex-medic turned Mars farmer. He raised the hopper in the zero-gee environment and started hauling a corner of the net out the hatch door. They were followed by the three other hoppers attached to the other corners of the net. They soon pulled the net free and were floating in space, connected only by four shroud lines that ran from each corner of the net to the cable spooling slowly off a reel bolted to the floor of the cargo hatch.

"Give us some slack, Donna," Roscoe said to a small, wiry

figure standing next to the large reel of high-strength stranded fiber. The motorized reel started to turn, letting out cable, and the four hoppers started flying out in front of the large lander, gaining speed. As soon as they were well clear, the lander pilot fired reverse jets and moved rapidly back away from them, the cable reel humming as it shot out line to keep the cable slack.

Five minutes passed as they continued their motion over the lunar surface, the lander just a tiny speck in back of them. Slowly the net started to change shape as the cable began to pull on it.

"Must be at about two hundred kilometers," Roscoe said. "Donna is putting on the brakes."

The pull of the cable slowed them down and they started to fall toward the lunar surface. It was only five kilometers down, but was zooming by at six hundred kilometers an hour. The pull of the cable increased and Tanya leaned forward in her seat harness to hug the control panel in front of her. She noticed Roscoe doing the same thing.

"Hold onto your helmet," he called. "This is going to be one rough ride!"

"I hope the cable holds," Tanya said.

"It should," Roscoe said. "It was made in Russia."

"Don't remind me," Tanya said, her voice strained as the deceleration level rose to three gees.

The seconds passed as the deceleration force from the in-reeling cable slowed them from orbital velocity down nearly to zero.

". . . fifty-four, fifty-five, fifty-six," Roscoe was counting.

Suddenly the deceleration stopped and they were in free-fall again. They were now only a few hundred meters above the lunar surface and drifting slowly over a crater that contained a huge parabolic dish built into it. Ahead, Tanya could see the large photon bucket. Off to one side were the observatory buildings and outside the buildings was a large clump of people.

"Over to the left!" Tanya shouted.

"I see them," Roscoe said. The four pilots activated the jets on their hoppers and started hauling the net toward the crowd. Far above them, where the four shroud lines from the net came together to attach onto the cable proper, was a yellow box containing a radar altimeter that radioed signals back to the take-up reel so that the box stayed roughly at constant altitude. That way they didn't have to cope with tangled shrouds and loops of cable all over the ground.

"There must be two or three hundred people," Tanya said, noticing that some of them were children. She switched her mike to the emergency channel and started giving instructions in Russian.

"The instant the net is on the ground, run to the middle and sit down. If your suit has a safety hook, attach it to the net. Holes in the net are large enough for children to fall through. Instruct them to hold tight to the ropes with arms and legs. We leave in sixty seconds."

The hoppers landed in a rough square, the net laid out between them. The first thing each driver did was cut his hopper loose from the net; then he stood there, one hand on the limp shroud line coming down from above, the other helping people into the large net. The lander zoomed past, five kilometers overhead, and the yellow box drifted slowly after it as Donna switched from pulling in cable to letting out cable. People continued to clamber into the net.

". . . . forty-eight, forty-nine, fifty . . ." Tanya was counting in Russian over the emergency channel. She looked around. Everyone seemed to be in and settled. "Our turn," she said to the hopper drivers in English as she started walking in toward the center of the net herself.

"Damn," Roscoe said quietly.

Tanya turned around. The shroud line had tangled around Roscoe's foot. It tightened and started to lift him. Tanya looked on with horror. The minute the shroud started to lift the massive load of people, Roscoe's foot would be amputated. Shortly after that— he would be dead.

"Help!" she screamed as she leaped for the shroud. She was able to grab it with her left hand just above Roscoe's tangled foot. Supporting her weight easily by one hand in the one-sixth lunar gravity, she managed to use her right hand to get enough slack to free his foot. He fell down into the closing pouch full of people. Suddenly, there was a jerk as Donna started the three-gee pickup acceleration.

The shroud line was plucked from Tanya's hand with a force that sent her flying across the gray crust of the lunar surface far below. The last thing she remembered before she struck the ground was seeing a string bag of arms and legs being lifted into the sky and hearing excited clamors in Russian and English coming over the emergency channel.

Donna had started her reel-in at the signal from Michael, the pilot. Actually, she was still reeling out cable, but at a slightly slower speed than the motion of the ship. She monitored the jury-rigged displays on the computer-controlled take-up reel as it adjusted the speed of the cable to keep the accelerometer in the yellow box at the shroud attachment point hovering around three gees.

The minute needed for acceleration finally ended. Donna looked out the cargo hatch door along the thin line of cable. Two hundred kilometers away was a tiny bright speck in the sunlight moving slowly toward her.

"We've got a netful, Mike," Donna said over the intercom to the pilot. "Too big to fit in the hold. Let's head for the mother ship."

"Roger," Michael Wolfe said, and started a long curving trajectory that pulled the ship and its trailing net of human cargo away from the Moon and out to an interplanetary ark, floating motionless in the waveless calm of the vacuum of space, the deadly gamma ray glow of its antimatter engines turned off in consideration of those approaching to embark.

During the long journey out to *Shalom*, Donna slowly shortened the cable until the net was a kilometer away. Far enough from the rocket engines for safety, but close enough so they could wave to each other. Then Donna began to worry. They had practiced and practiced the simulations of dropping the net on the Moon and picking it up, but how were they supposed to land their cargo? She had heard of situations where someone pulling in a cable with a heavy cargo had tried to reel in too fast toward the last. Oscillations would start, and before they knew it the payload had wrapped itself a number of times around the spacecraft like an errant yo-yo.

"Almost there," the pilot reported. "And they have the landing net out. Get ready to cut the cable."

Donna peered ahead along the side of the long truss structure of *Shalom*. Just in back of the crew cabin, right next to one of the cargo airlocks, was spread a large net, firmly attached to some jury-rigged booms.

"Easy does it," Michael said as he drifted their catch toward the net. The netful of human beings hit and stuck, a hundred hands reaching through the netting to make sure.

"Cable cut!" Donna said. "You can take off and dock." But Michael just floated there for a few satisfied minutes, looking at the scene taking place a few hundred feet away. The pouch of their catch had broken open, and at that distance it looked like a recently disturbed spider's nest. The little spacesuited spiders were clambering their way across the ropes and then disappearing into the cavernous cargo hold after waving good-bye to their rescuers.

"Get in here, Mike!" Gus yelled over the radio. "Missiles have been launched from Earth—and they're headed our way!"

"Right!" Michael said, and the lander pulled gees for its docking port on the *Shalom*.

"Tell Tanya that I want to see her as soon as possible," Gus continued.

"Ah—" Michael stalled, wondering how to break the bad news Roscoe had relayed to him during their long trip back to the *Shalom*.

CHAPTER 15

ESCAPE TO MARS

It was the loud, demanding, female voice and the throbbing head-ache that helped Tanya realize that she was not dead. She opened her eyes slightly and looked around. She was in a hospital room on the Moon, and a doctor was arguing with someone. It was a huge woman, dressed like a low-budget movie version of an Amazon warrior, all bare flesh and skimpy gilded brass armor, but the pseudo-Greek helmet had a viewer over the left eye like the Caps of Contact of the Unies.

"Although all she suffered was a concussion, it was a bad one," the doctor was saying. He was wearing a green Cap of Contact. "She isn't even conscious yet."

"Let me know the instant she's awake," the Amazon said. "I have orders to return her to Earth immediately. The Infinite Lord himself has matters to settle with her."

Tanya closed her eyes and feigned unconsciousness. But it would not be long before they found out she was awake.

You are in serious trouble, Tanya Pavlova, she thought, the ache in her head making it hard to concentrate. Now that Alexander is ruler of the whole Earth, no one can stop him from killing people that thwart him . . . He threatened to bomb those on the Moon that attempted to thwart his desires . . . And you have definitely thwarted him time and time again. There came an unbidden vision of the enraged look on Alexander's face as Gus forced his way into his office, preventing her rape. You'll have one last chance when you are brought before him . . . What will you do? First . . . to save your life, and then . . . to find some way to stop this insane, egotistical man. No, half a man. It was almost as if the two twins were two halves of a single person, one with all the good and one with all the evil.

No, it wasn't that simple. Her Gus was not an angel . . . She caught herself and kept her lips from smiling at the memories that thought evoked. And Alexander was not the devil. He was a man, just a man. And there wasn't a woman born of woman who couldn't twist any man around her little finger if she worked hard enough at it—especially if she had practiced earlier on a nearly identical model . . . She would have to swallow her dislike of the man and use all her wiles to keep herself alive and near him, where someday she might be able to do some good. As she fell off to sleep, the voices of the two Amazon guards drifted in through the open door to her room.

"What's the news on the escapees?" one said.

"They're heading for Mars," the other said. "But they're as good as dead. The minute the ship they're on tries to slow down, the missiles launched after it will catch up, and it'll all be over."

Two men floated on opposite sides of a circular railing that surrounded a large three-dimensional display set in the command deck of their spacecraft. At one side of the display was the growing globe of Mars, and in the center was the arrowlike icon of their ship, turned around and ready to decelerate to bring the ship and its precious cargo to a halt at their destination. But on the other side of the display were eight deadly red dots.

Colonel Yitzhak Begin frowned with concern. He looked up at the stocky figure on the other side of the display. His glance met that of Dr. Augustus Armstrong, steel-gray eyes half hidden by the arrowlike crow's-feet wrinkle pattern that formed when he was angry or concerned. He was both.

"That power-mad brother of mine isn't satisfied with the whole world—he's got to kill everyone that isn't under his thumb—including his own brother! Isn't there anything we can do?"

"We're in no immediate danger," Yitzhak answered. "I accelerated the *Shalom* until we were going slightly faster than the missiles, so we are actually pulling slowly away from them. We've reached turnaround and it is past time to start deceleration if we are going to stop at Mars. But, if I did that, they would catch up to us and it would be all over."

"Can we change course and lose them?"

"I tried that when we were under acceleration. They just changed course. These must be maneuverable antisatellite warheads that they hurriedly mounted on top of interplanetary launchers when they saw us coming on the rescue mission. Not nuclear, of course—counterproductive in near-Earth battles. Just a small amount of high explosive to spread out the dozens of penetrator rods. But those rods would make Swiss cheese of the *Shalom*. I could try some more maneuvers as a last resort, but we don't have much fuel left."

"This was designed as a warship," Gus said, brightening slightly. "Couldn't we use its defensive missiles?"

"All weapons on the *Shalom* were removed or disabled by the orders of General Alexander Armstrong before he left," Colonel Begin replied grimly. "He didn't want to leave U.S. secrets in the hands of 'foreigners.' That was silly, of course; many countries have missiles that are cheaper and often better than U.S. missiles. Israel for one—the Russians for another."

"The Russian antispacecraft missiles!" Gus said, right hand starting to manipulate the control pad in front of him. "The ones on Deimos! We must contact Mars at once!"

Twenty minutes later Chris returned their urgent call with a short video message.

"I talked to Boris Batusov, and he identified a Russian tech who helped install the missile system. They will both be leaving for Deimos shortly on emergency orbital flights along with anyone else who thinks they can be of help in deciphering the system and getting it operational. We'll do what we can, but it may take hours—or days."

"Or forever . . ." Gus said as he stared at the frozen face of Chris left at the end of the message.

"I'll adjust our course so we pass right by Deimos, then gravity-whip by Mars," Colonel Begin said. "We may be able to shake a few when they lose lock on us as we go behind the two bodies. I'll try to put us on a trajectory for Jupiter. We can do another gravity turn around there and come back. Maybe by then someone will have thought of something."

"Are our life-support systems designed for that kind of journey?"

"No," Colonel Begin admitted. There was nothing more to say.

Four hours later Gus and Colonel Begin received a message over the ship's comm links requesting their presence in the pilot's briefing room. When they got there, they found the sixteen lander pilots floating in or above their chairs. Their copilots were not there. Michael Wolfe spoke for them.

"The guys have been talking since we heard about the missiles on our tail," he said. "We feel our job isn't done until those people we picked up are safe on the surface of Mars."

"But you did your job perfectly! Every one of your pickups were successful." Gus paused for a long moment. "We only lost one person ... and that wasn't your fault."

"Nevertheless," Michael persisted grimly, "we're going to make sure everyone gets home safe. We sixteen request that Colonel Begin start deceleration to bring the *Shalom* to rest in Mars orbit. Toward the end of the deceleration period, we sixteen will disengage our landers and head for the enemy missiles." He paused and continued grimly. "If we have anything to say about it, they will not hit the *Shalom*."

"I can't let you go to certain death!"

"There's sixteen of us and only eight missiles," said one of the pilots in the back. "That's fifty-fifty odds—pretty good for a rear guard action during a retreat."

There was a pause as Gus thought.

"He's right, you know, Dr. Armstrong," Colonel Begin said seriously.

"Can't we just launch the landers under automatic control?" Gus asked, still not wanting to make a decision.

"Those missiles are locked on a two-kilometer-long *Yorktown* class spaceship. They are going to ignore—even avoid—lander-sized spacecraft," Michael said. "Pilots will be necessary to supply terminal guidance."

"I still don't like the idea," Gus said.

"Two thousand dead or eight dead is the decision you must make," Colonel Begin said.

There was a long silence as Gus thought.

"It must be done," Gus finally said. Tears welled in his eyes as he looked around the room. "Thank you. All of you."

He pulled Michael Wolfe into his arms and gave him a bear hug, then went floating around the room to hug and thank each pilot in turn.

Colonel Begin paused for a moment to use a comm panel.

"Initiate deceleration . . . That is correct. Initiate deceleration. Destination—Mars." He then followed Gus around the room, adding to the hug a European double kiss to both cheeks.

Smiling grimly, the pilots went down to their ships—alone.

Six hours later there was another message from Chris. Mars now was a visible disk and was rapidly growing larger. The pursuing missiles were closing in on them as the *Shalom* decelerated.

"Boris and the techs had trouble breaking into the secure portions of the missile control system," said Chris' image on the video message. "They've laid bypass wiring that will enable them to launch the missiles, but they haven't been able to change the pursuit programming to make sure they ignore the *Shalom* and the landers."

"I'll just change our trajectory slightly and bring them so close that the Russian missiles won't need accurate pursuit programming," Colonel Begin said to Gus with a grim smile. "What was that phrase you Yankees used at Bunker Hill?"

"Wait until you see the whites of their eyes," Gus replied.

There was a strange noise in the corridor outside the control room. Gus went to the door and looked out.

"Oh! Hi, Dr. Armstrong," Maury said. "Just taking the family out for a little stroll to strengthen their legs while we have some gravity." Behind Maury were a dozen yellow ducklings waddling along on their little orange feet as they followed Maury down the corridor.

"They hatched a little sooner than I thought they would," he explained. "Now they think I'm their mommy. It's going to be hard to sell them off when I get to Mars."

Gus couldn't help but grin as he went back into the control room and shut the door.

Boris Batusov floated on tiptoe above the sunlit gray dust of Deimos. He and his team of Martian techs and engineers had done what they could, but it hadn't been enough. There were too many uncertainties—and in space uncertain knowledge usually meant certain death. In this case, it could mean death for two thousand people.

Inside the control building his engineers were watching the action unfold on the radar screens. He, no longer needed, had felt compelled to come outside and see what happened with his own eyes, limited though they were.

Off to the left of the sun he saw a spot of reflected light in the sky. It soon became an elongated hyphen of light moving toward him. Sometime later a shiny head and red tail began to be visible. It was the *Shalom*, traveling backward, its antimatter engines off for the moment as it moved toward Deimos at relatively high speed. As the rapidly moving spacecraft drew closer, Boris could see the flare of the jets from the landers as they pulled away from behind the head of the *Shalom*.

"The people of Mars will remember you sixteen forever," Boris said to himself as he watched the landers move forward to form a protective cloud in front of the arrowlike spacecraft. The *Shalom* grew in size . . . then things happened almost too fast to follow.

The *Shalom* shot by the small moon, not twenty kilometers overhead, and immediately turned on its antimatter rocket at maximum gees to decelerate into an elliptical capture orbit around Mars. Even if it were hit, there might be a few survivors in spacesuits who could be rescued by orbiters. Next came the cloud of sixteen landers—also moving backward, although their rockets were blasting at maximum acceleration to move them away from the *Shalom* and toward the incoming missiles. One lander came so close Boris was sure he could see the pilot in the cockpit.

The engineers monitoring the radar system inside the control building had the launching triggers set. The second the landers passed in one direction, the long-dormant Russian antispacecraft missiles were launched in the other direction. The ground rumbled under Boris' feet, and dozens of streaks of light dashed outward. There was a flash in the distance as an invisible antispacecraft missile launched from Deimos met an invisible antisatellite missile launched a few days ago from Earth. Another flash, another, another . . .

"Seven . . ." Boris said, counting to himself and waiting for the eighth and last one. It did not come.

"One got through," said the discouraged voice of one of the engineers inside the control room. Boris saw the missile streak overhead directly along the trajectory that the *Shalom* had taken, its divert thrusters firing sporadically to keep it on trajectory. As it passed by, the ground shook with dozens of small explosions as the deadly rodlike debris from the warheads of the other seven missiles rained down on Deimos. One hit only a few dozen meters away from Boris and raised a fountain of dust interlaced with glowing droplets of rock and metal.

Boris turned around on tiptoe to look with concern at the rapidly disappearing *Shalom* as it headed for the limb of Mars. The swarm of landers in front of the *Shalom* suddenly developed a clump as four of the landers converged at a point.

There was an eighth flash.

The *Shalom* was saved.

Relieved, Boris allowed himself the luxury of going over to inspect the hole the antisatellite rod projectile had made in the surface of Deimos. The rod had probably been a few millimeters in diameter and thirty centimeters long and massed less than half a kilogram. But its kinetic energy content was greater than an equivalent amount of high explosive. The hole it had made in the ground was over three meters deep and two meters in diameter—with little slumping of the walls due to the low gravity on Deimos. He turned away from the hole and went inside the control center to see what had happened to the *Shalom* and the sixteen.

"The remaining landers were able to rescue three of the pilots," Gus reported over the video link from the *Shalom* to the various stations on Mars. "Their landers were only disabled by the shrapnel from the explosion. But Michael Wolfe must have hit that missile head on. There was nothing left of his lander." He paused, then continued on a positive note. "I want to thank Boris and his team. It could have been a lot worse."

"I only wish we could have gotten them all," Boris said from Deimos.

"Well, now you will have time to crack the security locks on the software and reprogram the rest of the missiles in case Alex sends another attack at us," Gus said.

"I'm afraid that can't be done," Boris said.

"Why?"

"Because we have no more defense missiles," Chris interjected from Olympus base. "We didn't know how well the missiles would perform, so I had Boris shoot all four dozen of them. It's a good thing I did. As it was, one got through the barrage."

"So Mars is defenseless," Colonel Begin said from the *Shalom*.

"I'm afraid so," Chris confirmed.

Tanya waited for two days in the plain, tiny room in the basement of the Potomac Palace. She had plenty of time to think, since the only reading material was the Bible of the Church of the Unifier. After skipping through the book and reading a few random paragraphs, her scientist brain rebelled at reading such illogical, emotional, guilt-laying garbage. The afternoon of the second day the door lock clicked and her Amazon room guard came in. Instead of food, this time the guard brought a half dozen other Amazons with her.

"Take off your clothes," the guard said.

"Why?" Tanya asked angrily.

There was no reply. The seven women advanced on her, roughly stripped off her clothing, threw her on the bed, and held her down. One of them, who obviously had some medical training, then searched every body cavity thoroughly, even tapping each tooth in her mouth. Large plates were placed under various parts of her body and flash X rays taken. The examiner looked at the glowing images on the self-developing plates, then nodded to the guard.

"Clean yourself up and put on this robe," the Amazon said, throwing a towel and robe at her. The rest of the women left, taking her clothing with them.

"You have five minutes," the Amazon warned as she closed and locked the door.

Tanya was ready and waiting when the door opened again. This time there were four Amazons behind the guard. If anything, they were even larger and more fanatical-looking than the others.

"Come with us."

Tanya didn't argue, but stepped rapidly to the door in her bare feet. She was taken up elevators, down long corridors, and through doors guarded by both computer and sentries. The longer they walked, the more ornate the decorations became. Finally they came to a hallway richly decorated in white wool carpeting embroidered with ornate designs in gold thread. Silvered mirrors in solid gold frames alternated along the corridor walls with gold candelabra holding burning white candles that gave a spicy tang of incense to the air.

They came to an ornate door that filled the end of the hallway. As they approached, the sentries there started opening the doors. One of the guards stepped behind Tanya and bent her arm behind her back.

"Bow," the guard hissed.

The guards and Tanya bowed as the door opened, and a familiar voice called from far away.

"Tanya, it is such a pleasure to see you again. Come here, my dear."

Tanya raised her head. Alexander was standing in the middle of a huge room. There was a gigantic bed along one wall. He was wearing his gold buttonless tunic with the broad space-wing shoulders, gold tights, and golden boots—with lifts, Tanya noticed. Alexander had gained a lot of weight and his face was almost as round and ruddy as that of the fat man standing next to him.

The fat man had a pompadour of white hair and was dressed in a white suit, white shoes, a wide white silk tie, gold brocade vest, and enough gold jewelry to sink a horse. Try as she might, Tanya couldn't recall ever seeing the man before. She walked forward and Alexander waved the guards away.

"That's all right," he said to them. "I handled her once before and I can do it again." The guards left and shut the door.

"Tanya, my dear," Alexander said, "I would like you to meet my good friend, Rob. You might say he is my right-hand man."

Rob looked at her suspiciously, nodded perfunctorily, and murmured, "Evening."

"My guards tell me that you were captured at Tsiolkovsky Observatory trying to help some of my disobedient subjects escape the will of the Infinite Lord. That was a naughty thing to do," he said, shaking his finger at her. "Now . . . you are here, and Gus is back on Mars. I'm sure my poor brother must be pining his heart out for you."

His eyes looked back and forth at her two nipples poking up under the thin white robe, rigid from the cold air in the room. His face turned into a leer and his voice harshened. "But to the victor belong the spoils." He grabbed her left wrist and started off toward the large bed.

He paused and turned his head to look back at Rob. "I'll see you later."

Rob nodded and started to walk off to a side door.

Alexander felt a pressure against his chest and looked back around. Tanya was now snuggled up to his chest, smiling at him. She raised her free hand, ran it through his hair, down behind his ear, and down along the side of his neck, snuggling her head closer to his chest.

Suddenly she stiffened.

"Hold still!" she cried, and put her hand on the side of his neck, feeling the pulse in his throat.

"What?" Alexander said, starting to back away.

"Hush! Hold still," she repeated, giving him a quieting kiss to the lips.

"Let me check," she said after a few seconds. She fumbled around on his chest and pulled open the front of his tunic, baring his chest. Soon her ear was pressed tightly against his chest, listening to his heart, while her cool hands were around behind his back, pulling him toward her. Alexander raised his arms in bewilderment at her actions. She suddenly raised her head and called toward the disappearing figure of Rob.

"This man is sick!" she yelled. "Get me a stethoscope and a blood pressure cuff!"

"What is this rot?" Rob said, coming back in the room. "He has a personal physician that checks him weekly. He always reports that Alex is in perfect health."

Tanya turned around and looked disapprovingly at Alexander. "Admit it, Alex," she said, tickling his chest hairs with one hand and waggling a finger at him. "Don't you have the slightest bit of high blood pressure?"

Alexander hesitated, then admitted, "Yes. A little."

Tanya turned to Rob and said firmly, "Get that quack in here—stat!"

Rob hesitated, then punched a short code on his wrist communicator. There was the slap of a distant door opening, then the sound of running feet. An elderly man with thinning hair half hidden by his purple and white Cap of Contact came bursting into the bedroom through the side door.

"Let me have that bag," Tanya said, yanking the doctor's supplies from his grasp as he stood there bewildered, trying to figure out why he had been so urgently summoned. She rapidly found the blood pressure cuff and advanced on Alexander.

"Off with your tunic," she ordered.

"I'm perfectly all right," Alexander objected.

"Off! Off! Off!" Tanya repeated, as she ran her arms under his tunic and extracted an arm. The blood pressure cuff was around his biceps and going though its preprogramed routine before Alexander could protest any further.

"Two hundred! Over one hundred twenty!" Tanya screamed when she read the indicators. "You could have died in my arms!" She turned to the doctor in fury. "What's been going on here!"

"I kept telling him he ought to take some medication," the doctor whined. "But he refused to consider it. He—he made me promise not to tell Rob or anyone else."

Tanya had been rummaging through the black bag and came up with a bottle.

"You have a beta blocker right here," she said, opening the bottle and taking out a pill. She walked over to Alexander.

"Here," she said. "Take this."

Alexander turned his head to one side. "No!"

"Why?" Tanya asked.

"The side effects," Alexander said petulantly. "You know . . ."

"I warned him it might make him impotent," the doctor said.

"It only happens in a small percentage of the cases," Tanya said angrily to the doctor. She turned and, holding the tiny pill between her fingers, walked up to Alexander.

"Besides," she said to him softly and seductively, "if I am your doctor, I will personally guarantee an erection every time." She moved closer, until the nipples under her robe were rubbing against the hair on his chest. She swayed back and forth and brought the pill closer to his mouth.

"You two can go now," Alexander said over her shoulder—then took the pill.

The following week there was a succession of storms along the east coast of the North American portion of the Unified States. Slush and rain and sleet and hail followed one on the other.

"I'm tired of this," Alexander said. "I much prefer my tennis outside."

"I'm not one for tennis inside or outside," Rob said. "But I'm working on a permanent solution to these bad weather days. I've ordered the island of Cyprus evacuated. It's right in the middle of the Mediterranean Ocean where the weather is always balmy. Security will be easier, too, since only high-level followers will be allowed on the island. We'll get rid of all those peasant hovels, and of course raze all the old Greek Orthodox churches—wouldn't do to have them on the Island of the Infinite Lord."

"I don't know," Alexander said. "When I was giving my speech in Turkey on that world tour you arranged, it was pretty hot."

"That's the nice thing about Cyprus," Rob said. "You can either stay down at the seashore and enjoy the ocean, or go up to the top of Mount Olympus and enjoy the cool mountain breezes."

"Mount Olympus! A fit place for a god. Build me a palace on the top of Mount Olympus."

"I'm already having the top three floors of the Olympus Hotel near the top of the mountain rearranged for our use," Rob said.

"I don't want a 'rearranged hotel,' " Alexander said, very annoyed. "I want a palace—at the top."

"I'm sure that Rob meant that the Olympus Hotel was just to be a temporary residence for us while the palace is being built. Weren't you, Rob?" Tanya suggested.

Rob glanced at the usually silent woman that had latched onto Alex. He didn't trust her, but so far he had nothing to complain about. At least she had Alex taking his medicine. Now she was helping *him* out of a minor difficulty. What was her game? Whatever it was, she wasn't going to hurt Alex. Her medical kit had been stripped of dangerous tools and drugs, and Rob had Watchers following her every move outside Alex's quarters.

"Tanya is right," Rob said. "We'll get started on the palace as soon as you tell us what you would like—besides being right on the top of Mount Olympus."

"Well," Alexander said, thinking. "It should have a tall tower, with a parapet on top, so I can go up and look out over my world . . ."

"Good morning, Alex," Tanya said brightly as she came into the master bedroom of the penthouse suite of the Olympus Hotel, carrying a pill and a pressure cuff in one hand and a crystal goblet of water in the other. She was wearing a sky-blue satin short nightgown and a white lace robe, for she had just come directly from her small bedroom down the hall—Alex preferred to sleep alone in his huge circular bed.

Alex groaned and sat up. She sat on the bed next to him and expertly slapped on the pressure cuff, which started in on its preprogramed routine.

"Time for your pill," she said firmly, handing him a pill and the goblet of water.

She watched him take the pill with a twinge of guilt. It was not the beta blocker he needed, but a placebo that she had laboriously fabricated in secret from an aspirin tablet. She took off the blood pressure cuff and smiled approvingly. Alex never looked at the readings on the indicators, but they now read 150 over 100—high, but not dangerous ... unless you knew that the indicators had been biased to read low. Steeling herself to make the next move that might be the means to bring this tyrant down, she tilted her head to one side, forcing herself to sound enticing. "Do you think you'll need an anti-impotency treatment this morning?"

"Not today," Alex said with another groan. "I've got a terrible headache."

"I shouldn't wonder," Tanya said, relieved. "You and Rob were really pouring down the whisky last night. You should do like Rob, stick with scotch instead of bourbon."

"I'll drink what I damn please," Alex growled.

"Of course, my Infinite Lord," Tanya said agreeably. "If you will excuse me, I'll go get you some aspirin."

"I still can't see why I can't blast Mars out of the solar system," Alexander said petulantly, going back over the previous night's discussion. "Surely my owlies could do that for me."

Tanya stopped and came over close to him. "I believe General Sam and General Jerry made it clear that they were certainly willing to try. But unlike the first time you conquered Mars, you won't have the advantage of surprise."

"Yeah," Alexander admitted. "As you pointed out, any incoming spacecraft would be sitting ducks for those Russian missiles on Deimos."

"And you remember what Rob said," Tanya reminded.

"Yeah," Alexander admitted again. "It would look bad in the history books for Alexander the Infinite Lord to lose a battle. That would make him second-rate compared to the Alexander the Great of Macedonia, who never lost any."

"Besides," Tanya said, running her fingers through his curly hair. "If you killed off your brother, then he would no longer know or care that *you* are bedding me down every day instead of *him*."

"Yeah!" Alexander said, brightening at the thought. "You're right. I'll leave Mars alone and just let my brother rust to death out there." He pulled her down to sit on the bed. "What did you ever see in that crip, anyway?"

"He was the closest thing I could get to you," Tanya lied, not avoiding yet another chance to kill this brute with kindness. She slipped off her robe and nightgown and, smiling enticingly, lay back on the bed. She steeled herself as Alex's flushed face moved closer and she began thinking once again of the lovely pink skies of far distant Mars as the clumsy hands started pawing her naked body.

CHAPTER 16

THE RIGHT HAND OF GOD

"Well, how do you like it so far?" Rob asked.

"Nice, very nice. You've done an excellent job, Rob," Alexander said. "You're to be commended."

They were on top of a square stone tower that rose high out of the palace building still under construction below them. It was growing dark and the evening Silver Scythe was rising up over the horizon. Alexander walked to the parapet and looked out over his world from the top of Mount Olympus, enjoying the cool evening breezes.

"I'm truly amazed that you could arrange for such rapid construction," Alexander said.

"It was easy," Rob said offhandedly. "The first thing we did was put in six- and eight-lane superhighways around the island and up and down the mountains. With the natives off the land and their villages torn down, we had plenty of room to straighten out the right-of-way. The tourist hotels make good dormitories for the workers; and, being faithful members of the Church of the Unifier, they work long hours for practically nothing except room and board and don't give us any union trouble."

"But all this stonework . . ." Alexander said, his hands brushing appreciatively over the sharp square edges of the massive blocks of stone that made up the parapet.

"That's the beauty of this island," Rob said, smiling. "It's full of blocks like that, all cut and ready to use. For instance, this stone tower you are standing on is made of stones from the Kolossi Castle, and the walls of the palace below are going to use the stones from the Curium Amphitheater and the various other old stone temples, forts, and buildings. And don't forget the hundreds of old Greek Orthodox churches. The rubble from each one we knocked down produced a few hundred good-sized building stones.

"Of course, we trimmed all the blocks square to get down to new stone without markings on them, and we used modern cements and connecting rods to fit them together." Rob gave the parapet wall a kick. "Even a major earthquake can't knock it down."

Tanya came up from below and stepped out of the central elevator house. Her long blond hair, now shoulder-length to please Alexander, blew in the light evening breeze. She was followed by four of Alexander's Amazon guards. Tanya came over to Rob and Alexander, while the Amazons went to the four corners of the tower to relieve the four guards posted there.

"Our quarters in the tower are snug, but very livable," Tanya said.

"Good," Alexander said. "I will stay here tonight. I'm tired of that hotel. I want to be here where I can look out on my world."

"Look!" Tanya said, pointing to the east. They turned and saw a number of the points of light in the evening Silver Scythe of God rising rapidly upward away from the rest of the points of light.

"Yes," Rob said, his normal ingratiating smile turning grim. "I was expecting that to happen at about this time tonight, Tanya. Some of your scientist friends at Novosibirsk thought they could fool me by pretending to be devout members of the Church of the Unifier, while all the time secretly constructing a long-range hypersonic nuclear missile designed to penetrate the air defenses around Cyprus and kill Alexander."

"Kill me!" Alexander exclaimed, perturbed. "I want those people punished."

"They were punished," Rob assured Alexander. "I dumped a few sail-loads of crowbars on the whole city. The few survivors will think twice before they try anything like that again."

"But surely not everyone at Novosibirsk was involved," Tanya protested. "To destroy a whole city of scientists because of the actions of a few—"

"I don't trust any scientist," Rob said. "They aren't real people. No emotions you can play on. Too honest. That's what gave me the clue something was up. They turned into Unies too fast."

"Kill me?" Alexander said, ignoring their conversation and shaking his head. "The Infinite Lord? I cannot be killed. I cannot die. I *must* not die!"

"If I hadn't caught that plot in time, you would have been dead, all right," Rob said, pleased with himself. "Infinite Lord or not."

"No! The Infinite Lord must live forever!" Alexander yelled. "Get me Jerry!" He fumbled with his wrist communicator. Rob raised his and tapped in the codes. After a pause he looked at the reply on the screen.

"Jerry was down in the basement control center working on the program for the security system for the castle. He'll be right up. I'm sure he will reassure you that every precaution is being taken for your safety."

"Good," Alexander said, still perturbed. He paced nervously away, muttering to himself. "The Infinite Lord *cannot* die . . ."

"As I was saying," Rob continued, talking softly so that only Tanya could hear. "I don't trust scientists. And that includes you!"

"I have done nothing," Tanya said calmly.

"I know," Rob said, turning pointedly to look at the still rising sails. "And don't even *think* of trying anything, or you'll be as dead as Novosibirsk. This setup is too good to lose."

The elevator door opened to an audible *whoosh-whoosh* and Jerry stepped out. He was wearing a white sweatshirt, running shoes, and trim swim trunks over tight muscular buttocks now nearly devoid of flab. Life on Cyprus as head of Alexander's Department of Applied Magic had been good for him. He flipped back the viewer on his white and purple Cap of Contact and trotted over to Alexander.

"Jerry!" Alexander said, brightening up. "You look in tip-top shape today."

"I owe it all to you, my Infinite Lord!" Jerry said, bowing slightly. "What can I do for you?"

"Someone tried to kill me today."

"Oh! No!" Jerry said, appalled at the thought. "The death of the Infinite Lord is unthinkable!"

"It must be made unthinkable," Alexander said firmly. "I want you to make a bomb—a doomsday bomb. It must be big enough to blow up the whole world! It is to be arranged so that if I am killed, everybody else in the whole world is killed."

"That would truly make your death unthinkable," Jerry said, pleased with the idea. "Let me see . . . We have plenty of nuclear warheads left in the missile silos in the American states and the EEC states—but I'm not sure they are enough to really do a good job on the whole world. What we need is something bigger—like the huge asteroid that wiped out the dinosaurs, only bigger, so that *nothing* survives."

"Just a minute!" Rob interrupted, beginning to get alarmed. "I don't mind spending any reasonable amount on security to make sure nobody gets to Alex, but this is ridiculous. Suppose he popped off because of a heart attack? Bingo! The world is gone. No way! I refuse to allow it!"

Alexander stiffened and raised himself up to glare over at Rob. "Who are *you* to tell the Infinite Lord what he can do and what he cannot do?"

Rob decided he'd had enough. "I'm the guy that made you— that's who! I made you—and I can break you! If I hear any more of this Infinite Lord doomsday bomb stuff, I'll have Eric cut off your comm links and deflate you so fast you'll be a nobody in three months."

Tanya had come up beside Alexander and was now stroking one of his cheeks, trying to calm him down. "You have the whole world, Alex, and me, too. Why don't you just enjoy it and let Rob and Jerry take care of the pretty details like security."

Alexander ignored Tanya's presence, and in the twilight his steel-gray eyes flashed black, as the deadly arrowlike furrows sprang up around them.

"You dare threaten the Infinite Lord?" he roared. "I warned you once before that I don't get mad at people, Rob. I get *rid* of them. You don't get a second chance." He turned and hollered, "Guards!"

The guards came running, gun-spears at the ready.

Rob, suddenly alarmed, started to back off. "Wait, Alex! I'm sorry about—"

But Alexander wasn't listening. Pointing to Rob he ordered, "Get rid of that man!" The four huge Amazons surrounded Rob and, grunting, lifted him into the air. One had him by the tie—choking him so he couldn't scream.

"Alex! Don't . . ." Tanya pleaded, pulling at Alexander's shoulders.

The guards walked over to the parapet, holding Rob high. They paused for a second to look back at Alexander. He glared, then deliberately turned his back.

Rob screamed for a few seconds as he fell down the tall tower. There was a thud, then silence.

Alexander turned to look at Tanya. His face stern. "Don't . . . what?" he asked menacingly.

"Nothing," Tanya said weakly, brushing an invisible piece of lint off his padded golden shoulders.

"Good. Go downstairs and get in my bed where you belong. I'll see you shortly."

"I'm looking forward to it," Tanya said, trying hard to make her smile look enticing instead of forced. As she took the elevator down to Alexander's quarters her mind was whirling. She would have to try harder to stop this tyrant—take more chances—find something sharp and an unguarded moment to strike. But even with Rob gone, the Watchers would be observing her every move—and Alex always sent her out of his room after he had finished with her and before he went to sleep . . . She would just have to try harder.

Alexander turned to Jerry.

"Y'know," Jerry said, musing, "when those guards were tossing Rob over the balustrade—it reminded me of that old idea that Newton wrote down in his Principia on the similarity between cannon balls and satellites. If the guards had thrown hard enough, Rob would have gone into orbit."

"Rob in orbit!" Alexander exclaimed—then burst into uncontrollable laughter at the image of the porcine Rob floating in space, arms and legs waving in the vacuum. He got himself under some control, then blurted out, "P . . . p . . . pigs in space!" and burst into laughter again. Jerry laughed with him.

"Anyway," Jerry said after they had both calmed down, "it gave me an idea for a terrific doomsday bomb. I'll take some of the orbital forts we have floating around in space, add some asteroid slag for mass, and tie them all together with the new high magnetic field superconductors into a giant artificial asteroid. Only *this* asteroid is going to be in the strangest orbit you have ever seen—a bouncing orbit."

"Bouncing orbit?" Alexander repeated, puzzled.

"The asteroid—we can call it the 'Mace of God' if you like—"

"I like it!" Alexander said.

"The Mace of God starts way up high above the northern hemisphere of Earth—I don't know the exact distance yet, it's probably out further than the Moon—but poleward. It drops straight down at the Earth, getting bigger and bigger—and scarier and scarier. Then just before it hits the Earth, you push a button and the asteroid splits into two pieces and goes flying apart, pushed by magnetic springs.

"The two pieces go orbiting around the Earth, meet on the other side, the magnetic fields clamp the two halves together again, and the recombined asteroid shoots upward over the southern hemisphere. If I time everything right, it will take half a week to climb up and half a week to fall down, so once a week you save the whole world from instant obliteration by the mere press of a button."

"People will really appreciate me then, won't they?" Alexander said, pleased.

"Yeah! And once I have the button keyed so that it only responds to *your* thumb, then no one will dare attempt to assassinate you!"

"You have done well for your Infinite Lord, Jerry," Alexander said, patting the young man on the back.

"I have not done it yet, my Infinite Lord. But I'll start work on it right away. It shouldn't take long. Most of what we need is already in orbit. One of the tricky parts will be the identification hardware and software to make sure that it is really you that pushes the button."

"Remember, I don't like that iris identification stuff. It's not dignified for the Infinite Lord to have to stare into a peephole like ordinary people."

"I am quite aware of that, my Infinite Lord. But tactile-plates are tricky to adjust. I hope you'll be able to give my assistant some of your time tomorrow?"

"Sure," Alexander said agreeably.

"His name is Bill Boswick. Sixth level and as sharp and hard-working a computer hacker you'll find anywhere."

"Tell your owlie to make an appointment with . . ." Alexander started. "Damn! Guess I'll have to get Eric to replace Rob. Can't be bothered with all these details . . ."

Saturday afternoons were Tanya's free days. Alexander liked boxing and spent every Saturday afternoon watching the fights put on for his benefit. The last fight was always a heavyweight fight—bare-knuckled—to the finish. Both winners and losers in the bloody contest were paid handsomely, but sometimes it was the next of kin that collected the loser's share. Tanya usually begged off and went shopping.

In one luxury store limited to seventh level Watchers and higher, she was looking over some sexy nightgowns to see if these were perhaps the key to a heart attack or stroke. There were only a few weeks left until Jerry would have the Mace of God operational. Once the Mace was in place and keyed to Alexander's hand, then she would have to shift her tactics to keeping Alexander alive and healthy as long as possible. She should also find some way to warn those on Mars, although there was little they could do.

The clerk serving her wore a fifth level yellow Cap of Contact and kept trying to interest her in a compact of eye makeup.

"I'm sure madam would find this most interesting," the clerk said, holding out the compact in front of her.

"I'm not interested."

"The design is most unique," the clerk persisted, opening the compact. "The mirror is removable." She levered the mirror forward out of its receptacle in the top. Behind the mirror was a yellow viking coin from Mars.

Tanya stole a furtive look at her ever-present Amazon guard. The guard was standing in the doorway to the shop, looking outside, obviously bored. Few of the clothes there would have looked good on that burly body. Of course, the shop had surveillance cameras, like every other place on Cyprus, but considering its clientele, Tanya was sure that the Watchers spent little time monitoring the activities in this store. Besides, mere possession of a Mars coin was not a crime. Many had been brought back as souvenirs.

"Very interesting color. I'll take it." Tanya reached for it, but the clerk pulled it away.

"That's just a sample," she said. "I'll get you a fresh one." She reached under the counter and handed Tanya a box.

"If you don't like the color, bring it back," the clerk said. "I'll replace it with another one."

CHAPTER 17

DESIGNING EDEN

Alexander had barred two-way communication with Mars. His ego, however, was such that the laser link from Earth still transmitted video programs from the Church of the Unifier television network. He hoped ultimately to convert those on Mars by the force of his personality, having failed using the force of his weaponry. Almost the only one who watched the programs was Maury Pickford. As one of his many jobs as part-time assistant to Chris, governor of Mars, whenever he had some free time he would skim through the day's worth of stored programs, passing over the commercials and sermons, to pay careful attention to the live coverage of Alexander and other church officials, trying to extract some real news for publication in his videotext newspaper, the *Mars Weekly*.

"The warnings we've been getting from Tanya through the Mars underground have finally come true," Gus said. He was gathered with a number of other scientists in the main lecture hall in the basement of the Sagan Mars Institute. During mealtimes, the lecture hall doubled as part of the base cafeteria. Now the chairs were all facing one way and everybody was watching the Church of the Unifier program on the large flatscreen in the end wall. It was Sunday on Earth and Alexander was preaching his usual Sunday sermon. Gus noticed that Alexander had lost some weight and no longer had an apoplectic color to his face. Tanya must now be doing all she could to keep him healthy. Today the views of Alexander preaching were interposed with views of a falling artificial asteroid.

251

The camera angles, taken from strategically spaced spacecraft and various locations on the ground, showed clearly that the asteroid was falling rapidly straight at Earth. Directly in front of Alexander was a large model of the globe, and above it, slowly moving down, was a miniature model of the falling asteroid.

"The world is sinful and needs to be punished," Alexander preached to the huge audience that had gathered to hear him in the gigantic Eurodome, built where the country of Monaco used to be. It was evening and the dome had been retracted to show the starry sky above. "So I have caused to be made the Mace of God. If the Mace of God strikes the Earth, it will destroy all that live upon it."

He paused, and a computer simulation showed the Mace of God falling onto Europe. First there came the searing heat and light from the shock-heated atmosphere piling up in front of the asteroid, then a gigantic explosion as it struck the surface and burrowed through the crust and into the Earth's liquid lava core. Huge tidal waves started across the Atlantic to ravage the coasts of North and South America, but long before they got there, the shock waves passed through the center of the Earth and produced gigantic earthquakes around the entire globe. Long-dormant volcanoes erupted, then molten debris from the impact started to fall from the sky.

Gus closed his eyes, unable to stand it any longer, but unbidden from his memory came the images from his own dream where he made a pact with the Devil. He quickly opened his eyes again. Now on the screen all the raging infernos covering earth were disappearing under a pall of dust.

". . . that will hide the Earth in darkness for decades. *Nothing* will survive.

"But!" Alexander continued, "If the people of the world will love and worship the Infinite Lord, their God, and be truly unified, then I will save them from the Mace."

He raised his arms to the crowd that stretched seemingly to the horizon in the two-kilometer-diameter stadium.

"Do you love me?" he asked.

"We do!" came the deafening roar. Alexander beamed.

"Will you follow me and worship me?" Alexander asked.

"We will!" the crowd roared.

"Will you obey me and cease being sinners?" he asked.

"We will!" came the reply.

"Then I will save you," Alexander said. He put his hand on the model of the Earth, interposing it between the model of the Earth and the model of the falling asteroid. As he did so, the model asteroid sprang apart into two pieces that started to circle around the model Earth, just missing it. The video then switched to cameras showing the real artificial asteroid springing apart. Inside could be seen the powerful superconducting magnets that supplied the strong repulsive forces needed to push the two halves apart with enough velocity that they would separate by more than the diameter of the Earth before they fell. The same magnets would act as a compression spring when the two halves met each other on the other side, soaking up the energy of the collision and storing it as compressed magnetic field energy for use the following Sunday when the Mace of God fell on the Southern Hemisphere of Earth.

Having saved the world, and with everyone obediently paying attention to his every word, Alexander launched into his usual Sunday sermon. He seemed to pay no attention as one half of the asteroid streaked through the upper atmosphere right over the open stadium with a blue-green glow that warned all once again how close they had come to a fiery death.

"That drag loss is going to build up, and some day Alexander isn't going to be able to save them," some scientist said from the audience.

"Our Mars underground contacts say that they make up the losses with onboard nuclear power plants that pump up the superconducting magnets after the two halves recombine," Chris answered.

"Isn't there some way our contacts can turn that doomsday machine off?" another asked.

"One of them was on the design team," Gus said. "He did what he could, but Jerry Meyer checked all the control codes himself. In addition, the asteroid itself is booby-trapped. If anyone unauthorized lands on it, it locks up and the next time it falls—good-bye Earth."

"We've got to do something!" Jay Plantagenet exploded. "We can't let the whole Earth die when the egomaniac dies."

"It would be great if we could figure some way to save Earth," Gus said. "If any of you have any good ideas, please let us know, and we'll see if they can be carried out using our Mars underground organization on Earth. But in the meantime, we had better start thinking about Mars. If the Earth goes, the few thousand people here on Mars are the last chance for survival of the human species."

"Dr. Armstrong is correct," Boris Batusov said. "We cannot survive indefinitely on Mars without aid from Earth. We do not have the technological infrastructure. Soon our medicines will be gone, then our electronics will fail, our machines will wear out, our buildings will fail, our population will decrease, and mankind will fade from the universal stage."

"We need to terraform Mars so we don't have to live inside pressurized buildings, vehicles, and Marsuits," Chris said. "Once we can live out in the open, we can let our population grow and become large enough to have the technological infrastructure we need."

"Great idea, Chris," Jay said tartly. "I presume you're going to do it in six sols, so you can rest on the seventh?"

"Well, it will take a little longer than six sols. But it might not take too long if we are willing to be satisfied with less than ideal Earth conditions."

"Anything is better than the near-vacuum we have to work in now," Gus said. "What are your proposals?"

"I've done some thinking about this before," Chris said, "being in atmospheric studies and all . . . We already know that many plants can grow at low pressures and temperatures. Not Mars surface pressure and temperature, but if we can get the pressure up above one hundred millibars—ten percent of an Earth atmosphere—and the temperature above the freezing point of water for part of the day during growing season, then many plants not only can grow, but can fix nitrogen from the three percent there is in the present Mars atmosphere."

"But people can't survive in one hundred millibars," Red Storm said from the back. "At least not for long. Air bubbles start to form under the skin and then the pain gets so bad you wish you were dead. You have to have at least two hundred millibars, and most of that has to be oxygen. I know—I once had to spend three weeks at that pressure to conserve air until I finally found the leak in my tug. A quarter atmosphere is better—that's what most belters use in their work suits."

"Somewhere between a quarter and a third of an atmosphere, 250 to 350 millibars, is what I've been thinking," Chris said. "The top of Mount Everest is at 350 millibars, and there have been some crazies who have actually climbed the mountain without using oxygen masks. A half atmosphere would be nice—but I'm afraid that will be tougher to come by."

"How are we going to get two hundred millibars, when all we have now is six?" Jay asked. "Not to mention that there isn't any oxygen in it."

"You gave me one idea, yourself, Jay," Chris replied. "We just go to the middle of Hellas Basin and dig a hole forty kilometers deep. The Martian atmosphere rushes in, and bingo, down in the bottom of the hole we have half an atmosphere. All we need to do is divert a large asteroid from the asteroid belt and drop it in. We might even get some volatiles that way."

"You're beginning to sound like the Great God Alexander!" Jay protested. "To get a hole forty kilometers deep, you'd need a seventy-kilometer diameter asteroid, roughly twice as big as the hole you want. That would raise a huge cloud of dust, crack the crust with earthquakes, and reactivate all the volcanoes."

"Reactivating the volcanoes wouldn't be so bad," Chris said. "We'd get some of those subsurface volatiles put back into the air. The dust cloud would absorb more sunlight, generally heating the atmosphere, which is good, although if it were real thick it would get temporarily cooler near the surface. Besides, Mars has plenty of experience with planet-wide dust storms. Remember the really bad one we had last fall? It only took ten weeks to clear up."

"It would take a good deal of time and effort to find and move the asteroid," Gus continued. "But it would be worth it if it gave us enough pressure that we could work without suits, even if we would have to have oxygen masks."

"I don't think you eggheads know what you are talking about," Red blurted from the back. "A measly little asteroid a hundred meters in diameter weighs a million tons. Just how the hell are you going to move that seventy-kilometer sucker you're so glibly talking about? What sort of delta vee are you going to have to give it to get it moving toward Mars—and what rocket ship are you going to do it with? My tug sure ain't up to it."

"Hmmmm . . ." Chris said, pulling out his vidofax and setting it in compute mode. "Getting an asteroid from the belt would mean a lot of delta vee. Maybe, if we are lucky, we can find a Trojan asteroid or a distant outer moon of Jupiter or Saturn that we can kick into escape with just a delta vee of one kilometer per second."

"I doubt it," Red said. "But so what if you did? Stick it in your computer and get ready to be appalled."

"I'll assume a density of rock," Chris said, punching the number icons on the face of the vidofax. "Ouch . . . Red is right . . . Almost ten to twenty-third joules. Wonder what that means in real terms." He punched some more, then looked up.

"Assuming fifty percent conversion efficiency, we would need twenty thousand one-megaton bombs . . . or a ton of antimatter."

"All the Earth's antimatter factories together produce only about a hundred kilograms a year," Gus said. "And we don't have all the Earth's antimatter factories. We'd have to spend a couple of centuries doing nothing but building antimatter factories, and we'd still be left in a hole."

"I didn't say it would be easy—or quick," Chris said. "There's another way to terraform Mars. It's more conventional, but it will take time. What we need to do is heat up the polar ice caps. It's long been known that there is plenty of carbon dioxide and a small amount of ammonia frozen along with the water ice in the permanent polar caps and the dust-covered layered terrain around the poles. If we can heat those areas, then enough carbon dioxide will be released to raise the air pressure at Mars sea level to almost 200 millibars—250 millibars in Hellas Basin.

"Once the carbon dioxide pressure reaches that level, the greenhouse effect will start and raise the temperature, melting the water ice all over the planet and releasing even more volatiles trapped in the water and on dust grains. The small amount of ammonia will complement the carbon dioxide since it absorbs in the infrared region between eight and twelve microns, where carbon dioxide doesn't. According to some old papers by Sagan, even one hundred parts per million of ammonia would be very effective."

"Hmmm," Gus said. "We could start by illuminating the poles using those reflective battlefield illumination mirrors that Alex left in orbit. We would want to build more, of course, which would mean that Red and the belters would have to look for asteroids with aluminum in them."

"Tin, copper, silver, even lead, aren't bad reflectors in space where they don't oxidize," Red said. "Maybe I'll find a solid silver asteroid next . . ."

"Dust from Phobos and Deimos dropped on the poles would darken surface of ice and increase absorption of sunlight," Boris suggested.

"We will want to help out the process by making a few thousand tons a year of other greenhouse gasses like the various fluorocarbons and the simpler hydrocarbons like methane, ethane, propane, and butane," Chris said. "The hydrocarbons will also help keep out the ultraviolet. If we are going to work outside, we'll need the protection. We should stop with butane, though. I understand that the next hydrocarbon, neo-pentane, smells like a mixture of yak shit and rotten fish."

"It's going to be bad enough with ammonia and methane in the atmosphere," Gus said. "But I suppose we'll get used to it."

"Our long-term objective will be to convert the carbon dioxide and water into oxygen and hydrocarbons," Chris continued. "That's what plants do, of course, and we'll want to start as many forests as we can, as fast as we can. It's still going to be a long time before we can do without oxygen masks."

"We don't need to carry tanks of oxygen as long as there is *some* oxygen in the atmosphere," piped up Martha Turner, one of the chief techs at the institute. "It would be simple to design a battery-driven turbocharger with the right kind of filters to separate out the nitrogen and oxygen for use with a breathing mask."

"Great," Chris said. "Work up a design and I'll give you a patent."

"Now comes the cruncher," Gus said. "The last terraforming idea turned out to require tons of antimatter. What do the numbers say for this idea? I would say that there may not be enough solar energy hitting Mars to heat up the ice caps in a reasonable period of time."

"I've already calculated that," Chris said. "To heat up the *whole* surface of Mars, not just the ice caps, to above freezing temperature, *and* to vaporize all the carbon dioxide from ice to gas, takes about two million joules of absorbed energy per square centimeter of planet surface."

"Ouch!" Gus said. "Well, I guess that takes care of that idea. No way are we going to get two million joules of energy for each square *centimeter* of Mars. I'd hate to calculate the equivalent amount of antimatter."

"No!" Chris protested. "That's not bad at all. Don't forget that in this case we can use plain sunlight as our energy source. And although only sixty milliwatts of sunlight falls on each square centimeter of the sunlit portion of Mars, just one Earth year's worth of sunlight is enough to heat Mars above the freezing point if all of it could somehow be absorbed in the planet. If we dust the ice caps and trigger the greenhouse effect, then one percent improvement in the absorption of sunlight means one hundred years before it gets warm. Two percent—fifty years; four percent—twenty-five years."

"That's beginning to sound interesting," Gus said. "How long before the carbon dioxide has been converted into oxygen and hydrocarbons, so we can go out without even requiring Turner's turbocharged breathing masks?"

"It's going to take a long time," Chris said. "Plants aren't very efficient at using sunlight to crack apart carbon dioxide molecules and rearranging them into something humans tolerate."

"How long?" Gus asked.

"A hundred thousand years," Chris admitted softly, then added, "We can speed that up a factor of ten by choosing the right types of plants."

There was a long silence.

"It'll have to do," Gus said. "Alex has left us with little other choice. Anyone have any better ideas?"

The room was silent. Finally Jay spoke up. "I think Chris' greenhouse approach is the one we should start working on. Being able to work outside and raise crops outside without being limited by high-tech pressure suits and pressurized buildings is going to make a big difference in our survivability. If Martha Turner can come up with a low-tech, low-weight, high-reliability turbomask, then we will be essentially as free of technology on Mars as an Eskimo is on Earth. That goal is worth putting in twenty-five to fifty years of effort—and the time it takes to reach that goal is short enough that people can stay motivated to work on it. I might even walk around outside without a Marsuit myself someday—if I'm lucky."

"We'll start working on Chris' idea immediately," Gus said. "I'll want Chris and others to go through the numbers carefully and come up with a detailed plan as soon as possible. In the meantime, if any of you have any new ideas or possible modifications to Chris' basic plan, please let me know."

"I'm going to model the formation of some smaller 'air hole' craters with my asteroid impact computer simulation," Jay said. "If we have fifty or a hundred millibars of atmosphere at sea level, which we might get after ten years of warming, then we would need a much smaller hole to get the pressure up. Also, if we lived in the hole with the plants, then we could keep the oxygen level higher than if the plants were trying to oxygenate all of Mars."

"You're still talking about an awfully massive asteroid," Red warned. "Don't forget that the mass goes up as the cube of the diameter, and you said that you needed an asteroid with a diameter almost twice the size of the hole you wanted to dig."

"Not necessarily," Boris said, raising his hand to interrupt. "I witnessed a penetrator rod from the antisatellite missiles strike Deimos. It dug a deep hole in crust. Very deep compared to either its diameter or length."

"That's why rods are used in warheads," Jay said. "They penetrate extremely well, even through armor. The French knights at Agincourt found that out the hard way when they met the arrows from King Henry's English longbowmen. Do you have any rod-shaped asteroids, Red?"

"I can find you lots of sweet potatoes, but no rods," Red replied.

"Maybe a closely spaced string of small asteroids would be just as effective as a rod," Jay mused, getting up. "I'll have to run it through my simulation."

"I never tried to deliver more than one asteroid at a time, especially to the surface of a gravitating body," Red said, also standing up. "I've got some calculating to do myself."

Gus stood, too. "Let's everybody do some calculating and modeling, then get back together tomorrow."

The room was shortly empty except for Gus and Chris. Maury, who had ducked out to the nearby Olye Olye Outs Inne bar toward the end of the meeting, wandered back in carrying a beer.

"Unless you have some objection," he said, "I'm going to make the results of this meeting a major feature article in the next *Mars Weekly*."

"No objection," Gus said. "The more people who are thinking about making Mars a better permanent home for mankind, the better."

"Say, Maury," Chris said. "This terraforming project is going to keep me awfully busy."

"I don't doubt it," Maury said. "I'll do all I can to take care of governor business for you."

"Thanks," Chris said. "But I was thinking of something else. Elections are coming up in eleven weeks. I've just decided I'm not going to run for reelection again. Three terms is enough. Why don't you run?"

"Why not?" Maury said, thoughtfully pausing to sip his beer. "It would give me something useful to do and let you scientist types have more time to save the human race."

"Good," Chris said, pulling out the violet-colored Globe Coin of Office from his shirt pocket and hanging it around Maury's neck on its frayed rainbow ribbon. "You can start being governor now. You take all the calls, you make all the decisions, and if something needs a signature, just shove it in front of me and I'll sign it. I'll take the blame if anything goes wrong, and the people of Mars can get a good look at how you operate *before* they elect you."

"But ..." Maury protested, picking up the violet coin to look at it, but Chris was already on his way out of the room.

"Say, Governor," Gus said, with a slight smile. "You have some delicate negotiating work ahead of you."

"Me?" Maury protested. "Negotiating? What? With whom?"

"If we're going to terraform Mars so it is more suitable for humans, don't you think we should inform the original inhabitants of the planet what we're up to?"

"But I thought the Lineups weren't talking to us."

"We at least ought to try and let them know," Gus persisted. "We'll go visit their North Pole enclave as soon as Chris, Jay, and the others have firmed up the detailed plan."

A few days later the lecture hall at the Sagan Institute was full again. They had moved the walls so that more of the cafeteria was included, but still there were people standing in the back. Nearly everyone on Mars was working on some portion or other of the terraforming problem.

Jay reported that a string of small one-kilometer-diameter asteroids would indeed be better than one large asteroid at digging an "air hole" in Hellas.

"When you drop a big asteroid on a planet it makes a big hole," Jay said. "But it also shakes up the ground so much that the dirt loses all its strength and it starts to flow like water. It flows in and fills up the hole. That's why you don't find any really deep impact craters on Earth or Mars.

"A string of small asteroids will dig a hole roughly equal to the length of the string, but the total energy deposited is down by many orders of magnitude, so the ground-shaking is less. Hopefully this means less fill-in afterward. We won't really know until after we try."

"How many asteroids will be needed?" Gus asked.

"Eighteen one-kilometer-diameter dense asteroids as close together as Red can get them," Jay said. "They'll dig a hole twenty-four kilometers deep, and I'm hoping it will only fill back halfway—leaving us twelve kilometers."

"But you are still talking about kilometer-sized asteroids—and eighteen of them, at that," Red protested. "We can get a net around them, but the typical sail will take hundreds of years to move that amount of tonnage."

"Depends upon the gravity well they are in and whether you can use gravity assist," Jay said. "Have you found any bodies that size near Jupiter and Saturn—but not too near?"

"I'm still collecting that data," Red said. "Been trying to get some of the astronomer-types out in 'Giant Land' to look for stones instead of stars."

"If worse comes to worst, we'll just have to wait a hundred years," Jay said.

"I'll let you know," Red said. "But it'll take a week or so to collect the data."

"I'm sort of held up, too," Chris said. "The gang on Phobos have gone out in an orbiter to look at the battlefield-illumination mirrors still floating around. But it will be awhile before they can check to see how many are operational. I'll need that solar influx data before I can do any more detailed calculations."

"Then perhaps it's a good time to go tell the Lineups what we are planning," Gus said.

"If they'll listen," Chris said. "I never felt so insulted in all my life as when that character 'Biddeliboop' told us to shove off and not only locked the door in our face, but sealed it shut."

"We still should try," Gus said. "I'll take along a laser communicator and try sending the beam through the door and up the tunnel. If that doesn't work, I'll break into their cable one more time and try contacting them that way."

"That sure brought them out last time," Red said. "By the way—we don't have to go to the North Pole to talk with them. They have at least five enclaves at various places all around the globe. Last winter I looked up maintenance reports on crawlers for 'optical fiber tangles' and found a number that couldn't have been caused by missile fibers. It didn't take long to go to the scene, find the fiber end, and track it down to their enclave. All of the enclaves are widely separated and buried deep underground. They almost never come out except to fix a broken fiber. They must use them to keep in touch."

"I wonder why they're underground, and so limited in distribution?" Max MacFadden asked.

"According to some of the biology-types I talked to, they don't understand it either," Red said. "The Lineups seem to have made little oases and are just trying to hold on, rather than trying to expand their population. Not the normal response."

"They also aren't normal in that they haven't evolved in two billion years," Gus said.

"The buried enclaves distributed over the whole globe make perfect sense," Jay said. "If you're trying to maintain status quo in a few oases over billions of years of time, then your real danger is asteroid strikes. You want deep cover so the small ones don't get you unless it's a direct hit, and you want wide distribution so you survive even a big one."

"They also avoid the volcanic regions," Red said. "The known enclaves are at each pole and near the impact craters Copernicus, Maunder, and Kunowsky."

"Kunowsky!" Jay said. "I did a traverse of that crater."

"According to the maintenance records, your crawler also got a wheel tangled in some optical fiber," Red said. She paused. "It wasn't missile fiber."

"Of course!" Jay exclaimed, shaking his head at his own stupidity. "It couldn't have been. We were thousands of kilometers from the nearest war action. It never occurred to me at the time—"

"You weren't the only one," Gus said. "But Red *did* pay attention and found the Lineups. Now, we'd better go and talk with them. Although Copernicus is closer than the North Pole, we should go to the North Pole enclave since we have regular hopiter flights to the base nearby. It'll save on antimatter."

"I want to go," Red said. "As you said, I found them. Besides, I haven't patted a hunk of diamond in a while."

"Well," Gus said, looking around, "a hopiter or crawler can carry a dozen—if not in comfort. Chris and Jay should go, in case the Lineups do talk to us and want to ask questions about the terraforming plan. Maury—apprentice governor. Some biologists, in case they let us in . . . Anyone else that doesn't have important work to do at the institute?"

When the director of the Institute put it that way, the number of raised hands in the room dropped dramatically.

CHAPTER 18

THE LINEUPS HELP

The eight that landed in the hopiter at Boreal Base included Antonio Fiat, a medical doctor from the EEC contingent that had been rescued from the Moon, and Chang Lu, a low-gravity biologist from the Chinese moon contingent. For the drive in the crawler over the dunes and glaciers to the enclave, they used Al Eisen, who had driven them there before. Phyllis Eisen used Al's influence to join them.

"If they let us inside," Phyllis said, "I want to record all the ice and dust layers those diamond tunnels pass through."

That evening, Gus looked for Viktor, in order to invite him along, too. He found him in the Bore Hole—drunk and crying. Red was sitting with him, trying to comfort him. She looked up as Gus came to their table.

"He just learned from the Mars underground that his wife was one of those killed at Novosibirsk," she explained.

"My heart, it is broken," Viktor burbled drunkenly, then started sobbing again.

"Maybe there's someone else that can take her place," Red said as she drew the sorry besotted head to her breast and rocked him gently. She looked up at Gus.

"I'd better get him to bed," she said. "I'll see you tomorrow morning at the base motor pool. I don't think he'll be in any shape to come."

"The crawler leaves at nine sharp," Gus warned.

A winter had passed since the last time they had visited the enclave. The crawler used autonomous guidance most of the way, but occasionally Al had to take over and chose a route past a slide or around a new crevasse.

When they came to the diamond door set in the face of the cliff, the circular door opening was visible once again, and the "porch" had been swept clear of snow. Red went immediately to the door and tried to turn it.

"It's locked," she reported. "Welded shut."

Gus got out the laser communicator and set it up so that it shot up the tunnel. A good deal of thought had gone into what message they could send that would draw the attention of the Lineups and get them to at least converse with the humans. The biologists had suggested one course of action based on the few comments the Lineup Badepi had made before it had so abruptly terminated conversation.

"Hello," Gus said. "This is Gus Armstrong calling Badepi. I have friends with me. Mars is too cold. Mars does not have enough air. Our equipment is failing. We cannot survive much longer. We need help. Please talk to us."

Gus took his thumb off the "talk" button on the laser communicator.

"A bit of a lie, but to a culture that has survived a few billion years, a few hundred years is 'not much longer.' "

There was a glimmer of laser light reflected from the floor of the diamond airlock and the communicator spoke.

"Replying to Gus Armstrong with friends is Kipape-bypepo-tumuro-badepi-pubemu. Coming am I. Waiting are you."

"It worked," Maury said. "It's coming."

"It's not the one we talked to before," Gus said. He replayed the response and listened to it carefully. "But there *is* a 'Badepi' in there."

"The creature you originally talked to was a single segment, sent out to do a simple mission," Chris said. "I bet that now it's linked up into a longer, more intelligent creature. Remember how the learning power of the Lineups increased as more segments plugged into the first group?"

"Here comes Kip-whatever," Maury said, pointing at the low door. The inner door of the airlock had been opened and the front portion of the long Lineup had its forward eyerods up against the door. Varicolored laser light flashed over them as the creature scanned their bodies.

"Finding of equipment of Gus Armstrong operational," came the voice from the laser communicator. "Finding of equipment of friends of Gus Armstrong operational. Understanding of statement of Gus Armstrong not."

"Our equipment is operational now," Gus said. "But within a few years it will not be. We humans will then die."

"Coming of humans, one of male sex, one of female sex, inside shelters then allowed. Remaining of others outside."

"Only one pair of humans allowed. These enclaves are the Lineup version of arks," Phyllis said.

"We must save *all* the humans," Gus said. "Please give us permission to increase pressure, increase temperature, and increase oxygen content of Mars atmosphere."

"Asking of permission needed not. Preventing of any creature from any action unthinkable."

"But we may melt the ice cap and destroy your protection. The increase in temperature and pressure might kill the plants you are protecting. Are you sure it's okay for us to change Mars until it is more like Earth?"

"Surviving of fittest prime directive. Controlling of environment on Earth enabled survival of humans in past. Controlling of environment on Mars enables survival of humans in future. Preventing control of environment of Mars by humans unthinkable."

"The quintessential ecologist," Phyllis said. "They would let us change their whole world rather than interfere with us while we're following our inherent nature to change the environment in order to be more 'fit' and be a survivor."

"The human race thanks you," Gus said. "We will get started on our work soon, but it will take many years—centuries—before we are done. In the meantime, would it be possible to come into your wonderful shelter and see some of the marvels there?"

"Continuing of tasks on inside of importance higher," the reply came, and the Lineup backed out of the airlock, screwed shut the inner door, and started to turn back up the tunnel.

"It's going back in again," Gus said, shaking his head. "I guess they really aren't interested in us except as specimens."

"What the hell!" Maury shouted. He grabbed the laser communicator control from Gus and shouted into it at the retreating figure of the Lineup. "Hey! Come back here!"

"Coming back," the reply came. The Lineup stopped and came to the inner airlock door and waited.

Gus and the others stood there open-mouthed.

"Open the door," Maury commanded.

"Opening," the Lineup said, and unscrewed the inner door.

"Open . . ." Maury started, but Gus grabbed the communicator control away from him.

"Opening," the Lineup said, and started to open the outer door of the airlock.

"Wait!" Gus yelled through the laser communicator.

"Waiting," the Lineup said, the six fingerlike protuberances around its snout paused in the holes in the circular door.

"It's obeying commands just like a robot!" Phyllis said.

"Very unnatural for a biological creature," Chang Lu said.

"I'd better be careful how I phrase things," Gus said. "Maury almost had him opening the outer door of the air lock before he closed the inner door."

"Close the doors, but leave them so humans can open them," Gus commanded. "Return inside shelter. Wait there for humans to arrive."

"Leaving doors," the Lineup said, backing up through the inner airlock door and rotating it shut. "Returning inside." They waited for a few minutes, then a fluttering of reflected laser light came through the diamond door. "Waiting for humans."

"Let's go!" Red said, starting to twist the outer airlock door by its six finger-sized holes.

"Scientists first," Chris said, holding up his air analyzer.

"He's been there before, Red," Gus said. "Let him go ahead and make sure the Lineup will really let us through the last door into the enclave proper."

After Chris had reported success, the rest cycled through one by one until only Gus and Al Eisen were left.

"You'll have to stay here to call for help in case something happens," Gus said to Al.

"I'll watch it all through Phyllis' helmeyes," Al said agreeably, pulling down the visor on his modified battle helmet.

When Gus cycled through the last door into the Lineups' enclave, he looked around to see that everyone had taken their helmet off except Phyllis, who was turning around slowly, recording everything with her helmeyes and at the same time giving Al a view. Gus raised his hands, unlatched his helmet, and took a sniff. The air was warm, humid, and had a hint of spice. The Lineup was right below his nose, but it didn't seem to have any particular smell.

The room was pretty much as they had observed before through Chris' helmeyes view from the airlock. Beds of plants were being tended by Lineups of varying lengths, while single units scampered here and there on errands. Gus then looked up to see some large black batlike creatures fluttering overhead. They were bigger than a kite, with two meter wingspans and bodies the size of an Italian sausage.

"What are those?" he said, pointing.

"I call them flutterbats," Chris said. "At first we thought it was a different creature, but then Phyllis pointed out the similarity between it and the 'wings' that the Lineup segments grow. Sure enough, Maury caught one of the Lineups growing wings and then letting them fly away free. The flutterbats seem to stay clustered over our heads. Perhaps we stink and they are air cleaners of sorts. I do note that when one of them passes close, the air has a fresh spicy smell to it."

"I'm starting to get a headache," Red said. "It's been fun, but on goes my helmet."

"Red's right," Chris said, raising his helmet, too. "There's plenty of oxygen to breathe in here, but there's too much carbon dioxide. A few hours of this and you'd be one sick dog."

"I'll need my helmet laser to talk to the Lineups anyway," Gus said, putting his helmet back on.

"While you talk to them, Chang Lu and I are going to have a look around," Phyllis said.

"I will go this way," Antonio said.

Gus put a firm tone into his voice as he spoke to the still-waiting Lineup through his suit laser communicator. "Humans will explore shelter. No Lineup is to obstruct humans. You will listen to Gus Armstrong."

"Obstructing of humans in exploration of shelter unthinkable," the Lineup said. "Listening is Kipape-bypepo-tumuro-badepi-pubemu."

"I will call you Kipape," Gus said. "I want to make sure you understand what we are planning to do to your planet. We humans are going to make a new atmosphere for Mars by warming up the polar ice caps using large reflectors of sunlight in space and darkening the ice with dust from the moons. We then are going to drop some small asteroids to make a hole in Hellas Basin to increase the air pressure."

"Making of new atmosphere from polar caps by humans take long time," said Kipape.

"A very long time," Gus agreed.

"Making of new atmosphere from polar caps by Lineups take one cold-hot cycle," Kipape said.

"One cycle?" Gus said in amazement. "You mean you could do all that in one Martian year!"

"Making of atmosphere and hole in one cycle with near certainty," Kipape said.

"Would you?" Gus asked, unable to believe in their good fortune.

Kipape didn't answer, but just stood motionless, his eyerods sweeping back and forth over the group of humans.

"All you have to do is give him the order and they will start," Maury said. "Gives you a sense of power, doesn't it?"

"A sense of foreboding," Gus said. "I feel like the Sorcerer's Apprentice."

"Or someone who has just rubbed a magic lantern," Maury said. "What's the best way to spend three wishes?"

"That's it!" Gus said. "Instead of us trying to think of the best thing to do, then telling them, why don't we ask the Lineups to help us figure out how best to use them!"

"Dear Lineups," Red murmured to herself. "Please design us an Eden on Mars."

"Commencing of design of Eden on Mars," Kipape said.

"Wait!" Red yelled in panic. "I didn't mean it!"

"Waiting," said Kipape.

"At least you can turn them off," Maury said.

"It's all right, Red," Gus said. "Provided they know what an Eden is."

"The Old Testament must be part of the Main Base library that they memorized," Maury said. "But all of those begats must have bewildered them when they got to that part."

"Continue," Red said tentatively.

"Continuing design of Eden on Mars," Kipape said. There were flashes of light from underneath his body as bursts of laser power shot back and forth from his coupling eyerods to light fibers lying on the floor of the cavern. Soon a another five-segment Lineup came and hooked into the end of Kipape, then a four-segment, then a seven-segment. The long body of the twenty-one-segment creature stretched across the room and around the beds of plants. It was strangely motionless as its twenty-one-segment brain cogitated the difficult problem. After a while, a burst of laser light flashed at Gus' laser communicator.

"Making of diamond tower into space take long time. Taking of Lineup of one segment by humans into space take short time."

"We'll be glad to take any number of Lineups anywhere in the solar system, if it would help," Red assured.

"Taking of one segment to near moon sufficient," Kipape said. "Continuing design of Eden on Mars."

When it was all over and the eight humans crawled back out of the Lineup enclave, they were followed by two Lineup segments. The two segments had simple stripe patterns around their middle that were very similar. Their names were similar, too, Babadi and Babado.

"It's hard to believe that those two creatures are going to terraform Mars in one Martian year," Maury said as he watched one of them start ripping up a nearby snowbank with its powerful claws and devouring the dirt and snow as fast as it could eat. The other Lineup went to the nearby crawler and waited patiently outside the airlock door.

"They aren't quite going to do the whole job in one mear," Chris said. "As they pointed out, the material just isn't there to make the atmosphere really Earthlike. They'll get us out of spacesuits in a mear. But to convert the carbon dioxide into oxygen, and dig up all the nitrates buried in the ground and turn them into nitrogen will take a little longer."

Al opened the airlock door to the crawler and waved at the Lineup waiting there.

"Hop in," he said. The Lineup stayed motionless.

"Forgot . . ." Al said. "Maury!" he called.

"Hop in," Maury repeated, coming up. The Lineup bunched its powerful legs beneath it and literally hopped into the airlock using all four feet.

"Hopping in," it reported.

Maury climbed in the airlock with the Lineup and Al cycled them through as Gus came up for his turn.

Al turned to Gus and said, "It's a good thing you gave the Lineups the general command that henceforth they are only to obey commands from someone who carries the violet Globe Coin," Al said. "Otherwise every offhand statement by a human could lead to trouble."

On the arrival of the crawler at Boreal Base late the next day, the Lineup caused quite a crowd to gather, but the Lineup ignored all the people and trotted to the orbiter waiting on the landing pad at the end of the base.

"Is it housebroken?" the orbiter pilot asked dubiously as he looked at the feathery-skirted piglike animal.

"Hasn't eaten a thing in over twenty-four hours," Maury assured him. "But just get him up to Phobos and stand back. It'll more than make up for lost time if it eats like the other one."

"No waist for a seat belt," the pilot continued, still dubious.

"I'm sure he can hold on with those claws," Maury said.

"I'll send you the bill for any rips in the seats," the pilot promised as he activated the outer airlock door.

"Hop in," the pilot said to the Lineup. It didn't move.

"Hop in," Maury said, smiling superiorly at the pilot.

"Hopping in," Babado said as it hopped into the airlock with a heavy thud.

"Hey! Take it easy on the equipment," the pilot said.

"Sorry. My fault," Maury said, stepping into the lock with the Lineup. "See you inside." The air lock door closed as the pilot stood there shaking his head.

Chang Lu and Antonio Fiat took two sols to gather together a few colleagues with backgrounds in biology—there weren't that many assigned to the supposedly barren Moon and Mars—some techs, and some equipment, then drove back out to the site of the Lineup enclave in a caravan of crawlers. Chris went with them. When they got there after the long journey through the spiral ice canyon, there were four Lineups, busy eating the snow and dust as fast as they could.

The Lineups were standing side by side, digging their way across the surface of a slope that would ultimately take them up on top of an ice ridge. From their backs extended long jet-black wings, soaking up the sunlight that was now pouring down almost twenty-four hours a sol. Behind them, in the broad trench they were making, the snow was covered with a dull black substance.

"Their feet now number eight!" Chang Lu said with obvious surprise. "I do not understand."

"They have grown much longer in the middle," Antonio said. "They seem to have grown the extra feet to support the middle section. They are almost as long as two Lineup segments."

"That is the answer," Chang Lu said. "They do not replicate by making smaller young through parturition or budding, but instead grow large enough to make two adults by bifurcation. Look at that one on the left. It has a seam all around its middle, and it has eyerods starting to come out, just as on a two-segment Lineup."

"Let us not sit here observing out the window of the crawler," Antonio said, noticing Chris out on the snow with his air analyzer. "We should be outside with our cameras and equipment gathering data."

Antonio read the readouts on his materials composition analyzer. He had just fed it a sample of the dull black ice that was ejected periodically from the rear of one of the hardworking Lineups.

"Almost pure water ice and elemental carbon," Antonio said. "The buried layers of ice they are eating contain twelve percent carbon dioxide and five percent ammonia frozen in with the water ice. But they are removing the carbon dioxide and ammonia and passing the ice on through after mixing it thoroughly with carbon black so it absorbs sunlight better. What is amazing is that the temperature of the eliminated ice is not significantly greater than the ingested ice."

"It's hard to get exact figures because of the background atmosphere and all the leaking human pressure suits around," Chris said. "But I'm pretty sure that they are turning the frozen ammonia and carbon dioxide into gases. About one-fourth of the carbon dioxide is left as it is, the other three-fourths is converted into oxygen, methane, and the carbon black they are mixing with the ice. They must have a pretty remarkable digestive system if they can selectively process all the other molecules, while essentially passing the water ice through unchanged.''

"Something's happening over here!'' a tech yelled. "One of the Lineups is doing the splits!''

Chang Lu, Antonio, and Chris ran over to where the Lineup lay sprawled on the ground. Its four front feet were all to the left side of the recumbent body, while the four rear feet were on the right side. The elongated body of the Lineup was twisted about the central section, where a full complement of eyerods jutted out between the seam. The Lineup twisted some more, then two clawed paws, one from each side of the middle, reached out to grab each other and increase the twist. Suddenly there was a giving of the middle section and the long, eight-legged Lineup segment became two short, four-legged Lineup segments.

"Identical twins,'' Chris said.

"Not quite,'' Antonio said. "The zebra stripe pattern is slightly different. The front one has an outer stripe that is black, while the rear one has an outer stripe that is white.''

"They all have the same basic pattern of stripes in the middle,'' Chang Lu said, looking around at the other Lineups. "But they are all different in the outer stripes.''

"Just like the old product identification stripes they used to use in grocery stores before computers got smart enough to read labels,'' Chris said.

"Very strange,'' Chang Lu said. "Much too orderly for a biological creature.''

"There goes another Lineup into a sprawl,'' Chris said, pointing. "Pretty soon we'll have eight instead of four.''

"Their replication rate is astounding,'' Antonio said. "It is only five days and they have replicated three times.''

"The first one probably started out pretty well fed,'' Chris said. "So it takes them two days to process enough ice and dirt to replicate. That's not surprising, the way they eat. They must pass a ton of ice a sol when there is lots of sunlight. All they need to do is find fifty kilos of good stuff in that ton.''

"With the chemical capabilities of their digestive system, all they need is carbon dioxide, water, and perhaps a few trace elements," Chang Lu said. "There is certainly all they need in the ice and dirt."

Chris had been punching the number icons on his vidofax. "The way I figure it," he said, "they will exceed the nearly ninety billion population of Earth in just thirty-seven replications—a little over ten weeks from now."

"They will completely cover the polar cap!" Antonio exclaimed.

"I think that's the idea," Chris said, putting his vidofax away with a smile.

"I said, 'Proceed with plan,' and the little bugger just snouted right into that gray dirt like it was honey," Maury said, taking a sip of Caldera beer in the Olye Olye Outs Inne bar. He looked down appreciatively at his glass. "They sure don't make good brew on Phobos like Jim does here. Must be the low gravity or something." He looked up at Gus and Jay again. "I stayed around to watch the first few replications, but after a while it got disgusting, so I took the next orbiter down."

"Disgusting?" Gus said.

"Well, the biologist types might find it interesting," Maury said. "But when the nose falls off a creature and wiggles into the ground like a worm, I call that disgusting. Especially since it grows a new nose and does it again. Pretty soon every Lineup had a couple of dozen groundworms helping it root through the loose dirt it had clawed up. Looking for the good stuff, I guess."

"It would certainly improve its efficiency at processing the soil," Jay said.

"That's not the most disgusting part, though," Maury continued. "After a groundworm is loaded up with as much as it can carry, it has to transfer that load of nutrients to the main Lineup . . ." He paused.

"Does it hook back onto the nose?" Gus asked.

"No," Maury said, grimacing. "Wrong end."

"Of course," Jay said brightly. "The Lineup segments connect together nose-to-tail to make longer segments, and the segments share a common bloodstream, nervous system, and digestive tract through that connection. Thus, they have a built-in place for the groundworms to hook into. Neat!"

"Neat to you scientist types," Maury said. "Disgusting to me. The groundworms crawling up the rear eyerod fans looked like fat maggots crawling up their skirts, then thin maggots dropping out again. I couldn't stand more than a few minutes of it."

"I'm sure many of the things we do look just as disgusting to them," Gus said. He turned to Jay. "What is the latest news from Phobos about the progress there?"

"The Lineups are doing real well," Jay said. "Their replication rate is higher on Phobos since they don't have to heat up ice. They have already started on the mirror-building phase."

"I still don't see how diamond can be made to reflect sunlight," Maury said. "Isn't it transparent?"

"Think of it this way," Jay said. "Even though a pane of glass is transparent, when you look through it you see a weak reflection of yourself in the front surface, like it was a poor mirror."

"Yes," Maury admitted.

"Well, there are actually *two* reflections," Jay said. "One off the front side and one off the back side. If you make the pane of glass real thin—a quarter of a wavelength of light thin—then the back reflection comes out in phase with the front reflection and they reinforce each other, making a single sheet of quarter-wavelength-thick glass a moderately good mirror. Then if you put another thin sheet a quarter of a wavelength behind the first one, it will not only reflect the light that gets through, but do it in phase with the first sheet, making the combination a slightly better mirror. The Lineups are going to use eight layers of diamond of slightly different thicknesses alternating with seven layers of vacuum. They expect to get better than three nines reflectance over the whole solar spectrum—much better than *any* metal mirror."

"Three nines?" Maury asked.

"Ninety-nine point nine percent," Jay said. "Less than one tenth of one percent of the sunlight will get through. They expect to do

better than five nines in their laser mirrors, since they can be tuned
to a single wavelength of light. They'd better; at the power levels
they're going to operate at, the diamond would convert to graphite
if much laser power got absorbed in the mirrors."

"When is the first laser launch?" Maury asked.

"Day after tomorrow," Jay said. "Won't be much to see except
the sail moving away. The laser line in the Martian atmosphere the
Lineups are using is in the long infrared. The Lineups can see that
color, but we can't."

A few days later, half of the humans on Mars were outside in Marsuits watching the large gossamer sail floating motionless in the sunlight above Mars. It was light enough that the sunlight was already
pushing it outward toward the asteroid belt, but the speed obtain-
able from sunlight was not fast enough for the Lineups. They were
going to illuminate the sail with their own artificial sunlight.

"Here comes the laser over the horizon," Gus said. He was
wearing a modified battle helmet and was watching the scene in the
infrared through the helmeyes in the top of his helmet. "I can't see
the laser beam from the output mirror, but I can sure see the scattered light glow from the laser light bouncing back and forth between the two mirrors."

Maury's helmet didn't have a helmeyes, and all he could see was
two flat mirrors orbiting slowly overhead. The distant sail started
moving as the gigawatts of laser power from the orbiting atmospheric laser bounced off it, pushing it outward to the asteroid belt,
carrying its single passenger.

"There goes the first interplanetary Lineup," Gus said. "At the
rate the sail is accelerating, the Lineup will be there and replicating
in a few weeks. Then watch out, asteroid belt."

"How is it going to stop once it gets to the asteroid belt?"
Maury asked. "Is there a laser there, too?"

"The sail going out is actually in two pieces," Gus said. "An
inner portion that carries the Lineup in a harness, and an outer ring-
shaped portion. When the sail gets near the asteroid belt, the two

parts are separated. The laser light being sent from Mars pushes the ring-shaped outer portion faster than the inner portion carrying the Lineup, so they drift apart. Soon, the laser light bouncing back from the ring-shaped mirror is striking the inner sail from the other side. The focused laser light reflected from the large ring sail is nine times brighter than the laser light coming directly from Mars, so the inner sail slows down and comes to a halt in the asteroid belt."

"I still don't get it," Maury said.

"There is a good book in the library files that explains it all," Gus said. "It's a science fiction novel, but there are diagrams in the back explaining how the multiple sail concept works. I think the title's *Rocheworld* . . . can't remember the name of the author."

"Years of work made worthless," Viktor said sadly as he watched the slush drip out the ends of the hundreds of coring tubes still stacked in the storage racks. Ernest Licon came over from where he had been supervising the crew that was dismantling the core storage building preparatory to moving it to a safe place off the polar caps. The distant horizon was covered with millions of Lineups eating their way toward them. Above the Lineups spiraled clouds of flutterbats, processing the gasses released by the actions of the Lineups and the groundworms. In polar orbits overhead passed thousands of large reflector mirrors, turning as they orbited to keep the region where the Lineups were working flooded with sunlight even though it was the dead of winter.

"At least you got pictures of every core," Ernest said.

"But the whole idea was to establish a chronology of ice and dust layers so that any future cores could be rapidly dated," Viktor said. "With the Lineups digging up the polar regions, there is no need for a chronology."

"We are all having to make sacrifices," Ernest said.

"I know," Viktor said sadly.

"You had better get to the hopiter pad and get out of here," Ernest said. "Although the Lineups like working under the equivalent of twenty Suns, your Marsuit can't handle it. We'll all have to be on our way before the wave of Lineups gets any closer. I'll see you at the 'bomb shelter' in Mutchville when my crawler convoy gets there."

"Don't be late," Viktor said. " 'Splat Sol' is only twenty-five weeks away."

Orbiting low over Mars, skimming through the upper regions of the atmosphere, were eighteen lasers, soaking up the energy stored in the sunlight-excited carbon dioxide molecules and turning it into eighteen beams of ten-micron laser light. The mirrors on the lasers were three kilometers in diameter—big enough to send their powerful beams all the way to the asteroid belt without spreading. There, the beams were picked up by eighteen similarly sized ring-shaped mirrors anchored behind eighteen one-kilometer-diameter asteroids. The ten terrawatts of repetitively pulsed laser power in each laser beam were focused onto the rear of each massive nickel-iron asteroid, turning it into a crude rocket. First a short pulse would turn a thin layer of metal into a thin cloud of vapor, then a longer, stronger pulse would explosively heat the vapor, pushing the asteroid along. Although there were Lineups riding along on the structure to adjust the focus for steering, the system was designed as a self-steering beam-rider, and there was little for the Lineups to do until the last few sols, when they would tie the asteroids together with diamond-fiber cables into a long metal arrow aimed at Mars.

"Twenty-four hours to Splat Sol," Gus said. "Is everyone out of the volcanic regions and into shelters?"

"Olympia, Tharsis Saddle, Elysium Saddle, and Hellas Basin are all deserted," Maury reported. "And of course the polar bases are closed down because of the Lineup activity there. We have Phobos and Deimos crammed to capacity, since they'll be the safest places. Everybody else is in underground shelters at Mutchville, Sinai Springs, and Melas. Some people wanted to stay at Isidis, but I felt that was too close to Hellas."

"All we can do now is wait," Gus said, strumming his fingers nervously on the table at the Too Mutch bar. The large flatscreen on the wall had an image of the approaching string of asteroids taken from a telescope on Phobos.

"Good thing we have lots of beer," Maury said, taking a sip. He looked at the flatscreen. "How come the asteroids are in an arrowlike configuration? I thought they were supposed to be lined up in a row."

"By putting a couple off to one side at the end, the Lineups hope to make a hole shaped like a butterfly," Gus said. "The 'wings' will be northeast and northwest. That will give us more sunlight down at the bottom."

"Let's hope it works," Maury said.

"They've been doing things right so far," Gus said. "They're only partially done at the poles and we already have sixty-five millibars of oxygen and a total pressure of 125 millibars here in the lowlands at Mutchville."

"Some crazies have even gone out for a few minutes with nothing but Turner Turbomasks on," Maury said. "I was going to make a law against it, but decided not to. Let 'survival of the fittest' operate to weed out the stupid ones."

"I guess the best thing for me to do is get plenty of sleep," Gus said. "Hopefully there won't be any emergencies tomorrow, but if there are, I need to be fresh."

"I think I'll have another beer, first," Maury said. "See you in the conference room tomorrow."

"Somehow, this just doesn't feel right," Gus said as he watched the large flatscreen in the conference room.

"What do you mean?" Chris asked.

"The Lineups are doing all the work for us," Gus said. "All we're doing is sitting around on our duffs, drinking beer and watching television, while the Lineups are making us a brand new world—out of their world—and handing it to us on a silver platter."

"I sort of agree," Jay said. "But we originally were planning on doing it all on our own."

"And they *are* doing it hundreds of times faster than we ever could," Chris said.

"That's a good close-up shot of the arrow coming in," Maury said. "How did they get that one?"

"Somebody took an orbiter out from Deimos in a high elliptical orbit a few days ago so he could travel along with the arrow for a portion of its track and get a good picture," Jay said.

"Say!" Gus yelled. "There are Lineups still riding on the asteroids!" He grabbed the controls to the flatscreen and zoomed in on a diamond cable. There was unmistakably a Lineup segment moving along the cable. "There's another . . . There are dozens, hundreds of them! Splatdown is only two hours away! They're going to be killed!" He grabbed a communicator. "Maury, quick—what's the channel for our optical cable link to the Lineup enclave?"

"Forty-nine."

Gus punched the icons on the screen of the communicator and spoke into it. "Hello! This is Gus Armstrong calling Kipape."

There was a short pause, then came a reply. "Replying to Gus Armstrong is Kipape-bypepo-tumuro-badepi."

"Some of your people are still on the asteroids!"

"Remaining on the string of asteroids are 648 segments."

"They must be taken off!"

"Remaining of segments on asteroids until impact is plan."

"They'll die!" Gus yelled, frustrated. "We humans can't allow the Lineups to sacrifice their lives for us!"

"Sacrificing of lives of segments not possible. Having of lives of segments not."

"They're not alive?" Maury blurted. "They certainly act plenty alive to me."

"I've always been suspicious," Chang Lu said. "Ask them if they are artificial life forms—robots."

"Are the Lineups artificial life forms?" Gus asked. "If so, who made you and when?"

"Making of Lineups by Masters many cycles ago."

"That explains many things," Jay said. "But that means we asked permission of the wrong people."

"Where are your Masters?" Gus said into the communicator. "We want to talk to them."

"Existing of Masters here at this time not."

"They are caretakers of the lifeforms until the Masters return," Jay said. "But the Masters didn't figure on one of the lifeforms learning to talk and giving orders to the Lineups. They won't recognize the place when they get back."

"Tell me about the Masters," Gus ordered.

"Telling about Masters permitted not."

"We'll have to work on that later," Gus said, turning off the communicators. "We have a hole to dig. I still don't like the idea of those Lineups going with it, robots or not."

Circling out in space, the well-shielded eyes of orbiting cameras watched the arrowlike string of asteroids plow down through the thickening Martian atmosphere and strike Alpheus Colles at the bottom of Hellas Basin. The strike had been timed so that both Phobos and Deimos were on the other side of Mars where they were protected from the X rays emitted by the shock-heated atmosphere compressed ahead of the leading asteroid. There was a gigantic thunderclap as the air rushed in to fill the vacuum in the hole punched through the atmosphere.

The string of metal spheres stabbed down into the soil. Their kinetic energy turned into heat as they plowed to a stop, and they blew up like a line charge of dynamite. A butterfly-shaped cloud of dust and rocks rose from the ground and shot into the air, where it would stay for weeks. A shock wave spread out to encircle the planet. It was felt with trepidation by the humans huddling in the underground shelters, but the hundred billion Lineups that now covered both polar regions continued to dig and eat the icy dirt without a pause.

CHAPTER 19

MARS REBORN

"The radio signals just stopped, sir," the tech said sadly.

"That's what comes from trying to fly at low altitude," Gus said resignedly. "Especially in a region where there may now be a mountain where there used to be a valley."

"Shall I send in another RPV, sir?" the tech asked.

"No," Gus said. "The dust is still too thick. Too thick to risk a manned hopiter, too. We'd better go in on land."

Gus put on his Turner Turbomask and switched it to the pre-breathing mixture to clear the nitrogen from his system as he walked down the long underground corridors in Mutchville to the motor pool area. The outer buildings at Mutchville had been depressurized from the original half-atmosphere pressure to a third-atmosphere. Now people who worked outside could switch back and forth between the quarter atmosphere around Mutchville at the bottom of Chryse Basin and the slightly more comfortable third atmosphere inside without having to put on Marsuits. There were some sensitive types, however, who couldn't take the low pressure—and it certainly stressed the children, who spent most of their time in the half-atmosphere core buildings where school was held.

Gus checked the sensors in his turbomask as the airlock went through its cycle. He was still putting out a lot of nitrogen and shouldn't say outside too long. He switched the turbomask to pure oxygen and stepped outside onto the surface of Mars. The sky was still the dark rusty red it had been for the last four weeks, with only a brighter area in the sky where the noonday Sun should have been. He walked past the greenhouse balloons, brightly lit from inside by the fluorescent lighting, his feet crunching loudly in the inches-deep dust and ashes still drifting down from the sky. It was cold and he hurried into the warmth and higher pressure of the motor pool maintenance hut to arrange for their journey south to inspect their new home.

The crawler convoy from Mutchville worked its way across the equator through the Ares Valley, down past the Beer and Newcomb Craters, then started over the Hellespontus Mountains. Although their average speed through the Chryse Plains had been good, as they got into the more cratered highlands south of the equator, they were lucky to average ten kilometers per hour. It took almost three weeks of continuous driving to cover the six thousand kilometers to Hellas Basin.

"I do believe the sky is getting clearer," Chris said, peering out the overhead dome in the cockpit section of the lead crawler. "I can actually see a disk where the Sun is supposed to be."

"The ground isn't getting any clearer," Al Eisen said. "Nice fresh boulders everywhere. Our average speed is now down to five kilometers per hour."

"What's that up ahead?" Chris asked. "Looks like something moving around in circles."

"Could it be a dust devil?" Gus asked, getting down from the jump seat in back of Al and climbing up to the observation dome in the central section of the crawler. "Or worse?"

"Moving too slowly," Chris said.

Gus activated the telescope and zoomed in on the distant motion. "It's a cloud of flutterbats!" he said.

"We're going over completely new ground, now," Al said. "The crawler's map has a half-kilometer hill at this point, with the top at minus two kilometers below sea level, but our navigation system has us at minus four kilometers and dropping rapidly."

"We must be starting down the crater," Jay said. "I wonder how deep it goes?"

"Take it easy, Al," Gus warned.

"The crawler can handle this slope easily, sir," Al said. "And the visibility is good out to a couple of hundred meters before the dust gets too bad."

"Let me go outside for a background atmospheric measurement," Chris said, putting on his sweater and slinging on his turbomask. "I need to calibrate the crawler instruments to take out the contaminants coming from the crawler itself." He cycled through the airlock, went a few dozen meters away, set up his analyzer, stood back while it made a reading, then brought it back in. Above him whirled clouds of flutterbats.

"Phew!" Jay said at the odor arising from Chris' clothing. "You smell like you have been rolling in a barnyard."

"That's life on the new Mars for you," Chris said, reading out the display on his analyzer. "Total pressure 290 millibars. Oxygen 146, carbon dioxide 90, nitrogen 43, methane 11, and a trace of ammonia. It's the methane and ammonia that give the air its tang."

"Cow farts and pig piss," Jay said.

"But they make great greenhouse gasses," Chris said. "And its already working. It was actually six degrees *above* freezing out there."

"Balmy," Jay said.

"Down we go," Al said, starting the crawler moving again. Phyllis came over to Chris and looked at his sweater.

"Hold still," she said. "What's this on your sweater?" She picked off a tiny brown waxy pellet.

"Flutterbat droppings," Chris said. "The ground is covered with them."

"Wonder what they contain?" Phyllis said to herself as she went to the analytical bench in the engineering section. A short while later she returned.

"Carbohydrates and ammonium nitrate," Phyllis said. "Organic material and fertilizer. We shouldn't have any problems getting plants to grow in this ground."

"I notice that the carbon dioxide, methane, and ammonia levels are all lower than what they should be for a well-mixed atmosphere," Chris said. "I think the flutterbats are converting them to useful solids, leaving just the oxygen and nitrogen for us."

"From the smell, they have a long way to go," Jay said.

"Coming up on a stream," Al said. They all went to the front to look out the window. A whole section of the hillside was wet with springs where the fracture zone from the impact had cut through the water table. From the base of the seep there flowed a good-sized stream that was cutting a virgin valley down the sloping side of a gigantic hole in the ground. Al led the three-crawler convoy on a ten-kilometer detour around the marshy slopes before they could continue on their way down.

"Ten kilometers below sea level," Al announced a few hours later.

"We're halfway down, if the hole comes in at what I calculated it," Jay said.

"Pressure up to 390 millibars," Chris said, "and a balmy thirty centigrade outside; don't even need a sweater. This would be a nice place to live."

"Except for the smell," Jay said.

"Well," Chris said, looking up through the dome overhead at the clouds of flutterbats that spiraled upward as far as they could see, "the flutterbats are working on that. Give them time."

The stream had grown into a significant river. Twice, they were forced to backtrack and ford over when they came to a fork where the river joined with another one.

"It's getting hotter," Phyllis complained. "Does this crawler have an air conditioner?"

"Are you kidding, Phyl?" Al said. "Heaters we got. The makers never thought we'd need air conditioners on Mars."

"Say!" Gus said, pointing slightly upward through the clouds of circling flutterbats that grew smaller as they faded off into the dusty air. "I think I see the other side. We must be coming to the bottom." Sure enough, off in the distance they could see the dark meander of a stream coming down the opposite slope a number of kilometers away. Al took them further down slope. The air, full of busy flutterbats, became clearer and clearer, until finally they could see the surface of a body of water far below. In the center of the brown steamy lake was a small peaked island.

"Splash Lake," Jay said. "Just where it ought to be, sixteen kilometers below sea level. Right now it's muddy and ugly and hot, but soon it'll be the resort spot of Mars."

"My prediction for the temperature down there is fifty-four Celsius," Chris said, "with a humidity to match. A veritable equatorial jungle. It would be a great place for plants, but I think I'll wait until it fills up to a more temperate level."

"It's hot and damp and smelly, but it's home," Gus said. "Let's call the 'bomb shelters' and tell everybody to start packing up the moving vans."

Gus looked down out the picture window in his new office at Dugout City to Splash Lake lying far below, surrounded by the lush fields and gardens of New Brazil. The huge pane of thin plate glass for the picture window had come from a window-glass factory started by some entrepreneurs, now that air pressures had risen to where unpressurized buildings were feasible.

Off to the left he could see Westside River meandering down through the young forests covering Westside Slope, while ahead of him were the lush pastures of New Switzerland, dotted with tentlike pens of grazing sheep, goats, rabbits, and barnyard fowl. The clear plastic tents were weighted down around the edges by large-scale versions of the Turner Turbochargers, for the animals were just as sensitive as humans to carbon dioxide. He watched as a crew of animal tenders moved a tent full of goats to a fresh patch of thick green grass. They still had no cows—Earth was still not communicating with them, much less sending cow embryos. It was recess time at the institute day school, for the hillside below him was covered with running and laughing children, each with his or her personal Turner Turbomask.

Some cumulus clouds were building up at the far end of the lake, where the Sun had been reaching down Eastside Slope to heat the already-warm waters. There would probably be the usual afternoon rainstorm. Above, on the surface of Mars, it was cold and

frosty as winter started in the southern hemisphere, but down here
in Dugout, the warm waters of Splash Lake always kept the small
band of humans warm and safe. He turned to go back to his desk
to tackle the problem that still awaited him there.

Carlo Vulpetti's accelerator team had finished building the first
section of their antimatter factory down Ius Canyon. Should they
start on a second section or work on an accelerator breeder to make
fissionable fuel for the nuclear reactors instead?

Just then Fred Whimple interrupted.

"There is an important message from the Mars underground
through our Tokyo laser link," Fred reported. "It's on your message file."

Gus pulled up the message. It was from Tanya.

Alex had minor stroke Sat night. Pleaded with Jerry to
turn off Mace. Says controls respond only to Alex. I was
able to pull Alex through enough to get his hand on globe
Sunday. Alex better now, but still obstinate—refuses to believe he might die. Can you talk sense into him?

The terrible dream of the world exploding into a ball of lava
came unbidden again to Gus and he could almost hear the echoing
laughter of the Devil as he accepted the Devil's offer of a world.

Suddenly Gus was racked with a physical shiver of guilt and
fear. He *had* accepted a world—Mars—and was now gloating over
its beauty, while all the time Earth was but a heartbeat away from
complete destruction.

He doubted that he could do anything to sway his brother—
obstinate was inadequate to describe him—but he had to try.

He touched a few icons on his screen and soon was in touch
with Tether Control on Phobos.

"I'll be taking the next tether shuttle up," he said. "Get ready
to activate Project Fireball." He reached into his desk drawer and
took out the violet one-thousand-Mars-dollar globe coin lying there.
"Fred!" he called at the comm unit. "Could you come in here,
please?"

Fred Whimple came meekly through the door. "Yes, Dr. Armstrong?"

"I'm going on a trip. A long one. I'd like you to run the institute while I am gone."

"I'll be glad to, sir, as long as I can reach you for important decisions."

"I'm afraid that will be impossible, Fred. You'll have to make all the decisions yourself—even the important ones."

"I can't do that!" Fred said, his chin dropping and his eyes widening. He started to shake in fear at the thought of all that responsibility.

"You *can* do it, Fred," Gus said firmly, getting up from behind his desk. He motioned to the chair he had just vacated. "Please sit down here."

"I couldn't do that, sir."

"Please," Gus repeated. Fred came over and slowly sat down at the desk.

"Now, as you know," Gus said, the badge of office of the Governor of Mars is the violet one-thousand-dollar globe coin."

"Yes," Fred said. "I have seen it. The only one ever made."

"No. There is one other." Gus held up the large, thick, violet-colored coin in his left hand and rotated it with his mangled thumb and finger so Fred could see both sides.

"It belongs to the director of the Sagan Mars Institute," Gus said. He handed the coin to Fred, who took it with a hand that trembled at first, but which steadied as he brought it closer to look at it.

"It's yours now," Gus said. "With that coin, you have the authority to make whatever decisions need to be made to run the institute. You can even command the Lineups.

"Of course," he continued, "it wouldn't really do to flaunt it about . . . sort of detracts from the authority of the governor of Mars."

"Yes. Of course," Fred said, smiling conspiratorially. He put the coin in his vest pocket.

"If you'll bring up the 'In' file on the console, you'll find your first problem waiting for you," Gus said. Fred quickly touched a few icons and the problem was once again on the screen.

"The solution to that is obvious," Fred said quickly. "Mars needs mobility more than fixed power sites. With the temperature rising and the ice melting, we'll soon have plenty of hydroelectric power and can hold the nuclear power plants in reserve. Why don't you tell—"

"Why don't *you* tell them?" Gus interrupted. Fred looked up at him, a panicked look on his face. Then he reached into his vest pocket, fingered the coin hidden there, and firmly turned to the console.

Gus went into the front office that held Fred's little secretary desk, picked up Fred's name plate, and returned to the director's office. As he placed the name plate on the desk and took his own off, he could see the last of the message on Fred's screen.

> Dr. Fred Whimple
> Director, Sagan Mars Institute (Acting)

"If I didn't know it was made of diamond, I wouldn't trust it," Gus said, looking at the thin strand stretching out into space away from Phobos. The diamond tether was zooming by below them as they rode it outward, braking their fall in the centrifugal force field by transferring energy to the superconducting cable wound in a spiral around the diamond tether core. They shot though the Deimos transfer station at the 940-kilometer point. A capsule released at that point would fly out to the inner tether hanging down three thousand kilometers from Deimos without having to use any fuel. They continued on to the launch station at the end, some one hundred thousand kilometers distant, passing Deimos' orbit at the fourteen thousand kilometer point.

"Since the orbital inclinations of the two moons are almost a degree different, Deimos only gets near the tether a few times each mear," the capsule pilot said. "Then we *twang* the first vibrational mode of the tether just enough to avoid hitting it."

Six hours later they were standing in the half-gee centrifugal acceleration of the end station. The strange ship of Project Fireball hung waiting at the bottom of the station.

"It'll be like living in a telephone booth for a month," Gus said grimly as he climbed down through the graphite tanks full of water and into the small central compartment.

"The smaller it is, the less likely it is to be noticed," said the engineer helping him with his equipment. "I made sure the central computer memory has plenty of books in it, plus all the information I could dredge up on Cyprus. Good luck, Gus."

"I'll need it," Gus said, closing the hatch.

Shortly thereafter, the swing of Phobos in its orbit was at right angles with the far-distant Earth. Grapples released and Gus shot off toward the inner solar system at twenty-three kilometers a second, higher than escape velocity from the solar system. If he missed Earth, he would never come back.

Now that the capsule was in free fall, specially designed nozzles released the stored water in a controlled spray that covered everything in tens of meters of dirty, frothy ice. Soon, another insignificant comet was on its way to a blazing death as a momentary fireball in the upper atmosphere of Earth.

CHAPTER 20

THE LEFT HAND
OF GOD

The bright streak of a falling fireball burned itself out in the upper reaches of the moonless sky. The radar warning net that surrounded the Island of God took note of the blazing column of plasma, trailed it for a while, since its trajectory was a little unusual, then dropped it from notice as the fireball seemed to break into pieces that were too small to reflect radar well.

The still-glowing pieces of the heat shield broke up around him, and Gus had a momentary sense of fear as the cocooning couch that had been surrounding him also began to come apart. The insulating, foamlike layer covering his spacesuit not only kept the heat out, but absorbed practically everything electromagnetic in the radar bands. Gus looked down at the uprushing Earth. Through his darkened visor he could see his glowing feet creating a shock wave of phosphorescence in the rarified air. Beyond them were patches of light from the cities below.

The glow around his feet faded away as the diamond-glass cable tethered to the massive "comet head" thousands of kilometers above pulled on his harness and slowed him down. The visor on his helmet adjusted automatically to the light level, and he could now make out the illuminated main road that ran around the island ahead. Minutes passed and Cyprus loomed large ahead of him, with Turkey off to the right. He pulled down the infrared visor and the scene turned from blackness to phosphorescent light, as if he had turned on an artificial green moon. He was falling more slowly now, as the slowly tilting cable brought him down closer to the surface.

The timing had been good. He was going to land in the water just offshore of Limassol. The automatic ultrasonic altitude indicator came on, and he felt the motor in his harness hum as it reeled cable in. His feet were now just inches above the rippling waves. He skimmed across the water toward the shore, the cable reel singing as it sucked in cable to keep him above the surface. He found the blinking blue light that marked the end of a long unloading pier that stuck out into the water.

Don't want to get too close to the perimeter guards, he reminded himself. He punched the release button, splashed into the water, and sank to the bottom.

"What was that?" the patrolwoman said, lifting her head. She put down her coffee, unstrapped her varigun, and stepped out the door onto the pier to look out onto the calm Mediterranean ocean. Her partner went out the other door. Themistocles Haloulakous raised his massive, curling eyebrows up on his Sun-weathered forehead until they almost touched his orange Cap of Contact. A well-deserved self-satisfied smile spread over his face. He glanced at the clock. Right on time. And he had lured the patrol inside so they didn't see anything.

It had taken months of cajoling and flirting with the patrolwomen to get them to include a stop at his pierside taverna in their patrol routine. But he had once trained show-horses to dance, and if you can teach a horse to dance, you can certainly teach a dumb patroler to drink on stimulus. He came out from behind his counter and walked out onto the pier. The patrolwoman had placed her varigun on the rail and was scanning the surface of the water with her infrared binoculars.

The other patrolwoman came over from the opposite side of the pier. "Do you think we should report it, Sergeant?"

The sergeant hesitated. They should not have been in the café for longer than it took to get a cup of coffee and use the toilet. Even then, one of them should have stayed outside looking.

"It was probably just some dolphins fooling around," Themistocles said, smiling broadly at the sergeant. "One of the male dolphins must have had a horny dream, and when he woke up, he tried to take advantage of some sleepy little virgin girl dolphin." He grinned and leered at the sergeant, twisting his large curly mustache in an exaggerated fashion. The sergeant blushed, then turned stern.

"Must have been dolphins, Private," she said to the other patrolwoman. "Whatever made that splash would have had to be big, and there's nothing out there now. Let's get back onto patrol."

"*Au revoir*, Michelle. *Sayonara*, Michiko," Themistocles said. "See you tomorrow night. I will have a new espresso with cream and chocolate in it for you next time."

He bustled around their patrol wagon, opening the doors for them and helping them into their seats, implanting a gallant kiss on the back of their hands as he did so. He stayed at the end of the dock, waving them good-bye until they were out of sight. It was nearly midnight and there were no customers in the taverna, so he sent the busboy home and locked the door. Just before he turned out the lights he looked around the taverna one last time. He would not miss it.

Themistocles' home was under the taverna. It was a lousy place to live, with no view during the daytime except that of the sides of boats unloading food supplies during the morning and taking away garbage in the afternoon. Damp, too. But at least he didn't live in the city where his every move would be observed by the Watchers.

He had video cameras in his apartment, of course. Everyone on the Island of God had cameras in his apartment, even the bathrooms. The salt water was hard on the cables and equipment, though, and the occasional failures had given Themistocles many opportunities over the years to get work done when the cameras were not reporting his activities back to the Watchers and their monitor computers.

As he opened the door at the bottom of the steps leading to his rooms, his elbow pushed firmly on a decorative tile set in the wall and a video recorder interrupted the signal coming from the Watcher camera inside the living room and replaced it with a video picture of Themistocles entering his apartment, fixing a snack, and after a long yawn and stretch with his head tilted way back looking at the ceiling, finally sitting down to watch a late-night movie on the television. Themistocles had written the script, so he went through the identical motions of making the snack, so that the eye in his Cap of Contact would report the same actions the substitute video signal was reporting. During the long stretch, when the cap eye was looking at nothing but ceiling, he deftly took the bust of Homer from his bookshelf, slipped the cap from his head to Homer's, and placed Homer comfortably on the back of his easy chair in front of the television. He backed away from the chair and into the walk-in closet at the opposite end of the room, quietly closing the door behind him.

He turned on the closet light and opened a small secret panel in the wall at eye level. There was a small mirror and in front of it was a pair of small scissors and a safety razor. As his hands reached to pick up the scissors they trembled a little, but it was not fear that made them tremble, it was rage.

"I will never forgive that blasphemous usurper of the Mountain of the Gods for making me do this. May Zeus blast him with a thousand thunderbolts!" He picked up the scissors, hesitated, then snipped off one magnificent half of his mustache. Another snip and his upper lip was quivering under two hacked-up patches of hair. He tossed the scissors back into the hole in the wall, picked up the safety razor, and finished the job dry. He ended with a small cut in the upper left corner of his mouth. He had forgotten to include some kind of astringent, but he was not about to go back to his bathroom, so he had to keep dabbing at the blood with his handkerchief.

He next removed from the hole a cap that had the purple and white pattern of the employees of the Household of God, but its electronics were useful for other things than sending video to and from the Watchers. He put on the cap and looked in the mirror. He looked naked, but not naked enough. Rage was still on his face and his eyebrows glowered most unlike a true devotee of the God Alexander. He sighed. It must be done. He picked up the scissors and trimmed his thick handsome eyebrows to a pusillanimous patch. He made faces at the mirror until he found a combination of wide eyes and drawn-down mouth that made him look sufficiently stupid to be a workingman-devotee of the Great God Alexander. A white working-man's smock-coat completed the change. Lastly, he took out a set of keys, a small, battery-powered metal ball, and a bundle of painted cloth with shaping wires. These went into his cavernous coat pockets.

The closet had a secret exit. It went outside to a catwalk that ran around underneath the pier. He took the catwalk to the stairway that went up on top of the pier. Seeing no patrolwomen around, he quickly climbed the steps and walked briskly down the boards. Most of the pier was taken up with a large refrigerated warehouse where the incoming food supplies for the House of God were unloaded from ships, inspected and sorted, then loaded onto refrigerated trucks for transport up the curving expressways to the top of Mount Olympus to feed the large crowd of people in God's Castle.

The keys let him into the warehouse. Over the months it had been simple to make impressions of the keys of the warehouse foreman as he moved the keys from one part of the taverna counter to another while cleaning up the spills on the counter.

Once inside the warehouse, Themistocles acted like he belonged there. He opened a door leading to a loading dock, found the keys to a refrigerated truck on the wall inside, and drove the truck up to the loading dock. He went into the walk-in freezer and used the overhead dolly to roll a few sides of beef out of the freezer, across the room, and into the refrigerated truck. Then he rolled the overhead dolly to a door that opened out over the water at the end of the pier. The door opened automatically as the dolly approached. Making sure his back blocked the view of the Watcher cameras, Themistocles attached the small battery-powered ball to the hook and lowered the ball down into the water below. Leaving the baited hook in the water, he returned to the job of loading the truck. There were lots of boxes of frozen pheasants, and he stacked them carefully in the back of the truck so that there was a hidden space in back of them that was large enough to hold a man.

Gus had been making time, but slowly. His suit had been carefully adjusted with weights before he left, but they had guessed a little bit on the heavy side and it was hard going walking across the sandy bottom through the water. He stopped to check his bearings. The sonar signal from the pinger underneath the pier was right in the middle of his visor in blue. The pinger gave off a low level pseudorandom noise that was indistinguishable from wave noise unless the receiver knew the pseudorandom code. The pingers to the right and left were also on his visor, but had been translated into yellow arrows pointing to the blue dot at the center. Suddenly, there was a brighter pulsating green dot, moving slowly down through the water, just to one side of the steady blue dot. Gus headed for the green dot as fast as he could move through the water.

Themistocles kept himself busy for an hour, then went to the door overlooking the water and tried raising the hook. The motor on the overhead dolly changed pitch as it started to pick up a load.

"I've caught a fish," Themistocles said to himself, "a big one." He raised the hook until he could see the dark shape hanging above the water in the darkness below the pier. Hiding his actions as well as he could, he unwrapped his bundle of painted cloth and shaping wires, got it around the cable, and dropped it down to cover the large shape below. Now that the cover was on, he raised what looked like a wrapped bundle of meat and used the overhead dolly to roll it across the room and onto the truck in full view of the Watcher cameras and their monitoring computers. He would soon know if the disguise was good enough.

Leaving his extraterrestrial visitor hanging, Themistocles finished loading the truck with more sides of beef until the truck was nearly full. Pretending to take an inventory, Themistocles moved through the beef carcasses to the back of the truck, where he unwrapped and unhooked the visitor, still in his insulated space suit, and restacked boxes of frozen pheasants to hide him. It was still a number of hours until dawn. He found the logbook for the trucks on the foreman's desk, forged an entry for a late special delivery to the castle, with return of the truck on the following day, and drove off into the night on the long trip up to the palace at the top of Mount Olympus.

"I hope whoever it is back there knows what he's doing," Themistocles said to himself as he drove. "Years of work getting myself established on this island, and tonight I'll be a hunted man."

It was early Sunday morning when Themistocles drove up to the delivery gate at the Olympic Palace. He caught the guard dozing at her post.

"What the hell are you doing here!" the Amazonian palace guard blustered, shaking herself awake. "Why aren't you at Sunday service like everyone else?"

"Just like you—some of us must keep things going even during compulsory services," Themistocles said. "I have a special delivery of frozen food for the kitchen. Must be a party coming up."

"I don't know about any party," the guard said suspiciously.

"Just obeying orders," Themistocles said, waving his arms and raising his eyebrows. Then he remembered he had no significant eyebrows left. He put his stupid face back on. "Guess I'd better take it back."

"No! Go on in," the guard said angrily, opening the gate. "But I have to inspect the load."

Themistocles opened the door to the truck with one hand while his other hand was on a wrench hidden in his pocket. The flood of frigid air pouring from the truck raised goose bumps on the naked flesh of the thinly dressed Amazon guard. She peered in through the frosty mist at the sides of beef and stacks of cartons and passed him on.

At the delivery door to the kitchen there was a tall woman with long blond hair standing on the loading dock. Themistocles recognized her as Alex's concubine, Tanya. Her left hand was by her side, signaling the hand sign of the Mars underground, index finger straight for the spear, and the thumb and remaining fingers formed into a circle for the shield. He returned the signal and backed the truck into the dock while she rolled up a container on wheels.

"All the kitchen staff is at Sunday service," she said.

"Then the first load off the truck is the important one," Themistocles said. He rolled the covered container into the truck and shortly thereafter rolled it back out again.

"Hard work," he said to her. "Think I'll go for a little swim afterward."

Tanya took the container and pushed it into the walk-in freezer off the kitchen.

"Gus!" Tanya said when the helmet came off. "I missed you so!" She hugged him, chilly space suit and all.

"Tanya!" Gus said, wishing that he were not in his space suit so he could feel the hug. He was content with the shower of kisses and the nose wet with tears nuzzling his cheeks.

"You may smell like an ancient astronaut, but you look beautiful to me." She reached for a bundle she had stashed inside the freezer and handed it to him. "A large damp towel and a change of clothing," she said. "I hope you don't mind satin underwear—your brother has developed some weird tastes."

"How is Alex?" Gus said, struggling out of his space suit.

"Not good, despite everything I could do to keep him well. He doesn't know it, but I saw him suffer another small stroke last week. We've got to get him to tell Jerry to turn off the Mace."

"Can't Jerry do it himself?"

"Alex has to authorize any change to the program personally, and he won't do it. He is sure he is immortal. Can you talk to him?"

"I'll try, but I can't promise anything. How do you plan to get us together?"

"After Sunday dinner, the kitchen staff is usually let off for Sunday evening classes to study for their next level. Many times he and I have come down late in the evening and made ourselves a snack."

"Yeah," Gus said. "We used to do that when we were kids. Mom would never be sure what would be left in the refrigerator the next day."

"I'll bring him down tonight."

"While I wait in the dark inside the freezer," Gus said. Tanya silently picked out a blanket from the bundle and handed it to him.

"You'll have to," Tanya said. "It's one of the few rooms outside Alex's private quarters that doesn't have a monitor camera."

She gave him one last kiss and headed upstairs.

"Stop snooping!" Alexander yelled at the monitor camera as he and Tanya came into the kitchen. The indicator light on the camera blinked off and Alexander went to the large refrigerator and opened the door.

"Cold pheasant and cold duck!" Alexander said. The Olympic Palace kitchen staff knew their master's habits well and kept the refrigerator well stocked with carefully prepared leftovers.

"Sounds delightful, Alex," Tanya said nervously. "But there is something else . . . very important . . ." She opened the door to the freezer and stood to one side. Gus was standing just inside the door.

"Hello, Alex," Gus said calmly. "I'd like to talk to you—brother to brother, twin to twin . . ."

Alexander turned. His eyes grew wide and his face turned red with fury. He glared at Tanya, then at Gus.

"I have no brother!" he yelled. "I am the Infinite Lord! I am perfect! Look at you! Mangled! Imperfect! You're no twin of mine! You're an impostor!"

"Guards!" he bellowed. "Guards! I want this man destroyed!" Then he remembered that the monitor cameras were off. He started fumbling with his wrist communicator. Tanya ran to him and grabbed his wrist. He struggled with her, then threw her through the freezer door into Gus. She and Gus both fell to the floor while the wrist communicator went skittering across the floor and through a slot in the wooden floor grating.

"I'll do it myself!" Alex growled, running into the freezer, grabbing at Gus' throat.

"Alex," Gus said, choking. "Stop!" He got his hands up to Alex's chest and tried to push him away.

"Go ahead!" Alex gloated. "Try and choke me, you crip! You can't!" He laughed, and the laughter took on a metallic tone as Gus began to loose consciousness. The image of the Devil laughing while the world turned into a ball of molten lava returned . . .

The pressure stopped . . . Gus felt a heavy weight roll off his chest. Tanya's face was looking down at him.

"I gave him a shot with a hypospray I carry in my medical kit," she said, putting the empty tube back in the little belt pouch. "He'll be out for a few hours."

"That little conversation didn't turn out very well," Gus said. "What'll we do? Make a run for it before he wakes up?"

"That will still leave the world his hostage."

"We've got to get that Mace turned off," Gus said.

"We have one slim chance," Tanya said. "Alex hated to have to stop and peer into an iris scanner for identification, so the central computer has been trained to recognize him by sight. Let's see if we can get you into his quarters. Once there, we might be able to contact Jerry and turn the Mace off."

She looked at the slumped body of Alexander.

"Where will we put Alex in the meantime?" she asked.

"I know a nice warm space suit he can use—secondhand. Even has a hook to hang him up with, so he won't walk away when he wakes up."

"Cold pheasant and cold duck!" the handsome man in the golden tunic and tights said to the smiling woman with the long blond hair hanging on his arm.

"But is was too bad you cut your hand, sweetheart," the woman said. "It was a good thing your doctor was there to bandage it up."

They came to a large double door inlaid with golden carvings. On either side of the door was a giant Amazon guard, their helmets reporting everything they saw to the central computer. The doors swung open and the couple entered the private quarters of the Infinite Lord.

"Now for the central computer," Gus said, putting down the food.

"Let me," Tanya said, going to the control console. "I've

watched him do it a couple of times." She touched a few icons and the computer spoke.

"You wish to change the operating parameters of the Mace of God?"

"Yes," Gus said.

"I beg your pardon for having to ask, Infinite Lord," the voice said. "But you did require me to request identification. Please put your hand on the globe."

Gus looked around. There was the globe of the world that Alex used each Sunday to save the world. It was floating in midair above its base—no doubt some sort of superconducting applied magic. Above it was the little model of the asteroid that Alex had saved everyone from that morning. It was on its way up to its apogee, from whence it would return next Sunday.

He walked over to the globe and confidently put his hand on it.

"The left hand please, Infinite Lord."

Gus hesitated, took a deep breath, and put his bandaged left hand on the globe.

"The bandage prevents complete identification, Infinite Lord, even though my vision program tells me it is you," the voice said. "Is it possible to remove the bandage?"

"Not at the present time," Tanya interrupted, switching off the console. The minute the computer saw Gus' stumps, it would know something was wrong. She muttered something in Russian.

"Damn!" Gus said.

"I said that already."

"Maybe Alex has cooled off enough that we can talk with him," Gus said with a sigh.

"It's our only chance," Tanya said, leading the way to the outer door. "Remember, when we go into the kitchen, if the monitor camera is back on, tell it to stop looking at you."

"He's not wiggling, so he must still be out," Gus said as he un-latched the helmet.

Tanya looked in at Alexander, then suddenly put her hand on his throat to feel his pulse.

"He's dead!" she said, her face terrified at what she had done.

They got him out of the suit as fast as they could and tried everything, but they were too late.

"The world has one week to live," Gus said dejectedly. He picked up the limp left hand of his brother. "From the way that computer responded, it seems like the only thing that can save the world is this hand—the left hand of God." He brushed lightly at the fingertips that had recently tried to throttle him. The hand was starting to cool off. "If there were only some way we could keep it alive . . ."

"There is," Tanya said.

Gus looked up at her quizzically.

"But it's going to hurt," she said.

Gus was feeling queasy after they returned from carrying the remains of Alexander's body back into the freezer. Lying on the butcher block, next to the meat saw, was Alexander's left hand.

"Now it's your turn," Tanya said. "Are you up to it?"

"Is there any sedative left in that injector?"

"I'm afraid not." Tanya was using a steel to sharpen up the butcher knife again. Gus watched the flickering blade with dazed fascination.

"Besides, we have to make it look like an accident. I'll cut the major tendons and nerves with the knife so they'll be easier to reattach, but the muscles and bone have to go through the saw to make it look good."

She put down the sharp butcher knife and picked up Alexander's left hand. She looked at the end of the stump carefully, noticing the specific position of the important nerve fibers in this particular genetic version of a human left hand. She then placed Alexander's clammy left hand on top of his brother's quivering left hand and scratched a ragged white line on the living flesh with the point of her blade.

"Ready," Gus said. He stretched out his arm on the butcher's

block and looked away. Tanya turned on the meat saw so it would
be running when it was needed, then picked up the knife.

As the ambulance wailed off into the night, Tanya turned to the
crowd of staff and guards.

"Don't just stand there," she yelled at them. "Get to the church
and pray for the immediate recovery of the Infinite Lord from this
tragic accident!" Obediently they turned and, voices chattering,
headed for the huge chapel at the center of the Olympic Palace
complex.

When they were all gone, Tanya turned on the giant-sized waste
disposal machine next to the butcher block, picked up a cleaver, and
headed for the walk-in freezer.

Early the next morning Tanya went to the Central Hospital. As she
was approaching the main entrance, an armored patrol helicopter
thundered in overhead and landed at the emergency room pad. She
watched as the medics pulled the bloody body of a man in swimming trunks out the side door of the helicopter and placed him in
a stretcher. Tanya recognized him as the man who had delivered
Gus to the castle in the freezer truck.

"See if you can bring him around," the patrol officer growled.
"We want to find out why he was trying to swim to Turkey."

"Then you should shoot fewer machine gun bullets," the medic
said, looking up. "He's dead."

Tanya had a little difficulty getting in, but soon was allowed a short
visit with the recuperating Infinite Lord. He was in a large suite in
the wing of the hospital reserved for the higher level initiates of the
Church. She was relieved to see that the room had no monitor
cameras, although there were plenty of them in the hallways.

"There is only one of you now," she reported grimly. Gus
didn't ask how she had arranged that. She looked carefully at his
left hand. It was swollen, but pink.

"The world has a new lease on life," she said.

"But only if we can keep up the masquerade," Gus said. "Once anyone in the upper levels of the Church finds out that I'm not Alex, there'll be a palace coup and the world will find itself under a new tyrant."

"The one other person who knew you landed successfully on Earth was killed by the patrol."

"Then Augustus Armstrong must die," Gus said. "That way no one will ever conceive that there's been a switch—even if I commit serious blunders or start doing things differently."

"Like acting rationally?"

"Send a message to the Mars underground asking why I didn't show up. Sooner or later the news that I was lost in space will leak to the Watchers. No resistance movement is leak-proof."

"I hate to do that. It's going to demoralize both Mars and the Mars underground with you gone."

"The sooner they learn to stop being dependent on one man to tell them what to do, the better," Gus said gruffly. "Tell them Gus Armstrong is dead."

"Very well," Tanya said. She got out a slip of paper and a pen, wrote a short note, and tucked it in back of the mirror in a compact full of violet eye shadow.

"I don't think violet is a good shade for me," she said, looking in the mirror. "I think I'll return this for another color."

CHAPTER 21

EARTH RELEASED

The following Saturday the Infinite Lord was brought back to the Olympic Palace in his private helicopter. It landed on the roof of the tall stone tower in the evening dusk and he took the elevator down to his floor. Tanya was waiting for him next to the floating globe of the world. Above the globe was the tiny model of the Mace of God—on its way down toward its rendezvous with the Earth Sunday morning.

"We can talk here," Tanya said. "Even the central computer is blind until you turn on its console." She came over to look at the bandage on his left arm. She took the hand and touched each finger lightly and professionally, then stroked the palm to watch the reflex.

"How does it feel?"

"Still sore and swollen, but I can move some of the fingers already." He demonstrated by curling the outer three fingers toward his palm. "Still can't get much reaction from the thumb and forefinger. Guess my brain doesn't know how to cope with them, having done with stubs for so long."

"It *is* still slightly swollen," Tanya said. "We had best put it to the test before the real crisis comes tomorrow morning."

"Yes," Gus said. "It ought to be easy to turn off the Mace now that I can command the central computer."

Tanya walked over to the computer console, activated it, and touched a few icons. The computer spoke.

"You wish to change the operating parameters of the Mace of God?"

"Yes," Gus said, walking over to the globe and putting his left hand on it.

"Very well, my Infinite Lord," the computer said. "What is your command?"

"Please arrange to have the Mace of God go into an orbit that will not intersect Earth."

"Given sufficient advance notice, the Mace can be made to drop down over any point on Earth where you are speaking to create the proper amount of awe in the congregation," the computer said. "But what you ask is not physically possible."

"Then arrange so that the Mace separates to miss the Earth even if I *don't* put my hand on the globe," Gus said.

"That would defeat the purpose of the Mace," the computer said. "It is not one of the possible options."

"But suppose I die!" Gus blurted, frustrated.

"That is not possible," the computer said. "The Infinite Lord cannot die."

Gus switched off the console before he lost his temper and gave himself away. He went over to sit down on the huge circular bed and shook his head.

"What are we going to do, Tanya? The insane zealots that wrote the Mace program even have the computer believing I'm immortal."

"Why don't you get some rest," Tanya said. "Fortunately, the computer recognizes your left hand, so we can activate the Mace tomorrow morning. That will give us another week to work on a solution."

She started to leave.

"Where are you going?"

"To my room," Tanya said. "Alexander preferred sleeping alone."

"I'm not Alexander."

"I'll put on my nightgown and be right back," Tanya said with a pleased smile. When she returned, Gus was undressed and lying waiting under the sheet. She climbed over the huge circular bed, lifted the sheet, and looked down under the sheet at him.

"Well, it may not be *infinite*, my lord," she said. "But it'll do."

Late that night Tanya was wakened by a whimpering sound. It was Gus having a bad dream.

"No! No!" he shouted out.

She reached over and hugged him, then stroked his face and reassured him until the dream went away.

Eric had already arranged for the Sunday sermon to be a rerun. Actually it would seem like a new one, since it would be a smoothly blended version of the best parts of some of Alexander's older sermons. It was still necessary, however, for the Infinite Lord to place his hand on the globe at the proper time in order to activate the separation of the Mace of God. Gus did that in private in his room and was relieved to see the model of the Mace split in two.

"It worked," he said. "We have a week's respite while we try to figure out how to get the world out of the mess that Alex left it in."

"The first task is to turn off the Mace," Tanya said.

"There is more to be done than that. We have to destroy the hold the Church of the Unifier has on the world. How do I call Eric on this console? I need some information."

"The Church controls over a hundred trillion dollars," Gus reported later with amazement. "More than a thousand dollars for every person on the globe."

"That's because they've gouged tens and hundreds of thousands of dollars out of every Church member," Tanya said. "It's a racket to enrich the franchise owners and the Watchers."

"But most of those people joined the Church of their own free stupid will," Gus said. "They were bamboozled with words, but no force was used on them. I don't think many would believe the truth about the Church even if I told them. The first thing I'd better do is destroy the power of the higher levels while I still have the Mace to hold over their heads."

"Don't forget the Silver Scythes," Tanya said.

The following Sunday, the Infinite Lord was ready. He gave a powerful sermon that assured all who listened that the world was finally
unified and saved. Since they were saved, they no longer needed
watching. In a dramatic gesture, he announced that the Winged Eyes
of God were henceforth blind. He thanked the Watchers for their
faithful labor over the years and not only relieved them of their
duties of watching, but formally retired them with large pensions
for being such good servants of God. A few Watchers, those who
were in it for the power rather than the money, tried to use their
Caps of Contact to carry out their usual snooping. They found they
were locked out of the control computer.

Then, to the dismay of the thousands of ninth level Leaders
around the globe that owned the franchises to the level instructional
schools in their district, the Infinite Lord removed all the security
blocks to the instructional courses needed to move from level to
level in the Church. Now anyone with a Cap of Contact of any
color had free access to all the mysteries that they previously had
to pay for. When the Leaders tried to complain, they, too, found
they were locked out of the control computer.

Finally, the Infinite Lord forgave all debts owed to the Church
and released the faithful of the Church from the requirement of
tithing. Gus would have liked to give them back the money they
had already poured into the Church, but most of it had already
been spent, and he was going to need the rest to keep the higher
levels bribed into submission.

Right after the sermon, the Infinite Lord broadcast a short message to the Caps of Contact of the ninth level Leaders and the eighth
and seventh level Watchers.

"We almost blew the whole gig two weeks ago. I'm closing the
operation down. Nines get a billion each, eights one hundred million, and sevens ten million. Take the money and run. In case any
of you are thinking about causing me trouble, the Silver Scythes
have *not* been deactivated. Alexander."

The next visit of the Infinite Lord was to the office of the head of the Department of Applied Magic down in the basement of the castle. Jerry arrived soon after they got there.

"Sorry I was so late responding to your call, Infinite Lord," he said. "I was skinny-dipping down on the beach with some unmarried sixes. What can I do for you, Infinite Lord?"

"Because of my recent experience, Jerry, I want to have the Mace disabled so it will no longer strike Earth—even if I happen to die."

Jerry looked bewildered at the thought of the Infinite Lord dying.

"Or lose my left hand."

"Yeah!" Jerry said. "That *was* pretty close, wasn't it. Never thought about that possibility." He paused to think for a while.

"Sorry. Can't be done. Wrote the codes myself. Crack-proof. But we have nothing to worry about . . . 'The Infinite Lord is infinite in both space and time.' Unified Scriptures 15:74, if I recall correctly."

"Isn't there some way to turn it off?" Gus pleaded, getting frustrated. He thought for a minute, then said, "I'm getting tired of having to show up every Sunday."

"I see . . ." Jerry said, thinking. "I guess that is a drag." He thought some more. "Nope. I can't think of a way to do it without triggering the circuits that lock the two halves together."

Gus ground his teeth in frustration and tried to hold on to his temper. Then he remembered his still-hidden white knight.

"Isn't there someone else that might have some ideas? Like Bill Boswick?"

"Yeah!" Jerry said, brightening. "Bill might be the one. Let's go see him."

When they entered Bill Boswick's office, Bill looked up from his console and stared strangely at the stocky figure of the Infinite Lord in his golden tunic and tights. Gus could see the suppressed emotion of raw hate in his eyes. Gus could understand why, for on Bill's desk was a picture of Bill's wife, a gorgeous long-haired blond—just the kind that both Gus and Alex liked—and in front of her were their two little daughters. Except for the skirt and curls, the older girl's face was almost identical to that of the Armstrong twins at that age.

Gus wanted to reassure Bill that things would soon be better, that Bill's Uncle Dave was here—hiding behind a golden costume. But that couldn't be done. Bill must never know, for Augustus Armstrong had to stay dead.

"The Infinite Lord wants a vacation from his Mace duties," Jerry said. "You got any ideas of how to turn the Mace off? Now don't count on that back door you hid in the code. I caught that when I did the final program check." Jerry turned to Gus.

"Every programmer I know sticks back doors in stuff that they write, so they can always access it later even if they don't know the password the customer has chosen for access."

"Then why don't we use your back door?" Gus asked.

Jerry looked shocked. "I would *never* put a back door in something I wrote for *you*, Infinite Lord," he said. "It would be unthinkable. That's why I took Bill's out. Besides, even if there were a back door, the options available for the operating parameters of the Mace do not include turning it off—as you found out. There was no need for it, so I didn't put it in the program."

"We've *got* to find a way to turn off the Mace," Gus said with emotion. "We can't let the world die!"

Bill Boswick looked quizzically at the man he hated more than any other in the world. Bill knew how close the world had come to dying last week. Maybe this vain crackpot now realized that, too, and was finally beginning to come to his senses.

"I might be able to think of something," Bill said cautiously. "But how do I know you won't just have it nullified and leave us in the same predicament as before?"

"I can understand why you don't trust me," Gus said. "But after my recent experience, I've changed. I apologize for any wrongs that I may have done to you. Please, if there is *any* way to rid the world of this terrible menace that hangs over us all . . ."

Bill hesitated for a while, then finally turned to his computer screen.

"I'm bringing up the portion of the program for the Mace that has to do with the timing gates."

Bill soon had a screen full of lines of programming code. He pointed to the screen. "The basic time interval is the seven days between Sundays, three and a half days up and three and a half days down. When the globe is activated at the right time, plus or minus a half-hour, then the signal it sends tells the two halves to fly apart and pass around the Earth. But when I was coding it, I think I made a little mistake," Bill said, looking at the screen. "What is the number of seconds in a week, Jerry?"

"According to what it says in the program here, it's 302,400."

"That's the little mistake," Bill said. "That number is the number of seconds in three and a half days. The number of seconds in a week is twice that."

"Why, you tricky little rascal," Jerry said with a pleased smile. "The Mace will accept signals not only when it is approaching the Earth, but also when it is at the peak of its trajectory at eighty-three Earth radii. If we spring the two halves of the Mace apart at that altitude they'll go into orbit about the Sun."

"Just what I want!" Gus said, relieved. "When?"

"Well, the Mace is normally set for your ten A.M. Sunday sermon every week," Jerry said. "So half that is ten P.M. Wednesday night."

Wednesday night Gus slept peacefully for the first time since he had arrived on Earth, no longer tormented by his "temptation" dream. Both the Mace and the Silver Scythes were gone from the skies. The two halves of the Mace were now in safe orbits about the Sun, while the sails of the Silver Scythes, their loads dropped into the oceans, were on their way out of the solar system.

"Now comes the tough part," Gus said to Tanya the next day. "Unselling the marks. I wonder how Eric is at making my sermons dull and boring."

The Infinite Lord, pleading fatigue, retired to his castle on top of Mount Olympus. Week after boring week, reruns of old sermons were played day and night over the Church networks until even the most devoted often left their Caps of Contact hanging on the hat rack. The television and newspapers started referring to the Infinite Lord as just Alexander, but still as Alexander the Greatest or Alexander the Unifier.

At the order of the Infinite Lord, all remaining weapons on Earth were destroyed. The Watchers had long ago disarmed the lower levels; now even the police were armed only with nonlethal, although highly technical, capture aids.

In taking over the world and forming the Unified States, Alexander had already eliminated national boundaries. Now Gus retired all his regents and formally broke the world into small, self-governing city-states, each made up of people with common languages and common customs. The city-states had local police and taxing power and provided the necessary services to their citizens. All the thousands of city-states sent delegates to a world congress, which—as a result—was so big and clumsy, and had so little real power, that it could do almost no harm. Diplomatic relations were restored with Mars and space travel was once again encouraged.

One evening Gus and Tanya were standing out on the tower rooftop enjoying the cool evening breezes blowing over the top of Mount Olympus. The steady bright red star of Mars was rising up over them. Gus gave Tanya's hand a squeeze.

"It seems to be working, Gus," she said, squeezing his hand back. "The executive secretary of the World Congress hasn't had to call on you to settle a dispute in over a month."

"Now, Tanya . . ." Gus said, turning to shake a cautionary finger at her. "The only way we can make this work in the long run is to make sure we always refer to me as Alexander. Gus is dead."

"It isn't fair," Tanya said angrily, tears welling in her face. "Alexander was an insane, bullying, murderous tyrant. It isn't fair that *he* is going to go down in history books as the unifier of the human race. It's you, dammit, not him, that should get the credit."

Gus gave her a hug. "As long as *you* know, that's all that counts," he said. He picked up her chin and gave her a kiss. "Since the world now seems to be able to run itself without Alexander, let's take ol' Alexander off on a long vacation—to Mars."

The shuttlecraft rose up over the rugged rampart at the end of Eastrise and glided slowly down into the deep basin. It was late afternoon and stacks of dark cumulus clouds filled the hole below. The whistle on the long wings grew louder as the shuttlecraft flew down into thicker air. The pilot found a break between two anvil-shaped clouds and swerved to pass through the gap.

"Those are pretty ugly looking thunderheads," the pilot said through the intercom. "It's going to get a bit bumpy, so keep your harnesses on."

"Those are beautiful-looking clouds to me," Tanya said as the plane dropped down into a valley made of gray-white cotton fluff. Gus leaned against her shoulder and looked with her out the window. Suddenly the cloud out their side lit up from inside and a fraction of a second later there was a loud crack of thunder.

"Wow!" Gus said. Then the view out the window was lost in racing rivulets of rain.

The shuttlecraft pilot landed at Westrise Airport near Augustus City. The rain was still falling heavily as they taxied toward the terminal.

"You'll have to wait until the welcoming committee comes on board," the pilot said. "The governor of Mars decided that because of the rain it would be better to take your arrival pictures in here, despite the crowded quarters, rather than after you're in the terminal building, but soaking wet."

The first one through the airlock was Maury. He was unusually quiet and reserved, very strange behavior for the normally outgoing Maury. His nose was still bulbous, but the red veining was gone. Gus noticed that Maury had neglected to completely close the inner airlock door, so that no one else could enter.

"I'm Maury Pickford, governor of Mars, your Lordship," he said uncomfortably, looking carefully at Gus' face as they shook hands.

"Titles aren't necessary anymore," Tanya prompted. "Alexander will do." Maury's face became even more somber when heard Tanya mention Alexander's name.

"Welcome to Mars, then . . . Alexander. I used to be a good friend of your brother, Augustus, before he was lost in space. Our capital city is now named after him." Gus had reached up his left hand to grasp Maury's arm and give it a firm squeeze in addition to the handshake. The scars above his left wrist were visible under the sleeve of his gold tunic. Maury suddenly released the handshake, took Gus' left hand, looked at the five stubby, but perfect fingers, stared at the scar pattern, then looked up into Gus' eyes.

"Are you sure . . ." he started. Gus remained silent, unable to lie to his old friend.

"Alexander will do," Tanya repeated firmly.

Maury looked at Tanya and hesitated, thinking. Still puzzled, he finally said pensively, "Alexander the Unifier of Earth, it has to be . . . so Alexander it *is*."

His demeanor brightened and he turned around and reached back into the airlock. "Got a present for you, Alexander, sir. We didn't used to need these, but there is a thriving cottage industry in them now." He handed a cloth-covered stick to Gus and to Tanya.

"Don't open them in the shuttlecraft, it's bad luck. Besides, then you can't get out the airlock. Wait! Almost forgot the pictures!" He panned a microvideo camera over the two of them, then opened the airlock door and motioned them in.

"Come on, Alexander. Mars is waiting to greet you. Here is a hand-held O-mask to get you to the terminal building. After that we will fit you with a turbomask."

Maury got soaked as he helped Tanya and Gus out the door and under their umbrellas. The three made a dash for the terminal building. The building was made of red Marsbrick and had an inflated dome roof that gave off a deafening roar under the beating of the raindrops. They had to wait between gusts to get the brief welcoming ceremony on video. The video would be sent back to Earth to let the people know that their God had arrived safely.

Maury introduced them to the line of people waiting there.

". . . and this is Dr. Fred Whimple, director of the Sagan Mars Institute."

Gus forced his face to look normal as he shook hands with Fred, who stepped forward with confidence and shook hands firmly with Gus. Gus noticed a large circular worn spot on one pocket of Fred's vest.

"The Sagan Institute thanks you for the most generous support we have received recently from Earth," Fred said. "Our scientists can once again return to their research activities."

After the ceremony was over, Maury took the video camera from the technician, changed the holocube, and sent the exposed one with the tech to the Earthlink station.

"We still have a lot of work to do here on Mars, Alexander," he said, "so I hope you don't mind if I just show you around the place myself. I don't know how to do anything but talk, so the techs are happier when I *don't* try to help." He went over to some cabinets near the exit door and got out some clear plastic masks, one small and one large, and handed them to Tanya and Gus. He then checked a row of Turner Turboexchangers, picked out two with fully charged batteries and emergency oxygen tanks, and handed them over, also.

Gus adjusted the elastic bands on his mask to make sure there was a tight fit around his nose and mouth. Then he checked the indicators and settings on the turboexchangers and adjusted the harness so the heavy apparatus would ride around in back above the waist where it would be out of the way. He finally hooked up the long hose from the turboexchanger over his left shoulder to the fitting on his mask, turned on the turbomotor, and checked the whole system for leaks.

Tanya was having trouble putting hers on.

"Here," Gus said. "Let me help you with the straps."

Maury watched him take her through the detailed procedure.

"Nice thing about being an omnipotent God," Maury said with a knowing smile as they finally finished. "You instantly know how to put on and check out a Turner Turbomask even though you've never used one before." Gus stopped and looked over at Tanya.

Maury deliberately ignored their concerned looks and led the way to the airlock. "Come on, God. I'm first going to take you down hole to Splash Lake. It's really beautiful country. Has the largest waterfalls in the solar system—maybe in the universe—but you'd know all about that, wouldn't you, God?"

"Look!" Tanya said, pointing across the lake. The rain clouds had parted for a few moments and the late afternoon Sun was shafting down Westrise to form a brightly glowing rainbow that stretched from one side of the lake to the other.

"Say! That's real impressive, God!" Maury said. "Got to get a picture of this." He ran uphill a ways, adjusting the field of view of the video camera as he went. He stopped, knelt down, and framed the whole scene in the viewfinder. The two were looking away from him at the rainbow.

"How about a statement for your people, God!"

Gus and Tanya turned and looked back at Maury. Gus hesitated for a second, then took a deep breath, took off his mask, and said in a voice that boomed over the land, "Come! Come follow me to the stars!"

A lightning bolt shot down from the cloud in back of the rainbow, striking the top of Splash Peak, now nearly buried under the rising blue waters of the lake. Maury Pickford brought down the video camera.

"Great speech, God! Couldn't have ended it better myself. You'll be a smash in Peoria when I downlink this video to the news pool back on Earth."

Gus wasn't listening. He had put his mask back on and had turned to look at the multihued double rainbow set against the distant green slopes of New Switzerland. He turned back again as

Maury walked up and handed him a thin booklet printed on per-mapaper.

"By the way," Maury said, "here is a copy of a brand new booklet I put together. It's called the *New Colonists' Guide to Mars*. You might want to read it carefully, God. We mere humans have changed a few things since you slapped Mars together some four or five billion years ago. For the better, too—if you ask me."

NEW COLONISTS' GUIDE TO MARS

by

MAURY PICKFORD

Governor

Territory of Mars

WELCOME TO MARS!

We hope the information stuffed into this little booklet will introduce you to your wonderful new home and keep you from getting killed. As a new colonist, you have come here at great expense and it would be a great shame if you expired from homesickness or the stupids before you had your passage worked out of you.

It is strongly advised that you immediately sit down and read every word in this booklet at least once. The words on safety matters should be read at least twice. Then keep this booklet in the pocket closest to your heart and consult it frequently as you transition from being one of those stupid new colonists who think they don't need such a guide, to one of those smart old colonists who constantly consult their dog-eared copy for guidance.

This first copy of the *New Colonists' Guide to Mars* is free, subsidized by the Territory of Mars. After that, they cost ten Martian dollars each, payable to Maury Pickford, author, publisher, and governor of the Territory of Mars.

DRY FACTS ABOUT MARS

On the next page you will find a list of the physical properties of the planet Mars and how they compare with those of Earth. You will see that Mars can be thought of as a small, cold, dry Earth. What this all means for the average new colonist is that unless you are an ex-Lunie, you should have no problem adjusting to the length of a Martian day, since it is almost the same as a day on Earth. With the axial tilt of Mars also almost exactly that of Earth, Mars has the same seasons as Earth. The Martian year, however, is nearly twice as long as an Earth year, so those seasons are going to seem like they drag on forever.

Radius (avg.)	3,386 km	(53% of Earth)
Land Area	1.44×10^{14} m²	(97% of Earth)
Mass	6.4×10^{23} kg	(11% of Earth)
Average Density	3.93 g/cc	(72% of Earth)
Surface Gravity	3.73 m/s²	(38% of Earth)
Escape Velocity	5.0 km/s	(45% of Earth)
Orbital Velocity	3.5 km/s	(45% of Earth)
Axial Tilt	25.2 deg	(107% of Earth)
Length of Day = Sol	88775.238 s	(103% of Earth)
Sidereal Sol	88642.663 s	
Length of Year	59355041 s	(188% of Earth)
	686.97964 days	
	668.59906 sols	
Solar Flux (avg)	590 W/m²	(43% of Earth)
Sun-Mars Distance (avg.)	228 Gm	(152% of Earth)
Perihelion	207 Gm	
Aphelion	250 Gm	
Earth-Mars Opposition Dist. (max)	101 Gm	
(min)	56 Gm	

MOONS

Phobos and Deimos are the two moons of Mars. They lost a little mass and got their corners rounded off when the Lineups processed them for carbon and other useful elements for making laser mirrors and various space structures. They are still in the same orbits with the same periods, however, and have roughly the same physical properties as before, which are:

	PHOBOS	DEIMOS
Orbital Radius (km)	9,378	23,459
(Mars radii)	3	7
Orbital Period (sidereal, sec)	27,554	109,075
Average Radius (km)	11	6
Average Density (gm/cc)	2	2
Approximate Mass (kg)	1×10^{16}	2×10^{15}
Surface Gravity (mm/s²)	6	3
Surface Orbital Velocity (m/s)	8	4.5
Escape Velocity (m/s)	11	6

So Phobos rises in the west and sets in the east some 4.5 hours later, usually disappearing into the shadow of Mars for a while during its journey across the sky. Deimos, like the Earth's Moon, rises in the east along with the stars, but since it rotates only a little slower than the planet (30 hours vs. 24 hours), it is nearly at geosynchronous altitude. It takes it some 60 hours to go from moonrise in the east to moonset in the west. Meanwhile the Sun has risen and set 2.5 times.

Both moons are tidally locked toward Mars, so that one face is always toward Mars, just as we see only one face of the Moon from the Earth. This means that the "days" on Deimos are over 30 hours long, while those on Phobos are not quite 8 hours long, plus additional periods of darkness when Phobos passes through the shadow of Mars.

The low gravity on the two moons is a cause for caution. The usual "lunar lope" is much too vigorous for use on these bodies, and you will have to learn a lighter step using just your toes to push yourself along. Since orbital velocity at the surface is about as fast as a person can run (if you could get the purchase to get up to speed), you are really travelling in a series of suborbital arcs. But until you have built up a lot of experience on these moons, take it easy! . . . and move at moderate speeds. It may be fun to run off the edge of a cliff and float to the other side, but fun can turn into danger if you start to tumble halfway across and land on your helmet.

Despite the scare stories some old-timers might have told you, it is *not* possible for the average person in a space suit to jump into an escape orbit from either moon. Given just a little mechanical assistance, however, like holding onto a tether attached to a piece of moving machinery, or a punctured oxygen bottle in your lifepack, or a stuck thrustor on a hovercraft you are riding, and you could find yourself in your *own* orbit about Mars.

Also, don't show off by throwing pebbles into an escape orbit. Four hours later (15 hours on Deimos), that pebble will be coming back to strike somewhere on the moon with the velocity at which you threw it! Your arm may have temporarily thrown the pebble out of the gravity well of the moon, but your arm isn't strong enough to throw the pebble out of the gravity well of Mars. That pebble will go into a slightly elliptical orbit about Mars that intercepts the orbit of the moon halfway around Mars on the other side of the orbit. Its the gravitational equivalent of "spitting into the wind."

CLOCK AND CALENDAR

The Martian clock and calendar are significantly different than the Earth clock and calendar, although we tried to keep things as much like home as possible. Fortunately for those that have strong body rhythms, the

Martian day is nearly the same as the Earth day, so you shouldn't lose any sleep over the shift in planets. But the extra 39.5 minutes is enough different that it causes problems. If Mars had been colonized by businessmen, we would have just slowed our watches down by 3% and continued using sols with 24 hours, hours with 60 minutes, and minutes with 60 seconds. The only difference would have been that the second on Mars would have been 3% longer than the second on Earth.

Unfortunately, this is heresy to a scientist. A second is no longer 1/86,400th of an Earth day, but is defined as the duration of 9,192,631,770 cycles of a certain frequency of radio waves from a cesium atomic clock. Since Mars was colonized first by scientists, we are stuck with the system that they developed, where a Martian second is exactly equal to an Earth second, so the scientists on the two planets can talk straight to each other. You will have to put your Earth watches away and get a Mars watch.

The Martian day is called a sol. The Martian sol is divided into 24 increments called maurs (for Martian hours). [Despite some snide comments by erstwhile friends, the maur is not named after me.] Each maur is roughly the length of an Earth hour so students still have one hour class periods and people still work eight hour shifts, only now they are eight maur shifts.

Now comes the real difference. Instead of a maur being made of 60 minutes of 60 seconds each for a total of 3600 seconds per hour, there are 60 marmins (Martian minutes, of course) of either 61 or 62 seconds each (remember a Martian second is identical to an Earth second). The shorter marmins are the 00 and 01 marmins in each maur and every marmin divisible by 3, for a total of 21x61 + 39x62 = 3699 seconds per maur. Then, three sols out of four, the 02 marmin of the 00 maur has only 61 seconds to give 3698 seconds for that maur and a total of 88775 seconds for the sol. The fourth sol does not skip that leap second and is 88776 seconds long. This gives an average for the four sols of 88775.25 seconds, close enough to the physical sol that the difference over a Martian year can be included in the leap seconds the scientists add or subtract occasionally anyway to adjust for the slowdown in the planet's spin rate and changes in the shape of its orbit. Fortunately, you don't have to worry about memorizing where the leap seconds go or don't go, all the leap seconds are programmed into the timing circuit of your digital Marswatch, along with the various holisols and leap sols to keep the yearly calendar on track with the seasons.

Another major difference between timekeeping on Mars and on Earth is that, because of the greater distance of Mars from the Sun, the Martian year (called a mear) is nearly twice as long as an Earth year. Because we have no slow-moving moon to make "moonths" important, we have done away with them. But we *have* kept the 7-sol week. (T.G.I.F.

means the same thing on Mars as it does on Earth.) A Martian calendar year consists of 95 weeks of 7 sols each for a total of 665 sols.

To round the calendar up to the nearly 669 sols of the physical mear, we add four seasonal "holisols" outside the weekly calendar as near the physical equinoxes and solstices as possible. They are: the perisolstice, the apequinox, the apsolstice, and the periequinox. The following sol starts a new week, so is always a Sunsol. Thus everybody gets two sols off in a row.

The mear is really about 668.6 sols long, so every 2.5 mears, starting from M001.25 or the apequinox of M001, we have either a "springmear" and spring forward over the periequinox into the new week, or a "fallmear" and let the apequinox fall off the calendar, so the start of each new mear stays on track with the seasons. That should keep us on track until way past M999 (about A.D. 4000) when everyone will have to buy a new watch anyway.

The 95 weeks are divided into seasons. The seasons are not equal in length because of the high eccentricity of the orbit of Mars. Since the main human habitation here on Mars is now in the southern hemisphere, we designate the seasons by what is happening here. Those that live "Up Over" have the opposite seasons, of course. The year starts with the perisolstice, the solstice that occurs when Mars is close to the sun. This starts the short, hot summer in the southern hemisphere and the short, warm winter in the northern hemisphere. This southern summer season is 22 weeks long. There follows the apequinox and a 27-week fall, the apsolstice and a 26-week winter, and then, as Mars starts back in toward the Sun, is the periequinox followed by the shortest season of all, the 20-week spring.

The seasons are not used in writing down dates. The standard order for a date is a letter M to indicate that it is a Martian date, immediately followed by the number of the mear, with M000 coinciding with the Earth year 2000, when the starting times of the Earth year and the Mars year were very close. (They weren't perfect, but let the scientists worry about those little details.) Then comes the number of the week from 00 to 95, the three letter code for the sol of the week (SUN, MON, TUE, WED, THU, FRI, SAT), the maur, the marmin, and the second. If the date happens to fall on a holisol, the five letter abbreviations PSOLS, AEQUI, ASOLS, and PEQUI, are used instead of the week and sol. In this nomenclature, the start of the mear is M025/PSOLS/00:00:00, while the last second of the mear is M025/95SAT/23:59:62.

MONEY

We do have money on Mars, although there are no bills. Bills wear out too fast, so we use coins of hardened anodized aluminum. The diameter and thickness of the coins are proportional to the value of the coin, while the colors of the coins follow the colors of the rainbow. Around the picture on the front of the coin are the words: Territory of Mars. There is no date, since there are no plans to make any changes, and we want to actively discourage collectors.

VALUE (M$)	THICKNESS (mm)	DIAMETER (cm)	COLOR	FRONT PICTURE	BACK INSCRIPTION
0.01	1.0	1.0	Red	Deimos	1 Cent
0.10	1.5	1.5	Orange	Phobos	10 Cents
1	2.0	2.0	Yellow	Viking	One Dollar
10	2.5	2.5	Green	Olympus	Ten Dollars
100	3.0	3.0	Blue	North Pole	100 Dollars

There are no plans for larger denomination coins, since transactions that large should be carried out by iris-certified bank account computer transfers anyway.

The artificially low (and subsidized) exchange rate of one Mars dollar equalling one-hundred U.S. dollars that was set up by the founding fathers before Alexander the Unifier brought Earth under one rule, has fluctuated wildly depending upon the diplomatic relations (or lack of them) between Earth and Mars. Now that The Unifier has allowed self-government again on Earth, things have stabilized and the present rate is one Mars dollar equals 280 Earth credits.

A helpful hint for those caught without a ruler but having a pocket full of change: A stack of five vikings or a red on edge is one centimeter, while an oly is close to an inch across.

ATMOSPHERE

The original atmosphere of Mars when the Viking spacecraft first landed was significantly different than what it is now after the Lineups processed the polar ice caps and raised the temperature and pressure. The total pressure was only about 8 millibars, compared to about 1000 millibars (that's 1 bar) for Earth, and the 500 millibars at the bottom of Dugout Crater. The triple point pressure for water is 6.1 millibars, so any open water on Viking's Mars would not only have been frozen, it would have been sublimated away. If you had gone out for a walk back then without your space suit, you would have found yourself a little short of breath, and pretty soon you too would be frozen and sublimating away.

Not only wasn't there enough air to breathe, what little there was wasn't worth breathing. The atmosphere consisted of 95% carbon dioxide, 3% nitrogen, and 1.5% argon, with oxygen only 0.1%. The water vapor content was variable, from nearly zero in the winter to 3% in the summer. This is to be compared to what you were used to back on Earth, which was 78% nitrogen, 21% oxygen, 0.9% argon, and only

8

0.03% carbon dioxide; then, depending upon the humidity, the water vapor in the air would be from 0 to 3%, displacing the other gases.

The atmosphere down at the bottom of Dugout Crater is certainly not earthlike, but it is better than what we started with. It contains 48% oxygen, 35% carbon dioxide, 13% nitrogen, 3.5% methane, and trace amounts of argon and ammonia. The argon came from the original Martian atmosphere, while the methane and ammonia were deliberately put in when the Lineups processed the poles. The methane and ammonia make it smelly, but they are good greenhouse gases and help keep us and our crops warm down at the bottom of Dugout Crater.

The partial pressure of each of the major components of the atmosphere changes with altitude in a slightly different manner, with the heavier gases, like carbon dioxide, falling off faster with altitude than the lighter gases like methane and ammonia. That means these greenhouse gases form a higher percentage of the atmosphere at high altitude, where they can do the most good. The following table gives the partial and total pressure with altitude. Take a good look at it before you start on a trip.

The temperatures given are the average daily temperatures in the midsouthern latitudes for summertime in the south. They can vary ±20 degrees C during the sol. Fortunately, the Lineups warmed things up somewhat from the original Martian temperatures when they processed the ice caps, and the increased pressure and the greenhouse gases are continuing to warm things up.

The amount of water vapor pressure given in the table is the maximum for 100% humidity. Usually, however, the only time you run into 100% humidity is down around Splash Lake on a hot, muggy summer sol, but that is soon relieved by a thunderstorm.

(Normally, a guidebook like this would also give you another table based on the average winter temperatures, but you shouldn't be traveling when it is winter in the southern hemisphere.)

ATMOSPHERIC PRESSURE WITH ALTITUDE

ALT. (km)	TYP. PLACE	AVG. SUMMER TEMPERATURE			MAX H_2O (mb)	PARTIAL PRESSURE					Tot
		(°K)	(°C)	(°F)	(mb)	O_2 (mb)	CO_2 (mb)	N_2 (mb)	CH_4 (mb)	NH_3 (mb)	(mb)
+27	Peaks	186	−87	−125	0	15	4	6	4	0.1	29
+10	Tharsis	237	−36	−33	0	65	30	21	7	0.1	123
+5	Elysium	252	21	−6	1	89	46	28	8	0.1	171
+2.5	Melas, Olym.	260	−13	9	2	104	56	32	9	0.2	201
0	"Sea" level	267	−3	27	3	119	68	36	10	0.2	236
−2	Lowlands	273	0	32	6	132	79	39	11	0.2	261
−4	Hellas Basin	279	6	43	10	146	90	43	11	0.2	290
−10	Halfway Ter.	303	30	86	42	191	130	55	13	0.3	389
−14	Augustus	319	46	115	100	224	161	63	14	0.3	462
−16	Splash Lake	327	54	129	150	240	178	67	14	0.3	499

As can be seen from the table, the total atmospheric pressure at the bottom of Dugout Crater is 500 millibars and exceeds 290 millibars for a few hundred kilometers distance around Dugout at the bottom of Hellas Basin where the altitude is below − 4 km. These pressures are high enough that you don't need a pressure suit outside.

You can put on a pressure suit if you want (and you *must* if you leave Hellas Basin), but in the basin and especially down in Dugout, all you will need is your Turner Turbomask with its miraculous molecular microfilter. A battery-powered turbofan sucks in the low-pressure outside atmosphere with its 48% oxygen, 35% carbon dioxide, and 13% nitrogen plus other noxious and smelly stuff at 500 millibars and creates some 3 atmospheres (3000 millibars) on the high-pressure side of the filter. The magical molecular microfilter passes nitrogen and oxygen through to the other side and prevents the carbon dioxide and smelly stuff from getting through. You get to breath the filtered air on the other side through your mask. The turbomask delivers 58% nitrogen and 42% oxygen at a little over 500 millibars, giving you the same amount of oxygen per breath as Earth's 1000 millibar atmosphere with 21% oxygen. A slight bit of excess pressure inside the mask not only makes it easier to breath, but helps keep the nasty stuff out.

Up at Breakout, where Getout Slope merges with the bottom of Hellas Basin at − 4 km altitude and the total pressure is only 290 millibars, the turbomask is delivering a 72/28 oxygen to nitrogen ratio, or 210 millibars of oxygen and 80 millibars of nitrogen. This is roughly the same mixture that was used in the first American SpaceLab in the early space exploration days.

In an emergency, it is possible to use a Turner Turbomask (set on pure oxygen) for your air supply and your skin as your space suit up to about 2.5 km altitude, where the total air pressure has dropped to about 200 millibars. Don't stay outside too long, or the surface of your skin will be one large hickey.

Now . . . if you are new to Mars, and the last time your body experienced the effects of too much carbon dioxide was back on Earth when you chug-a-lugged a warm cola and experienced a painful burp . . . then widen those scanners and put the next section into permanent memory.

CARBON DIOXIDE POISONING

Carbon dioxide can kill you.

I repeat . . . **CARBON DIOXIDE CAN KILL YOU!!!** It can get you two ways. First, it can displace the oxygen you need and suffocate you to death. Second, even if it can't get you that way, it will sneak up on you and poison you to death.

10

Most of the medical information on the dangers of carbon dioxide poisoning was obtained back on Earth when workers went in to clean out the vats in breweries. Exposure to high concentrations, such as 25% of an Earth atmosphere (partial pressure of 250 millibars), causes convulsions and coma within *one minute*. Exposure to concentrations near 10% (100 millibars) for only a few minutes will produce coma and subsequent asphyxiation. Since the partial pressure of carbon dioxide at the bottom of Dugout Crater is 178 millibars and at the top is 90 millibars, you can see what just a few minutes of breathing without a mask can do to you.

Inhalation of concentrations from 7 to 10% (70 to 100 millibars) produces difficulty with breathing, headache, dizziness, and queasiness. Five percent produces shortness of breath and headache in many individuals. After several hours of exposure to just 2% (20 millibars), most people develop headaches and have difficulty breathing after only mild exertion. So if you have a headache, or have difficulty breathing, or otherwise don't feel well, immediately suspect a leaky mask combined with a faulty CO_2 warning system.

What is happening to you is not a lack of oxygen. Instead, the carbon dioxide (called carbonic acid gas on the label of your cola can back on Earth) is building up in your bloodstream, slowly turning your blood into carbonated vampire beverage and lousing up your delicate internal pH balance.

So—keep those breathing masks on tight and make sure that every breath you take has come through the filter canister on your turboexchanger. If your mask is not on tight, you may be getting enough oxygen to breathe and feel all right, but at the same time you may be getting too much carbon dioxide. Before you know it, you will be confused, weak, sick, or go into convulsions from acid blood.

When you are in an air-filtered building or work compound with the 40/60 oxygen/nitrogen ratio that makes exercise at 500 millibars possible, and even fun (according to some—never could see it myself), keep your turbomask or an emergency oxy-mask on you at all times. (There are some indoor sports where it is allowable to keep your masks on the bedside table.) If the structure is breached, allowing the outside atmosphere in, get to a high point until you can get your emergency mask on.

It is important to note that carbon dioxide, with its molecular weight of 44, is heavier than oxygen and nitrogen. When there are windstorms up on the surface of Mars, the winds are often made up of carbon dioxide that is evaporating from the polar caps. The airflow can stream down Getout Slope, get denser as it moves into the higher pressure regions near the bottom of Dugout Crater, and puddle in low lying areas, displacing the air with the 48% oxygen that you need to breath. Your

11

turboexchanger and filters may be working just fine, but no oxygen in—no oxygen out. As you move around outside, keep a watch on the oxygen-level indicator, and don't commit yourself to a fast descent into a depression unless you are carrying an oxygen bottle in addition to your turbomask.

FIRES

The other reason we need carbon dioxide in the atmosphere is to keep from burning the place up. We could have had the Lineups generate us a pure oxygen-nitrogen atmosphere with almost no carbon dioxide in it. Unfortunately, the amount of nitrogen readily available in the ice caps (as frozen ammonia clathrates) was limited. The total nitrogen partial pressure that could be generated was 36 millibars at Martian "sea level" and 67 millibars down at the bottom of Dugout Crater. Combining that with the present 240 millibars of oxygen in Dugout would have produced 307 millibars total down at the bottom of Dugout. This pressure level would be high enough that space suits would not be needed and with sufficient oxygen partial pressure and no carbon dioxide, no turbomasks would be needed.

Unfortunately, an atmosphere of almost all oxygen may be fine for breathing, but it can be deadly if a spark or match flashes. Especially since we wanted to put some methane in the atmosphere to act as a greenhouse gas to warm the place up. An atmosphere made up of oxygen and methane would be fine—until someone lit a match! We need some nonflammable gas to keep the oxygen percentage down. Unfortunately, the only thing available was carbon dioxide.

With the present mixture of 48% oxygen, 35% carbon dioxide, 13% nitrogen, and 3% methane, the atmosphere won't burn all by itself, since the flammability range for methane is over 5%. The relative amount of oxygen is quite high, however, more than twice that on Earth. Although the lower air pressure helps keep fires down, you *must* be careful about matches, sparks, and open fires. We have invested too much in our trees to lose them in a forest fire.

PLACES

There are lots of places to go on Mars. After all, Mars has the same amount of land area as the dry land surface area on Earth. Unfortunately, there aren't too many places to go that have people. Here is a list of the main cities, and the camps that have shelters and life-support facilities, but no permanent occupants.

CITIES:

AUGUSTUS (aka Dugout) [– 39 S 303 W – 14 km, pop. 4500]. Capital of Mars. On a crescent-shaped terrace 2 km above Splash Lake at the bottom of Dugout Crater. There are a number of suburbs of Augustus (such as Halfway Terrace at – 10 km) at each of the terraced levels at increasing elevations until we get to Breakout Base at – 4 km in the Hellas Plains (aka Hell's Flats) at the top of Getout Slope. Over the decades, Augustus will move upward and finally disperse as Dugout Crater fills up and starts to spread out into Hellas Plains to form Hellas Sea. The debris from Dugout Crater covered over the original USSR base Novosibirsk that was nearby.

MUTCHVILLE [+ 24 N 45 W – 3.5 km alt., pop. 250]. City in the middle of Chryse Plains, the second lowest basin on Mars. One of the spaceports of Mars. The altitude of the basin is low enough at – 3.5 km, that the post-Splat air pressure of 28% Earth pressure is sufficient for people to operate outside without pressure suits—just a turbomask. Mutch Memorial is 100 km away to the southwest. Primary activity of the personnel is studying shorelines of the ancient Martian Boreal Ocean. Duplicate samples of all Mars-adapted plants are also kept here in case some catastrophe hits the nurseries at Augustus.

ISIDIS (aka Insidious) [+ 14 N 272 W – 1 km alt., pop. 200]. A small city in the third lowest basin on Mars. The air pressure, however, is only one-quarter of Earth pressure. Unless you are an old-timer and know what you are doing, don't assume that your skin will serve as an adequate space suit and wear a pressure suit outside. (Most old-timers got to be old-timers by wearing a pressure suit even when they didn't really have to.) A base for exploring the northeastern portion of Mars.

OLYMPUS [+ 14 N 130 W + 2.5 km, pop 200]. Previously USSR Novomoskovsk and original capital city of Mars. At the base of Olympus Mons just below the southeast scarps. One of the spaceports for Mars. There are a number of camps around and on Olympus Mons that are attached to Olympus city. About 100 km due north of Olympus city is one of the two near vertical cable lifts up onto the Olympus Mons ramparts. This one goes straight up almost 5 kilometers. The cable-lift from the northwest campsite goes up almost 8 kilometers. Saves a lot of climbing. (The cable-lifts only put you at 10 kilometers, however. It is 17 more kilometers to the top of Olympus Mons!)

MELAS [– 10 S 73 W + 2.5 km, pop. 200]. Previously USSR Novokiev. At the bottom of Valles Marineris in the Melas Chasma. Low altitude base for exploring the western end of Valles Marineris. Very close to Sinai Springs.

BOREAL BASE (aka Boring) [+ 79 N 48 W 0 km, pop. 150]. Previously USSR Novomurmansk. Right at entrance to Chasma Boreal. Main scientific base for exploration of the North Pole of Mars.

13

AUSTRAL CANYON (aka Bottom) [−84 S 262 W 0 km, pop. 150]. Previously USSR Novovladivostok. Deep in Chasma Austral. Main scientific base for exploration of the South Pole of Mars.

HALFWAY TERRACE [−41 S 303 W −10 km alt., pop. 1000]. Halfway is one of the cooler, and therefore popular, suburbs of Augustus that is halfway up Getout Slope, 6 km up and 100 km south of Splash Lake.

HELLAS BASE (aka Breakout) [−42 S 303 W −4 km alt., pop. 250] Breakout is at the top of Getout Slope, 12 km up and 200 km south of Splash Lake. Going from Splash Lake to Breakout is like climbing an inside-out Pavonis Mons. One of the spaceports for Mars.

SINAI SPRINGS [−8 S 84 W 8 km alt., pop. 100]. Continuously occupied base despite high altitude. Major activities consist of water engineering projects trying to tap the large water reserves and the potential energy difference between the top and bottom of the nearby cliffs into Valles Marineris.

NORMALLY UNOCCUPIED CAMPS:

THARSIS SADDLE [−4 S 117 W +10 km alt.]. In the flat spot between Arsia Mons and Pavonis Mons. Originally set up as a base camp to explore the three mountains on the Tharsis Ridge.

ELYSIUM SADDLE [+29 N 211 W +5 km alt]. Formerly USSR Novoleningrad. In the flat spot between Elysium Mons and Hecates Tholus. Originally set up as a base to explore the Elysium Ridge.

SOLIS LACUS [−26 S 80 W +6.5 km alt]. Formerly USSR Novobaku. Early radar studies of Mars by Earth seemed to indicate this region produced specular microwave reflections, as if liquid water were on or near the surface. The USSR set up a base here to look for the water. Water oriented activities were later shifted to Sinai Springs and this camp abandoned.

HELLESPONTUS (aka Hellsbridge) [−30 S 315 W +3.5 km alt]. Another site where Earth radar detected liquid water.

MARINER LAKE (aka Drainhole) [−7 S 36 W −2 km alt]. Lowest part of Mariner Valley. Post-Splat air pressure of 26% Earth pressure and average summer temperature above freezing, is enough to allow pools of water to form in the summer. (I have some lakefront property for sale.) Base is used during summer for scientific studies of permafrost melting, valley dynamics, and lake formation.

MUTCH MEMORIAL (Viking 1 Lander) [+22 N 48 W −1.5 km alt]. A must for every tourist to Mars. 100 km southwest of Mutchville.

VIKING 2 LANDER [+48 N 226 W −1.5 km alt]. A long way from everywhere.

ABOUT THE AUTHOR

Dr. Robert L. Forward writes science fiction novels and short stories, and science fact books and magazine articles. He is also a consulting scientist specializing in exotic physical phenomena and advanced space propulsion. Dr. Forward obtained his Ph.D. in Gravitational Physics from the University of Maryland. For his thesis he constructed and operated the world's first bar antenna for the detection of gravitational radiation. The antenna is now at the Smithsonian museum in Washington, D.C.

For thirty-one years, from 1956 until 1987, when he left in order to spend more time writing, Dr. Forward worked at the Hughes Aircraft Company Research Laboratories in Malibu, California, in positions of increasing responsibility, culminating with the position of senior scientist on the staff of the director of the laboratories. During that time he constructed and operated the world's first laser gravitational radiation detector, invented the rotating gravitational mass sensor, published over sixty-five technical publications, and was awarded eighteen patents.

From 1983 to the present, Dr. Forward has had a series of contracts from the Phillips Laboratory (formerly the Air Force Rocket Propulsion Laboratory) of the U.S. Air Force Systems Command to explore the forefront of physics and engineering in order to find new energy sources that will produce breakthroughs in space power and propulsion. He has published journal papers and contract reports on antiproton annihilation propulsion, laser beam and microwave beam interstellar propulsion, negative matter propulsion, light-levitated perforated sail communication satellites, cable catapults, LEO to lunar surface tether transportation systems, space warps, and a method for extracting electrical energy from vacuum fluctuations.

In addition to his professional work, Dr. Forward has written over eighty-five popular-science articles for publications such as *New Scientist, Analog Science Fiction/ Science Fact, Encyclopaedia Britannica Yearbook, Omni, Science Digest, Science 80,* and *Galaxy.* His most recent science fact books are *Future Magic* and *Mirror Matter: Pioneering Antimatter Physics* (with Joel Davis). His science fiction novels are *Dragon's Egg* and its sequel *Starquake, The Flight of the Dragonfly* (recently reprinted as *Rocheworld*), *Timemaster,* and *Martian Rainbow.* The novels are of the "hard" science fiction category, where the science is as accurate as possible.

Dr. Forward is a fellow of the British Interplanetary Society and editor of the Interstellar Studies issues of its journal, associate fellow of the American Institute of Aeronautics and Astronautics, senior member of the American Astronautical Society, and a member of the American Physical Society, Sigma Xi, Sigma Pi Sigma, and the Science Fiction Writers of America.

DEMCO